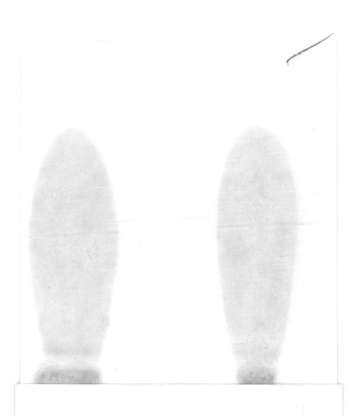

THE
GLAD
RIVER

ALSO BY WILL D. CAMPBELL

Brother to a Dragonfly

THE
GLAD
RIVER

WILL D. CAMPBELL

Holt, Rinehart and Winston
New York

Published by Holt, Rinehart and Winston,
383 Madison Avenue, New York, New York 10017.
Published simultaneously in Canada by Holt, Rinehart and
Winston of Canada, Limited.

Library of Congress Cataloging in Publication Data
Campbell, Will D.
The glad river.
I. Title.
PS3553.A488G59   813'.54   81-6969   AACR2
ISBN: 0-03-059898-2

First Edition

Designer: Amy Hill
Printed in the United States of America
10 9 8 7 6 5 4 3 2 1

Grateful acknowledgment is made for use of the following:
Lyrics from "Good Friday Morning" by S. R. Campbell,
copyright © by S. R. Campbell. Used by permission.
Lyrics from "The Whittling Room" by S. R. Campbell,
copyright © by S. R. Campbell. Used by permission.

For Brenda and Harlan

And I will gather the remnant of my flock out of all countries whither I have driven them, and will bring them again to their folds. . . .

—Jeremiah 23:3

There is a river, the streams whereof shall make glad the city of God. . . .

—Psalms 46:4

THE
GLAD
RIVER

*C*laudy Momber was born near Claughton Station in Claughton County, Mississippi, on February 29, 1920. His mother did not want to name him Claudy because in Mississippi in 1920 Claudia was pronounced "Claudy," and that was a girl's name. His father gave him the name but did not call him by any name at all until he was almost a year old. When the first sounds he made were d$\overline{oo}$, instead of buh or duh, he called him Doops. The day he started to school, his father went with him and wrote his name on the blackboard. CLAUDY. He told the teacher and eleven frightened first-graders that what he had written was pronounced "Claudy," and that was a boy's name. He wrote "Claudia" underneath it and told them it was pronounced "Claud-ee-ah," and that was a girl's name. Then he erased both names and stood his son up on the teacher's desk and told the startled teacher and first-graders that the boy's real name was Doops. He walked out the door leaving his son standing on top of the teacher's desk. No one called him anything else again. He was inducted into the army on May 1, 1942, as Doops Momber.

Kingston Smylie was named Kingston Smylie by his mother three days after he was born near Cummings, Mississippi. She knew that she would never see her baby's father again and decided that her baby's grandfather, who had brought her there from Frilot Cove, Louisiana, when she was four months pregnant, was not going to give him a name.

Fordache Arceneau was born about seven miles from Mermentau, Louisiana. Nobody knows for sure who named him. Perhaps his grandmother. She spoke only Cajun French and told the boy's mother that no other good French names were left because they had had so many babies.

Cecelia Geronymus was born in 1513 in Amsterdam, where she lived all her life, except for the four years she was in a convent in East Fresia. She was drowned in a bag in the Amstel River in the spring of 1550, having been found by the state to be guilty of sedition on account of her religious beliefs and practices.

The exact date of Pieter Boens's birth is not known. From all available records, it is thought that he was born about 1510 in Alsace. He was executed by fire in Amsterdam, one hour after Cecelia died.

Goris Cooman was the son of a Dutch soldier and a Spanish Moor. He was born in Antwerp in January 1498, and died with Pieter Boens.

They were related by blood.

1

Doops was sitting on a dead cypress tree, uprooted years before by one of the hurricanes that periodically blow in from the gulf and wear themselves out as they seek to accomplish the same wrack in the thickets and timberlands as they inflict upon the towns and villages along the shoreline. It was his first week at Camp Polk, Louisiana. He was pretending that the Kisatchie National Forest where he was sitting was the jungles of some South Pacific island and that he was about to go into battle for the first time, when he heard a subdued sobbing in the distance. He knew from the beginning that it was the sound of a soldier far from home, a new soldier feeling exactly what he was feeling. At first he tried to ignore it. But as the soft whimpering became louder, grew into almost hysterical weeping, Doops began walking toward it. As he moved along he hummed and whistled a tune. As he drew closer he began singing the words out loud.

> "Move it over. Move it over.
>   Move it on over there.
> There's another dirt load
> Coming down the road,
>   So move it on over there."

He saw a soldier standing alone in a small clearing. The soldier did not stop crying and when Doops walked up beside him he did not seem to notice. Doops did not speak, just stood beside him, not even looking at him. When the man stopped crying, turned away and blew his nose between his thumb and forefinger, Doops put his hand on his shoulder. "I know the feeling, neighbor." The soldier did not answer, but did not move away either. Doops ruffled a pile of cypress needles and sat down, watching the man at the same time. "I know the feeling, neighbor," he said again.

"I'm sorry," the soldier whispered, his voice cracking. "I'm real sorry." He backed away a few steps and sat down too, facing Doops.

"Sorry for what?" Doops asked.

"I'm just sorry. Real sorry. I never cried before. I never cried before in my whole goddamn life."

"What about when you were a little boy? You ever cry then?"

"I reckon. Not much though. My mamma said I never did cry much. Said I didn't even cry when she borned me. Said the doctor kept hitting me on the rump to make me cry and kept on smacking me till the nurse grabbed me away from him and said, 'For God's sake, he's breathing. Leave him alone.' I'm okay though now. You can go on." Doops did not move. "I guess you'll tell everybody in this chickenshit army that you saw me crying," the soldier said.

"Here," Doops said, handing him his handkerchief. The soldier took it without embarrassment, wiped both his eyes, blew his nose again, and handed it back. Doops opened his barlow knife and began to whittle a toothpick from a small twig.

"They call me Doops," he said, putting down the knife and extending his hand. The man stood up and bent over to shake his hand. Good breeding, Doops thought, standing up too. Good folks always stand up to shake hands.

A small army plane, part of the Louisiana maneuvers, moved out of the treetops above them, dropped a small sack filled with powdered chalk, banked sharply, and flew off. The sack landed in a bayou fifty yards away, breaking open when it hit and spreading a film of white dust over the dark water. The sound of the plane faded in the distance and died away.

"That's a bomb," Doops said. "If the war umpires find you with any of that flour on you they declare you dead. Or hurt, depending on how much gets on you, I guess."

4

"What they have to find on you to declare you missing?" the man asked. " 'Cause that's what I'm fixing to be. Slam gone."

"I suppose if we have to have a war, that's the best kind to have," Doops said, not commenting on what the man had said. "Just drop chalk on one another and then count up the score. Count up the dead ones and the hurt ones and declare a winner."

"Yeah, I guess so," the man said. "But I wish they had of dropped it on me back home." He moved a step closer to Doops and shook his hand again. "Had of. Some grammar, huh? And me been to college."

"Talking is to make folks understand you," Doops said. "You can do it any way you want to. At least, that's the way I always figured it. Particular if you know better. That's the way I always figured it."

"My name's Kingston Smylie," the man said. "I'm a Redbone."

"It's a *redneck*," Doops laughed. "And I'm one too."

"No, it ain't *redneck*. It's *Redbone*. Redneck is white. Redbone ain't nothing. Redneck is cracker. Redbone ain't even nigger."

"Redbone?" Doops asked.

"Yeah. Redbone. That means I don't exist."

Doops had never heard the word before and the disparaging manner in which the man spoke of himself, using a word Doops had never heard before, made him uncomfortable. "Is that something like a bluetick?" Doops laughed.

"Yeah. I reckon it is. Yep, it's a lot like being a bluetick hound."

"Well neighbor, I don't know what a Redbone is. So why are you telling me you are one?"

"Because you saw me cry. And when a man sees another man cry that means he knows all there is about him. It ain't that way with women. My mamma said men like to see women cry so they can call them weak, but they won't cry themselves so they can think they are strong. I don't know. But I know nobody else ever saw me cry before and nobody else knows I'm a Redbone. Just me and you know that." They were sitting on the ground again and Doops was chewing on the toothpick he had whittled. "And now I've got to tell you the rest of it," the man said.

"The rest of what?" Doops asked, spitting the toothpick out.

"The rest of my story. I've got to tell you the rest of it." They began to walk aimlessly about the area. Doops wished that the soldier would not tell him whatever it was he was about to tell him, that they could just walk back to the camp together. But as the soldier began to move in the opposite direction from the camp, motioning for Doops to follow, Doops knew that what he was about to hear was very important to the man and would probably be important to him as well. They walked for several minutes before the man began. When he did speak, it was as though he were reading from a book, as if he had rehearsed the words. Doops hurried to keep up, listening. But for a long time he did not understand what he was hearing.

"My daddy told me all this stuff I'm going to tell you when I was sixteen years old. On the very day I was sixteen years old he took me in a brand-new pickup truck he had just bought and we rode to New Orleans. It took us three hours to get there and four hours to get back. When we got to New Orleans, he drove all the way down Canal Street to the ferryboat and then he drove the truck onto the boat. Halfway across to Algiers, right in the middle of the Mississippi River, he got out of the truck and told me to get out too. Standing there on the deck of the ferryboat in the middle of the Mississippi River he handed me the keys to that truck and said I was a man now and said that brand-new pickup truck belonged to me. He told me to get behind the wheel and I did. When we got to the other side of the river, he told me to turn around and get back on the ferry. That we were going back home. Man, you know, I had been driving tractors and old trucks around the farm since I could remember, but I sure as hell had never driven anything off and on a Mississippi River ferryboat, and never in all that New Orleans traffic.

"But that's what he told me to do and that's what I did, jerking and stopping and starting and honking the horn with one elbow out the window, just like a real dude. And just as soon as I started to drive that brand-new pickup truck, even before we got off that ferryboat, he started to talk to me. I don't reckon he had said a thousand words to me before in my whole life. He just never did talk much.

"When I was trying to turn around on the Algiers side of the river, we got caught right smack dab in the middle of a parade. You ever been to New Orleans? God bless, they have parades

6

about everything. Here was a nigger church parade with nigger cowboys on white horses and a nigger queen sitting up on a high truck they called a float, waving and smiling and throwing little things off the side and people fighting and scampering trying to catch them. You ever been to New Orleans? Everybody blowing brass horns and beating drums and twisting and turning this way and that. Well, there I was, caught in the middle of the Greater Pilgrim Rest Baptist Church parade in a brand-new pickup truck and my daddy fixing to tell me something that would scare the living shit out of me."

Doops stopped walking and took the soldier by the arm. "Wait a minute, Smylie. You sure you want to tell me all this? Man, we don't even know one another."

"You got half of it right," Kingston said. "I don't know you. But you know me. I didn't ask you out here in the middle of the woods where I was. My daddy told me to listen real good. And that's what I'm telling you to do now.

"And then right off he told me he wasn't my daddy, that he was my granddaddy. Well, I had noticed, you know, when I got big enough, that him and my mamma didn't . . . well, you know . . . act like married people at night and all that. When I was little, my mamma slept in the room and in the bed with me. But then when I got bigger, she slept in another room. But I'll tell you the truth, I never did think too much about it.

"Well, it scared the hell out of me and I didn't know what to say, didn't even know what to call him if I needed to call him something all at once. All my life I had been calling somebody Daddy and now all of a sudden I'm supposed to call him Grand-daddy. Or something. I didn't say a word and he kept on talking. He told it real slow and it wasn't until we had crossed the river to Algiers and gone back through New Orleans and was getting off the Airline Highway heading up 51 outside of LaPlace, almost to Manchac Pass, that I began to make any sense out of what he was saying."

Doops made a quick turn in the direction of the main camp but when Kingston realized it he turned and caught up with him, nudging him in the opposite direction.

"I thought we had always lived on this big ole farm outside of

Cummings, Mississippi. That's the only home I ever knew and I thought that was where we had always lived. But he said we had come there from Frilot Cove, Louisiana. And to tell you the truth, that ain't too far from where we are right now. He said he had a big plantation at Frilot Cove that his daddy had left him. He said his wife, who would have been my grandmother—I got so mixed up I didn't know one from another anyway—died when my real daddy was born and he raised him there by himself. He said he raised him right, made him work, and took him to the Baptist church. But somehow he broke bad when he was just a yearling boy, started running around at night with a bad crowd, drinking beer and wine, and fighting and getting in all kinds of trouble and wouldn't go to school. But he said he never did whip him or anything, just tried to get along with him and raise him right. We were up past Hammond by then and he said he needed to go to the rest room and told me I better check to see if my truck needed some gas. I swear to you I was so mixed up I thought about jumping out of that truck and running like hell. But I just sat there. And when he got back in the truck he picked up right where he left off."

Doops slowed almost to a stop. "Kingston. I really don't think you ought to be telling me all this. I mean, I really don't get it. Why don't we just forget the whole thing. You really haven't told me much yet and . . . well, hell. So what! So I saw you crying. Everybody cries sometimes. But that don't mean you're disgraced, that you've got to spill your guts to a rank stranger." Kingston paid him no mind.

"And that's when he told me about the Redbone folks. He said his boy, my daddy I reckon, started messing around with this Redbone girl. I didn't know what a Redbone was. You know, like you said, I've been called a redneck by the town shits who lived in the big city of downtown Cummings, but I hadn't ever heard of a Redbone. He said they were a bunch of people who stayed pretty much off to themselves and didn't mix with other people. Sort of a clan like. He said the main people—he didn't say white people, but I knew that was what he was getting at—wouldn't let them go to their schools, and the Redbones wouldn't go to school with the colored people. So they had their own schools and

8

churches and lived off to themselves. He said folks just called them Redbones, he reckoned because they was supposed to have Indian blood in them. He said a lot of them might be real dark and look like colored people and some of them had blond hair and blue eyes, but he said most all of them had big stubby noses and used to go around pinching their noses to make them look like the main people's noses. He told me folks thought they was a mixture of Indian and white and colored. They wasn't white and they wasn't colored. They was just . . . Redbones. And that's what everybody called them. Redbones. Everybody except them. He said if you wanted to start a fight you could call one of them a Redbone to his face. And if you really wanted to start a fight you could call one of them a nigger."

This time it was Kingston who slowed down. "You still want me to quit talking? If you don't want to hear the rest of it, you don't have to. I'll stop right now and you won't ever be bothered with me again. Just tell me what you want me to do."

Without saying anything at all Doops quickened his pace and Kingston resumed talking.

"Well, anyway, you know, his boy was running around with this Redbone girl, and everybody was talking. You couldn't do that. Then one day this Redbone girl's daddy came over and called the old man outside and told him that his boy had done his daughter wrong, that she was in a family way. He said he took the girl's daddy inside his house, something you wasn't supposed to do either, and called his boy in and asked him in front of the man if he had done that Redbone girl wrong. His boy denied it at first, just said why would he want to mess around with a Redbone girl when there was plenty of good-looking white girls around. But he knew he was lying and right there in front of that man he beat the tar out of his boy with a plow line until he told him the truth. Then he beat him some more because he had lied to him and then he beat him some more because he had messed around with a Redbone girl. Finally, he said, it was her daddy who caught him around the waist and held him and wouldn't let him beat him anymore. Said that wasn't doing anybody any good."

Suddenly Kingston stopped walking and grabbed Doops by the collar, jerking him toward him.

"Hold it," Doops said. "What's your problem? Now I didn't ask you to tell me all that. Tried to get you not to tell me. You just started talking. So why you riled all of a sudden?"

"Never mind who asked and who didn't ask. I want to know what you're thinking. Right now!"

"What I'm thinking? You really want to know what I'm *thinking*?" Doops asked.

"Yeah. I really do. And tell me the honest to God truth. What are you thinking right this very second."

"Okay. I'll tell you the honest God truth what I was thinking just the very second you grabbed me."

"Tell me," Kingston said.

Doops began to laugh and jostle the man playfully. "I was thinking," Doops said, "I was just thinking about asking you to let me check your moons." Doops stopped laughing when he saw that Kingston didn't think it funny.

"Yeah. I know about that too. I guess you're kidding me. I reckon I hope you are. But my daddy, that's my granddaddy, told me that's what the main people at Frilot Cove used to do, used to say. They always said if somebody had one drop of nigger blood in their veins, no matter how little and how far back it went, their fingernails would have half-moons on them. Well, here you are. Take a good look, Private Doops." He opened both hands with the palms down and thrust them at Doops.

"I've got moons! Now what are you thinking?"

"I'm thinking you got moons," Doops said, not laughing. "So go on."

"Well, anyway, the next morning the boy, my daddy, my real daddy I reckon you might say, was gone. He had stolen a thousand dollars the old man had hid in the house because he didn't trust banks and he was clean gone. He said he didn't even look for him, knew his boy wasn't ever coming back again. So that very same day he went down and advertised his place for sale. Then he went to the girl's daddy, my mamma's daddy, my other granddaddy I reckon you might say, and told her what he was going to do. He told him he wanted to adopt the girl, legally you know, and finish raising her and raise the baby. Me. Well, he said they was real poor. I mean he said they lived in a house worse than his chickenhouse. So my mamma's daddy and his wife both went

10

with my granddaddy to Baton Rouge and they all signed some papers and then my mamma was his daughter. Then, soon as he sold the place, he went to Mississippi and bought that big farm where I was raised. He moved up there and joined the Catholic Church, I guess because the Redbones was all Catholic, and they've been living there ever since. And still live there. Even though my mamma was just fifteen years old at the time, she was a big girl and looked a lot older. He said he didn't tell folks anything, you know, that she was his wife or she wasn't his wife. But everybody just thought she was and since she had his name then, they would naturally think that, and he never told anybody any different."

Kingston stopped talking as abruptly as he had begun. Neither of them spoke again for a long time. They continued to walk, wandering, going nowhere. Finally Doops broke the silence.

"That why you were crying out there in the woods?"

"No. I never even cried the whole time he was telling me all that. Maybe I was so proud of that brand-new pickup truck, but I never did cry. I almost cried when it finally dawned on me what he was saying. But then I started laughing like hell. My grand-daddy asked me what was so funny. I said, 'It sounds like you're telling me I belong in the Greater Pilgrim Rest Baptist Church parade.' He didn't think that was funny worth a cuss. But then he never did laugh at anything. I've never seen my granddaddy laugh. Never in my whole life. But he's a hell of a man. One hell of a man. I was crying out there in the woods because I'm so goddamn homesick for him I could die."

"Homesick?" Doops asked.

"Yeah. Home *sick*," he answered, dividing the word into two words.

"Well, like I told you," Doops said, "I know the feeling."

"And the hell of it is, I don't even have to be here. I mean, legally I'm not really in the army. My daddy—I just kept calling him Daddy even after he told me all that—told me when the war started that if I didn't want to be drafted I could go back to Frilot Cove and live with some of my blood kinfolks down there and I never would be drafted. He said the colored people and the white people didn't get put together in the army and the draft board down there just left the Redbones alone. I mean, there's an army for white people and an army for colored people. But there ain't no army for Redbone people. So he said they just left them alone, pretended they weren't there."

"Did you really want to get drafted?" Doops asked. "Hell, I *had* to come. I didn't want to come."

"Well, I didn't exactly want to get drafted but it's kind of funny putting one over on this chickenshit army. I mean, those guys over there in that quartermaster outfit, across the bayou, from the lightest mulatto to the niggerest nigger, they're over there because they knew what to tell the draft boards to put on their records. And then when the army got them, they knew where to put them, what to do with them. Just look at the forms the draft board filled out and you've got a soldier or a niggersoldier. But they go by check marks on a form. They don't go by moons on your fingernails. So I screwed 'em. Maybe I ought to be across the bayou."

"Yeah, I guess that is kinda funny," Doops said. "Yeah, that's just as funny as hell." But neither of them was laughing.

Doops put his hand on the man's shoulder and turned him around, looking directly into his eyes. "Do you trust me, Kingston?"

"Yes. I trust you, Doops. Do you trust me?"

"Yes. I trust you." They stood shaking hands again, looking each other squarely in the eyes.

"Then are we buddies?" Kingston asked. Neither face showed any expression.

"Yes. We are buddies. I'm your buddy."

"Are you my friend?"

"Friend?" Doops replied. "Friend." He repeated the word but no longer as a question, his voice dropping. "That's a stronger word. We'll have to see. But we're neighbors. Like I say, we're neighbors. I know that much."

"I ought to cut you with my knife," Kingston said, laughing out loud and slapping Doops on the back.

2

Doops and Kingston were reading over the shoulder of a soldier who was studying a notice the company clerk had just tacked on the bulletin board outside the orderly room. The man was having trouble understanding it, pointing to each word with his finger and mumbling the words to himself in a language they didn't understand.

M E M O R A N D U M

For: All members of Company D
SUBJECT: Assembly and Secret Mission

1. All members of Company D will stand formation on 19 June, 1942 at 0100 hours. Uniform will be fatigue, helmet, full field pack, and web gear.
2. Company will procced to Motor Pool for transport following formation and inspection.

> Roger L. Fenton
> Capt. U.S. Army (Inf.)
> Commanding

"O-one-hundred hours," Kingston said. "Now why can't they just say one o'fucking clock in the morning?"

"Because then everybody would know what it meant. I don't believe you understand how this man's army works. They want to confuse everything so they can chew your ass out when you get something wrong."

"I'll bet you five bucks I can tell you what that's all about," Kingston said as they were walking away.

"Wait a minute." Doops stopped and looked back at the soldier studying the bulletin board. "Ain't that the Cajun fellow? Damn sure is. You know, the guy the sergeant has been giving hell every chance he gets."

Fordache Arceneau was the only man in the platoon from Louisiana. When they first came, the sergeant mispronounced his name at roll call and when he didn't answer, he was marked absent. After a few days, the soldier who stood next to him would nudge him when it was time for him to answer. Later, the same soldier, older than most of them, explained to the sergeant that he wasn't pronouncing his name correctly. After that, the sergeant, enraged by the prompting, would scream the name at reveille: "Ford Ar-*sinew*!" Sometimes on the drill field, when Fordache missed an order and didn't turn on command, getting bayonets tangled with the man behind him, the sergeant would scream, "*Dumb coonass*," or whatever he thought would embarrass and humiliate him.

Fordache generally took the harassment in stride, doing his best to keep up. Some of the soldiers began calling him "Model T." At first, he disliked the mascotlike attention from the soldiers, but when he saw that they meant no harm, understood that they meant Model T Ford, he began to enjoy it. When he got confused in close-order drill, he would go into a routine of roaring, backfiring, sputtering, shifting gears, and clattering until he caught up.

He did not look the way they thought Cajuns were supposed to look. His hair was reddish brown and his skin had an almost albino quality about it. His beady brown eyes seemed dull in contrast to the bright freckles clustered around his nose. An impish grin and the jerky, roosterlike movements of his body gave the impression that he was always on the verge of saying something funny. But because his English was so poor, he said no more than was necessary.

"I think we ought to help him read that damn notice," Doops said. "Whatever the hell it means."

"I know what it means," Kingston said, hastening to catch up with Doops. "I told you I already know."

"Hi, neighbor . . . uh, Model T," Doops said as the man looked around at them. "You're the one they call Model T, ain't you? That's a friendly name, I think, but if you don't want me to call you that, I won't." The man didn't answer.

"They call me Doops. And this one here is Smylie. Kingston Smylie."

Fordache extended his hand to both of them but still didn't answer.

"You want a beer?" Doops asked. "Me and Kingston are fixing to go get a beer. Come go with us."

"*Mais*, ah'll have tuh t'ink about dat." Fordache gestured to the notice on the bulletin board. "*Ton parle!* Ah don' understan' dat, me."

"Come on," Doops said, tugging at his sleeve. "We'll explain it."

"Is he cussing us?" Kingston whispered as they started walking toward the PX.

"Who cares. I think we might like him."

"We?"

"Yeah. We. Me and you. I think we might like him."

"**Y**ou know the damned officers," Kingston said after they got a table and the private at the bar had brought their beer. "They think we can't hear, I guess. They talk in front of us as if we're not even there. Well, I was on clean-up duty at the officers' club last night and heard Fenton talking to his girl friend, bragging about how he was going to be the only company commander at Camp Polk to show his troops some Japs before they got to combat. He told her his brother was a brakeman for the Southern Pacific Railroad and that his train was hauling thirty-nine carloads of Japanese from California to the relocation center in Arkansas. It'll be passing through DeRidder at two-thirty tomorrow morning. That's what the order is all about. We're going to DeRidder to see Japs."

Fordache had trouble understanding a lot of what Kingston was saying. Doops explained as best he could, taking plenty of time. He could see that Fordache was beginning to relax, beginning to feel comfortable with them as he understood what Kingston was telling them.

"I know a good idea," Doops said, feeling the beer. "Let's start a hot rumor in the morning that we're going to war in DeRidder. The captain will get up there at o-one-hundred hours and lay all that bullshit on us, tell us we're going to see the enemy. So we'll just take it a step further. We'll start a rumor that we're going to war. We'll just quietly pass the word to a few guys on the truck that we're going to kill some Japs."

Doops noticed a sudden change in Fordache's face. He looked worried, and began frantically waving his hands, trying to make them understand him.

"*Mais, poo yie!* Ah got tuh say you somet'ing, me." He pushed the beer back and began chattering in French. Kingston and Doops sat looking at him, not knowing how to respond. Finally, as he slowed down and began putting some of the words into English they realized that he was telling them he wouldn't kill anybody. When he was satisfied they understood, he pulled the beer toward him, took several long gulps, and leaned back.

"O hell, Model T—mind if I call you Model T? Hell no, we're not going to DeRidder to kill anybody. None of us is going to kill anybody. We're just going to make a joke. You know, ram it up the captain's ass."

The captain, slapping his leg nervously with a swaggerstick, fingering a service revolver strapped to his waist with a Sam Browne belt, stepped intently to the front of the formation as soon as the first sergeant called them to attention. "All right men, I want you to listen carefully. Now we're going to march to the motor pool, load on the troop carriers, and ride to DeRidder— that's only twenty miles from here—to see some Japs. Now that's all I can tell you. I can't answer any questions, so don't ask any. Just be good soldiers. This is war, you know."

Confusion comes easy at one o'clock in the morning among a tired and groggy group of new soldiers far from anything familiar. No one spoke as they were marched to the motor pool and loaded, one squad at a time, onto vehicles that looked to them like cattle trucks. When everyone was on, the convoy leader signaled for the engines to start and all the vehicles moved out as one. The rolling of the wheels churned clouds of red dust all around them, the powdered Vernon Parish dirt losing its color and consistency as it blended with the night fog rising from the cooling creeks and bayous, the mixture forming its own color and consistency, drifting above them in a hazy pattern that seemed to fit the occasion.

"Where the hell we going?" one of the soldiers asked as soon as the convoy began to move.

It was the cue Doops wanted. It was, in fact, the very question he had told Kingston to ask if no one else did. "We're going to war," he said, looking at the soldier as if the man had just asked what planet they were on. "The Japs are in DeRidder. We're going to war." He said it matter-of-factly, as if it were something all of them should have known.

After a brief silence, a few twittery giggles sounded in the lurching truck. Then, as the soldiers clustered in small groups, talking hurriedly among themselves, a cycle of humorless questioning began. Fordache and Kingston stood close beside Doops in the very middle of the vehicle. One by one, the small groups began calling questions to Doops. Most of the questions were the same: How did the Japs get to DeRidder, Louisiana? They still did not believe it, but as they discussed it and recalled the unexpected attack on Pearl Harbor and what they had been told about the cunning Japanese, they no longer completely disbelieved it either.

"Gentlemen," Doops began as the small clusters began to break up and face him. "We have with us a native." He put his hand on Fordache's shoulder. "A man who knows every beach, bayou, and tributary in this part of the world. I present to you Mr. Arceneau, known to some of you as Ford, to others as Model T—may I call you Model T? Mr. Arceneau, will you explain to these distinguished soldiers exactly how the crafty enemy has invaded our shores?" He spoke slowly and deliberately, not for Fordache's benefit, for he had already told him what he would ask him to do.

As the convoy moved along the narrow macadam road, the giant cypress trees and loblolly pines admitted occasional light from the full moon, then darkness again as the oncoming shadows seemed to lunge at them in silent outrage. Fordache shuffled his feet around, beating his clenched fist into the palm of the other hand.

"*Sacré misère! Fut putain! Sacré misère!*"

"Now, we don't know what that means," Doops said, smiling and nodding at him. "It may be cussing, for all we know. We just want you to tell us how the enemy got to DeRidder, Louisiana. Speak American, neighbor." Doops patted his shoulder in a patronizing, almost cajoling fashion, winking quickly as the shadows allowed a moment of light.

"*Sernis Japons!*" he exclaimed, looking at Kingston, who was watching and listening now as earnestly as the others. "Dey pass tru de Sabine. *Peut-être* Anacoco Bayou. Could be Bundick Creek. Dey'll be dere fuh shore. Ah'm tellin' you de trute." He kept pounding his fist in his palm, making a sort of whimpering noise in his throat between words.

Doops kept questioning him, getting pieces of answers, turning often to the others to explain what Fordache was saying. He interpreted with measured control, sighing with deep resignation as he spoke. "What he says is that the Japs probably landed first at Sabine Pass. That's down close to Port Arthur. From there they could come up Black Bayou to Bundick Creek. Or maybe, he says, they landed at Cameron—he knows where that is—and came up the Calcasieu River and hit Bundick Creek that way. Or maybe, he says, they came up the Sabine River from the pass and got off at Merryville."

By now the soldiers were pushing and jostling for position, straining to hear Doops above the roar of the convoy. "So, gentlemen," he concluded, "there you have it. We're going to war."

Doops was pleased by what happened next. But also a bit daunted.

"War?"

"Sonofabitch."

"Goddamn sneaky slopeheaded bastards."

"Just like Pearl Harbor."

"War!"

"The Japs are in DeRidder."

"Six weeks in the fucking army and I'm going to war!"

All of them were speaking at once. Doops, appearing now as frightened as the rest, stood watching them. Suddenly he realized that he was frightened, not of Japanese in DeRidder but of the captain in the jeep at the front of the convoy. They had been assiduously informed, by lectures, films, and posters, of the perils of malicious rumors. And the penalty. He knew it was time to turn the joke around.

"Look," he shouted, waving his hands above his head for quiet. Fordache had backed up against the cab of the truck, his hands folded across his chest, watching it all with obvious satisfaction. When Kingston, laughing hysterically, stumbled by Doops, trying to get to where Fordache stood, Doops whispered, "When I get them quiet, you tell them the truth."

"It's your picture show, hoss. I don't know anything," Kingston said as he moved on, still laughing.

"Look, you guys! Listen to me! Look! Look!" He was screaming, moving about, touching everyone he could reach. "Look. We're bullshitting you guys. Now, there may be some Japs in DeRidder and we may be going there to see them. But we sure as hell ain't going there to fight them."

The response was a renewed babble of confusion and protests.

"You don't know!"

"Model T knows."

"Model T knows this country."

"Soldiers don't go nowhere this time of morning except to fight."

"I'm jumping off this thing."

"We going to war!"

Seeing that he would get no help from Kingston, Doops thought of another way to convince them he had been joking. "My dear friends and colleagues in the fine art of war," he began, once they had quieted down. "Mr. Smylie. Mr. Arceneau. Distinguished gentlemen." A few of the soldiers laughed. "Did it occur to any of you that if we are on a mission of slant-cyed carnage, we are missing something?" His mention of slant-eyes brought a sprinkling of applause. He bowed politely and continued. "Now. We got shelter halves, we got tent pegs, and we got mess kits. We got blankets and K rations. We got little rolls of toilet paper in our full field packs and we got canteens full of fresh water. We got laced-up leggings, and we got salt tablets. We got steel helmets." He paused for effect. "But we ain't got no bullets. And we ain't got no guns. Now what the hell kind of war is that?"

There was a general rumbling of agreement, but it was short-lived. The older soldier, the one who stood next to Fordache at formations, spoke from the darkness. "Sometimes they don't issue the guns until you get to the front lines."

"Yeah, that's right!"

"The guns may be in that truck with the canvas top on it."

"Hell, we *are* going to war!"

The excitement was not so intense now, but Doops knew they were getting close to DeRidder and if the captain found out who'd started the rumor, he would be in trouble.

As the trucks pulled alongside the depot at 1:55, the murmuring was still going on. When the engines stopped, Fordache, who hadn't moved from where he was standing against the cab, took a step forward, indicating that he wanted to say something. "*Mais*, I got to say you somet'ing," he said, the impish grin stretching the freckles on his nose and cheeks. "If de Japs hadda came de way I say y'all, dey woulda had tuh leave de gulf befo' dey bomb de Pearl." They were convinced.

"What do you think of the little Cajun?" Doops asked Kingston, who had joined him at the tail end of the truck.

"We'll watch him," Kingston said.

"He knows something we don't know," Doops said, shaking his head, thinking of how close he had come to getting in serious trouble with the army.

The trucks formed a parallel to the tracks, the sides next to the depot in the light, the far sides in the shadows. The captain moved from one vehicle to another, explaining to the soldiers why they were there. "Just stand in place where you can see good. I'll talk to my brother, get him to delay the train with some engine problem or other. That way you'll be able to get a good look. Now, remember, these people are still American citizens—some of them—most of them I suppose. So don't laugh at them. Don't point and don't talk. Just look. Pay special attention to the shape of their eyes, their size, their color, and the way they talk and move around. The next time you see somebody that looks like them, they'll be trying to kill you."

The stationmaster pushed his visor up and looked out, then turned to someone behind him. "There ain't a troop train due in here for two days. Go see what them bozos want."

A Negro man, dressed in a neat Pullman porter's uniform, came out of the light toward them.

"Cap'n wants to know what you boys want."

"We've come to see some Japs," Doops said, his control regained.

"Yeah, I know. That's what we've all come to see. First they came to see us at Pearl and now we've come to see them. He don't mean why'd you leave home. He means what you want *now*. Here at the depot. He ain't talking about the war."

The porter pulled himself up on the tailgate and climbed on over, then moved down the vacant side of the truck and faced Doops.

"Now, the cap'n in there wants to know what y'all want, son. Now, what y'all want?"

"Like I say. We've come to see some Japs. Go ask our captain. He's right up there in that jeep."

"Well, I guess you ain't supposed to tell me. Military secret, huh?" he said, teasing. "None of my business, huh?"

"Where you from?" Doops asked him, wanting to change the subject.

"Me? Centreville, Miss'ippi. I'm from Centreville, Miss'ippi."

"You from Centreville, Mississippi?" Doops asked. "I'm from Claughton Station. That ain't far." The porter looked at him without answering.

"How come every Pullman porter in the country comes from Centreville, Mississippi?" Kingston asked. "I rode a train to North Carolina one time and the porter told me he was from Centreville, Mississippi. And when they shipped me down here from Hattiesburg, the porter on that train told me he was from Centreville, Mississippi."

The man shrugged his shoulders. "Don't know 'bout them other boys. I just know 'bout me. And I'm from Centreville, Miss'ippi. And if anybody wants to bet, I can prove it."

"How you going to prove it?" Kingston asked.

"I know how," Doops said. "I'm going to ask you three questions about Centreville, Mississippi, and if you can answer two of them, that's where you're from."

"Five says I can answer all of them," the porter said, reaching into his back pocket.

Doops took a five-dollar bill out of his wallet and wedged it between the slats of the truck rack. Kingston took out two dollars, placed them under one foot, then reconsidered and put one of them back in his pocket. Model T pulled a Golden Grain tobacco sack from his shirt pocket, untied the drawstrings, and took out three quarters.

"Anybody else?" The porter motioned for them to put their money on the floor of the truck. Most of them did.

"Wait a minute!" someone called. "How we going to know who's telling the truth?"

"Easy," the porter said. "He knows the truth. And I know the truth." He moved directly in front of Doops, glaring into his eyes, straining in the poor light. "And I just believe me and him going to tell the truth. Ain't we son!"

"Yes, sir," Doops said, glancing quickly at Kingston as he said "sir."

Doops wrote the three questions on a piece of paper, the answers on another, and handed them to one of the soldiers.

"First question. How far is Centreville from Gloster?"

"You trying to trick me, son? They's two ways to go. Which way you mean?"

"The shortest way," Doops said. "I forgot about the other road."

"Ten and a half miles. Sign to sign," the man said.

"Question two. Which side of the post office is the cotton compress on?"

"West side. Two blocks west."

No one asked Doops if the man was right.

"Okay. Last question. Who owns the Jitney Jungle grocery store?"

"Gimme the money, boys. Gimme the money. Everybody knows that. Old man Patterson. Mr. Ira Patterson owns it. He owns everything in Centreville. Every *thing*. And every *body*.

Least every colored body. And that's why so many Pullman porters come from Centreville, Miss'ippi. Don't no one body own a Pullman porter. Now. Gimme the money."

He moved about the truck collecting the bills. Seeing that he had forgotten him, Model T walked over and handed the man the three coins. No one asked to see the answers the soldier had in his pocket.

The stationmaster had moved away from his desk and stood outside under the gooseneck light, ignoring the bugs as they hit the hundred-watt bulb and dropped onto his shoulders and into his hair. He seemed disturbed at the banter going on between the porter and the soldiers. The porter pretended not to see him.

"Okay, boys. Now we're friends. Right? I don't bet with nobody unless he's my friend. We all bet with one another. So tell me what y'all doing here?"

Doops answered as if the question had not been asked before. "We've come to see some Japs."

"Come on now. I don't really care," the man said. "It don't make no difference to me one way or the other. And the cap'n there. I ain't telling him nothing. He ain't got nothing to do with me. I'm just here waiting for my train. I don't work for him. You heard of Mr. A. Phillip Randolph? Well, that's my man. That's who I work for. What you boys doing here? Tell me."

"Really," Doops said. "I'm telling you the truth. Captain Fenton said there was a train coming through here tonight with three thousand Japanese on it. He said he wanted us to see what they look like. Said next time we see them they'll be shooting at us. That's what he told us."

The man's face changed from a very dark brown to a reddish copper. Doops had never seen a Negro blush before. At Claughton Station, the white people said a Negro couldn't get sunburned, couldn't blush or turn red. And that adhesive tape wouldn't stick to their skin. Doops didn't know what he had said wrong, but he sensed the change, saw the rapid shift of mood. He glanced at Kingston, and Kingston caught his eye, winked, turned away.

The porter started climbing over the side of the truck.

"Sheee-it" he mumbled, drawing the word out as long as his breath of air would hold out.

"Sheee-it," he said again, as if spreading what he was pronouncing over every square inch of everything around him. "Goddamn concentration camp!" He turned and spit hard on the ground. "Wonder why they didn't tell me what train I was catching?" he mumbled. "But I reckon I know. I'm just a goddamn . . ."

None of the soldiers understood.

He started to walk away, then slowed down, stopped completely. The soldiers watched him. Suddenly he turned around and moved back to the truck.

From his front pocket he took all the money he had won and placed it on the floor. Moving back a few steps, he began to speak again.

"Which one of you is Model T?" Two of the soldiers pushed Model T to the front, facing the porter. "And where's the one I heard y'all call Kingston?" Kingston stepped up beside Model T.

"When I left Centreville, Mississippi . . ." He pronounced each word and syllable now, the way Doops thought all Yankees talked. "When I left Centreville, Mississippi, I moved to Los Angeles. Got married out there. My wife died and the grandparents got the young. Wife died when the last one was born. There are three of them."

He moved back to the edge of the truck. "How much did you bet?" he said to Kingston.

"One dollar, sir." The man did not seem surprised that Kingston addressed him as "sir." He picked up one of the dollar bills he had returned to the floor of the truck and put it in the same pocket he had taken it from.

"And how about you?" he said to Model T.

"Six bits."

He picked up the three quarters and put them in his pocket with the dollar bill. "Like I say, I don't bet with nobody ain't my friend." The reddish copper color was gone from his face. He gazed in the direction the train would come from.

"Nine. Eleven. And thirteen. Two girls and a boy." Speaking to Kingston and Model T he did not acknowledge the presence of the other soldiers.

"And they'll be on that train. That's the last load. They'll be on that train with their grandma."

He began walking toward the depot but turned back again.

Kingston and Model T were still standing side by side, everyone quiet.

"And . . . God . . . damn . . . Mr. Patterson," the porter said, walking away again, looking dourly over his shoulder at all the others whose money he left on the truck.

As soon as the man disappeared into the depot, some of the soldiers began picking up the money, each one taking no more than he had bet. When they had finished, a five-dollar bill remained on the floor.

"Don't you want your Lincoln, Doops?" one of the soldiers asked. But he did not answer. And no one picked it up.

It was almost daylight when the train finally arrived. Since the porter left, Doops, who had moved to the dark side of the truck, stared into the darkness, saying nothing, feeling strange. Kingston and Model T stood beside him but did not talk. He had felt this way before, but he couldn't say exactly how it was he felt. It was somewhat like homesickness but seemed more haunting. And more intense. One night in the barracks they had talked of homesickness and one of the recruits said his parents had been killed when he was two years old and he had never lived in any one foster home for more than six months since. Yet he seemed to be the most homesick of all. Doops tried to imagine how the man felt, remembering getting a bellyache one time when he had eaten two quarts of homemade ice cream. Like getting the bellyache without the ice cream, he thought. But that wasn't what he was feeling either. He didn't know what it was. He had been happy and he had been sad. It was neither of those. It was more like someone else had been somewhere else and had seen something else and had tried to tell him about it and he was sure that he was seeing exactly what they had seen. Whatever it was, it always made him hold his breath. When he did that as long as he could, he was overwhelmed by a strange sort of dizziness, a feeling that he was close to passing out. But he never did.

That was what he was feeling when the train moved into place and stopped.

"There's the slopeheads. There's the sombitches. Thirty-nine carloads of 'em," one of the soldiers said.

There were small-town noises and sights and smells all around.

A lone taxi driver had heard the train come into town and made his way to the station, moving slowly under the giant live-oak branches, breaking the night's work of hundreds of spiders, their threads and nets giving way and clinging to the morning wetness of the taxicab.

"Reckon one of them Japs ordered a cab," someone said. "Maybe it's Tojo," another replied.

A herd of dairy cows, already milked and on their way to pasture, lowed in the distance, their smell floating through the morning, mixing with the smell of the train's coal smoke. A small Negro woman, wearing a maid's dress, carried a blue porcelain nightjar from her back door, emptied it across a barbed-wire fence on which clothes were draped, placed the chamber pot on the porch, crossed the railroad tracks at the front of the train, and started into town.

"All right, men. This is it. Everybody up!" The captain tried to muffle his yell. Doops had not moved.

The other soldiers stood silently against the cattle rack, straining to see. The flashing signal lights at the crossing formed weird and changing patterns as the fog floated slowly to the east.

"That must be the captain's brother. That's the brakeman," someone said.

Slapping his leg with his swagger stick, the captain walked briskly to the man climbing down from the giant engine. They shook hands, the captain talking hurriedly to him as they did. The brakeman glanced at the engineer, who was watching the line of trucks parked beside the depot, nodded his head to the captain, and began peering underneath the engine, kicking on one, then another of the big eight wheels as if inspecting the tires on a secondhand car.

"Reckon he's fixing to buy that damn thing?" someone asked. No one answered.

The crew members busied themselves with the refueling and oiling, checking couplings, not hurrying. All the doors of the Pullman cars were shut and every curtain was pulled down.

"That damn train is probably filled with rich people going to New Orleans," one of the soldiers said. "Probably been to Mexico."

A sliding door on a car about midway along the train began to move. It was a big door, in the center of the car, not located in the front or rear as on the other cars. They could see someone peering out as the door opened wider.

"Here they come," the captain yelled, louder than he intended, then quickly repeated the words in a whisper, as if his whisper could wipe out the yell. The soldiers fidgeted in place, calm now, jostling one another, making noises in their throats which the captain could not hear.

Flanked by Kingston and Model T, Doops still had not moved from his place on the dark side of the truck. He leaned against the top slat of the rack, which was breast high. His hands were locked behind his head. Every few seconds, he leaned his head over the rack and spit a long stream of light thin saliva into the dust.

When the door was fully opened, a small figure moved to the center of the opening, paused, jumped to the ground. It was a young girl, perhaps in her early teens, though they had been told that all Japanese look the same age. Her skin was darker than they had expected. Her hair was long and very black, not straight but wavy like a fine mare's tail.

As soon as she was on the ground, other hands and arms appeared from each side of the door opening, pushing large metal trash cans to the center. The girl began to pull the heavy cans to the ground. Then she emptied them in a wooden bin nearby, beating the bottom of each one to make sure nothing was stuck.

They had not noticed that the porter had come out of the depot and was standing about midway down the train, waiting to board. When he saw the girl leave the train, he dropped his bag and stood between where she was working and the convoy, standing protectively, moving as she moved, trying to block the view of the soldiers. Even the persecuted persecute, Doops thought, watching the girl empty the garbage. She paid no attention to the convoy or the porter.

When all the cans were emptied and back on the train, four hands reached down and pulled the girl up into the car. The porter stood in place until the door was completely closed. He stared at the spot where she had disappeared until the whistle sounded and the train began to move.

Doops did not turn around as the others watched the man quicken his pace in time to grab hold of the railing on the caboose and swing himself up, throwing the duty bag onto the platform.

Kingston and Fordache seemed obliged to stand with Doops, not to turn around either.

"Dey call me Cayenne back home at Mermentau," Fordache said, looking first at one and then the other. "*Mais*, Ah t'ink y'all bes' call me Model T." He put his hand on their shoulders.

"Thanks for saving my ass," Doops said. "And you, Smylie, can *kiss* my ass," he added, returning Kingston's sheepish smile.

3

"**O**kay, Mr. Private Doops. What was that all about?" Kingston asked him. The captain had told the platoon that they could sleep for two hours before reassembling for morning drill. Doops had wandered outside the barracks and Kingston and Model T followed.

"What's what all about?" Doops said.

"You know damn well what I'm talking about. What was going on in that truck?"

"You know what was going on. That porter found his kids. And we didn't see any Japs."

"We saw one," Kingston said. "At least half of one. Wonder what she's got on her fingernails."

"Half-moons on one hand and rising suns on the other, I guess," Doops said, not laughing.

"Maybe so. But what the hell was the matter with you. You looked like a ghost," Kingston replied.

"I felt like a ghost," Doops replied.

"You ever felt like that before?"

"Yeah."

"How many times?"

"Lots of times. Lots of times. But skip it. I don't want to talk about it. Skip it!" Doops walked away but Kingston and Model T followed.

"You didn't let me skip it out there in the woods that day. The other day when you found me crying my ass off. Now, I want to know what was going on."

"Hell, I let you skip it. I didn't want you to tell me all that stuff. You wanted to tell me."

"Yeah, I wanted to tell you after you saw me cry. So now, I've seen you cry. Or I saw you do something. Now tell me. You said we were friends."

"I said we were buddies," Doops said.

"Well . . . buddies. Tell me what was going on."

"I don't know what to tell you. I just felt weird, that's all. I felt funny. Like I was going to pass out or something. My heart felt like it was slowing down. Like it was going to stop. Like my blood was being diluted. Like I was drowning."

"Drowning? And what else?"

"Nothing else. I just felt funny. I've felt that way sometimes ever since I was little. Like I'm looking for something and can't find it and I don't even know what it is anyway. You ever been lost? I remember one time we were burning brush heaps in a new ground at night. I thought the house was in front of us and it was directly behind us. Just confused. I thought I was mad, losing my mind."

"What you looking for?" Kingston said. "Me and Model T here, we'll help you find it."

"If I knew that I could probably find it myself," Doops said.

"You ever see a doctor?"

"No! No, I never saw a doctor. What the hell would I tell him? That I felt funny? Hey, doc. I'm drowning! Save me! Hey, doc. I'm looking for something."

Doops changed direction and started walking toward Kisatchie Forest, pretending unconcern. Kingston and Model T followed, Kingston talking, Model T saying nothing.

When they reached the edge of the forest there was an awkward silence until Doops began to speak.

"Sometimes I think it has something to do with the way I was born. I almost died. Fact is they thought I *was* dead. But I didn't die. I didn't die or I wouldn't be out here in this godforsaken place learning how to kill somebody I don't even know. I almost died. But I didn't die."

There was silence again as they walked on. The sun was bearing down on them in the early Louisiana morning. The newly mown grass clippings from the parade ground they'd crossed were sticking to their boot soles and hanging in the hooks of the canvas leggings they had not taken the time to remove. Finally Doops spoke again.

"Nobody ever actually told me what happened. I just put the pieces together. Here and there, you know. When I was growing up. Every time I got a cold or something, somebody would mention the night I was born. And that's all I know how to tell you."

"No it ain't," Kingston said. "That ain't all you can tell me." He spoke as if Model T were not even there. "I want to hear all of it."

"I don't know all of it. Don't you understand that? I don't know all of it! I can't tell you something I don't know!" He tried to move away.

"But you can tell me what you *do* know. What you heard. What you put together."

Doops took a breath, sighed hard, and began walking in a straight line into the forest.

"I kept hearing them talk about it. I never did ask them what happened, and they never did tell me. Seems when I was about to be born, when they took my mamma to the hospital, something happened. Finally, when I was about fifteen years old, I took all the little pieces I had put together, wrote little notes down on a piece of paper and made a doctor talk to me, tell me what it meant. I hitched a ride to Crosby and found a doctor's name in the telephone book. I just went to his office and told the woman I wanted to see the doctor. When she asked me what was wrong I just told her I needed to see the doctor. I had saved up eight dollars and I told him I would give it all to him if he would tell me what the notes meant. He read everything I had on the paper two or three times, asking me some of the words he couldn't make out. Then he said he knew what I was getting at but that that couldn't have happened to me or I would be dead. He used a lot of big words and wrote some of them down. I went to the library in Crosby that same day and looked the words up, the ones I didn't understand. They had a big medical book and I found what I was looking for in it. The doctor tried to put it in real plain English so I could understand, but I missed some of it."

Occasionally Doops would repeat what he had just said, knowing that Model T wasn't understanding all of what he was saying and wanting him to hear it too.

"When you're inside your mamma, you're just sort of floating around all the time. But you're tied on to her, sort of, by a cord. The umbilical cord. You're inside a little sack thing, but you're just sort of floating. And all the time you're swallowing water."

Model T began to wave his arms excitedly.

"Aw, *non, vieux! Ca c'est pas vrai.* You drown youself in no time like dat."

"Knock it off, Model T," Kingston said. "You don't know your ass from a hole in the ground."

"Mah ass, dat's wat it is—a hole in de groun'."

Kingston started to say something else to Model T, stopped short, stammered, and turned to Doops. "What'd he say?"

"And the Lord made man of the dust of the ground," Doops said laughing approvingly. "That includes his ass. I told you he knows something."

Doops began talking directly to Model T, continuing to explain.

"The reason you don't drown is because you ain't actually breathing. Your lungs ain't working. You get the oxygen from your mamma. It's sort of like deep-sea diving. You're down there in all that water but the tank on your back, or the line going back to the boat, gives you the oxygen. Not really like that but something like that. Anyway, sometimes the sack you're in comes loose from the womb. And the cord tears loose. And that's what happened to me. The doctor came flying out in the hall and told my daddy that something was wrong and that he didn't have but a few minutes to cut my mamma open and get me out of there. But he said he had to have the proper permission to do it. My daddy went running in the room past the nurses and everybody and said my mamma was not asleep and that she would have to give the permission. I guess my mamma was all excited or something, but she never would tell him to cut her open and get me out. She just kept saying she'd have to think about it. Said she didn't believe in things like that and that she would have me the natural way. By that time the doctor said it was too late, that I was already dead and all they could do was wait for her labor pains to bring me out, but that I would be dead. But about fifteen minutes later I was born. And here I am."

"Wut de devil was de matta wit you dum' ma-ma?" Model T whispered.

"Shut up, Model T," Kingston said. "You don't talk about somebody's mamma. He told you he didn't know. So he doesn't know."

"Watch it," Doops said. He had become more and more irritable as they walked. Now he turned abruptly to Model T, his mood changing. "Hey, Ford! What do you do back home? How you make a living?"

"Me? Ah most de time do wut mah pa-pa do. Ah trap de nutria. Fish. Catch de muskrat. Ah pick de moss, too. Pick lotta moss."

"Moss?" Kingston said, trying to sound pleasant. "What do you do with moss? What kind of moss?"

"*Mais*, tree moss," Model T said. "Dat's de kin' a moss ah wanna mean. Dey stuff dat moss in t'ings like some mattress, an' t'ings tuh set you on. T'ings like dat. Dis man come all de way from Lafayette. He buy de moss, him. Yah, me, I pick a lotta moss."

"Do you trust me?" Doops said, looking at him in a friendly but strange sort of way, a way Model T had not seen before.

"Wut de devil? Wut you t'inkin' about?"

"I mean, are you my buddy?"

"*Mais*, wut you t'ink? *Mais*, hell yaah! Ah'm gonna tole you. Me an' you, we buddies, *hein*. An' dat's de trute. Ol' Kingston too, him."

"Is that right, Smylie? You and him buddies?"

"Sure," Kingston said.

"Then tell him. Tell him what you told me. You know, about your daddy."

"You think he would understand?" Kingston asked.

"Yeah. He'll understand. Tell him."

"If I do what you want me to, will that make us friends?" Kingston called over his shoulder, walking several steps ahead of Doops and Model T.

"No!" Doops snapped, his face flushing, the volume and inflection of his voice surprising both of them. "And don't ever ask me that again."

"Jesus," Kingston said. "What the hell is that all about? Okay, okay, okay. I just asked. The other day you said we were buddies. When I asked if we were friends you said we'd have to see. Well, when we going to see? Maybe I'm tired of being buddies. I think to get through this goddamn war somebody got us into I'm going to need more than buddies. I just asked, that's all. So skip it, hoss. Skip it."

"I didn't say skip it," Doops said, composed now. "Or maybe I did. But look . . . " He hurried to catch up with him. "Being friends doesn't have anything to do with somebody doing something or not doing something. It just happens. My daddy used to say you had to eat a peck of salt with somebody before you could be their friend. I guess I never did believe that. That's a hell of a lot of salt. And before you could eat that much salt . . . well damn, you'd die of high blood pressure. Maybe friend is impossible. You don't ever know till it's over. Like, I mean, it's a forever thing, I suppose. That's all I'm talking about. But we'll be neighbors. We'll be a neighborhood, me and you and Model T. You know, a community. And we'll make it."

"Well, you jumped a lot of rabbits with that one and I'm not sure I bagged any of them. But all right, I'll tell Model T." And putting his arm around Model T's shoulder, he talked as they walked along. Doops dropped far enough behind so that he could not hear Kingston talking. Model T showed no sign of missing any of what he was hearing.

4

Their training at Camp Polk was both minimal and routine. In three months they did calisthenics, ran obstacle courses consisting of old automobile tires, scaled high walls with hemp ropes, crawled under barbed-wire entanglements with real bullets just above to keep rumps close to the ground. There were all-night marches with carrot sticks to eat and salt water to drink, and endless days on the firing range learning to shoot M-1 rifles, carbines, and Browning automatic weapons—all called "pieces."

"Do you think the Japs do it this way?" Kingston asked when they did some particularly foolish exercise.

"I hope so," Doops answered. "Then they'll be just as stupid as we are."

For three months they faced slant-eyed figures—dummies, sacks filled with straw and looking more orangutan than human, stabbing at them repeatedly with bayonets while screaming *"yiah!"* "Wonder whatever happened to the Germans," Kingston would say, noticing that they never seemed to be mentioned during their training.

They were marched to a dark and musty room called a gas area where a tremulous little major, said to have been a victim of a gas attack during the bombardment of Ypres in 1917, explained the horrors of chemical warfare. Using charts, diagrams, and formulas they didn't understand, he made them remove their gas masks long enough to sniff and identify lewisite, adamsite, and phosgene, smelling to them like geranium, newly mown hay, and long-dead fish. "*Mais*, dey kill me dead, *hein?* *Mais*, dey kill me dead, *hein?*" Model T said when he didn't understand the order and got too much of the tear gas in his eyes.

They stormed and screamed from what the officers called a Higgins boat but which was nothing more than a flat barge pulled manually with a steel cable and a windlass by squads of black soldiers from a quartermaster detachment on the back side of the camp. Their ocean was a craggy and shallow lake, little more than a pond, cypress knees protruding everywhere except in the narrow channel that had been cleared for the back-and-forth passage of the barge. In five minutes, they were on the other side, storming and screaming and cussing at nonexistent Japanese. Preparation for a war they could only imagine, a war, they were constantly told, that would take their lives if they did not take the training seriously.

In thirteen weeks it was over and in an elaborate ceremonial of bands, flags, and generals, they were declared soldiers. Ready to kill. "Or be killed," the general said.

"Hurry up and wait. Hurry up and wait," Kingston said. After a brief furlough, they returned to Camp Polk to be assigned to organized units. The shipping orders were posted daily on the bulletin board and the men gathered to see where they would be going. At first the lists were long—seventy-five to the 137th Infantry Regiment at Camp Blanding, fifty to Camp Joseph T. Robinson near Little Rock, ninety to Fort Ord, California. As the days and weeks passed, the number posted each day grew smaller. A new word had been born—*snafu*. Situation normal, all fucked up. Generally there were no explanations, no reasons, no one to ask when a soldier's name still did not appear. He simply waited. There were exceptions, valid causes why someone was not shipped out: he was being considered for Officers' Candidate School, a special assignment, misplaced orders, perhaps health reasons. But those were few.

After five weeks, eighteen men from Company D had still not been shipped out. Doops, Kingston, and Model T were among them. They had long since been moved to other quarters because the old barracks space was needed for new recruits. They were called to battalion headquarters and told that they had been classified as "holdovers," a designation Doops explained as meaning they no longer existed.

"What the hell do we do now?" Kingston asked as they walked back to the barracks.

"You've said it before," Doops replied. "Hurry up and wait."

The waiting was long, mostly boring, but sometimes adventuresome. They learned early that holdovers were looked upon with disdain—a nuisance, as if they were a disease upon the body, as if it were their own fault that they were still there. They also learned eventually that their records were lost. Doops was right: they no longer existed. And neither did their pay.

"Okay, neighbors," Doops told Kingston and Model T, "we have to go into business for ourselves. PX beer is cheap but it ain't free."

Model T came up with the idea of substituting for soldiers with money who might not want to do certain assignments. The risk of being found out was minimal as long as they watched Company D's NCOs. Since they had little to do, they could get passes to go to Leesville whenever they asked for them. For two dollars, they would give a soldier their passes and let him use their dogtags. If he didn't plan to get back before bed check, one of them would lie in his bed with the covers pulled over his head. That was a dollar extra. KP duty was five dollars. Once a week, all the new soldiers were marched to the dispensary to be examined for venereal disease. They called it short-arm inspection. If someone suspected that he was infected, one of them would serve as a surrogate. The price was eight dollars. "You pay for the risk," Kingston told them. Whatever they made was put in their treasury and all of them could draw from it.

It was a lucrative scheme and worked well for three weeks. Then Model T took on a KP tour. What they hadn't thought about was that sometimes mess sergeants were transferred from one company to another. On this particular day, the mess sergeant had been eyeing Model T, puzzled and suspicious but unable to place him. Duty was about over and the sergeant, who had formed all the KPs in a line, was instructing them to flood the entire area and scrub the floor with huge long-handled brushes. Just as Kingston and Doops arrived at the mess hall to pick up

Model T, the sergeant remembered where he had seen him.

"Okay, you coonass sonofabitch!" he screamed. "So you like to pull KP. All right, buddy, I'll just show you how it's done."

He called the other soldiers, already starting to work, back to where he was standing. "Gentlemen, we have a man with us today who just loves to scrub floors. So it would be a shame for the rest of you to cut him out of the fun." He reached up to an overhead shelf and pulled down a small string mop, used ordinarily to swab sauce or butter onto large pieces of meat.

"This ought to be easier for you, Freckles. Now God damn it, you get your scrawny Cajun ass out there on that floor, on your hands and knees, and I want you to scrub every board in this hall, one at a time. And the rest of us are going to stand here and watch you do it!"

Model T stood for a minute looking at him, making no move to take the mop from his hand. Doops and Kingston thought he was going to refuse to do it, expected him to turn and walk away. The sergeant shifted nervously, obviously uncertain what he would do if Model T defied him, looking him in the eyes. Model T held the stare, all the other soldiers forming a semicircle around them.

"I believe it's your move, sergeant," Kingston said from outside the circle. The sergeant didn't answer. Model T studied the sergeant, watching him the way he might watch an alligator in the swamps of Mermentau.

"You gave him an order," Kingston said, moving closer, Doops trying to quiet him. "Now it's your ass or ours." When Model T heard Kingston, and heard Doops trying to control him, he reached out and took the mop and began scrubbing the floor as near the sergeant's feet as he could get.

"*Sacré misère,*" he said, glancing at Doops and Kingston for the first time.

Doops led Kingston away and the sergeant followed them outside.

"You getting smart with me, Slim?" the sergeant said.

"Come on," Doops said, still walking. But Kingston turned around to face the sergeant.

"You said it was my ass or yours. Which one of you wants to be first?"

"Come on," Doops whispered, pulling at Kingston's sleeve.

"I said, 'It's your ass or ours,'" Kingston shouted, ignoring Doops. "Now it's just your ass or *mine*. They're not in it. I'll be first."

"Tomorrow is my day off. What time?"

"Five o'clock," Kingston said. "We'll leave from right here. I ain't fighting on army property."

"Better bring your buddy to tote your ass back," the sergeant called as they walked away.

"Don't tell Model T," Kingston said. "I don't think he ought to know about this."

"Don't tell Model T? And why the hell not? He's part of the neighborhood."

"Why do you have to tell him?" Kingston asked, looking away. "Does he have to know everything we do?"

"I told you why," Doops said. "And that's why. Now are you going to tell him or you want me to do it?"

Kingston stopped walking and leaned up against the orderly-room wall, poking the ground with the toe of his boot. "Why do you think I don't understand how things are?" He looked hurt. "I mean, I don't try to dress it up, but Redbones aren't necessarily stupid, you know. Just because a guy has moons on his fingernails doesn't mean he doesn't have feelings, that he's a shithook. Is that what you think?"

"Oh, for Christ's sake!" Doops said. "I didn't mean it that way. I just . . . well, sometimes you're pretty rough on the little fellow."

"'The little fellow'?" Kingston said. "Well, he's not 'the little fellow.' He's Fordache Arceneau. You make it sound like he's a goddamn pet monkey."

Doops started to say something but didn't.

"So I'll tell him," Kingston said. "Okay? It's my place. I'll tell him I almost screwed up the neighborhood."

"I didn't say you were screwing up the neighborhood," Doops said, almost apologetically.

They stood looking at the ground between them for a minute or two.

"I ought to cut you with my knife," Kingston said, smiling. "Let's go get drunk. That coonass will know where to find us."

"**Q**uo *faire* . . ." Model T began, then switched to English. "Why he did dat?"

"It's called pulling rank," Kingston said, pouring him a beer from the pitcher on the table. "Here, you're three behind. I ought to kill that cocksucker."

"No, you won't," Doops said.

Kingston started to answer, thought it wasn't the time to talk about the fight, and said nothing.

"Hey, I know a good idea," Doops said.

"You know a good idea?" Kingston said. "Well, that's a first time. What's the good idea?"

"Let's all of us tell the saddest thing he ever saw."

"Jesus," Kingston said. "I ought to cut you with my knife! What the hell for?"

"No reason," Doops said. "Let's just do it. Just for the hell of it. You first. Then Model T. Then me."

"Bullshit!" Kingston laughed. "You're stacking the deck. Except you don't have a full deck to stack." He punched Model T. "Ole Doops here, he's got something he wants to tell us. He don't give a damn what we say. Well, I never saw anything sad in my whole life. Not till I met you anyway. You ever see anything sad, Fordache? Tell Doops something sad. Ole Doops wants to cry in his beer. Tell him about the time your grandma got her tit caught in the sausage grinder. That must have been pretty sad."

"Naw, come on guys. I'm serious. I don't mean anything real personal. You know, like somebody in your family dying or something. I don't mean something like that. Just something you saw. Anything."

"You writing a book, Doops?" Kingston said. "Hey Model T, Doops is writing a book. Tell him something for his book."

"Maybe I am," Doops said. "I always wanted to."

Model T began to scratch his head, reaching over with his left hand to the opposite side, playing "monkey" for them. Then he grew serious and began to tell about the time he and his daddy found a dog caught in a steel trap. They had set the trap themselves, set it and fifty others for nutria, little rodents whose pelts they sold for fifty cents each to a New York furrier who'd told them they were going to be more valuable than mink as soon as they caught enough of them to make them scarce. The day after they set the traps it rained so hard the marshes flooded and they couldn't run the traps for more than a week. The dog had not been badly hurt but it couldn't get away and drowned.

"The saddest thing about that story is the way that Yankee sonofabitch lied to you and your pa-pa," Kingston said.

Doops told him it was Model T's story and it was for him to decide what was sad about it. "Okay. Now it's your time, Redbone boy."

"I told you I ain't playing. And if I do play, I'll be last. It's your time."

Doops did not hesitate. "The saddest thing I ever saw, I believe, was five pennies and two dimes in a roadhouse urinal."

"You better chase that one across the creek again," Kingston said, laughing, running his hand back and forth across Doops's crewcut cowlick. "Yeah, you'd better run that one by me again."

"You heard me," Doops said.

"I heard you. Yeah, I heard you. Model T heard you too. But just what the hell is sad about five pennies and two dimes in a beer-joint pissery?"

"Well, I stopped in this roadhouse when we were hitchhiking back from Shreveport that time. Remember when we had that three-day pass and me and you got split up and that carload of soldiers couldn't take but one of us? I made you take the ride and the next guy who came along was smashed as a skunk and I drove him all the way to Leesville except he had to stop at every dive on the highway. We were up about Mansfield around midnight and this guy wouldn't leave until closing time. I went to the john and there in this country beer-joint urinal were five pennies and two dimes. I got to talking to the barkeep and he told me about them. Said they had been in there four, maybe five years."

Kingston was interested now and leaned forward, both elbows on the table, chin resting in his hands, not touching the beer while Doops talked. Model T rubbed the brass buckle on his belt, pretending not to listen.

"He said this big pulp wood hauler came in one night about that same time. Said he was already looped and between beers tried to fight everybody in there. Cussing and yelling and trying to jerk folks off the stools of the bar. Man, he said he was the crudest, vilest fucker you ever saw. After he went to the john, the next one in there found that money. Five pennies and two dimes. They had heard him throwing them in one at a time. The poor befuddled bastard thought the pissery was a wishing well. Thought he was throwing coins in a wishing well. A pulp-wood hauler throwing pennies and dimes in a wishing well. Well, they thought that was about the funniest thing they had ever seen. After he passed out on the floor and somebody loaded him in his truck and drove him home, they took bets on what he was wishing for. You know, just making jokes and talking about women."

Kingston motioned for Model T to pay attention.

"Next day they heard the guy's little girl had leukemia. They took a solemn pledge that they wouldn't ever take the pennies and dimes out of his fountain as long as the little girl was alive. And from then on every time one of them bought a beer he paid for two. They poured the pickled eggs out of this big jar and every time somebody drank a beer he put twenty cents in that jar. Said they raised quite a bit of money for the little girl."

Model T had stopped rubbing the brass buckle and sat with his eyes closed, his head against the back of the chair. "*Sacré misère*," he whispered under his breath. Kingston sat straight up, his eyes wide open.

When he finished talking, Kingston and Model T continued to sit in silence, the glow of the hops intensifying what they were feeling.

"Ah t'ink it's you time, Smylie," Model T said, trying to sound casual as he opened his eyes and stretched. The private first class who ran the bar was pouring another pitcher of beer, the head running over and forming a puddle in the middle of the table.

"I t'ink bes' I say you my story de nex' time, me," Kingston said, trying to sound like Model T.

They took turns going to the bathroom and when they finished, Doops began again. "Hey, I know another good idea. Let's talk about kinfolks. You got any kinfolks, Model T? I know this Redbone fucker's got lots of them, but hell, he don't know who they are." He put his arm around Kingston's shoulder. "Hey, Model T, you know what? This here ole fucker don't know his daddy from his grandpa. So how the hell is he going to talk about kinfolks. So who wants to talk about kinfolks?"

42

"You do," Kingston said. "You brought it up. Tell him about your kinfolks, Model T. You got any kinfolks?"

"*Mais*, wut you t'ink, *mon ami*? Alsonse, Etienne, Théobale, Léonce, Viola, Marie Louise, Auguste, Emmeline, Bé Bé, Ti-Joe, Ti-Gris, Nanainne, Papite, Antoine, Cécile . . ."

"Cécile?" Doops asked, a startled, bewildered look on his face. "Cécile," he said again, softer, not as a question. "Is that your mamma?"

"Dat's mah sister."

"Cécile," he whispered.

"What the hell's the matter with you. You crazy? You look like you just got hit in the face with a wet possum," Kingston said. "All them folks got the same last name?" he asked, turning to Model T.

"*Mais*, wut you talk about? Dey Bourque, Le Blanc, Laviolette, Comeaux, Guilbean, Dupré, Boudreaux, Dupuis, Bordelon, Gauthier—dey got lotta behind name. Lotta Arceneau too. Me, I got lotta kin, ah'm gon' say you."

Doops was drinking the beer in long, quick gulps. When he tried to pour another glass for each of them he spilled some of it, leaned forward to wipe it up, and almost fell off the chair.

"You got any kinfolks, Doops? Tell us about your kinfolks?"

"I got . . . a . . . first cousin once removed. . . . My . . ."

"What the hell is that? First cousin once removed. I've heard that all my life and I never knew what it means," Kingston said.

Doops was waving his hands in slow circles on each side of his head, looking confused.

"This fucker is drunk," Kingston said to Model T, taking Doops's glass and pushing it away from him.

"A . . . firs' cousin . . . once removed." He stopped as if he had forgotten the question, then continued. "Tha's when . . . your mamma's brother . . . has a kid and then he has a kid. So . . . I got . . ."

"Bullshit," Kingston said. "That's your second cousin."

Doops kept gesturing, trying to explain the difference between a second cousin and a first cousin once removed.

Model T picked up Doops's glass, drank part of the beer himself, and poured the rest in the pitcher, patting Doops on the shoulder as he did. "Me an' you an' Kingston could be more closer kin den dat, *hein?*" he said.

"Yep," Doops said, hiccuping and trying to stand. "We just might be. Cécile," he muttered.

The guy who ran the bar was blinking the lights to signal last call. Three soldiers were standing at the end of the bar playing "Chattanooga Choo Choo" on a trombone, tenor saxophone, and clarinet, imitating Glenn Miller, each one in turn stepping to a standup microphone for his solo, the microphone not even plugged in.

Model T and Kingston took Doops by the arms, trying to pull him up. He shook free and motioned for them to sit down.

"Now jus' a fuckin' minute," he said. "I got to . . . say something . . . to this audience." He was slurring his words but turned around so he could see everyone in the bar. No one paid him any mind.

"Let me tell you something," he began sternly. "You don't *get* in a fucking community!" He stood up and wobbled about the room, talking loud. "It ain't something you get voted in and kicked out of. Ain't something you join." The words were coming faster. There was a pleading quality to his voice. "You're just *in!*" The bartender winked at Kingston and motioned for them to get him out. "Hell . . . I don't know. Maybe you're born in. Shit . . . I don't know. But you don't choose it . . . an' I'm gon' tell you one more time." Kingston and Model T made no move to stop him, to take him out, motioning to the bartender that they would in a minute. "You don't take somebody in . . . an' you don't keep somebody out. . . . If . . . they're in . . . well, there ain't a fuckin' thing you can do about it . . . an' tha's jus' the way it is."

"You're a mess, Mr. Private Doops," Kingston said as they led him through the door. "I ought to cut you with my knife."

"And you ought to get your hair conked," Doops said, leaning on first one and then the other. "But . . . tha's . . . jus' . . . the way it is."

The next morning they were called to the orderly room of Company D and told that their records and transfer orders had been located in Fort Ord and that they were to report there for an overseas assignment.

5

They arrived on New Caledonia two weeks before Thanksgiving. As they waited for a combat assignment, they walked the beaches of white-silver sand, whitened even more by the deep blue-green coral reefs glistening in contrast through the miles of salty water, pacifying as the name itself.

DANGER: WATCH FOR FALLING COCONUTS. Army-posted signs in the palm groves stood in sad and grim mockery of what the trails they walked must have looked like before the Frenchmen came to establish the island as a prison colony almost a hundred years earlier.

Nouméa, the only town of any size on the island, was a gaudy caricature of the boomtown outskirts of Leesville, after Camp Polk came. Part county fair, part parasite. Its streets held rows of curio and souvenir shops, seashell beads, brass vases made from spent 50-millimeter shell hulls, aluminum bracelets cut and fashioned from destroyed or abandoned B-24 and P-38 fuselages, fake shrunken heads made from unripe coconuts, painted black and carved to look more Negroid than Melanesian. Coca-Cola bars and stand-up counters where a fried egg sandwich cost a dollar. Frozen custard, sno-cones, and cotton candy. A big USO building with a glass booth where for fifty cents a soldier could get sixty seconds of his own voice put on a paper-thin disc to send loved ones at home, and a pavilion where French hostesses, descendants of the early colonizers, danced one dance with each soldier on Friday and Saturday nights and women in Red Cross uniforms passed out doughnuts and gave away little boxes with five Chesterfield cigarettes inside.

"What does *sacré misère* mean?" Kingston asked one of the French women.

"What?" she asked, saying it as if he had said something improper.

"*Sacré misère.* What does it mean?"

"Well, that's two words but they don't go together," she said. "*Sacré* can mean 'sacred.' And it can mean an ugly word I won't repeat."

"No offense," Kingston said.

"*Misère* just means 'misery.' But the two don't go together. Why?" Her accent was more English than French.

"I just wondered," Kingston said, letting her go when the music stopped and joining Doops and Model T outside.

A short distance from the carnival itself, but part of it, stood a huge, castlelike structure called The Pink House, taking its name from the color it was painted. They stood and watched the double line of soldiers—all white—completely circling the building. For five dollars, a navy corpsman handed each entering soldier a kit containing a bottle of purple liquid and a bulb syringe filled with a stinging solution. After that he was allowed three carefully timed minutes with a woman, guaranteed to be of Chinese, not Japanese descent. When the three minutes were up, the prophylactic was repeated before the soldier was free to leave. Neither Doops, Kingston, nor Model T considered going in.

"Guaranteed!" Doops said. "Great God!"

"If that's making love, I've got a fist named Betty Grable," Kingston said. And that was the end of it.

While they waited, they spent some of the days and nights walking the tawdry streets, sometimes amused, sometimes melancholic, sometimes horrified by the ugliness of it all. But most of their time was spent in camp, sitting on canvas cots arranged in rows in the long, hot thatch barracks with roll-down canvas sides, open on each end like the hallway of a giant barn.

To pass the time, Doops suggested that they enroll for some

courses from the Armed Forces Institute, a correspondence school operated for the military by the University of Wisconsin. It took four weeks for the first lessons and books to arrive. Doops chose advanced Latin and a course on English poets. Kingston chose a college-level class called Agronomy of the Future. Model T registered for a course in Reading and Speaking. Kingston told him there was an expression teacher in Cummings and his granddaddy had paid fifty cents a week for him to take lessons from her on Saturday mornings so he wouldn't have his mother's accent. He said he would help him with the exercises if Model T would begin teaching them how to speak Cajun French.

"We'll swap out," Kingston said. "We'll learn to talk like you talk and you learn to talk like we talk. That way, everybody is everybody else."

Model T was excited about it. "*Mais*, ah'm gonna tell y'all. Ah'm gonna talk jus' like dat man on de radio. Could be ah'll get me a job on dat WWL station wen ah got back. Sell dat good ol' Dr. Tichenor's—'bes' annaseptics in town.'"

"It's mostly a matter of verbs anyway," Kingston said. "Your nouns and pronouns are okay. It's mainly your verbs. Just watch your verbs."

"And his adjectives," Doops added. "Nothing more important than adjectives."

"Just watch your verbs, T," Kingston said, frowning playfully at Doops and pointing a schoolmaster finger at Model T. "Doops never studied elocution. I did. Just watch your verbs."

They worked hard on the lessons every day, asking each other questions. Kingston listened to Model T's enunciation of "How now brown cow" and read Carl Sandburg poems about Abraham Lincoln aloud with him. Model T drilled them in Cajun French.

"*Sacré misère! Sacré misère!*"

"What the hell does it mean?" Kingston asked, repeating it over and over after Model T. Model T said it meant just about everything and anything. He said they could take their hands and those two words and talk to any Cajun in Louisiana.

"But what does it mean exactly?" Kingston wanted to know, still repeating after him. "A woman at the USO told me it could be something holy or something insulting."

"*Mais*, hell yeah!" Model T said. "An' dat's de trute. Dat's wut it mean. *Sacré misère!*"

After five lessons they were shipped out. They were important lessons—bonding, uniting lessons. Covenant. Things they had never known.

They had not been told that they were going to Guadalcanal until the convoy of ships was two days out of Nouméa. Then, for reasons they did not question, it was the chaplain who told them. The chaplain was a short, rotund man of about forty. There was a Scot's burr to his speech, appropriated and adopted by him, cultivated and brought back from the year's study at the University of Edinburgh that rounded off the three years he had spent at Union Seminary in Richmond, Virginia. This combination of speech and academic preparation made him an authentic Presbyterian. He was seldom seen by the troops on the ships, but was popular with his fellow officers. Kingston, temporarily assigned to the officers' wardroom, said that it was because he had been allowed an extra trunk to bring communion elements and the trunk was filled with four cases of Scotch whiskey. There were two services on Sunday. One was at nine o'clock for Catholics. There was no mass, but one of the officers led the troops in the rosary.

The other service was held at eleven for Protestants. There, the chaplain presided and offered communion. Doops went, stood on the fringe of the gathering, but did not participate in any of the hymns, responsive readings, or prayers and did not take communion. The wine was a pint of water with one ounce of the Scotch whiskey, roséd with red cake coloring.

"Did you play 'swallow the leader'?" Kingston asked Doops when he joined them after the service.

"Nope. I didn't choose to play."

It was after the service that the chaplain told the men where they were going. Moving in a navy skiff from one Liberty ship to another, all of them made in Pascagoula, Mississippi, and with names like *Mermacwren*, *Olymphia*, and *Essex XI*, he spoke with a bullhorn from the captain's deck, giving the same prepared speech each time.

"Gentlemen, we are gone now from the warm and mansuetudal French and are sailing into the romance and pageantry of
Spain. The Isles of King Solomon. Not many years after our own
beloved America was founded by an envoy of Queen Isabella of
Castile and Aragon, another nobleman, Don Alvaro de Mendaña
de Neyra, going forth in what was at once the promotion and
defense of his country, discovered the fabled islands which had
been the source of all the gold of King Solomon's Temple. It is
now the sanctuary of our perfidious and crafty enemy. He expects
to meet us there. And meet him we shall. And the victory, in the
name of all that is holy and civilized, will be ours. His purpose,
yea his promise, is to lay waste the treasured glory of the West.
The outcome is as secured as the bosom of Abraham. Christian
soldiers, onward! For we know what goeth on before. And we
know the banner will prevail."

As the soldiers stood watching him he traipsed back and forth
on the captain's deck high above them, basking in his assumed
eloquence, rambling on about the virtues of wresting this sacred
island of verdant green from the yellow of the rising sun, saying
more than he knew as he talked of the giant Lever Brothers co-
conut-palm plantation serving now as airfield for the jaundiced
Nipponese, equating Lux soap with the purity of America's heart,
finishing finally with what he thought would bring cheers from
the soldiers as he recited the words of a song about another legen-
dary man of the Lord. "Gentlemen," he shouted, holding his right
hand high above his head in a charge position, "praise the Lord,
and pass the ammunition!"

"I never did trust Presbyterians," Doops said.

"What?" Kingston said.

"I never did trust Presbyterians."

"Why not?"

"I don't know. I'm not sure there are any left. Like Baptists.
None left."

"What does that mean?" Kingston said, looking at Model T and
then back at Doops.

"I don't know. Don't know what it means. I'm just not sure."

"How corny can a bastard get?" one of the soldiers asked aloud.

"Mansuetudal?" another said. "What the hell does that mean?"

"I think it means rupturing your houseboy's spleen," the first soldier said. "That's what I saw one of the warm Frenchmen do one day. The kid died a week later. Twelve years old. Kicked to death for dropping a goddamn ashtray. Yeah. Warm and mansuetudal."

Doops leaned over the rail and opened his mouth. A long rope of thin liquid drooled into the ocean.

"You sick?" Model T asked.

"He's got the symptoms," Kingston whispered to Model T. It was what he had started calling the strange drowning sensations that Doops continued to have.

"No," Doops said, not hearing Kingston. "Just spittin' in the ocean. I never did trust Presbyterians."

"I thought it was 'pissing' in the ocean," Kingston said.

"Could be that too," Doops said. And turned away.

"Why don't you trust Presbyterians?" Kingston asked, squinting and looking back and forth from Doops to Model T.

"Damned if I know," Doops answered, squinting curiously as Kingston had done, looking back and forth at Model T and Kingston in the same manner. "I told you I didn't know. I just don't trust them."

Doops had bent a forty-penny nail into a hook and tied it to a string. For hours after the chaplain's talk he sat on the stern of the ship, holding the string, the weight of the nail dragging in the water, keeping it taut.

Model T and Kingston had learned that when Doops had the symptoms he generally did not speak. On those occasions, one of them would speak for him when an outsider tried to talk to him.

Hundreds of soldiers filled every inch of available walking space on the upper deck. One standing near Doops asked, "What you doing?"

"Fishing," Kingston answered.

"Fishing?"

"Yeah. Fishing."

"What for?"

" 'Cause I want to," Kingston said.

"No. I mean what's *he* fishing for?"

"That's what for. 'Cause I want to."

The soldier thought of another way to put it. "What kind of bait does he have?"

"No bait," Kingston said, still speaking for Doops, standing as close to him as he could get, his voice taking on the deep quality of Doops's own voice. "Fact of the matter is, there ain't even a hook. Just a big ole bent nail on the end of that string."

The soldier worked his way through the crowd mumbling to others as he went, shaking his head.

Half an hour later, a second lieutenant came and placed one hand on Doops's shoulder, smiling and patting his head with the other hand.

"You fishing, soldier?" the officer asked, bending his body so that he could look Doops in the face without falling over the rail.

"Yes, sir," Kingston replied.

"I'm talking to him!" the officer snapped, no longer smiling. "When I ask him if he's fishing, you let him answer me. You understand?"

"Yes, sir. But he's fishing for me. It really ain't him fishing. I'm fishing. That's why I said, 'Yes, sir,' sir."

The lieutenant wore a brass caduceus on his collar. The letter *A* was attached to it, the insignia of the Medical Administrative Corps. Kingston knew that meant he was not a doctor. He'd been in the army long enough to have discovered just how much confusion the regulations and standardized tests and procedures had created within the medical profession. General surgeons and internists, orthopedic surgeons and ophthalmologists were drafted as professionals. Unless they were women. Podiatrists, chiropractors, and osteopaths were drafted. But they were not allowed to practice their profession. Optometrists were not drafted. Female nurses could not be drafted but might enlist as second lieutenants. Male nurses were drafted as privates but did not serve as nurses. Pharmacists were drafted but not as pharmacists, though they were generally assigned to a hospital unit after basic training. Psychiatrists were drafted but many of them did not pass the examination for emotional stability under battle stress conditions, tests given to them by other psychiatrists, so there was always a shortage of this specialty. Gynecologists and obstetricians, also drafted as professionals, with little to do treating young

WACs and WAVEs, were often assigned as psychiatrists. Keeping all that straight required a separate professional category called the Medical Administrative Corps. In addition, if a problem arose—a soldier fishing with a bent nail and no bait—which could not be matched with one of the specialties, a medical administrator was expected to handle it.

"Look boys," the lieutenant said, all his patience gone. "You can't catch a fish with a nail with no bait on it tied to a string that would break if you did. Now, knock it off or I'll haul you both to the brig."

Model T had been standing close by, but had said nothing. Four soldiers sat on the deck cross-legged, playing poker. There had been a general announcement made when they boarded the ship that no gambling was allowed. So there was no money in the circle. Just cards. Model T moved beside the lieutenant, tapped him on the shoulder, and pointed at the four soldiers.

"Wut dey doin', captain?" he asked in his Cajun manner. With his elocution lessons he was speaking better English but when he was mad or excited he talked the way he always had.

"I'm not a captain. But I'd say from the cards in their hands they're playing poker. So what? They're playing poker!"

"*Mais*, wut you t'ink dey gonna win, *hein?*"

The lieutenant walked away, trying as best he could to return all the salutes as he made his way through the crowd, finally giving up and holding his hand to the bill of his cap until he disappeared into the officers' half of the ship.

The exchange had brought Doops back from wherever it was he had been. When Kingston and the soldier were talking, he had not even heard them. But he had heard Model T's words.

"Mr. Arceneau. My friend." Then changing it to "Monsieur Arceneau. *Mon ami*," the way he imagined Model T would say it back home. He extended his hand and Model T shook it, smiling as he did. "*Ah oui, frère Doops, mon bon cher ami.*"

Kingston stood looking at them, a dim pained expression on his face. Model T made a quick motion in his direction, making sure Doops saw him but Kingston did not.

"And *Monsieur* Smylie, *mon ami* also," Doops said, taking Kingston by the hand.

Kingston shook his hand firmly without comment, turning in-

52

stead to Model T. "You stupid coonass. How'd you know how to knock that lieutenant on his ass?"

"Ah jus' say, '*Mais*, wut you t'ink dey gonna win, *hein?*' An' dat's all wut ah said, me."

Doops began to pound him on the back and laugh. "Yeah. Dat's all wut you said," Kingston said. "And he never knew what hit him. You can't catch a fish with no bait. And you can't win at poker with no money on the table. But you can do both if you damn well want to. '*Mais*, wut you t'ink dey gonna win, *hein?*' "

The three of them found a vacant area about midship and sat down on the deck. Most of the other soldiers were already in line for the evening meal. Two meals were served each day and some of the troops spent most of their waking hours standing in the long line. The alternative was to lie on the canvas bunks stacked six high in the hold, or wander aimlessly about the deck. Most of the soldiers had grown accustomed to strict regimentation and felt more secure in the lines. But the three of them generally waited until the single file of soldiers had dwindled to a few, even though they knew that sometimes there would be little food left.

Model T had been on KP duty and told them he had a gallon of ripe olives in his duffel bag and that could be their supper.

"You dumb coonass," Kingston said. "You don't just walk out of the galley with a gallon of olives under your arm. You fixing to get thrown in the brig?"

Model T explained the way it happened. The petty officer had told him to take as many cans of the olives as he could carry to the officers' mess when he went off duty. He said they had been stored there by mistake, that enlisted men didn't eat ripe olives. Model T said that as many as you can carry was not any certain number. "*Mais*, ah can't bring no mo' den five, me. But ah got six. Dat makes one mo' den ah can carry. So de one dat ah can't bring, ah lef' it close tuh de lifeboat. Dat officer, he's gonna be plenty mad if ah come up dere wit mo' olives den ah can carry."

"You're one smart Cajun, Model T," Doops said. "That's why I like you. I never did like stupid people. Soon as we teach you to talk a little better you're going to be a prize. Blue ribbon at the state fair."

"Don't worry about my speech," he said, slowly and perfectly, resonating the words the way Kingston had taught him to do with "How now brown cow." Kingston smiled but said nothing.

"Anyway," Doops said, "it's probably beans, prunes, and corn bread again."

"Yeah, Yankee corn bread at that," Kingston said. "They put sugar in it. Nobody but a Yankee puts sugar in corn bread. Let's eat Model T's olives."

They decided they should wait until it got dark.

"Let's talk about the glorious future," Kingston said. "What we're going to do when it's over over there—over here. Hell, we're not over there yet and we're not here. Man, we're nowhere."

"Let's talk about the glorious past," Doops said. "What is past is prologue. That's Shakespeare."

"How the hell you know all that?" Kingston asked. "You learn all that at LSU?"

"In two years I should have learned something," he said.

"Yeah, in a year and a half I should have learned something at Holmes Junior College, too. But I didn't learn all that stuff you know."

"When you're weird you wind up learning stuff," Doops said.

"Weird? You're always saying you're weird. Man, you don't know what weird is."

Doops began to talk about his childhood. They had heard most of the stories before but they listened as if they hadn't.

"Yeah. Weird. They said I read too many books. Spent most of my time in the county library. Didn't help my daddy on the place much and didn't play with other kids. That was weird. At least that's what they said. Great big coarse woman named Jewell ran the library. The WPA built it. The WPA and the Geringer Lumber Company together. When it first opened, she wouldn't show me anything but the Big Little Books. Remember them? Wash Tubbs. Little Orphan Annie. Stuff like that. I didn't want to hurt her feelings so I would look at them for a few minutes and then drift on to the next room. One time I tried to check out *Pilgrim's Progress* and *The Last of the Mohicans* the same day. She said I wouldn't understand them. Told me I would enjoy Zane Grey westerns. She thought Zane Grey was a woman. 'That Zane Grey, she's a mighty fine writer. I've read every one of her books.'

I wanted to tell her Zane Grey was a man, but I never could do it. I guess just knowing it meant something special to me. Yeah. Weird.

"And that part about not wanting to be drafted. They thought that was weird too. I was twenty-one years old, and they started looking at me kind of funny like when I didn't race down and sign up. Hell, I thought they taught me in Sunday school that believers didn't kill. One of our neighbors wrote the draft board that I wasn't a believer, that I hadn't even been baptized. You know, if you get to be ten and haven't been baptized, you're some kind of a deviant. Weird. Yeah, man. I went down to the draft board and tried to tell them why I hadn't ever been baptized, but they just laughed at me. Then they got mad when I said I didn't believe in killing people. Told me about how Jesus drove the money changers out of the temple with armed might.

" 'You're cute, son,' one of them told me. 'Did your mamma ever tell you you're cute?' They teased me about my cowlick. Said it made me look like an owl. Said they ought to put me in the Air Corps because I could fly already. Another one said I ought to be in the intelligence department because I was wise. 'You bet your ass. He's a wise little booger. He goes to *college!*' "

Model T and Kingston were stretched out on the deck, listening without interruption as Doops talked, still as if they had never heard it before.

" 'The testimony of the witness strains the credulity of this board.' That's what the chairman read to the secretary out of the Draft Board Manual. They told me I could appeal it to Jackson and my mother said she would go with me if I really wanted her to, but she never mentioned it again and I didn't either. They can send me where they want to but they can't make me kill somebody. Yeah, gentlemen. Weird. If you don't want to kill and you don't want to get baptized either, that's weird.

"And Latin. Miss Helen Fiveashe taught it. Her daddy owned two sections of land and sent her to school across the waters. She never was married, never had a boyfriend, and went to the Episcopal church where she paid a priest from Port Gibson to conduct services one Sunday evening a month. So she was weird too. When we got a new principal and he found out she didn't have but two students, he said Latin was a dead language and let her go.

That old woman liked me, and I sure God liked her. She asked me if I would like to come to her house once a week and go on studying Latin. But she died not long after that. Yeah, if you don't want to go to war, don't want to get baptized, and like to study a dead language you're weird, boys.

"For a long time I hung around with the preacher. He hadn't been to school much, just sort of educated himself. He had books all over his house. All kind of books. And he knew all about how the Baptist Church got started. But then he started to harangue me about being baptized too. Said a lot of people thought I would one day be a preacher too. Yeah, men. I'm strange."

Doops, his reverie winding down, stood up, stretched, and began to pace around the area. Model T and Kingston didn't move.

"Hey, why don't we all go to LSU when we get back?" Doops said, sitting down again. "That way we would all be together. You know, keep the neighborhood going."

Kingston nodded approval. For Model T it was unthinkable. "*Ecoute ici, vieux*, you know ah can't go at LSU, me. Ah din' even finish de high school in Mermentau. *Mais*, wut you talkin' about, LS and U college?"

"There are tests you can take. You can go to college without finishing high school," Doops told him. "Me and Kingston, we'll teach you everything you need to know. There really isn't much to it anyway. Hell, I knew a guy who got a doctor's degree in physical education. I think he majored in push-ups."

Model T wasn't convinced. "Ah t'ink it would be more better if ah go an' trap wit mah pa-pa, me."

"You guys believe in reincarnation?" Doops asked. The question came from no place in particular and was not related to anything they had been talking about. They had seen him reading the same book for several days. He was holding it in his hand as he spoke, flipping the pages with both his thumbs, making a noise like shuffling playing cards. When neither of them answered he asked again. "You guys believe in reincarnation?" Model T didn't understand what the word meant. Anytime he didn't understand something he would say, "*Mais*, dat's pretty strong stuff, yaah." So Doops and Kingston talked about what the word meant, Kingston pretending he didn't understand either until he was sure Model T did understand.

"You mean sometimes you feel like you have been somebody else?" Kingston asked after Model T understood.

"I didn't say that. Maybe sometimes I feel like somebody else has been me. Or maybe sometimes I feel like I'm trying to be somebody else and can't. I just asked the question. Do you believe it or don't you?" When they didn't answer he said, "An' das all I ax," mimicking Model T, patting him on the back as he did.

"Well, I don't know," Kingston said, reaching over and taking the book from Doops. "You read too many books, hoss."

"Never mind the book," Doops said, taking it back. "Do you believe it or don't you?"

Kingston sat rubbing his head, looking as if he'd rather they didn't talk about it at all. "I don't know. I mean, sometimes something happens to me and I know that I've been there before. Sometimes I even know what somebody is going to say next. We had a teacher talk about that once. She explained how it happens, though. But I don't remember what she said. Something about how thought patterns work. Or something. I forgot. Anyway, she didn't hold with it much. Psychology teacher. Strong stuff, Model T. *Mais*, dat's pretty strong stuff! Freshman psychology at Holmes County Junior College. Strong stuff."

Doops knew Model T was about to say, "Let's wade out of this bayou," the way he usually did when he wanted them to turn from something serious. He interrupted him as soon as he began. "No, wait a minute. Tell me what you believe. Just tell me what you think. Never mind your Holmeass County Junior College. What the hell would she know?"

"And how the hell would I know either?" Kingston snapped, his voice rising. "It's your question. Tell us what you think. I mean, I don't believe in it and I don't not believe in it. I don't know! Can't you understand that?" He looked over the rail and pretended to study the flying fish jumping and gliding over the water near the ship, then he started to sing.

> "On the road to Mandalay
> Where the flying fishes play . . ."

Turning to a bawdy parody of the song, he sang in a half shout, the words leaving Model T giggling as he pounded both his fists on the steel deck, pretending he was accompanying the song with a drum.

"Okay," Kingston said, serious now. "Okay. Do you mean do I believe there are just so many souls or whatever in the world, and they just sort of get passed around? Like they just float around, waiting to be reissued, like a pair of GI boots from a dead soldier? Somebody has it one time and maybe a hundred years later, or two thousand, God, or the Great Whoever, reaches back in the soul quiver and shoots it on to some new little baby? That what you thinking about? That He just flat made more bodies than He can outfit with souls? Like Coca-Cola. They have more Coke than they have bottles. So you have returnable bottles. That what you thinking about? Jesus! This *is* strong stuff, Model T. Or as we would say in Cummings, thick cream." He started to laugh again. "I used to know a half-wit back home, everybody called him Jeremiah. He made a living picking up bottles along the highway. All day long he just walked up and down the road pushing a wheelbarrow, picking up bottles. Turned them in and got two coppers apiece for them." Kingston rubbed his hands together, trying to think of another way to break the spell. "Hell. Remodeled? You ain't never even been modeled. You ain't never been baptized. How you going to get reissued when you never been issued? Ain't that the way our bunch would figure it, T?" he said, slapping Model T on the back.

Doops scowled with disapproval. Kingston turned his back to him and spoke directly to Model T. "Hey, Model T? You know how we used to wonder how the priests made money. How they drove those Chevy coupes with knee action, overdrive, and a rumble seat when all they got to spend was a few dollars a month. I bet that's how they did it. They get two pennies for every soul they pick up and turn in. Redeemable souls. Ain't it a mess, Model T! Returnable souls. No throwaways."

Doops had stood up and walked away while Kingston was talking to Model T. When Kingston finished, he returned and sat down again, the expression on his face not changing. Model T sat snickering at the thought of getting a refund for turning souls in like empty Coke bottles and getting two cents for each one. When they saw that Doops was not laughing they sat up straight, placing their hands beside them and looking directly at him waiting.

"I guess what I really believe is that neighborhoods get reissued. You know, the community." Model T, confused, asked Doops if he meant that maybe Mermentau used to be in Japan or somewhere.

"You know what 'community' is," Doops said, his voice rising with impatience. "It's a bunch of folks getting along for some reason. Something holds them together. Generally something bad. Like me and you and Kingston. Hell, if we had met at the circus we probably wouldn't even have liked one another. But this damned army, this idiot war, holds us together. Being miserable seems to hold folks together. But when they're easy and everything is going right, they drift apart. Everybody goes home for a funeral and that's all."

Kingston dropped his head, the look on his face that of a little boy caught in mischief. Doops's last words made him think of home, of his mother and grandfather. He felt a sadness but now he did not want Doops to stop, nodded his head for him to go on.

"And that's all I'm talking about," Doops continued. "Nobody needs nobody when they're happy. But it just happens. We don't make it. We don't make community any more than we make souls. It's created."

"And you think we were around somewhere else? Some other time?" Kingston asked, looking at Doops and Model T as one, in a way he had never looked at them before. Neither of them appeared to notice.

"I said the *community* was around," Doops said. "Maybe, as you put it, there's a neighborhood quiver. And the Great Whoever reaches back and shoots off a dose of community from time to time when one is needed somewhere. When it fits His gameplan. You know, maybe there's only room in the world for just so many communities. Not souls. Communities. Like, the Lord not only created planets. He created communities. A solar system and a community system. And they go on spinning. All in place. All where they're supposed to be and when. Each one pushing the other away and holding it close at the same time. And they go on spinning. Different times maybe, but they go on."

"What's the difference between a community and a country?" Kingston asked.

"Size," Doops said. He answered quickly, as if he'd been wait-

59

ing for the question, wanting it to be asked. "And kings. A community doesn't have a king, a ruler. Everybody is equal. Now, it might start out as a community. But then somebody wants to improve on it, make it better because it gets bigger. And when it starts choosing captains, whammo! No more community. And that's when it gets put back in the quiver. Waiting to get reissued.

"Or maybe the difference between a community and a country is that a community has a soul and a country doesn't. Because God created the community and man created the country. Some king sees all these communities around and says, 'Hoboy! Let's put 'em all together and rule over 'em.' And then he promptly fucks it up."

No one spoke. They sat together in silence, each one staring at the space immediately in front of him.

The navy gunnery crews were checking their equipment, firing at imaginary aircraft in the distance. The ocean was as smooth as desert sand, the convoy of Liberty ships moving along like little boats in a shooting gallery. The hundreds of soldiers going and coming paid the three of them no mind. They just sat. Not embarrassed. Not awkward or uneasy. It was a silence that spoke of the three of them together. When the gathering night provided enough darkness for their olive supper, it was Kingston who spoke again.

"*Mais*, wut you t'ink, *mon ami?*" hugging Model T's shoulder, pulling him to him.

"*Poo yie*, ah t'ink it's time to open up de club." It was their expression for going to the PX to drink beer. But there was no PX and no beer. Just olives.

6

The major battles of Guadalcanal were over when they got there. However, they were told that thousands of enemy soldiers had refused to surrender. They assumed that they would storm the beaches, jumping from the Higgins boats the way they had jumped from the barge pulled across the river by black soldiers using a windlass, rifles held high, screaming and shooting as they went. The officers had not told them that, but that was the way they had imagined it would be.

They did go to the beaches in Higgins boats but only because the water was too shallow for the ships to get close enough for them to wade ashore. Instead of storming the beaches with their rifles blazing, all weapons were put in one boat and returned to them two days after they arrived. Instead of meeting hostile Japanese they were greeted by wildly cheering Marines whose places they had come to take.

The Marines told them the stories. Bloody Ridge and Matanikau Village. Night-fighting with trench knives and fists and teeth on the banks of the Tenaru River. Slashed throats and bayoneted buddies. Nightly air raids of Washing Machine Charlie, and constant bombardments from ships close enough to throw rocks at. Stories of the smell of death as two thousand human bodies lay bloated and rotting in the Sunday morning sun, of friendly heroics of big Melanesian natives with names like Vouza and Voula, or designations, not names, like Willie Motorcar.

They were entertained by the Marines' tales and amused by their braggadocio. Doops, more than the others, absorbed them to the point of almost believing they were his own. But when he heard the Marine battle cry in early morning formations, as they did calisthenics or played touch football on the beaches, it brought back what he had felt at DeRidder and on the troopship after the chaplain's talk. And on other occasions as far back as he could remember.

"Geronimo! Geronimo!"

At the first sound of it he would try to get out of hearing. But it was impossible. The shouts carried along the shoreline and since their company was not allowed to walk into the jungles, he could not escape the sounds. "Geronimo! Geronimo!"

Kingston and Model T soon noticed his confused and agitated behavior, had learned to recognize the early symptoms, and when the screams were heard they would try to occupy him with something else. Kingston tried to talk about it but Doops wouldn't. Even when Model T said it made him feel creepy, and Kingston said it was strange, what hearing it did to him, Doops dismissed it, just said he guessed there were some things they would never, weren't supposed, to understand.

There was more than just the stories of the Marines and the mysterious feeling all three of them got from hearing their battle cry. They would see for themselves as they gradually wandered inland. Japanese soldiers still unburied, bodies swelled, teeth protruding, looking to them like the groundhogs they had been taught all Japanese looked like anyway. Miles of what had once been palm trees, now jagged stumps and scattered branches, palm trees shattered into tiny pieces, shot down by guns friendly and unfriendly.

They were on the island for more than a week before anyone mentioned their going into combat. It was midafternoon and most of the soldiers were lolling around the beach, some writing letters, some sitting in the shade of pup tents, cleaning their rifles, others dozing in the sun. A messenger moved about the area on a Japanese bicycle, trying to figure out the gear pattern as he pedaled. He was passing the word that everyone in the first and second squads of Company D had to gather in front of company headquarters, a pyramidal tent on the edge of the jungle, in half an hour. That was all he was supposed to say, but when he was asked why they were gathering, he told them they were going into combat.

Doops and Kingston went looking for Model T and found him a quarter of a mile down the beach, kneeling behind a disabled tank, saying the rosary with beads made of black beans. He had bought them in Nouméa to send to his mother but had decided to keep them when they were told their unit was moving out. As the two of them approached they could hear him praying in French, the west wind blowing the sound of his voice through the gun turret above him, his voice mixing with the wind and the sound of the ocean, making a sound like a child singing through a kazoo. "Salut, Marie, pleine de grâce, le Seigneur est avec vous, vous êtes bénie entre toutes les femmes et Jésus, le fruit de vos entrailles, est béni." When they recognized what they were hearing, they slowed down, then stopped completely when they thought they heard him crying as he spoke the words. Kingston began muttering the words in English, pausing when Model T paused, not sure that he was in unison. "Hail, Mary, full of grace. The Lord is with you. Blessed art thou among women, and blessed is the fruit of thy womb, Jesus." When he supposed that Model T was about to the end, he whispered to Doops, and they began moving toward the tank again, arriving just as he finished. They told him what the runner had said. Their squad was being sent on a combat mission. He began to beat one fist into the other palm, whispering as he did.

"Everything is going to be okay, neighbor," Doops said. "Don't be afraid."

"I'm not afraid," he said.

Doops did not notice that he had spoken in perfect Kingston-Doops English.

"Attaboy, Fordache," Kingston said. "Watch your verbs! Watch your verbs! You're doing it."

"I am not afraid," Model T repeated.

"Let's go," Doops said, taking him by the arm. "We have to go."

"One minute. We'll go in a minute. Ah got to say you some-t'ing, me."

"I have to tell you something," Kingston corrected. "Watch your verbs." He spoke softly, winking at him as he did.

"I will not kill anybody. I will not run, I will not turn back." He was speaking slowly, weighing and forming each word perfectly but with little inflection. "But . . . I will not kill."

Kingston tried to make a joke. "Cut 'em with your knife. No harm in that, huh Doops?"

"It's time to go," Doops said, moving ahead of them down the shoreline, stopping occasionally to pick up a shell as the tide moved in, throwing it back into the ocean, trying to make it skim along the water the way he used to do rocks on the ponds when he was a little boy, the waves claiming each shell on the first hop.

He didn't look back but he could hear them walking behind him, the rubber-soled GI boots on the wet sand making a creaking sound with each step, like new saddle leather. He could hear Kingston speaking softly to Model T in gentle, reassuring tones, telling him that the three of them would stick close together, that they probably were sending them out just to give them something to do, that he had heard some of the Marines say there wasn't a single Japanese soldier left on the entire island. He had an urge to drop back and join in their conversation but was suddenly overwhelmed by the kind of lonely feeling he experienced so often when he was a boy. He remembered how he used to yearn for close friends, for a brother or sister, someone to tell his secrets to, even someone to go to the library with him and sit quietly on the other side of the table as he read. He thought of Miss Jewell and wished now that he had been able to tell her what he knew that she did not know, that Zane Grey was not a woman. He visualized all the people at home who thought he was peculiar because he didn't like to hunt and had a doll when he was ten years old. Now he was missing them. He wished that he could sit again in the room with the draft board, could tell them about finding Kingston crying in the Kisatchie National Forest, and hearing Model T's piteous prayers behind a knocked-out Sherman tank, and bodies lying in the sand with their eyes open. Homesick for loneliness.

The lieutenant facing them said that Guadalcanal was far from secure and that it was their time to encounter the enemy. He said their assignment was a scouting mission to find out if there were any substantial number of enemy soldiers left in the area they were to search. He said they would ride from where they were, Point Cruz, to Henderson Field, and leave there at dusk. Henderson Field, an airstrip started by the Japanese but taken and held by the Marines after many casualties, was built on the plantation where Lux soap had once come from. They would go there on troop carriers, already lined up on the edge of the beach, exactly like the ones they had ridden to DeRidder, looking for some Japanese then as now.

The lieutenant briefed them with maps, compasses, and diagrams he drew with his finger in the sand. Most of it they didn't understand but it was what the lieutenant had been taught to do in Officers' Candidate School before a combat mission, so that was what he was doing.

What he did next did not seem in keeping with his earlier manner. But he had been taught to do that also. He began a shouting but unconvincing harangue about the treacherous nature of the enemy, how sneaky and cunning and vicious they were, how they would tie themselves to trees so that even when they were wounded they could go on shooting. A body found in the jungle should be bayoneted or shot because they could prolong the last breath of life until an American passed close enough to be stabbed or shot. Every souvenir was a booby trap. "Trust nothing," he screamed in a voice that sounded more like words of a leading man at dress rehearsal than reality. "Kill the bastards. They are mad dogs. Animals. Every last one of them. The deadest among them is out to get you."

Doops, Kingston, and Model T stood side by side with the rest of the two squads. Except for the half-whimpering sound coming from Model T's throat there was no sound at all. Hundreds of other soldiers and a few officers formed a double line around them, listening, observing it all with mounting interest. As the lieutenant stepped away a staff sergeant moved to where he had stood. He explained that they would go four miles up the Lunga River, then move due east and to the highest point of Mt. Austen.

A native scout would meet them there and lead them back through an area suspected of harboring an unknown number of Japanese soldiers, hiding in caves. These were troops that could not be found during the confusion of the massive withdrawal, or who were such fanatics that they had defied orders and stayed. The assignment was to kill all of them who were armed, take prisoners those who were not. Large groups were to be noted but not challenged.

After the short ride to Henderson Field, while they waited for the sunset another sergeant reviewed all the bayonet maneuvers they had learned in basic training. He began by yelling the commands in order. "Short thrust. Withdraw. Long thrust. Vertical butt stroke. Slash. Horizontal butt stroke. Smash!" Then he demonstrated them all with his own rifle and bayonet, explaining again what each movement was expected to accomplish.

"Short thrust. You step off on your left foot and nick the sombitch with the point, throwing him off guard." He had pulled one of the soldiers out of formation to stand as a target for his demonstration. "Now you jerk back instantly on the short thrust. That's not the one you kill him with." He jabbed the bayonet, the sheath still on it, directly at the wincing soldier's throat. "Now with the long thrust you lead off with your left foot and follow through on your right. You send that twelve-inch piece of naked steel plowing right into the bastard's belly—try to aim at the belly button. That is, if Japs have belly buttons. As far as I'm concerned, buzzards laid them and the rising sun hatched them." As the soldier backed away, the sergeant pretended to ram the bayonet into his navel. "Now you pull it out in a hurry before his slimy flesh clamps down on it like a vise. Soon as you do, you come up with the stock like this. You catch the yellow fucker smack under the chin and you break his goddamn jaw. Wham!" The sergeant was so excited the soldier had to dodge to keep from being hit. The sergeant was talking faster and faster, louder and louder. "If the dumb shit is still standing you slash him in the jugular . . . *swishhh!* That's about an inch above the collarbone. It's called the clavicle, but you don't need to remember that. Then you catch him with the butt of the rifle on the temple. Then you start smashing him straight in the rabbitass teeth." The soldier was running round and round in circles, the sergeant chasing him. "And by that time you got you a dead Jap. One more yellow sombitch in history and we're that much closer to fried chicken and Mom's apple pie."

The soldiers stood staring at the ground, not moving. When the sergeant told them to break into small groups and practice the bayonet moves, they continued to stand, appearing not even to have heard him.

When the ranks did begin to fall away, most of the soldiers drifted off alone. Doops, Model T, and Kingston sat down on the running board of one of the troop carriers. "*Mais*, wat you t'ink dat Jap gon' to done all dat time?" Model T said after a while.

"Watch your verbs," Kingston said. "Before you go to work on him you're supposed to ask him to kindly stand still. The sergeant forgot to tell us that."

"**S**o this is war," Kingston said as they moved out, walking along beside Model T, Doops right behind. They marched in columns of two until they reached the Lunga River. Then the lieutenant told them they would walk in a staggered formation so that they would not be an easy target. They had been told to fill their canteens from the Lister bag, a twenty-gallon canvas sack hanging from a tripod. Doops fell back as they were fording the stream and emptied his canteen on the ground, and began to refill it from the river. Kingston and Model T did the same without asking why. "That water tastes like Absorbine, Jr.—stuff we used to pour between our toes for athlete's foot," Doops said, watching the river water swirling into the mouth of the canteen.

"Who farted in the bathtub?" Kingston said as the last of the water bubbled and gurgled, the three canteens going *valoop* one by one as they were full.

"Won't you ever be serious, you stupid hybrid?" Doops asked.

"Hope not," Kingston said. "It makes you crazy."

Some of the Marines had told them the Lunga was the river that had flowed livid red on the Sunday morning following a day and night of the heaviest fighting, blood mingling together from the bodies of Americans and Japanese, becoming one blood as it made its way over rocks and crustacean fossils, the blatant red becoming an inconclusive pink as it made its way to the sea.

"This will be better for us," Doops said as they hurried to catch up with the others.

Doops moved to the head of the formation and began talking to the lieutenant. He was a tall, thin, wizened-faced man of about thirty-five. His tousled hair, looking as if it had never been combed, was a deep shade of pink, which had once been red, now faded by the sun. The combination of his hair, old acne scars, and unusually large freckles was somehow suggestive of Halloween. He was not one of the regular officers and most of the men had never seen him before that day. Doops felt comfortable with him.

"I see you smoke Picayune cigarettes," he said to Doops. "I never heard of that brand. Could I have one of them when we stop?"

"Sure. They're made in New Orleans. Strong buggers. They say they mix chicory with the tobacco. Like they do with coffee. I heard they started doing that during the Civil War, when tobacco was scarce, you know. Some folks liked it, so they just kept on doing it. Don't know if that's true. Here. Take two. I've got some more."

"Accidental cigarettes, huh?" the lieutenant said. "Did you know that's the way bourbon whiskey got started? By a guy trying to cheat his neighbors?" Doops said he didn't.

"Yep. That's how it got started. This fellow, come to think of it he was a Baptist preacher, in Georgetown, Kentucky. He was a farmer too, big landowner, owned a lot of slaves. Made whiskey to sell to the folks who lived around there. And for his own use."

"A Baptist preacher?" Doops asked.

"Yeah. You know, nobody thought whiskey was a sin back then. It got to be a sin when most of the things that were a sin got to be the good things and the preachers needed some new sins to stay in business. Anyway, one winter there was a flash fire in this preacher's barn, where he had the empty whiskey barrels stored, and there wasn't enough time for the slaves to make new staves and barrels, so the preacher just figured nobody would know the difference, so he stored the new batch of liquor in the old charred barrels. When he drew it off next year the people said that was the best whiskey he had ever sold them, wanted to know how he did it. Well, he kept it a secret for a long time and was the only one who knew how to make it. And that's how bourbon whiskey got started."

"I reckon the Lord works in mysterious ways," Doops said, smiling, thinking he would have to remember to tell his mamma that bourbon was invented by one of her preachers.

"I can tell you're from the South," Doops said. "Where'd your daddy hunt?"

The lieutenant told him that he had been reared in an orphanage in South Carolina, that his mother died when he was born and he never knew his father. He had a brother in prison in North Dakota, and a sister who went to Bible college in Oregon but he had lost track of her. He was almost adopted when he was ten years old but the couple who wanted him were Greek immigrants and the case worker said they should not adopt a child with red hair and freckles and blue eyes, and that she would find them one more suited to their background and religion. The orphanage let him visit the couple on five successive weekends before the decision was made. When he was thirteen he took his file from the cabinet one day when he was cleaning the office and found another notation by the case worker. It said that each time the couple returned him on Sunday afternoons the woman cried when she hugged him good-bye and that was seen as a mark of emotional instability.

An unexpected cloud covering had moved in and they were not able to see far enough ahead to follow the azimuth projections of the compass. The lieutenant said they would bivouac where they were until dawn. They found old foxholes dug by the Marines who had fought for this same ground.

The officer gathered all the men around him and addressed them in a whisper. "We will not unroll our packs and will sleep in our clothes. We will post five guards and they will rotate every two hours. Five men awake, fifteen asleep. If we are fired upon, the guards on duty will do the fighting. Everyone else lie low or get away. We are not here to hold the ground. We are here to scout enemy troops, find out where they are and how many." There was a gentleness in his voice now, in sharp contrast to the toughness he tried to show during the afternoon when he made the pep talk to them.

They heard the lieutenant tell the sergeant to take the first watch. He would take the second. They heard him slowly call the names of those on the first watch. "Stelling. Rucker, Wardlow, Kasnud, Zurawski."

They heard him walk softly away. And then a loud explosion, a blasting, blinding, earth-rocking explosion.

"Mamma?"

The one word they heard was not an expletive, more the plea of a child, a bedtime plea for one more drink of water, one more story before the lights are turned off. It was the lieutenant's voice, his last voice, fading into and blending with the settling silence which separated the explosion from the screams of the soldiers. It might have been a word uttered by him as a terror-stricken little boy spending his first night in the cold strangeness of a South Carolina orphan's asylum. Or it might have been uttered as the secret of his every journey, in every drunken barroom, every brothel and college fraternity brawl, on every Christmas Eve caroling hayride and Sunday school weiner roast, in every military distinction and new ribbon and graduation from OCS. Whatever it meant, it was all they heard.

"Mamma?"

A land mine had been placed in one of the foxholes, covered lightly with ferns and palm branches, branches of hosanna, branches of death now as then. The light step of the lieutenant had been enough to unleash the compacted hell long held impotent by the same vulcanian muscle that could and did turn one footstep into nocturnal and malicious carnage.

"Japs!"

Everyone and each one screamed, each one hearing not his own scream but the combined screams of everyone.

"Japs! Run for your life! Japs! Japs!"

The lieutenant had told them to get away if they were fired on. But that was not why they ran. Rather, they ran because of the primordial instinct one word can evoke.

7

Doops did not know how far he had come, running, walking, calling. He remembered stumbling in the darkness, remembered twice taking Gideon drinks from stagnant lagoons, not touching the canteen he had filled from the Lunga River. He knew that he did not sleep at all the first night, and that he had continued to look for Kingston and Model T throughout the day, sometimes whispering their names, sometimes yelling as loudly as he could, until he fell at sunset, spent, his body used up.

He was not thinking of them as he was awakening now. He felt refreshed and as the morning breeze of the tropics touched his skin he was thinking only that a warm shower would be nice. When he fell exhausted he had not taken his shoes off, had not even slipped the full field pack from his shoulders. His rifle lay a few feet from where he had slept and he realized as he saw it that this was the first time he had been aware that he had it with him. As he sat up he slipped the pack from his shoulders and rolled it off to the side. Before he stood, he removed his boots and socks. He took one of the socks and rubbed it back and forth between his toes. As he struggled to his feet, feeling the soreness from his night and day of fighting the bush, he tossed the two socks in a pile beside his pack. "Laundry day, Mamma," he said. He had a whim to take all his clothes off, lay them all in a neat stack, then put them on again.

"Mamma?" he asked himself aloud. "Did I say that?" Reaching hurriedly and almost frantically for the socks and stretching them back onto his feet, he said again, "Mamma?" still not believing.

He buttoned his shirt and laced his boots. He had not eaten since they left Henderson Field and considered opening one of the K-ration packets. As he reached for the pack, he had the sudden and curious feeling that he was not alone, that someone was watching him. Without even looking around he picked up the field pack and put it on, shaking his shoulders slightly so that it fit exactly in place. He slung the gun over his shoulder, noticed that there was no clip in it, but did not bother to load it. He opened the canteen and took a long, slow drink of the Lunga River water. Then he looked around.

Less than twenty feet from where he had slept and where he was now standing was a Japanese soldier. Doops was not startled by the sight of him. It was as if he had been fully expecting to find him there. The man was sitting in a shallow pit made in the ground by an exploding mortar shell. He did not try to stand when Doops began walking toward him, just sat watching him as he approached. He had no gun and there was nothing near him. His only clothing was two square pieces of cloth in front and behind, held on him with a small satin sash. He sat in a puddle of what looked like a thin pea soup. The scent, rising in acrid vapor and in appearance matching the early morning fog, told its own story. In addition to his dysentery, there were large swellings under his arms. Lumps around the groin jutted from beneath the loincloth like large olives. Doops recalled the medical briefing on the ship, warning them of exposure to mumu, or elephantiasis. His color and the shaking of his frail body meant that he must have malaria too.

"This man must be sick," Doops said aloud. Then chuckling at his overstatement, he said, as if to cancel the thought altogether, "God, what a case of the turkey trots he's got."

The five feet, seven inches of Doops's own body loomed like Heracles over the undersized figure in the hole. The bayonet drill the sergeant had put them through didn't cross his mind as he unslung the rifle and let it fall to the ground.

There was a feeble stirring in the pit, the man shifting as if

72

trying to stand. Instead he slid back into place, refocusing his sunken eyes on Doops. He held the fixed and steady gaze, without blinking—a sort of plea—for what seemed a long time. When he did blink the stare changed into a weak consternation.

"Well, I've got me a Jap," Doops said. "I've found me a little Jap."

The thought of what he would do with him had not yet occurred to him. Gradually, though, it did occur to him. And when it did he felt consumed and overwhelmed by the same inner gnawing he had known before, the symptoms, the same seeing through blind eyes, the same consciousness rising out of knowing everything and nothing at all, dizziness so intense that it begot stableness, profusive nothingness engulfing and becoming all in all. The drooling, however, was absent, and he could not induce it. And when he tried, he felt that he was being drawn into the liquid vat with the little man. When the feeling passed he stooped beside the enemy he had found.

"Well, here we are . . . little buddy."

He had almost said, "Here we are, neighbor," stopped short, changing it to "little buddy." It was the first time he had spoken to the man and he talked to him as if he expected an answer.

As he spoke to the man in the pit he was thinking of Kingston and Model T. He began an imaginary conversation with them, speaking out loud for each one in his turn.

"*Poo Yie!* Wut you t'ink we gon' do?" he said.

"Guess Redbones don't know much about sick Japs," he said for Kingston.

"I t'ink dis man need some *boudin*, me." Model T used to tell them that *boudin*, a blood pudding made at hog-killing time, was a cure for almost any ailment.

"Come on, you guys," Doops said for himself. "What the hell are we going to do? This little Jap can't walk and we can't tote him. And if we could there ain't nobody to take him to. And if there was somebody to take him to we don't know where they are. And he's too sick to kill."

The imaginary Kingston spoke again. "This little Jap is going to die. All we have to decide is whether we're going to help him die."

Doops remembered something his daddy used to tell him. "Treat everybody as if they're gonna die tomorrow and you'll never be sorry for the way you treated anybody today."

That ought to be easy enough, he thought. But on the other hand, maybe it won't be so easy. For just how the hell am I going to treat him?

He thought about the time he shot a crow when he was a little boy. His daddy told him they were eating the newly planted corn seeds. They would circle the field, light in nearby treetops and, as the little green shoots broke through the ground, they would swoop down, take one row apiece, and simply go down it, pulling the swelled and softened kernels out of the ground. His daddy said they would ruin the entire field. Doops had heard that if you killed one of the crows and hung it on a nearby fence, the others wouldn't come back. The one he shot was far away and all he could see was a black something on a tree limb. But when he shot it, the crow didn't turn around and fly in the opposite direction as wounded crows are supposed to do. And it did not fall to the ground. Instead it circled in his direction, almost falling as it took an uncertain and tottery perch just above him. And, as the crow looked down at him, pleading, he had thought, to be finished off, he could see the glistening of the black feathers in the sunlight, saw eyes, a beak with tiny holes to breath and smell and taste, little feet with toes and nails on them for clinging to a limb or scratching in the dirt, even a tiny tongue he could see as it tried to caw, no longer a hunk in the distance. Not *the crows* now. *A* crow. Alive and hurt. He recalled that he hadn't shot the crow again. He pushed it off the limb with a long pole and fixed the broken wing with some adhesive tape and two wooden ice-cream spoon handles. He kept the crow in the smokehouse until he supposed it was able to fly again. He remembered, looking down at the man sitting in his own body waste, how he had felt the day he climbed to the highest point of the barn holding the crow, wishing with a part of himself that it would not be able to fly at all. He watched it lose altitude at first, almost touching the ground, but then stretching the injured wing to full length, gaining its balance and disappearing through the trees.

He was twelve years old then. After that he began following the hunters and rescuing the wounded game they left behind. The smokehouse became known in the neighborhood as Doops's Health Center. His Sunday school class gave him a little wooden plaque which the teacher's husband, a cabinetmaker, had made, inscribed *EPHESIANS 4:32*. The night after the draft board denied his petition, Doops heard his father say to his mother, "Yeah, when he used to nurse half dead 'possums they gave him a humane award."

"But he was twelve years old then," his mother replied. "And it wasn't 'possums that bombed our ships."

"Just seems strange," his daddy said. "And Ephesians is still in the book."

That was when Doops made up his mind to go, not to pursue the appeal.

Doops walked round and round the pit where the man sat, the simplicity and gravity of the situation still gathering. The sun was casting a lustrous gleam through the tangle of jungle foliage. A short distance away the mutilated remains of a thatch hut lay scattered. Just beyond it was a sagging bamboo bridge across a shallow lagoon.

This used to be someone's home, he thought.

Behind the hut he could see a stand of untended pineapple plants, denied harvest by the locusts of war.

As he squatted beside the enemy he had found, he supposed this was the war he had been trained for, that this was the war the lieutenants and captains and colonels had been talking about. But it was not the way they had told him it would be. And it was not the way he had imagined it. He had not thought of the Pullman porter and the little girl emptying the garbage for a long time. But now that he had found the enemy, he did. The captain had taken them to DeRidder and all they had seen was a long train with all the curtains pulled shut. And one little girl. The captain told them later that the Japs were in there all right. Scared to show their faces. Japs, he told them, were sneaky, cunning, not brave the way Americans were brave. All of that and all of his training passed quickly through his mind as he hunkered there in the jungle looking at the man he had found.

By noon the little man still had not stirred. Doops looked inside the K-ration packet for the first time, saw nothing he wanted to eat. He opened his canteen and sat studying the water. "Wonder if that young fellow would like a drink?"

"Hey fellow, you want a drink of water?" The man's face was devoid of any expression at all. His tremulous body had become more steady. The chill he had earlier had given way to furious fever. Every inch of his body was dripping with sweat, dripping into and mixing with the bile in which he sat.

He heard Kingston's voice again. "What he needs is a long pull of a three-sixes bottle." Doops visualized the 666 signs on the sides of barns back home and the bottle his mamma used to make him drink in the spring to ward off malaria.

"I said do you want a drink of water?" For the first time Doops felt hostile toward the man, an anger born of something he didn't try to understand.

"You better speak to me, boy! I asked you if you want a drink of water."

He moved closer to the moribund captive. "You're a prisoner of war. Or you can be. A prisoner of the United States Army. You're my prisoner! Or you could be. Don't you understand that?" His screaming surprised him, the stench coming from the pit driving him back. Neither his screaming nor the stench seemed to concern the man.

"Don't you know I can kill you? I'm supposed to kill you. I get paid fifty dollars a month just to blow your ass off the map. Now, I want to know if you want a drink of water!"

As quickly as it had come the anger left him. He moved in closer still, trying to ignore the smell, and spoke again. The words were calm now, but did not seem to be his own words. He sat down facing the man in a cross-legged position. The words came out but it was as if he were not saying them. "I will not betray you. The list. You had the list. We will not betray you." That was all he said.

The night before they left New Caledonia, they had seen *The Phantom of the Opera*. When it was over, as the credit lines were being shown and the soldiers were making their way down the side of the mountain that served as their outdoor theater, he had sat on alone, feeling he was losing his mind. He couldn't get the picture of Claude Rains, running wildly through the balcony, out of his head. He had that same feeling now.

Without standing up he folded a palmetto leaf into the shape of a paper cup, the way he used to do with notebook paper in school. He filled it half full of water from the canteen and held it to the man's mouth. Slowly, and as if in great pain, the man's eyes closed. He parted his lips and Doops thought he was going to drink, thought he had closed his eyes to give him strength to open his mouth. His head bobbed from side to side and up and down. Doops tried to follow the movements with his hand, keeping the cup close to his parted lips. Then, striking like an adder, the man's hand hit the palmetto cup, splitting it in pieces, the water splashing into the outpouring of his bowels in which he sat.

Doops felt somehow absolved and began to reflect on the words which had come out of him. Betray you? What the hell does that mean? What list? Jesus! I must be section eight. I'm going loony as a bat. Betray you! Jesus H. Christ! The mild eruption seemed to relieve his mind and he turned again to thinking of what he should do.

Taking the man with him was out of the question. That left leaving without him. The lieutenant had said to kill every Jap they saw who was armed. And to take prisoner those who were not armed. This man was not armed but there was no way to take him prisoner.

If I kill him I am defying orders, he thought. And if I don't take him prisoner I'm defying orders. He faced the man in the pit and sighed deeply, speaking aloud as he did. "And you know what? I couldn't kill you if you were tickling my tonsils with a howitzer."

He had never missed anybody in his whole life the way he missed Model T and Kingston. "I need me a coonass and a Redbone," he said aloud. He imagined that a coconut tree, shot off about six feet from the ground, was Kingston. And a shorter one was Model T. "Okay. We've got to have a community meeting," he said, looking first at one and then the other. He fantasized the two of them standing there with him and imagined what each one would say. He already knew what Model T would say. He had told them before he left that he would not kill anybody. Doops wasn't sure about Kingston. He stood there looking at the two jagged tree trunks and suddenly realized that it was almost dark. He had wasted, or spent, an entire day.

"Thank you, *mon ami*," he said, and turned around.

He walked over to where he had left his rifle and picked it up. That morning, when he realized he had the gun with him, he'd noticed that the clip was not in it. He still had not replaced it. Now he pulled a full clip from the ammunition belt lying on the ground and put it in place, pulled the bolt back, and heard a bullet slam into the chamber. As he walked back toward the man, holding the rifle at a stiff port-arms position, the man followed him with his eyes but showed no interest in what he was doing. Doops stood over him and began to speak.

"You, an unnamed soldier of the Army of the Rising Sun, are now a prisoner of the United States Army, Twenty-fifth Division, Major General J. Lawton 'Lightning Joe' Collins, Commander. Under the terms of the Geneva convention you are required to give no more than your name, rank, serial number, and military unit. You may be questioned but you may not be tortured. At the cessation of hostilities you will be returned to your country in accord with the terms of peace." They had learned the words correctly during the training but he could not remember them exactly now.

With that he unrolled the canvas from his pack and went to sleep.

With the dawn, Doops sat upright at a sound he hadn't heard before. The sound seemed to dart from place to place, never coming from the same place twice. He had been dreaming that he and Kingston and Model T were brothers and that they were at a county fair with their father. The man in the dream did not look like his father. Children were gathered around them laughing and jeering because their father was insisting to the carnival barker that he be allowed to ride the merry-go-round without a ticket so that he could make sure the three boys did not fall off. The sound Doops was hearing had the ring of a calliope and as the dream mingled with the meropic haze of just-opened eyes he imagined that he was seeing the gaudy steeds of the carousel whirling round and round and that the sounds were coming from them.

As the dream faded and gave way to more manageable images, he saw that what he was hearing was a pair of macaws squealing, screaming, playing, mating in the treetops.

Without looking in the direction of his prisoner he walked away, relieved himself on the ground, realizing as he did that he had hidden himself from the man in a patch of high grass.

"Good Lord!" he laughed.

He walked over to the dugout and, without looking directly down at the man, began to speak, hoping that there would be no one there to hear him.

"Good morning, Reuben. How's the collywobbles this fine day?" Looking down at him now, he saw that the man was not sitting cross-legged as he had been before but was reclining against the parapet-like ledge.

When he saw Doops standing over him, he raised his head, putting his hands down beside him as one would do to reach a standing position and, for a moment, Doops thought he was going to get up. Instead, he shuffled his buttocks deeper into the pit, a pit that looked to Doops like the wallowed-out troughs used back home for feeding hogs.

"Well, I guess I'd better fix us some breakfast. It's just a simple Continental but it beats nothing." He walked over to the pack and picked up the K-ration packet. He took out a small bar of chocolate and two hardtacks. The chocolate was made for the tropics, so hard that the most piercing heat could not melt it. The little biscuits were just as dry and hard.

All at once he dropped the packet and exclaimed, "Reuben!"

It had not occurred to him that he had called him that.

"Reuben. Well, I'll be damned! Now, where did you get that name?"

Somehow having a name made a difference. He wished that he hadn't said it. He walked back to the pit and spoke to the man the way he had at first, omitting the name. "Good morning. How's the collywobbles this fine day?" But it was too late. The man had a name and it was Reuben.

"Okay, Reuben. Why don't you talk to me? Tell me some news. Tell me where you came from. And how the hell did you get in this fix? Tell me something, Reuben. How 'bout it?"

He took a quick drink from his canteen. He folded another leaf as he had done the day before and poured some water for the man.

"How 'bout some o.j.?" He leaned over and offered the water. The man made no motion to accept it. But a sort of glaze seemed to cover his eyes at the offering.

Doops picked up a handful of dry twigs and stacked them into a small pen, just big enough to hold the palmetto cup. He dropped one of the hardtacks into the cup, watching it swell as it soaked up the water like a sponge. When it was wet through, he took it out and ate it, dropping the other biscuit in and adding more water. His prisoner was shaking with the hardest chill Doops had seen him have. He could hear his teeth chattering, making a sound like a machine gun in the far distance. The trembling of his frail body sloshed the liquid he sat in like the agitator of a washing machine. Doops had intended to offer him the soaked biscuit but decided to wait until the chill passed. He can't take many more of these, Doops thought. When the fever sets in he's liable to be gone.

The thought of death brought to his mind the first funeral he had attended. He remembered it was 1927 and his daddy had taken him with him because the dead man, Mr. Dalbo Sessoms, was a neighbor who used to tease and play with Doops a lot. He was an old man, almost eighty, a fisherman. Doops had seen his Uncle Roland and Mr. Grady Salters pass their house with Mr. Sessoms in the backseat. He was sitting upright but there was a bandana tied under his chin and over the top of his head and he didn't have his glasses on. Doops told his daddy that Mr. Sessoms looked like he was dead. His daddy had already heard that Uncle Roland and Mr. Salters had found him on the Homochitto River bank. He said he still had a grabbing hook in his hand and they figured he was trying to get a catfish out of a log and when he got to hurting he had stumbled onto the bank and died. They said his mouth was open and they had tied it shut with the bandana so the undertakers wouldn't have to break his jaw when they laid him out.

At the cemetery, Doops had moved in front of the circle of mourners so that he could see what they were doing. The coffin was a plain wooden box the man's sons had made and the preacher presided over every detail of the burial. The pallbearers were to lower the casket with two well-worn plow lines, cotton ropes borrowed from someone's mule harness for this use. The preacher instructed the men to hold the casket even with the ground while he prayed. Doops remembered what he had said.

The men had struggled to steady themselves as the ropes cut into their hands and the weight strained their muscles while the preacher prayed. He was careful to remind the Lord of all the man's well-known good deeds, saying nothing of the bad ones, making sure that each member of the family was blessed by name, ending finally with "dust to dust, ashes to ashes." When he finished with the prayer, he turned to direct the men in the lowering of the casket.

"Down now. Slow. Slower. Slower yet. Slow now."

They grimaced as the ropes slid through their palms. But it could not be rushed. The grieving wife and children must have time to see, to know, to experience that their lover and sire was leaving them forever. The preacher gave the command to hold when the widow swooned on the bosom of her firstborn daughter, a tall, thin woman looking as old as her mother. The preacher was masterful, balancing the lowering of the body with the level of composure and acceptance, so that finally, when the box came to rest on the bottom of the grave, coming to rest there without a thud but more as if it had been tenderly placed on a feather mattress, a kind of submission and relief could be felt from the seated mourners. And when the preacher turned to the family and asked them to return to their cars and buggies until the grave was filled and mounded with the flowers, the widow was able to say with a strong and steady voice, "I promised to go with him as far as I could go and I won't leave till the last shovel of dirt is throwed."

Doops thought of the scene a long time as he moved aimlessly about the pit where the man sat. Then he suddenly laughed out loud, remembering a story Kingston had told him of another funeral. He suspected that Kingston had made the story up, or that someone else had told it to him as a joke. But he liked it anyway. When they were holdovers at Camp Polk, Kingston was given military-escort detail for a soldier who had died at the base. The dead soldier, shot by accident on the firing range, had come from a remote area of the Missouri Ozarks. Kingston described it as Lum 'n Abner country. His duty was to fold the flag into a triangle at the conclusion of the service and hand it to the mother. The family was a large one and not all of them could be seated under the mortuary tent. A younger brother, about thirteen, was one who stood outside the tent. The grandmother, old and much too large a woman for the small folding chairs provided by the funeral home, was seated in the middle of the front row. None of them had ever attended a military funeral before. The bugler and firing squad were stationed out of sight in a grove of trees over the hilltop, so that the mournful strains of Taps would move in echelons, cascading over rocks and through smaller valleys, returning finally to them as a haunting echoing serenade.

When the first loud crack of the rifles was heard, before the echoes could begin, the frightened grandmother jumped straight up, coming down as quickly, the weight and suddenness of her body smashing the chair, dumping her into the laps of those behind her and finally onto the ground. The young brother outside the tent, as surprised and unforewarned as his grandmother, screamed, "Gawd-damn! Now they've shot Grandma too!"

Doops noted that the chill was done and the fever had commenced. The biscuit in the water had disintegrated into a gruel-like consistency. He stirred it round and round with his finger, added a little more water, and stirred again. Then taking a small bite from the chocolate, so hard that it took all the strength of his jaws to crack it, he held it in his mouth and let it gradually dissolve in the warm saliva. He swished it between his cheeks and teeth so that there would be no solid pieces left, then held it a while longer in his mouth until it was as thin as the mixture in the cup. Turning quickly away from the man, he spewed it into the leafcup.

"Damned, if I ain't a mother pigeon," he mumbled to himself. He stirred it all again and walked over to the prisoner.

"Here we go, Reuben. It's good for what ails us." Then, thinking that the man might be more apt to take the potion if he saw Doops drink first, he took a gulp of it himself, not letting the taste

82

of it show. He thought the man moved his head slightly forward as if to accept it. But when Doops touched his lips with it, he moved away. Doops did not persist.

"Okay, little Nipper. I'll leave it right here. The sun will heat it up for us." He placed it back in the holder he had made.

"Now, what the hell are we going to do all day?" He circled round the man the way he had before.

He was beginning to feel annoyed again that his prisoner would not speak to him. He knew that the man could not understand what he said but that did not excuse him. He could just shrug his shoulders. He could wave a hand at him or even blink his eyes, anything to acknowledge Doops's presence.

In his pack he had a small checkerboard his mother had sent him. It was a metal board and the red and black checkers were magnetized and would not slide off. It was a war notion, designed to be played in camp or even while marching along. He sat down facing his prisoner and placed the board between them, close enough for the man to reach if he wanted to.

"Your first move, Reuben," he said, nodding his head at him. Without pausing he reached across and moved one of the black checkers for him.

"Bad first move, son. Never make the first move to the right. Always to the left. Remember the left to keep it holy." Then he moved for himself. Again for the man.

He began to giggle. "Reuben, you're setting yourself up. I'm fixing to clean your plow." He made a double jump and placed the small discs on the ground beside him. Wondering what the hurry to end the game was, he sat and studied the board for a long time.

"Ain't you gonna move, little buddy?" he asked after a while. Then thinking, wonder what I would do if that damned little slopehead suddenly said in perfect English, "Why don't you kiss my ass?"

After four games, each one winning two, he tired of playing and put the set back in his pack. He noticed for the first time the man's toenails. They needed cutting and the nails on the big toes were heavily calcified. That was the way his grandfather's toes used to look, and he wondered how old the man was. He remembered how he and his grandfather used to sit out on the back-porch steps on summer nights and take turns washing each other's feet before going to bed. It was where he learned of the Milky Way, the Big Dipper, the North Star, and phases of the moon. And who his grandfather was.

"Okay," Doops said. "Recreation period is over. Time for you to take your soup." He looked back at the amber mixture but decided the man would not drink it. He picked it up and moved it farther into the direct sunlight.

Doops wondered how the man could stand both the fever and the sun, which was almost unbearable. He watched him as the sweat steamed in continuous lines from his body, dripping into the fetid bath. Seeing it reminded Doops of something he had intended to do earlier. He shook two of the rounded salt tablets from the K-ration packet, rubbed them in the palm of his hand, and sprinkled the powder into the cup. He took two of the tablets himself, washing them with water from the canteen.

"Greetings from the salt mines of Avery Island," he said to the man. "I guarantee you'll never die from a goiter."

He poured the rest of the salt tablets onto the canvas and counted them, then did the same with the Atabrine tablets. Putting them one by one back into the bottle, he began to sing a parody of Johnny Mercer's "Tangerine."

> "Atabrine,
>   for ma-lay-re-ah.
> That's the pill
>   that keeps the chills
> Away."

Boredom was becoming more oppressive than the heat. "I need a project," he said aloud. "I'm going out of my gourd."

Without really planning it, he took his machete and began to cut down armloads of green, slender bamboo poles from beside the shallow creek. With his pocketknife, he carefully sharpened each one to a needle point, sticking them into the ground in a row. When the last one was done and in place, they formed a line about eight feet long on the south side of where the man sat, each pole about six inches from the next one. He laced the gaps between the poles with huge palmetto leaves, the leaves reminding him of fans used by some of the women at revival meetings. They were status—delicate, tan, ribbed announcements that the owners had once visited Panama City or New Orleans or that their children worked there, that the women were somehow separated from the others who fanned themselves, minding the gnats and flies, with cardboard rectangles, thin wooden handles stapled on, pictures of Jesus in Gethsemane on one side and "Jennings Funeral Home" on the back. And separated too from the younger women who flaunted their coyness as they tittered behind the folding- and collapsible-type fans, sometimes made of silk but more often of paper, always bearing some festive pagoda scene.

The project took him well into the afternoon and he was tired. Occasionally he had walked over to the little creek and doused his head with the warm, stale water. He also ate a coconut, cracking it only after he had punctured one of the eyes and sucked all the milk out. When the wall was finished, he tied small vines to the top of each pole and wove them into one string. With this he could bend the entire structure over the man's head, sheltering him from the rain. When it stood erect it cast a long pattern of shade over him. By pulling it down in the opposite direction he could let the sun shine on him. "That's the chill position," he said to the man. He drove tent pegs into the ground behind and in front of the structure to anchor the string to.

"Okay, Reuben. Behold the Great Wall of Chills and Febris," he said, not remembering the Latin for "chills." The man paid him no more attention while he worked than he had before. Seeing that the fever had passed, and thinking that a new chill would soon set in, he pulled the wall away from the man, letting the warmth of the sun hit him directly.

"Siesta time," he said, crawling underneath the space between the palmettos and the ground. He lay there for the rest of the afternoon. It was cool there on the damp leaves, the wall hiding him from the heat. He felt better than he had since the explosion had sent them scampering into the jungle. A single mosquito, buzzing and singing about his head, kept him from sleeping.

"They say the ones that sing don't bite," he said, trying to trap the mosquito in his hand.

"Where did that guy get the name of Reuben?" he wondered as he lay there in the comfort of his bastion. "Whoever heard of a Jap named Reuben?"

He remembered a boy from Kentucky, with him at Camp Polk, who was married to a Chinese woman. At least they called her Chinese. Actually her ancestors had been Americans for generations, brought there by rich white men to build the railroads to bring the coal out of the mountains. But she looked Chinese and the boys used to ask her for chopsticks when she served them milk shakes at the Dairy Queen where she worked. She had sent her husband a picture of their baby, born three weeks after he was drafted. Doops recalled looking at the picture of the mother, lying in the hospital bed with the infant beside her, wrinkled and pink and squinting.

"What's his name?" he had inquired of the grinning father.

"Daniel Boone Elmore," the soldier replied.

"Daniel Boone?"

"Yep. She named him that. She and her mamma. I wanted to name him Jael. That's a Bible name."

"Jael?" Doops said. "That might not have been too good. Jael. Daniel Boone might be better."

"Jael is a Bible name," the soldier said again.

"Yeah, I know," Doops said. "But Jael was a broad. Drove a fucking tent peg through a general's head after she fed him buttermilk. After she had rescued his ass from the enemy, or he thought he was rescued. And cooed him off to sleep with sweet talk. Naw, I think Daniel Boone might be better."

Suspecting that Doops was ridiculing his son's name, he flushed with anger. "So what's wrong with the kid's name, buddy? What would you have named him? Sun Yat-sen?"

"Nothing wrong with it, Elmore. Nothing. Good name. Daniel Boone Elmore." Placing his hand on the boy's shoulder and jostling him around so that he would know he was teasing he said, "Like I say. I like the name. A Chink named Daniel Boone. The melting pot is still melting. Daniel Boone Elmore."

Doops could visualize the baby's picture as he lay there under the green shelter he had made. He reached out to fondle one of the tent pegs he had driven into the ground. "Jael! Maybe they should have named him that. Maybe they should have named *me* that. Jael. Great God!"

As he lay there he thought about a woman he had met on a Greyhound bus when he was returning from furlough. He wished that she were there with him, that she were lying there beside him under the bamboo and palmetto blanket. She had not been subtle with her flirtation, and he wondered if he would respond to her the same way now as he had then. He had felt so good about it at the time. She was traveling with her five-year-old son. She was a pretty girl with long dark hair and she smelled of talcum powder, the kind his mother used to buy from the Rawleigh man. The tattoo of a heart, pierced by an arrow, on the back of her hand did not detract from her natural charm but did give Doops some uneasiness.

"I'm on my way to Muscle Shoals to live with my parents," she said. "I was living with my husband at Camp Fannin, Texas. Tyler, Texas, really. That's where Camp Fannin is, you know. Rose capital of the world, you know. Real pretty in the summer. We got a divorce, though. So I'm going back home to live with my folks." Doops wondered what she was doing on a Natchez-to-Alexandria bus if she had been to Tyler, Texas.

Reaching over and taking Doops by the hand she added, "And my heart's just breaking right in two." As she leaned close to make him hear above the roar of the engine, her breath smelled of too much cigarette-smoking.

Thinking that he might understand her to be saying that she was still in love with her husband, she quickly added, "I don't mean for me. I mean for the little boy. No daddy and all, you know. I never really loved the guy. I mean, not really. I was awful young. Not even out of high school. And we had this baby right off. No, it's best for me. I'm really kind of glad to be shut of him."

When Doops did not respond, she continued. " 'Course, everybody gets lonesome sometimes. For companionship, I mean. But I figure there's more than one fish in the sea." When Doops still did not respond, she touched his hand again. "Don't you, honey?" Doops said yeah, that he figured it that way too.

He had told her that he had a five-hour wait in Alexandria and when they got there, instead of continuing on her bus, she got off with him.

"My folks don't have no idea when I'm coming in. So they won't be worried about me. I mean, you know, I'm a big girl now."

Doops asked her if she and the boy would like to go to a movie with him to kill some time. She replied that the little boy was fussy and tired and she was going to check into the old hotel near the station for a few hours. When Doops said that he was going on to the movie and that maybe they could have some coffee before his bus left, she said that they would go with him after all, that the kid could sleep on the bus later.

He bought popcorn for the two of them and Cracker Jacks for the boy, secretly slitting the top of the box with his knife and dropping a half-dollar inside, removing the little blue plastic duck that had been the prize. He remembered the little boy's ecstasy when he discovered the half-dollar prize, how he had hollered so loud that she threatened to spank him if he didn't quiet down.

Later, he got a letter from her, telling him that she was in love with him, that no other man had ever treated her like the lady she was, and asking if she could come to see him. But he never replied.

Maybe it was thinking of her that made him remember the Trojans.

"Wat de damn hell dese be fo'?" Model T had asked.

Before they left the Liberty ship, there had been a full field inspection. Each soldier had to display the contents of his pack, placing them in a specified order. Tent pegs, mess kit, socks, underwear, soap, first-aid kit—everything had to be spread out on the unrolled canvas so that a quick glance from the inspecting officer would tell him that it was all there. If anything not authorized was found, it was confiscated.

At the time of the inspection, other items were issued—salt tablets, three K-ration packets, and a bottle of Atabrine tablets. The medical officer explained in irksome detail that they were going into an area where an enemy more dangerous and prevalent than the Japanese roamed in abundance—the Anopheles mosquito. Malaria, he told them, had caused more casualties in the

88

South Pacific than any battle. Taking the Atabrine was not an option, it was an order. Failure to take the pills meant a summary court-martial. He had the men take one while he talked, the dry, gall-tasting pills gagging some of them as they had to swallow them without water.

"Now all of you have heard that these pills, if you take them long enough, will turn your skin yellow. That is true. But it is a temporary thing and your skin will return to flesh color a few weeks after you quit taking them."

"His flesh or mine?" Kingston whispered to Doops.

"Watch it," Doops said.

Kingston continued to tease. "Reckon they'll fade my moons?"

"Watch it," Doops said again, seeing the officer looking at them.

The doctor continued with his lecture, pretending not to notice the talking. "And some of you have heard that these pills will make you impotent. And that is *not* true. That is a rumor and you are to forget it. You can take the whole bottle at one time and still do anything you have ever been capable of doing."

"I wonder where?" Kingston said.

"Watch it," Doops said.

"They will temporarily turn your skin yellow. But so will malaria. And malaria may kill you to boot."

The company commander standing nearby interrupted him. "Another thing you'd better tell them, captain, is that I know they've heard stories about how some soldiers in the past have not taken the Atabrine just so they would get sick and be sent back to the States. You better tell them that if anybody gets malaria in my company they'll be court-martialed for malingering. You'd better tell them that."

"I did," the captain said, obviously annoyed at the interruption. "Now, I repeat. These little pills *will* change the hue of your skin. They will *not* affect your sexual potency!"

"I'd say he wants us to take them damn pills," Kingston said.

As the men lined up, packs rolled tightly now and on their backs, they were told that they would be issued one other item. A corporal with medical-department insignia on his collar stood at the hatch with a cardboard box in his hand. As each man passed him he was handed a small red envelope.

Every man knew at once what they were, had at least seen

them in filling-station or bus-station rest-room vending machines. And everyone except Doops thought it was funny. The bedlam in the ship's compartments, the laughter and jokes, recitation of latrine rhymes, thundered up the ladders and onto the deck.

"Wat de devil dese be fo'?" Model T asked, speaking again in his Cajun manner.

"I don't know what de devil dese be fo'," Doops answered. "But I aim to find out."

To see the chaplain, a private had to go through channels. "I want to see the chaplain," Doops said to his sergeant.

"What do you want to see him about?" the sergeant replied.

"Personal problem. I don't have to tell you. I'll tell it to the chaplain."

"Oh. You want your TS card punched maybe? That why you want to see the chaplain."

"Never mind. I have the right to see the chaplain and I want to see him."

Next morning the sergeant told him to report to the bow of the ship, that he could see the chaplain. At the door of the officers' wardroom, Doops found a frail-looking corporal wearing an arm-band with a felt cross on it. "What can I do for you?" he said to Doops.

"You can take me to where the chaplain is."

They found the chaplain seated at a small table with silver settings and linen cloth. A Negro sailor, messboy, was pouring his coffee.

"What can I do for you, son?"

Doops motioned with his head for the corporal and messboy to leave. When they didn't leave, the chaplain waved them away.

"What the hell kind of a joke is this?" Doops asked as soon as they were gone, pulling the Trojan envelope from his pocket and handing it to the chaplain. The chaplain glanced at it, stirring his coffee with one hand, pouring cream into it with the other.

"Watch your language, soldier!" he snapped. "And I don't believe I heard you say 'Sir.' "

"Sir," Doops said, saluting smartly as he did. "Sir, we're going to an island where there hasn't been a woman since God only knows when and where we would be court-martialed if we touched one of them anyway. We don't know how long we're going to be there and how many of us will get out alive. Now, I just wondered what kind of a cruelty joke this is—"

Before Doops could finish, the chaplain slapped his hand on the table. "Well, if you must know, private, you've come to the right man. It was my idea and it's a very good idea. Last night at dinner one of the ship's officers said they had a lot of them in the sick bay and that because they were so old and it would be a long time before their crew got shore leave again, they were going to throw them away. I told your CO that given the rumor that Atabrine causes impotency, it would be a good idea to pass them out just as a reminder that someday the men would need them again. What's wrong with that?"

When Doops didn't answer, the chaplain began to laugh, beckoning to someone who had taken a seat halfway across the compartment.

"Hey, major. Come over here, major. What kind of an army do we have here? Do I have to give my birds-and-bees lecture all over again before we land? This laddie wants to know what this is for." He continued to laugh but the major did not join him. He looked at the red wrapper in Doops's hand, patted him on the back, and said, "You're okay, son. Hang in there." Doops started to walk away but the chaplain grabbed his arm, told him he had something serious to talk to him about.

"Just before we left I got a letter from your mother. She's terribly worried about you, son, and I wrote her that I would talk to you."

"What about?" Doops said, only half sitting in the chair.

"About the fact that you've never been baptized. Of course, there's not a baptismal pool on board but, well, I'm Presbyterian, and I'm not trying to proselyte. Your mother wants you to be a Baptist and I want you to be whatever you want to be. But how would you feel about being baptized by pouring? Or sprinkling, as some people call it? I know that Baptists accept only a baptism that dunks you all the way under the water. But, well, you know, in time of war, in an emergency, how would you feel about my just baptizing you the way we do it in my church?"

"The original Baptists didn't worry about how you got baptized," Doops said. "That came along later. It never made much sense to me. They always said that it wasn't baptism that saved you, that baptism was nonefficacious. But it seems that baptism by immersion is the only efficacious nonefficacious baptism. Never made much sense to me."

"Hey now," the chaplain said. "What have we got here? Where you been hiding out? You're pretty smart. How did you know all that? I mean, I knew it. But I've been to theological school. How did you know that about the Baptists?"

"I don't know," Doops said, starting to get up. "I just knew it. I thought everybody knew it." The chaplain motioned for him to sit down again.

"Tell you what. Let's make a deal. Your mother wants you baptized. You don't care how it's done. I need a chaplain's assistant. Get the picture?"

"No, sir." Doops said, standing up again. "Guess I'm not as smart as you think."

"Sure you are. Fellow uses words like that. What I mean is . . . well, I've got an assistant. But you saw that fruity little fellow who brought you in here. How would you like having him following you around all day? And he's plain dumb. Dense. I need somebody bright. It's a mean ole war we're moving toward. Folks are going to get killed. You could be my assistant. I know you can type. Saw it on your record. But it wouldn't look good to have a chaplain's assistant who hadn't been baptized. That way, you'll be baptized, your mother will be happy, I'll be happy, and you won't get shot at. What do you say?"

Doops snapped to rigid attention, saluted the chaplain again, did a perfect about-face, and left without answering.

Back in the hold, he told the others that he couldn't find out why they had been given the rubbers.

Whether it was the thought of the woman on the bus or the memory of the Trojans, he crawled from underneath the bamboo shelter with a frivolous notion.

He checked to see if his prisoner was chilling or fevering. The man's skin was dry and had a wrinkled, leathery quality about it, but he was not shaking. Maybe the malaria has run its course, he thought. The man seemed to have trouble holding his head up and Doops wondered why he sat up at all, why he didn't simply lean back against the ledge as he had done during the night. I guess it's the mumu, Doops thought. He's afraid to go to sleep.

He touched the mixture in the cup with his finger and it was still warm. A double trail of large black ants moved to and from it, the line stretching farther than he could see. Flies and smaller insects swarmed about it but didn't seem to bother it.

"Too much for them I guess," He walked along the line of ants, dousing them as he emptied his bladder. "Now you're pissants," he said to them.

He fished the Trojan rubber from his pocket, pulled it out of the tiny package, and unrolled it completely. "My compliments, sir," he said to some imaginary man as he saw the full length of the condom.

He was aware that the man in the pit was watching him but he did not rush what he was doing, giving him time to follow him, to observe him, moving like a movie in slow motion. He shook the dry powder off the Trojan and began to blow it up like a balloon. He watched the prisoner from the corner of his eye. The balloon made a stretching screech as it grew bigger. When he decided that it was as big as it would get without bursting, he tied a knot on it and held it high above his head, pretending that the giant balloon was pulling him into the sky. He danced in Ray Bolger fashion, clicking his heels together as he jumped, clowning, pretending first to be a butterfly, next doing the only ballet positions he knew. He sang and whistled "We're Off to See the Wizard" as he danced until, exhausted, he made his final jump directly at the piteous creature before him, the balloon bursting with the sharpness that only a bursting balloon can make as it touched a sharp twig, a noise he heard as thunderous ovation.

As he straightened up from his overstated bow to his audience, a bow he followed with a more modest curtsy, he saw the tiniest hint of a smile, a painful trace, a slight parting and stretching of the lips of his prisoner sitting there.

Gotcha, Doops thought, smiling back at the man, bowing low twice again, knowing that in the man's condition what he had really seen was tantamount to a hearty belly laugh.

Don't rush him, though. Do something else first, Doops thought as he busied himself cleaning up the area, picking up the pieces of bamboo he had not used, straightening his pack. All the while he did not look back at him. When he finished his housekeeping, he casually walked over to the mixture in the palmetto cup and picked it up, strolling slowly back to the man. He did not coax him, just squatted nonchalantly in front of him and extended the cup. The man closed his eyes, parting his lips as he did, and moved his head forward.

"Drink ye all of it," Doops said, meaning it both caduceanly and sacerdotally. As the man's head leaned farther and farther backward, Doops emptied the last drop of the gooey porridge into his mouth.

"Thank you, Mr. Reuben. Thank you."

Suddenly he heard Kingston's voice, muffled and far away. But distinct. "How do you get in the community?"

"Great God!" Doops said.

"Ah t'ink we on de road tuh Jericho," Model T said, louder and closer than Kingston.

"Great God!" Doops said again.

Doops unfolded the cup and threw it on the pile with the other trash. "Now, what was all that about? What'd I do that for? One more round of shakes and hots and he would probably have been finished off." He looked back at the man, who was breathing harder now, totally exhausted by his first meal in a long time.

"Oh, well," Doops muttered, starting to clean the area some more. "It ain't gonna cure him. Anyway, so what! I did it. I got the little slopehead to drink it. When I tell my prisoner to do something, by God, he'd better do it."

Darkness was moving toward them. Three palm stumps, sheared off about six feet from the ground by cannon fire, farther away and in the opposite direction from the two he had consulted earlier, looked like three men huddled close together, outlined by the sun's closing words of the day, a glowing, orange-red fiery furnace that was the whole of the western sky.

Doops began to sing. "Shadrach, Meshach, and a big Negro."

He had intended to reconnoiter the wreckage of the thatch hut but had yet to do it. He took his bayonet from its scabbard and put it in place at the end of the M-1 rifle. After formally taking Reuben prisoner he had removed the cartridge clip and put it back in the ammunition belt. Now he reloaded, slamming a bullet into the chamber again and releasing the safety catch. As he made his way to the pile of rubble that had once been someone's home, he wondered what he was looking for. He remembered the dozens of training sessions he had attended called Know Your Enemy. Some of the films they were required to watch had scenes similar to this one. The same frame would hold for a full minute while the viewers searched the screen for booby traps, generally enticing souvenirs—binoculars, a samurai sword, wine bottles—always with a hidden string stretching to some hastily devised explosive contraption. Most actors who played the parts of Japanese were really Mexicans dressed in Japanese uniforms and with plastic buck teeth fastened onto their own teeth, the real Japanese actors having long since been hauled off to Arkansas and Arizona, to the relocation centers. During one of the films, a young Mexican-American soldier called out at the most exciting point, just as a fighter plane was diving in, strafing a column of troops, "That ain't no Jap. That's my cousin. I picked tomatoes with him in California and now he's a Jap. Holy shit!"

Doops approached the ruins of the hut with the caution he had been taught. With the tip of his bayonet he carefully began lifting layer after layer of the thatch, flipping it to the side. When he was almost finished, he struck something solid. Uncovering it with his hands, opening a cardboard box, he saw that he had found a small cache of food. The writing on the box was in Japanese but he could tell that the small flat cans were some kind of meat or fish. There were several larger round cans which he assumed to be fruit or vegetables. He recognized two canned-heat containers and there was a bag of black tea. Tied to the tea was a small wine bottle, half filled. The bottle had no label and no mark of identification. He removed the cork and sniffed it. "No smell," he said. "Wonder what it looks like?" He tipped the bottle until he could see inside. "Not pink enough to be called pink. No smell and no body." He placed it back in the box with the other things.

The wind was blowing hard and as it blew across him he could feel the dampness. Walking back toward his prisoner he could see the palmetto screen swinging in perfect cadence, the late evening sun adding a congenial tint to the richness of the green. Downright pretty, he thought.

As he made a neat stack with the cans he had found, he felt a hard object underneath his foot. He picked it up and wondered why he had not seen it before. It was a small pocketknife, almost small enough to conceal in the palm of the hand. Its one rusty blade was open. Doops snapped the blade shut, making a sharp clicking noise. Tossing it up and down in his hand he stared at the man in the pit. The man returned the stare, holding it as long as Doops held his, telling him nothing.

"So you really *were* armed, eh Reuben?" Doops said. "Well now. That puts a little different light on the subject. The Geneva convention is very clear on that subject. And so was the captain. My orders were to kill you if you were armed. Take you prisoner if you weren't. And you were armed."

"But he ain't armed now." It was Model T's voice. Doops even turned around to look for him this time.

"But he was armed when I found him. This knife here. He could have had it in his hand and stabbed me to death when I first offered him a drink." Doops waited for a reply.

"But he didn't," the voice said. Doops didn't turn around again.

"The community ain't something you join. You don't get voted into it. It just happens!" It was Kingston now.

"Okay. Okay. Jesus Christ! I know he didn't stab me," Doops said, answering Model T, ignoring Kingston.

He placed the knife back on the ground exactly where he had found it. Then moved it an inch farther away, measuring the man's arm length with his eyes and then noting the distance from where the man sat to where the knife lay. He pondered the two lengths until it was almost too dark to see. With the last bit of light he opened the knife and looked at the engraving on the blade. *Case*, it read. He started to throw it into the bamboo grove behind them, then placed it back on the ground where he had found it, the blade open as it had been before. He took the wine bottle from the box and placed it beside the knife. "Now I have a choice," he said. Then quickly added, "And I've made it."

The air felt even damper now. And in the distance he heard an intermittent rumbling. He could not tell if it was thunder or gunfire. Deciding that it was thunder, he pulled the bamboo and palmetto hedge down over the man and secured it to the tent pegs, forming a roof over him as he had done for himself in the afternoon.

"Good-night, Reuben," he called under the shelter. "Sweet dreams." He heard a slight sloshing sound and a soft thud. He wondered if the man had fallen backward against the parapet, into the sleeping position he had found him in that morning. Or if he had suddenly died.

It was beginning to rain. Doops rolled himself in his canvas and tried to go to sleep. But the indescribable smell was overwhelming, stronger than it had ever been before. Without the stirring of the air to dilute it, share in it, the vapors collected under the bamboo shelter in potent concentration, drifting from under the eave formed by the ends of the bamboo stalks, funneling into the nostrils of Doops with nauseous proficiency. He thought of the gas-mask drills at Camp Polk. He got up and started to put his mask on to protect him against the nidorous rage from the palmetto tent. He could see the man's head outlined against the ledge, could see that his eyes were open and blinking.

"Aw hell," he muttered. "That would be downright uncivil. Going to a man's house and wearing a gas mask."

He threw it back in the direction of the field pack, the canister striking the butt of his rifle, the hose uncoiling with the weight of the mask itself, coming to rest with the large plastic eyes of the facepiece presenting a Martian caricature.

"Great god," he said aloud, crawling back underneath the canvas.

His stomach retched and ached even more than before and his whole body jerked with spasmodic horror. As his throat could not turn back the bilious juices, as the choking mixture of poorly chewed coconut, hardtacks, and chocolate poured out his mouth and through his nose, he struggled to free himself from the canvas, tripping, falling away from where he lay, his insubordinate insides heaving and twisting until finally he pitched forward, lying tortured on the ground. The rain furiously beat him in the face, the same sweet rain which finally succeeded in refreshing and reviving him. As it did he thought nostalgically of his mother. And of the one present she had never exacted from him—his own baptism.

Toward midnight, after the rain had stopped, Doops heard a noise not far to the west of them. He could not tell what it was but it sounded like someone moving about in the jungle brush. Then he heard talking sounds, loud whispers, but could not make out what they were, not even the language. Suddenly there were similar noises to the east, sounds like people rushing about in confusion. There was no talking in that direction, just the constant sound of people in motion.

He peeked under the bamboo shelter and whispered, "Believe we got company, Reuben." He wondered if they were Reuben's people or his. "Probably some of both," he thought. He considered crawling toward one group or the other, close enough to tell which ones were speaking English. He reached for his rifle and quietly shoved a clip into place. As he considered his move he thought of some advice his father used to give him.

"Son, don't go over there where they're playing cards. But if you do go, don't go in the house. If you do go in the house, don't play. But if you do play . . . well, cut, shuffle, and deal!" He wondered how much dealing he could do with dripping-wet clothes and a rifle just as wet, a rifle he had not fired in months and never in anger.

Before he could decide, he heard a new sound, one he had been taught at Camp Polk to recognize, *whoosh*, directly overhead. He knew the next thing he would hear and even as he thought it, the sound was there—the hissing, like the last ball of a roman candle, and then the lighting up of the area where it landed as the ground flare exposed everything and everyone within its reach.

There was the same routine moving in the opposite direction, both flanks blazing now, looking like the giant brush heaps his father used to burn at night when clearing new grounds.

As the firing began, just as Doops knew it would, he dived under the bamboo shelter and twisted his way into the pit with his prisoner, keeping his own head low and at the same time pushing the man's head down too, not even aware now of the stench that a few hours earlier had overcome him.

"Move over, Reuben," he whispered.

The warmth of the liquid in which the man sat, warmth from the sun and the body of the frail little man, retained by the constant heat the jungle rocks held year-round, penetrated his clothes, and the contrast to the cold he had felt from the rain and wind outside brought a strange comfort.

As he lay there, the constant chatter of automatic rifles, punctuated by the single shots of the .30- and .25-calibers, tore through the bamboo overhead, the tracer bullets drawing straight white lines as they riddled the house that Doops built.

The man, startled and confused by the sudden presence of Doops and the sounds of war, struggled fiercely, lunged and lurched, trying to sit up or stand.

"Stay down, Reuben. Stay down." Doops was shouting now, knowing that he could not be heard above the gunfire. Suddenly the man relaxed and with a hushed but audible sigh sank down, the two of them nestled together in the pit as closely as two people could fit.

It was the first sound Doops had heard him utter and even with the continuing blanket of firing over their heads he felt a certain thankfulness for the human sound he had heard, the sigh.

As quickly as it had begun, the shooting stopped, both sides quiet as one. Doops could see that the flares on both sides still reached into the darkness, outlining the long bodies of the palm trees, their branches casting phantom shadows through the night, the shadows from the west meeting those of the east in flirtatious rendezvous, directly over where the two men huddled.

Both men were breathing hard, Doops thinking thoughts he could not bring into focus, his prisoner lying close beside him. Doops knew now that the Americans had been the ones on the west flank. He could not distinguish the sounds of their Browning automatic rifles and the automatic rifles of the Japanese. But he could tell the softer sound of the Japanese .25-caliber from their own M-1 .30-calibers. He supposed that a second scouting party had been sent out to clear the Japanese from that area. Or, perhaps, they were searching for him and the others when they encountered the Japanese. Whatever had happened, he was relieved they had survived the furious cross fire of the two parties, their people. Enemies. He also felt some kind of alien ease that he had not been rescued. And he remembered the sigh.

"Do you reckon they're gone?" he asked aloud. "Or do you

reckon they're dead?" He knew there was no way to find out until morning. After lying there for a long time he edged his way out of the quaggy pit and stretched out on the wet leaves in front of the opening of the bamboo eaves, where the smell still funneled out to him.

As he was falling asleep again he had a thought: I wonder if my mamma would settle for that baptizing.

8

It was the heat of the sun that awakened him this morning. His watch had stopped running but he supposed that it must be past seven. As he opened his eyes the dense vapor from the brumous mixture of rainwater and scours hovered over him like a heavy fog. The stench did not bother him as he struggled to his feet. He looked at the sun and set his watch at 7:08. "Close enough," he said.

The first noise he heard was from the jungle insects. They reminded him of the coming of the locust in 1937 when he was seventeen. Wherever one went that summer there was the steady thrum of thousands of locusts. Branches of fruit trees were chewed halfway off the trunks, and locust shells, those transparent outer casings of the cocoons from which the mature cicada crawls, could be found clinging to the giant loblolly pine trees they had to walk past to get to the fields. Young girls would hang dozens of them onto the front of their blouses, calling attention to the little nipples which already teased and tantalized the younger boys, boys who would playfully steal the shells from the blouses, pretending that it was the fragile shells they wanted to touch and mash between their fingers. The locusts were thought to be some kind of omen.

Miss Flora Milam was considered a witch in their community.

She was asked to interpret the meaning of the locust swarms. She told some of the boys to catch a dozen of the locusts alive and bring them to her, without damaging their wings.

Miss Flora had moved to Claughton Station when she was old and no one knew much about her. She ran a store where she would sell ready-rolled cigarettes to schoolboys for a penny apiece and a slab of bologna and two pieces of light bread for a nickel. Her hair was tightly braided and wound into a large bun on top of her head. Women went to her with corns or bunions on their toes and some people said women went when they didn't want to have a baby. She had high cheekbones and a sallow complexion. Some folks called her a gypsy.

On the day the locusts were brought to her, she explained that they appeared every seventeen years and always brought a message on their wings. She reached her hand into the sack they had brought them in and pulled one out. She tore off a wing and examined it carefully. She did the same thing with each of them. As she tossed the one-winged locusts out the door, they bounced and darted about the ground, unable to fly or balance themselves. The small children chased them as they skipped and fluttered.

"There's a *W* on every last one of them," she said when she had finished. "That means war. We'll have a war. This country will be in a war before the locusts come back again. Next time they come they'll have a *V* on their wings."

Guess Miss Flora was right, Doops thought as he got up. At least about part of it.

Without checking on his prisoner, he walked over to the shallow lagoon and took all his clothes off, threw them into the water, and waded to the deepest part. He sloshed the dark water onto his face and head, using the slimy silt as soap. When he had scrubbed his body, he began washing the clothes, dipping them up and down and rubbing them briskly on a rock sticking out of the water. When he had squeezed as much of the water out of them as he could, he moved back to the camp area and hung the clothes on bamboo stalks. The weight of the wet clothes would not let the canes spring back to their upright position and they reminded him of scarecrows.

The clean underwear he took from his pack felt fresh and soft against his skin. He pried the lid off the canned heat and lit it. The Lunga River water in his canteen was almost gone. He poured the last of it into the metal cup, stirred some of the black tea he had found, and placed it on the fire.

"Better check on Mr. Reuben," he said as he untied the strings from the tent pegs, letting the bamboo shelter spring up. Some of the poles had been riddled by the bullets and would not stand up. He cut them with his knife, some of them falling on the man's head. Doops cleared them away and spoke to him.

"How's it going, Reuben? How's your mammannem?" It was an expression that had nothing to do with one's mamma. It was just a simple greeting from his childhood, the equivalent of hello. It was generally followed by such things as, "Y'all got anything to boil?" which was a way of asking about the spring garden. Doops could see already that the man was worse than he'd been the night before. The swellings under his arms and around his groin were much larger, almost double what they had been before. His eyes were all one color—iris, pupil, and whites all running together and looking like the small gumballs Doops had seen in vending machines placed by Lions Clubs, the money going to crippled children. Flies and other insects sucked at his eyes and mouth and filled the air about him, the man making no effort to shoo them away. The scatophagous bugs that had been multiplying daily ate at the edges of the pit. His skin had lost its yellowish tinge and taken on a dull ashen gray.

Doops picked up one of the giant palmetto leaves that had fallen from the wall he had built and fiercely fanned the insects away. Then, tearing his handkerchief in half, he dipped it into the boiling tea, waved it about to let the air cool it, and began wiping the man's face, arms, and shoulders.

"This ain't the day to die, Brother Reuben. This just ain't the day to die."

Doops was not feeling well himself. He felt weak and achy all over. He had thought the day before was Sunday, though he was not sure, and had spent an hour or so reading from the Bible, a red-covered pocket-sized New Testament with Psalms, which the American Bible Society had issued to those who wanted one. The chaplain's assistant, who had passed them out, had told them a story of a soldier whose life had been saved when an enemy bullet pierced the Word of God instead of his heart. It was added incentive to accept and carry the Bible into battle. Doops, noting the back cover was made of steel, tore it off and handed it to a Jewish boy standing next to him who had not accepted one of the New Testaments himself. "Here. You take the steel and I'll take the shield," he said. The soldier laughed, stuck it in his pocket, and patted Doops on the back.

As he bathed the man's brow, assorted and disjointed words kept repeating themselves in his consciousness. Some of them were familiar and some were not. "Wherefore let him that thinketh he standeth, take heed lest he fall . . . Emanuel went forth from his father's kingdom into this world . . . and hath determined the times before appointed, and the bounds of their habitation . . . grace, peace, joy, gladness, consolation, good assurance . . . if the blind lead the blind will they not both fall in the ditch . . . whatsoever things were written aforetime . . . O then Adam, what hast thou done . . . the disciple is not above his master . . . even as Cain slew his brother Abel . . . Judica." None of it came into clear focus for him. "Damn it, I'm going off my rocker for sure. Squatting here in this goddamn jungle, washing a slopehead's face, thinking thoughts I don't even think. Just what the hell am I doing here? And just why don't I get the hell out of here?" He did not deal with either of his questions.

Instead, he walked over and fished the tiny book from his pack and searched for a passage that had stuck in his mind the day before when he was reading. When he was a boy, he used to pray a lot, even though he would not join the Church and be baptized. Since he had been in the army, he had not prayed at all. He kept flipping the pages until he found what he was looking for. He stood up and turned his face to the sky.

> Let the sighing of the prisoner come before thee; according to the greatness of thy power preserve thou those that are appointed to die.

At first he read it over and over in silence. Then, moving his lips, he read the passage in a whisper. Finally, with all the words

104

memorized, standing in the jungle almost naked, he shouted with all his strength, a strength he knew was beginning to wane. "LET THE SIGHING OF THE PRISONER COME BEFORE THEE: ACCORDING TO THE GREATNESS OF THY POWER PRESERVE THOU THOSE THAT ARE APPOINTED TO DIE!"

As he put the little book back in the field pack, he recalled the sigh of the man, the only audible sound he had heard from him, released during the height of the night battle. And he recalled that his own sound was a yell, not a sigh.

Doops took his spoon and dipped most of the tea leaves out of the heavy black brew, snuffed out the fire with the lid, and opened one of the larger round cans while the tea cooled.

"Prunes," he said to himself. Then to Reuben. "Don't guess you need these." He ate some of them himself, laid the can aside, and opened another.

"Pears. Good deal." With his fork he mashed the pear halves into a purée, mixing it with the juice. While he was doing this he noticed three lines of ants going and coming from the pit where the man sat. There were large and small red ones and middle-sized brown ones. He remembered a small bottle of denatured alcohol in his first aid kit and found it. Beside it was a bottle of iodine. He emptied the two bottles into the quagmire, stirring it all together with a stick. Dozens of small maggots were tumbling around the edges of the puddle. He watched the three lines of ants to see what they would do. The two lines of red ants got to the edge of the now reddish liquid, hesitated, then moved away. The brown ones continued to bring their cargo out. But as each one got a few feet from the pit, it would veer out of line, running and trembling crazily, then stop, quivering, rolling over paralyzed.

"Too yie! Red ant smarter than brown," Doops said, mimicking Model T.

He drank part of the tea himself and then stirred some of the mashed pears into the metal cup. He knew the man was too weak to hold the cup, probably too weak even to drink from it. He took a small amount in the spoon, touched it to his lips to see how hot it was, and offered it to him.

"Here we go, Reuben. Let's have some breakfast." The man opened his mouth and moved his head forward to receive it.

"Good boy, Reuben. Now let's try it from the cup." The man drank it all, more rapidly than he had drunk the potion Doops had fixed the day before. Doops tipped the cup farther and farther back, not rushing him, watching his bony Adam's apple move up and down.

"Which one of us does this stuff belong to?" he said, looking down at Reuben. "It has your brand on it. But it's in my corral. Guess it really doesn't matter. We'll share it. Community of goods. Share with the brethren. Yeah. That's what we'll do. Food belongs to the people. I heard somebody say that one time. But damned if that doesn't sound downright subversive, don't it Reuben?" He started to laugh. "You know what we are, Reuben? Me and you? We're a couple of subversives. We're a couple of Communists. But don't tell Sergeant Gaines. He would have us both drummed right out of the corps. Wouldn't that be a bitch! Me and you thrown out of the service."

Sergeant Gaines was a master sergeant at Camp Polk. Everybody knew he had an office at regimental headquarters but no one knew what he did. About once a week he would show up at each platoon and summon a trainee out of the ranks and they would walk around the quadrangle out of hearing of the other soldiers. Sometimes they would ride off in his jeep. Not long after they had started the cycle of basic training, Doops was told by his platoon commander to remain in the barracks after the others had gone for the day's training, that someone was coming from regimental to talk with him. When they had all gone, Sergeant Gaines made his way down the long aisles of neatly made bunks and sat down on the bed next to Doops, facing him. For a few minutes he just sat there, looking squarely at Doops, saying nothing. When he did speak it was with a mysterious air that made Doops uncomfortable.

"You're the one they call Doops?"

"That's right."

The sergeant looked over his shoulder in both directions. "May I see your dog tags?" Somehow it reminded Doops of the first time he saw Kingston's moons. He pulled the chain with the two little metal identification tags over his head and handed them to him. Sergeant Gaines sat there looking at them, turning them over and over as if the blank side might hide some code or secret.

"You were inducted at Shelby?"

"That's right. That's what the second number means. Eighth Corps. In my case, Camp Shelby, Mississippi."

The sergeant seemed both pleased and surprised that Doops knew that. "How did you know that?" he asked.

"I don't know. I thought everybody knew that."

"Well, they don't," the sergeant said. "What's your serial number?"

"You just looked at it," Doops replied. "It's on the tags. 38483013."

"You a Protestant or a Catholic?"

Doops did not answer for a moment. He sensed that the questions he was being asked had nothing to do with why the man was there. "I guess I'm neither. I'm neither Catholic nor Protestant. I never joined. But all my people are Baptist."

"But there's a P on your dog tag. Why not a C?"

"They asked me what I was and I told them the same thing I told you. And the guy stamped P on it."

"Why do you suppose they did that?" the sergeant asked.

"Well, I guess in America you have to be something."

Doops dropped his head and thought for a while about what he had just said. "Seems strange though, doesn't it. I mean, that everybody has to be something. In America, I mean." The sergeant did not comment. "But I guess the real reason is that when you get killed the priest does the words over the Catholics, the rabbi over the Hebrews, and the preacher over everyone else."

"You mean over the Jews. They're called Jews." Doops noted the scorn in the sergeant's voice.

"Then why do they put H on the dog tags?" he asked, not really sure that it was true.

"Oh, I guess that's sort of a courtesy thing. They're very sensitive, you know. Some people have to be humored. Even in the army." Doops did not respond.

"Well, never mind all that. I think you're my man. You're pretty smart, aren't you? I need smart soldiers. Your record shows an IQ of 136. That's high."

Doops looked down at his boots but said nothing. He knew

already that whatever it was the sergeant had come there to ask him, he wasn't going to do it. There was something about him he didn't like, didn't trust.

"You know, Doops—is it all right if I call you Doops? In time of war we have to fight with all kinds of enemies. Foreign and domestic. And with all kinds of weapons. Not everyone who is in this barracks is here to defend America. There are people here intent on doing us harm. I want you to help me find out who they are. In exchange for your services you will be rewarded. The reward can't be obvious. It will have to be something that will not make the other soldiers suspicious of your new duties. But the reward will be worth it. It'll be worth the wait."

He began to lecture Doops on what he was expected to do. He told him he was a natural for the job because he was friendly and outgoing and people were inclined to trust him. That he was a natural leader. And observant. And a lot of other things. He said he wanted him to look for any suspicious signs in any of the soldiers in the platoon. Any hint of disloyalty. Any suggestion that they were in any way un-American. Simple army bitching was not important but anything that seemed to be organized, any effort to enlist other soldiers in one's personal gripes should be noted. Some of them might be reading things out of the ordinary. Or getting mail from unusual places and people. All of that should be noted. Any subversive signal should be remembered. None of it would be written down. If it seemed important enough he should come directly to regimental to see him. Routinely they would meet once each week for his report. When he finished he offered Doops a cigarette, which Doops refused, lit one himself, and began to stroll up and down the aisle. "Any questions?" he asked.

"No," Doops said.

"Then we're all set. I'll see you again next Thursday. And every Thursday thereafter."

"I said no questions," Doops said. "I didn't say no answers. My answer, Sergeant Gaines, is no."

The sergeant came over and sat down again. He was trying to appear calm but his breathing was faster, his face a bit flushed, and his voice pitched an octave higher.

"No? No? You don't say no in the army, soldier. Now, that's an

108

order. An assignment. You'll do it and you'll do it well or you'll wish to hell you had. Am I coming through to you? Now, you sit there and let me tell you all about the program and then you sit on your ass and say no. Well, you'd better get yourself a new word and the word is *yes*. Is that plain enough for you?"

Doops was impressed with his own composure, a composure made easier by the sergeant's confoundedness. But he did not wish to disturb him more and began to talk again as if reconsidering.

"What exactly are we looking for, sergeant? Are we looking for Krauts and Japs in the barracks?"

The sergeant's voice lowered again and he seemed pleased. He talked some more about the program, pretending to let it slip that one of the considerations for his services was a good shot at Officers' Candidate School at Fort Benning. Doops feigned interest now, deciding that it would be best to slip away from him in a less abrupt fashion. He had not forgotten that the sergeant had assured him at the beginning that the program was voluntary, that it could not be a part of his permanent record if he took the assignment or if he didn't. But he would not remind the sergeant of his words. He tempered his terms now, asking him again if they were looking for German or Japanese sympathizers in their midst. The sergeant lit another cigarette. Doops took one of his own Picayunes from his pocket, placed it in a long silver-plated holder that the woman at the pawn shop in Leesville had told him was a souvenir from the last Democratic national convention. He held it in his hand, making sure the etched signature of Franklin D. Roosevelt could be seen by the sergeant.

The sergeant took a long draw from his cigarette, held it deep within his lungs, and answered Doops as he let the smoke out. "Actually, Doops, we aren't looking for Krauts and Japs. They're easy to spot. What we're really looking for is Communists." The last of the smoke drifted slowly from his mouth after he had said the last word. He said it as if he considered it the most important and heinous word in the language.

Doops leaned closer toward him and stared him directly in the eyes. "But I thought they were our allies." He spoke as if the sergeant had just made him privy to a well-kept national secret.

The sergeant answered him with equal graveness. "Son," he

said, placing his hand on Doops's knee, "everybody goes to bed with a whore. But *nobody* marries one."

The session soon ended with Doops playing on a childhood virtue he described as being so ingrained in him by his parents that he was sure he could not do credit to this important assignment. Nobody likes a tattletale. The sergeant seemed to understand this better and soon departed, advising Doops to say nothing of what they had discussed.

"Yeah, Brother Reuben. Me and you are a couple of Communists. Holding all our worldly goods in common. Let's form a party and take over the world. Make us a kingdom. Me and you. But what the hell would we do with it? Talk to me, comrade! What the hell would we do with it?" He started some other words, "My kingdom is not of this world . . ." then trailed off to silence when he couldn't remember the rest of it.

The man had not been in the usual cross-legged position while they ate. His back was against the parapet, one elbow resting on the level of the ground. But as Doops talked to him the man reached his hand forward and by pulling and pushing and pulling managed to get back into the sitting position.

Doops opened one of the flat cans. It was some kind of shredded fish. The taste was strange to him but he ate it all. And one of the hard biscuits. He thought about walking a ways in each direction to see if he could find any signs left from the battle. "Nope," he said. "They got their war. And we got ours."

He sat down directly in front of the pit. The man was looking at him in a way he had not looked before. Doops felt uncomfortable and wondered what it meant. He got up and moved around but each time he returned the look was the same. It was as if he wanted to speak to him, to tell him something.

"You got something you want to say, Mr. Reuben?" Doops said. The man's expression seemed to change. "Okay, okay. Out with it. You got something to say, say it. I'm all ears."

When the man did not move Doops began to nod his head up and down, as if agreeing with what the man was thinking.

Slowly and deliberately the man's left hand began to move. He touched his fingertips to his chest. Just as slowly he extended his hand toward Doops. Doops sat watching him until he repeated the gestures several times.

110

"Are you saying thank you?" Doops asked. "Thank you! You said thank you to me, didn't you? Greatgodamighty! You said thank you!" Doops was laughing out loud, had jumped to his feet and was dancing round and round the area.

"Did you hear that, Model T? Hey Kingston! Did you hear that? My little Jap said thank you! Greatgodamighty! He said thank you!"

Doops felt an urge to say something in return. But nothing came. As he continued to move around he could see the same effort, the same trace of a smile he had seen when he had done the Trojan dance.

It had taken all the strength Reuben had. The remission was over. He fell backward, his head resting on the ledge. His breathing was the same but Doops could tell that he was asleep. "When you wake up I'll have something to say to you," Doops said.

While the man slept Doops walked over to the little creek and dipped a helmet full of water, lit the canned heat, and began boiling a cupful at a time, pouring it into his canteen when he thought it was ready. He added some of the black tea to the last cup and put the fire out and watched the tea steep.

He was still feeling pleased that Reuben had talked to him. He turned from watching the tea to watching him. Suddenly he noticed the man's left cheek begin to twitch. At first it was hardly noticeable. But it seemed to gain momentum, like a car rolling down a hill out of gear, until every muscle on that side of his face was vibrating. It reminded Doops of the way he had seen a horse's flesh quiver to rid itself of a horsefly. He had marveled that a horse's nervous system could pinpoint such an area and send the spasm so directly to it, never missing.

As he looked at the continuing convulsion he heard the man mumbling something. He was hearing words but they did not sound Japanese. They came from deep within his throat, harsh guttural sounds, not like the crisp, unblunted noises he assumed all Orientals made when they spoke. It occurred to him that he had never actually heard a Japanese speak before. He had never even seen a Japanese before, except the little girl in DeRidder. He had heard the words in the training films but those were words spoken in broken English by Mexicans trying to speak broken English the way they imagined a Japanese would.

As the man spoke, Doops moved closer, putting his ear almost to his mouth, as if being closer to the sounds would make them intelligible to him. The sounds stopped and Doops noted that the convulsion had stopped also.

He moved back to the same spot and continued to look at the sleeping man. "You know," he said to himself, "yesterday wasn't Sunday. Yesterday was Saturday." He measured the days backward, re-counting them by what had happened each day since he had left Henderson Field. "Today is Sunday. And tomorrow is Christmas Eve. Guess we ought to have church."

When he was a child he never liked to go to church. No one could understand why. He was always a good boy, read the Bible, actually read it all the way through twice before he was ten and could recite long passages by rote. He was always the one they would call on to pray. Once, a visiting evangelist had announced that during that particular revival no one who had not joined the Church and been baptized would be called on to pray.

He wearied of the prodding, the downright threats and harassment, but he never relented. His mother became openly hostile about it at times, saying that the reason he didn't join the Church was for spite, was because he didn't love her. He never told her, never told anyone, except Kingston and Model T once when they were drunk and talking about religion, why he would not give in.

"Guess if we're going to have church I ought to get dressed," he said. He swung the bamboo canes he had hung his clothes on down to where he could reach them. The pants were still damp but he put them on anyway. Before he did he made a rough crease down the center of the pantlegs with the nails of his thumb and middle finger. When his combat boots were neatly laced he took the rag he had bathed Reuben's face with and wiped them clean.

While he was getting dressed, he thought about the Christmas services they used to have at the church back home. He remembered that there was always a holly tree with red berries, which they would cut down and place right in front of the pulpit. The only decorations were sweet gumballs, which had been painted different colors by one of the Sunday-school classes. And there were small candles that were stuck on the prickly holly leaves.

When they were all lighted, generally by the preacher's wife, the dying away of the Delco power plant could be heard from down the hill. It was the only source of light for both the church house and schoolhouse. When it was started, the lights came on. When it was turned off, the lights went off. There were no switches inside the buildings. He used to marvel that one man, an uncle who was in charge of the Delco plant, held the power of light and darkness over them all. Doops felt again what he used to feel when the last sound of the Delco was heard and the light bulbs hanging from the ceiling by a twisted cord had faded away and the only glow remaining was from the little birthday candles on the holly tree. And he remembered the rapid shift of mood from the deep melancholy that only little children seem to have the capacity to feel in its most rapt and genuine form, a melancholy which turned to exultation as the names of the children were called to come forward to receive the little gifts. Once he heard someone say that the preacher's children got no presents at all that year because he had spent all his money to buy toys for the children at church. Doops remembered that feeling too, and recalled wishing that he had not heard it said at all because he felt guilty playing with the little toy he got.

When he was fully dressed he got the little Bible and walked out of sight to the north, the direction their house was from the church. Then he turned and walked back to where the man sat. Sitting down in front of him again he began to sing:

"Jesus loves me, this I know,
   for the Bible tells me so.
Little ones to him belong,
   they are weak but he is strong."

When he finished singing he opened the Bible and began reading out loud, not looking for any special passage, not reading the Christmas story, which he could have recited from memory, just reading at random, and not remembering what he had read when he stopped. He was about to sing again when Reuben opened his eyes and again pulled himself to the same sitting position. Doops began to sing.

"On Jordan's stormy banks I stand,
  and cast a wishful eye
To Canaan's fair and happy land
  where my possessions lie.

I am bound for the promised land.
I am bound for the promised land.
Oh, who will come and go with me?
I am bound for the promised land."

The man appeared impatient and began making signs to Doops.
"Okay, Reuben. Amen. Now. What you got to say to me?" The
man was pulling at his chin with his left hand, stroking his
skimpy beard. Doops thought he was indicating that he was an
old man, and kept shaking his head that he did not understand.
The man kept repeating the same motion. Then, pulling and
stroking the threadlike beard on his chin again he leaned backward and folded his hands across his stomach, like one laid out in
a casket.

Doops moved around him, encouraging him, egging him on
with his own gestures like people excited in a game of charades.
"Old man? Old man? Dead? Dead? Yeah. Old man dead? Old man.
Father?" Then jumping and waving with his hands he shouted the
answer. "Your father is dead!" Then he nodded his head that he
understood and there was the same half smile, Doops thought, a
little more distinct than before.

He thought the man was going to sink back as he had done
before when he knew that Doops had understood him. Instead
the man began rocking his hands back and forth as if coddling a
baby. Doops didn't get it. "Baby? You have a baby? Little baby? No.
Tell me some more." He motioned with his hand for the man to
go on. The man continued to rock, then held the imaginary baby
to his chest, patting him on the back, motioning upward then
with both palms.

"Baby? Baby? No. Not baby. Mother! That's it! Your mother.
But what about your mother?" The man made the upward motion
with his palms again. "Your mother, your mother is standing up.
Got it! Your mother is alive!" His words came in rapid bursts.

The man's head dropped down on his chest and his body

114

swayed from side to side. Doops thought he was going to fall. But suddenly he straightened up again. There was something else he wanted to tell him. So far Doops knew that the man's father was dead, his mother was alive, that he was grateful, and that he was left-handed. That's more than he knows about me, Doops thought. But maybe he knows a lot more than I realize.

The man cupped his hands in an oval shape, moving them slowly along like a canoe on water. "That's it!" Doops shouted at him. "You came here on a boat." The curving of the man's lips was convincing now. He was smiling. Pleased.

Now he pointed at Doops's rifle and shook his head gently from side to side. "Rifle? You have no rifle?" He kept encouraging the man as he had done before. "You mean, don't kill me?" The man pointed again at the rifle and then to every object on the ground which had to do with soldiering, then back to himself, shaking his head from side to side.

"You mean you're not a soldier?" Doops wasn't sure. He put his helmet on, put the rifle on his shoulder, and began to march in close-order drill, calling out each command.

"Hup, two, three, four. Hup, two, three, four. To the rear, march! By the right flank, march! Hup, two, three, four. To the rear, march! To the rear, march! To the rear, march!" Doops was whirling around in a circle now as he called the commands in rapid succession. Coming to a stop directly in front of the man he called out, "Squad, halt!" He brought the rifle down beside him until he was standing at rigid attention before the man. He smiled again in the same pained fashion and shook his head. Doops knew the answer now. The man was not a soldier.

"Well, if you're not a soldier, what in the name of Tojoshit are you doing here?" He need not have asked. The man sat back, pooching his belly out as far as he could. He folded his hands and brought them up in front of his face, bowing his head as he did. Doops knew what he was saying. Even before the man bowed his head he knew.

"You're a priest! Well, I'll be a kiss my ass. My little Reuben is a priest." Then almost to correct himself he said, "My little Jap is a priest. I've done taken a preacher prisoner. How 'bout that, Model T? We got us a holy man."

Doops wondered why it was so strange to him that the Japanese army would have chaplains the same as they had. He had never thought about it before. All the training, the lectures, the Know Your Enemy films had depicted them as obdurate savages, as devoid of human kindness as a cobra. He thought about it for a long time while he waited for the man to tell him something else. He thought, too, about the chaplain on the troopship.

But that was all the man was able to tell him. Now his head fell back against the ledge and his eyes closed. Doops checked carefully to see that he was still breathing. He added to the list of what he knew about him. "His father is dead. His mother is alive. He came on a boat—ship, I reckon. He's not a soldier, he's a priest. Some kind of a priest anyway. He's left-handed. And he's grateful."

"And his name is Reuben." It was Model T's voice again.

Without turning around this time, Doops replied, "Cut that out, Model T! We don't know what his name is. Never will know what his name is. I just call him that." And then to himself, "I guess we're like that. If we don't know something's name, we just make it up. And then start treating it like its name. Reckon I should have named him Judas."

It was almost dark and Doops wanted to keep the man conscious long enough to get some more tea down him. So he didn't bother with the phantom Model T. He kept talking out loud while he lit the canned heat to warm the tea. He opened another of the flat cans but it was not fish this time. He wasn't sure what it was. It looked like potted meat but he didn't recognize the smell. Touching his finger to it and tasting, he decided it was some kind of soybean concoction. He put some of it into the tea and stirred it. "Needs something else," he said after taking a small sip. He opened another can of the fruit. "More prunes. The way my gut is beginning to feel I don't need any more of them. And I'm damned sure he doesn't," he said. He opened the last can. "Pears again. That ought to do it." He was speaking louder than usual, trying to keep the man awake. He kept talking as he mashed two of the pear halves the way he had done before.

He knelt down beside him and shook the cup back and forth to mix it. "Come on, Father Reuben. Suppertime. Nursie has some nice broth for you. Come on now. Sit up for the nice nurse." But

116

he did not respond. Doops tried some more but knew the man could not hear him. He watched the rising and falling of his chest and checked to see if the spasms had returned to his face.

"Well, I reckon he knows more about himself than I do. I guess he knows that he needs rest more than nourishment." Wishing that he hadn't added the soybeans to the mixture, he turned the cup up and drank it all without stopping. His head was hurting and his throat felt dry and scratchy. He checked the clouds in all directions, pondering if he should pull the bamboo shelter down over the priest. Deciding that it was not going to rain, he lay down on top of the unrolled canvas, put his head on the pack, and went immediately to sleep.

9

When Doops awoke he was not aware of how bad he felt. He did not remember being awakened by the sun or by any particular noise. There were the usual jungle sounds—insects, small birdcalls, and the two macaws were back darting and squealing, beaks and genitals touching briefly in midair. But he paid them no mind. His eyes were fixed on the man in the pit. The man's body was moving from side to side like a metronome and Doops was counting silently in four-four time. One, two, three, four. One, two, three, four. His own body followed in cadence with the movement of the man's body, as if on command. When the man's body stopped swaying Doops stopped too. That was when he first realized that he was awake. And that he was sick.

He felt a tearing pang in the left side of his chest. It was more severe when he breathed deeply and was almost unbearable when he coughed, something he tried hard not to do. He wondered if he could be coming down with malaria. They had said if he took the Atabrine the way they told him he wouldn't get it. He knew that he had not missed a day taking one of the bitter pills. He decided that he must have something else. He wondered if it might be the early stages of mumu. He recalled the pneumonia epidemic in Claughton County in 1929 and remembered hearing some of the survivors talking about how they'd felt.

118

"I'll bet I've got pneumonia." His own words made him angry and he pawed the ground like a bull, turning in first one direction and then another. "God damn it, I'm going to die of pneumonia! In an idiot war I didn't help to start on some sonofabitch island I never heard of, alongside some nakedass Buddhist who believes God only knows what about God only knows who." The female macaw almost flew into him as she swooped down to further tempt and tease and tantalize her mate. "That all you guys know how to do?" Doops yelled at them as they touched again. Then, "Why the hell not? Everybody ought to leave some issue." He turned to speak to the man in the pit. "You got any issue, Reuben? No, guess not. They feed you guys saltpeter, I reckon."

He had taken nothing off except his boots when he went to sleep and now he struggled to get them on. "God, I feel terrible," he said as he bent over, the blood rushing to his head, making him feel faint. "God, I feel terrible," he said again, regaining his balance.

He snapped the lid off the canned heat and when he did, the man shifted his position, the movement making a sloshing in the execrable pit, causing the vapors to rise in layers like smoke signals. "You got anything to say to me this morning?" Doops said to him. The elation he had experienced the day before when the man was talking signs to him was gone. He felt a pestering aloneness now and his head hurt the way it once had when he and Kingston and Model T drank two pints of homemade whiskey Kingston had brought back to Camp Polk from Mississippi.

"I wonder which one of us is the sickest," he said, looking down at the man. "Hey, I know a good idea. Let's see who can die first. The survivor gets the kingdom." The rising and falling of the man's chest seemed to come in short, shallow jerks. His mouth was open and his tongue moved with the breathing like a dog panting.

While the black tea was boiling he tried to eat some of the prunes he had opened the evening before. He choked on one of the pits and went into a fit of coughing. The can flew from his hand, scattered the prunes on the ground. He started to bend over to pick them up, remembered how his head hurt when he bent over, and let them lie where they had dropped. "It's tea and pears from here on in," he said. He remembered that he had not said good morning.

"Howdy, Reuben." He said it casually as if they were meeting on the street and neither of them intended to stop. He mashed some of the pear halves into a pulp again. His stomach was churning and he felt dizzy.

The pears and tea mixed together smelled like Jell-O. It reminded him of a time when he was riding a bus from Camp Polk to Mississippi and had watched a soldier saying good-bye to his girl friend and mother. From the conversation, Doops gathered that the soldier was leaving to go overseas. The girl was crying with abandon, hanging on to her man with furious purpose. The mother lagged behind, shushing her own crying behind eyes already dulled with hurt, containing it all with a pride the girl would probably never know. The mother had fixed a lunch for her son and the Jell-O dessert was already melting, running through the paper sack at the far end of the bench beside his duffel bag. As the girl and the soldier kissed and touched, in places too intimate for the Newelton, Louisiana, bus station, the mother pretended not to look, letting her, who had not borne him, had not fixed his croup kettles nor left him brokenhearted and alone at the door on his first day of school, get the final cuddle before he went to war. Some fix the basket, and some go on picnics, Doops remembered thinking. He watched the last passionate and prolonged embrace, watched the soldier climb onto the bus, forgetting the lunch his mother had fixed, leaving the soggy bag with the pink Jell-O dripping onto the floor. "Somebody's always leaving," Doops said. It was the name of a song and Doops hummed the melody as the bus pulled away, leaving the girl sobbing incoherently, the mother staring silently, hearing the last muffled sound of the big machine as it moved toward Alexandria.

Doops thought of the scene as he smelled the Jell-O smell and waited for their breakfast to cool. When it did he drank his half first. He thought it might settle his stomach. As he drank the man began motioning for him to come to him. Doops thought it strange but went to him anyway. Before he started to offer him the tea the man extended his hand to receive it.

120

You giving me orders? he thought. But he did not say it. What he did say was, "Here we are, Father Reuben." It occurred to him that he did not know for sure what kind of a priest the man was. He wondered what he would be called in his own country and among his own people.

The man seemed to be forcing himself now, exerting himself with a strength he did not actually have. He acted stronger than before but looked weaker. Doops knew that something was not the same but was too sick to give it much thought.

When they finished the breakfast brew, Doops tried to police the area. "Maybe I'll feel better if I tidy things up a bit," he said to the priest. But he got no further than putting the empty cans in a pile. He felt too weak to stand. He sat down in front of the man, closer than before, sat in the same cross-legged position the man was in. The eye contact, the fixed, steady gaze each had on the other seemed to be drawing Doops to him. Without interrupting the stare the man lifted his palms upward. Without questioning or even thinking Doops stood up. When the man turned his palms downward Doops returned to the same cross-legged position. "The disciple is not above his master." These words kept coming back, nagging, urging, as if he were supposed to recite them. But he didn't.

After they sat for an hour or more, the man not once taking his eyes off Doops, he pointed toward the empty canteen and then motioned toward the lagoon. As Doops stumbled along, he had the near delirious notion that the priest was going to baptize him in the lagoon and that he didn't have the strength to resist. He made his way to the lowest part of the bank, pushed the bottom of the canteen down into the silt, and watched the water swirling into its mouth, the nits and wiggletails flowing round and round as they were sucked in by the whirlpool. When he got back he started to strain the water through the piece of handkerchief to catch the larvae. But the man motioned for him to stop, to boil the water without straining it. Doops lit the canned heat, noticing that it was almost gone. The man gestured for him to sit down again. It was what he had meant to do and somehow he did not resent being directed to do something he was about to do anyway.

The pain in the left side of his chest was constant and had

moved lower down. He was sweating all over and each cough produced a series of sonorous outrages in his chest, rattling and hurting throughout the region between his ribs and backbone.

"Yeah! My testimony before the draft board strained the credulity of their hearing. Well, by God, I'd strain more than their credulity if they were here now. They're the bastards who drafted me. I didn't want to go. Never did intend to go. I don't believe in killing folks. And if my mamma had gone with me to the second hearing maybe I wouldn't be here right now. Dying of pneumonia. Come the morning I'm liable to be fucking dead! And who gives a shit!"

The anger was overwhelming him. He got up and pranced round and round the pit where the man sat. The priest followed him with his eyes but made no move to quiet him down. And when at last Doops did sit down, exhausted, his wrath and rage extinguished by some potent something outside and beyond himself, he came to rest on a spot behind the bamboo wall he had built to protect his prisoner from the rain and sun, a spot where he could not see the prisoner and the prisoner could not see him. He was breathing deeply and the pain was so fierce and so intensified by the harsh breathing that he almost wished for each breath to be his last.

He sat there for a long time, subdued by the alternating breathing and pain. And the anger came back. Then, as suddenly as it had come, it was gone, and he was speaking out loud the way he had talked that first day, when he couldn't get the man to answer him. Words he didn't understand. Words not really his own. He was aware that he was speaking in an unusual manner but this time he did not rebuke himself for it as he had done before. Instead he got up, walked to the front of the pit, and sat down facing the man again. The man did not move, made no gestures for Doops to follow, just sat with penetrating eyes fixed on him.

When he did move he held two fingers up to his lips the way one smoking a cigarette would do. Doops remembered that he had a fresh pack of his favorite Picayunes, which he had hidden in his gear the night they left Henderson Field. He tore it open from the bottom. He couldn't remember where he'd put his Zippo lighter the last time he had started the canned heat. The man pointed to the cigarette and then to the flame of the canned heat, a flame beginning to flicker its last.

The long, deep pulls of the strong tobacco smoke seemed to soothe his throat and lungs at first. Then it sent him into an attack of coughing. The man reached toward the cigarette and Doops handed it to him. He handled it awkwardly, like someone who had never smoked before. Doops watched the smoke rising between them. There was no breeze, and it drifted straight up, the trembling of the man's hand producing a sort of corkscrew effect. As they sat, eyes fixed intently on the eyes of the other, the smoke curling, spiraling between them, Doops felt a light exhilaration sweep through his body. He could not judge what the man was feeling and did not try.

They sat until the shank of the afternoon, the man occasionally directing Doops to do some piddling, meaningless chore. Once it was to pour water from the canteen into the helmet and then return it to the canteen. Another time it was to light the fire. Then immediately snuff it out. Twice they had tea. There were no more pears to add to it. "All we got now is your wine, Reuben. Just your wine to go," Doops said to him.

The pain and fever were too intense for Doops to think his own thoughts. When the man's body swayed from side to side, like the pendulum of a clock, Doops counted and swayed with his own body, as if to echo the movements he was watching. The convulsion on the man's face had returned, and Doops felt that his own face twitched in the same way. He followed all motions, whether voluntary or spasmodic, more with preoccupation than intent. The bile puddle in which the man still sat was thicker now, viscid, the clammy caking breaking into individual pieces as the man's body moved, like thin ice cracking on a small pond. "Guess his scours is over," Doops thought as the man appeared to doze for a moment, looking weaker.

Doops felt burning hot all over. His muscles ached but the worse pain was in his chest. He was coughing more, most of the time bringing up a thick, green sputum that clung to his tongue and lips as he fought to expel it.

"It ain't something you join. You don't get voted in or out. Maybe you're born into it. Hell, I don't know." He heard the voice directly behind him from the west. At the same time, he heard a second voice, an echo, coming with the same words as if spoken from deep within the jungle. It was Model T who spoke first. The echo was Kingston. He did not answer the voices, just mumbled to himself. "Fordache Arceneau and Kingston Smylie. Thanks for dropping by." He did not hear the voices again, and he felt terribly alone.

When the man dozed again, Doops felt a return of that strange feeling he'd lived with all his life. It was back—the indescribable feeling of fear that begat bravery, a dying that brought more life, of being all and nothing, anxious and indifferent at once, a sinking that was a floating into and beyond an unconsciousness in which there was awareness of everything, of sitting in a room with no door but seeing everything that happened in the next room. As he felt it, the stream of thin, waterlike saliva drooled from his mouth. It was clear and free of the heavy phlegm he had been coughing up.

Then the feeling passed and he was still sitting on the ground in the same cross-legged position. He noticed that the man was awake and watching him. Doops's coughing returned and with it, the same shortness of breath, rattling, headache, hotness. He listened for the late afternoon sounds that had brought him brief comfort on other evenings, but he did not hear them. All he heard was the rapid panting of the man in the pit and the rattling and wheezing in his own chest.

Suddenly the man stopped panting and did not breathe at all for a moment. His eyes were fixed in place and Doops thought he was dead, expected him to fall backward on the ledge. Instead he began to breathe deeply, slowly and deliberately. He indicated with his hand for Doops to join him in the breathing. He made a motion like unloosening a belt and Doops let his own webbed belt slip through the tarnished brass buckle He unbuttoned his collar without the man directing him. He watched the man settle back slightly and close his eyes and did the same. As the man began to breathe deeply through his nostrils, letting the air go all the way down to his stomach, Doops followed him. The two of them sat together, breathing in and out, in and out, slower each time. But deeper, deeper, and longer, Doops feeling the air soaking in. The man brought his hand up to his forehead and let it drop, as if he'd been about to make a sign of the cross. Doops had half expected him to make the sign but he didn't, just touched his forehead in the same way again. Doops did the same and felt a lessening of the pain in his sinus region, a drooping of the muscles around his eyes and all through his head. He felt strange, an unfamiliar strangeness that left him more awe-inspired than frightened or confused. He watched the man's chin drop and felt his own chin sagging. Muscles in his cheeks and mouth seemed to turn loose and his arms and elbows, wrists, hands, and fingers felt disjointed, as if each one were separate and did not depend on the other at all, his body totally exsanguine yet fiercely alive from some mysterious transfusion of support, his whole being anchored to some benign imperialistic mooring.

The metronomic motion of the man's body began again and Doops counted, not in cadence this time, counting one . . . two . . . three . . . four . . . five—up to twenty before the man stopped and motioned Doops to his feet. There was a singularity in his countenance that Doops noted with concentrated sanction. Without meaning to, without thinking, Doops started to walk away. He took five steps and stopped abruptly as if he had encountered some immovable object. He turned and walked back toward the man, stopping just as sharply before he reached him. He walked in all four directions. Each direction was the same, as if he were caged, hemmed, fenced in. He pranced like a lion, moving back each time from the boundaries drawn around him. He was not annoyed or agitated by the confinement, and did not stop until the man motioned to a clump of palmetto near the lagoon. Doops walked directly to them, passing without effort the line he could not cross before. When he turned, he saw the man make a breaking sign with his hand. Doops began to snap the brittle fans from the stalk. He spread them on the ground near the pit like a mattress, following the man's direction.

As he lay stretched out on the palmetto bed he had made, he visualized the Twenty-third Psalm. He saw clearly the shepherd, the green pastures, the still water, ". . . thou preparest a table before me in the presence of mine enemies. . . ." he saw it all. Not the words.

When those images passed he began to visualize the Betsy Ann Branch, a tiny brook that flowed behind their house in Claughton County when it rained. As he lay there on the pallet, surrounded by the green ferns and palm leaves, the cane poles he had built to protect his prisoner bumping together and sounding like wind chimes, he saw again the barefoot prints he used to make in the pink clay that lined the basin. Once, when he was thirteen, it did not rain hard for several months. He had made a deep imprint of his right foot while the branch was still damp and covered it with handfuls of the fine white sand that settled in the lowest spots. The hot sun baked it until it was almost like a piece of ceramic tile. When the next rain came and washed the sand away, leaving the foot track exposed like a fossil from some prehistoric era, he made another impression of the same bare foot beside it, measured it with a Coca-Cola ruler Miss Flora Milam had given all the children who came to her store, and found that the foot had grown almost an inch in just one summer. He remembered that he was not especially excited by the discovery. Just somehow strangely fed and calmly affected by the evidence of steady and uneventful flowing of a human foot, his own, an indenture in a piece of ground he had no reason to doubt would belong to them forever.

The brook had been named for his grandfather's mother, a woman he knew only from stories. She had come to Mississippi when the entire family migrated from North Carolina in covered ox-wagons, come to homestead in the Mississippi Territory, land still belonging to the Choctaws. The violent rivers, the deep and ever-running creeks, the shallow fords, had all been named for pioneer menfolk, each matched with his particular fashion and manner, the occasional tributaries not named at all. Because she had never done harm to anyone, was such a gentle woman, they had named the little branch for her. But only after she died. The six men who carried her coffin rested in the cool of the tiny basin before continuing to a spot designated as the cemetery when they had first come to Mississippi, a spot which already held the generation before her. And three of her own young. It would be her only eulogy, for they had no preacher. "This will be the Betsy Ann Branch," one of the pallbearers had said.

Doops knew the exact spot where they had crossed, where they had christened the Betsy Ann Branch. He would sometimes spend an entire spring day lolling and piddling there, imagining that it was an ocean beach, arriving in early morning and not leaving until it was too dark to see. He used to find Betsy bugs, those huge black beetles grown from larvae that bore holes in fallen trees and grow to maturity in rotting logs when winter comes, bugs called "sawyers" everywhere in the world except Claughton County, where they were called "Betsy bugs." He would take six of them to the Betsy Ann Branch and try to make them follow the trail in formation, pretending that they were carrying with them his great-grandmother's casket. Sometimes he would follow them as they made their way into the forest, in the direction of the cemetery, and once his father found him long after nightfall sleeping beside her grave, a grave he knew only from proximity to more recent, marked ones, the grave of blood kin he had never seen. And once he had built three little windmills beside the branch, and a waterwheel with a piece of poplar sapling for a shaft. He designed the waterwheel himself, but modeled the windmills from one his father had bought and installed to pump water for the cattle during dry spells.

As he lay there in the jungle, he imagined that this was the scene he was seeing. A soft and tender wind was blowing from the direction of the cemetery, a south wind. The thick cedar blades he had whittled for the windmills became full-size in his mind and turned steadily. A trickle over the waterfall moved the wheel round and round.

The scene was so far removed from anything he had experienced recently, so quiet and wonderfully relaxed, his own body so loose and light, he felt like going to sleep.

The man gestured for him to turn on his side and face him. When he did, he saw that the man was staring directly above him at an unusual crook at the very top of one of the bamboo poles. Doops had seen it when he was building the shelter and remembered thinking that it reminded him of a walking cane. The man continued to look at it, holding his head in that position the way one might do trying to entice a group to look for some imaginary object in the sky. Doops began to watch the spot the way the man did. As he held the comfortable stare he became more drowsy, more and more tired, his eyelids heavier, his entire body relaxed. The man began to make a noise but it was not talking, more of a droning, humming sound, a monotonous sound with no inflection at all. Doops's breathing was deep and regular. Every muscle, every bone and fiber in his body felt loose and limp, floppy, as if he were floating on the one billowy cloud moving slowly against the background of blue sky. When the droning of the man's voice stopped, Doops was asleep.

He dreamed that he was in the cemetery beyond the Betsy Ann Branch and couldn't get out of it. The boundaries were set the way they had been when he tried to walk away from the man earlier. He was nervous now, agitated that he could not walk beyond a certain point in any direction. He looked for Grandma Betsy Ann's grave and couldn't find it. There were three small graves and he stood looking at them, not recognizing the single names chiseled crudely upon rough fieldstone. Diann. Vester. Vernie. On the very edge of the prescribed boundary was a border of three large graves, all in a straight line. He tried to walk across each of them and couldn't. Though the markers were made of the same fieldstone, the lettering was different from that on the small graves, as if formed in some other language. CECILIA. JORIS. PIERROT. The sight of them was discomforting. As his eyes focused and held on the grave marked CECILIA, he was especially confused and upset. Sweating and shaking in his confoundment, he was not aware of the man, the pitifully dependent mooring, watching him all the while.

When the droning of the man's voice commenced again, Doops awoke, jumped to his feet, and began to stack the palmetto fans in a neat pile. He was mumbling something under his breath. ". . . and hath appointed aforetimes the bounds of their habitation." The man was not watching him now, appeared to be ignoring him completely. Doops did not feel tired and the late afternoon breeze blowing across his dripping skin was soothing, though all the pain had returned, worse now than it had ever been.

At the moment he was thinking of making tea again, the man motioned for him to light the fire. When he did, the Zippo lighter

128

slipped from his hand, into the canned heat. He didn't bother to fish it out, just followed the man's directions through each stage of the tea-making, pausing, turning back to him like a little child learning something for the first time, waiting to be told what to do next. When the tea cooled, Doops sat in front of the man and they passed the canteen cup back and forth, neither one sipping more than the other. When it was finished, Doops continued to sit in the same spot, the man looking at him.

As the man's body began the pendulum-like swaying again, Doops counted, his own body not swaying. Before he reached twenty he was asleep, not aware, not dreaming, his head settled back against the field pack, his feet almost touching the man in the pit.

And the morning and the evening were the fifth day.

Doops had not heard the struggling, the striving, the grunting and heavy breathing, the getting halfway up and falling again as the contending sun cut its way into the jungle and through a gentle rain. And he had not heard the shuffling as the man had reached for the canvas Doops had drooped beside the pit. He seemed to be aware before he was awake. He was not startled, not surprised by what he saw. It was as if he had expected it.

The man, who had not moved from the pit since Doops had found him there, was standing up straight. He had not left the pit, was standing in it, but not wobbly, his body not swaying. Doops did not move from where he lay. The man was looking down at him, his eyes fixed in the same steady gaze he had held most of the day before, the same monotonous drone in his throat.

Doops was not mindful of how he felt at first, did not think about it, and made no effort to get up. The loincloth the man had worn lay at his feet. The sash which had held it in place, too rotten to withstand the pull from the gelatinous quagmire, had broken as he made the final exertion to get to his feet. The rain beaded in places on his oily skin, the beads rolling together to form a steady trickle down his front and back, eroding the filth which still clung to his midsection, the small gullies forming circuitous patterns, looking like a map depicting land configurations. He made no sound, just stood there like a defamed statue, looking down as Doops had looked down.

He seemed to be standing without effort. It was as if he were held in place with guy wires, buttressed with braces and underpinning. When he lifted his hands for Doops to stand, not breaking the fixed stare, Doops did not hesitate. But the tearing in Doops's chest, the feeling of harpoon barbs being ripped from his lungs, the splitting of his head when he coughed, the dry and crusted sputum congesting his throat and clogging his nose, the throes of violent fever, all made the getting up slow and difficult. When he succeeded, he turned to face the priest squarely. He was taller than Doops had thought, a little taller than Doops himself, and his firm muscles stood out from his emaciated body like hefty tumors, indicating that he was once a strong and healthy man.

The two men stood like fragile puppets—fragile, yet held secure by some spectral wire neither of them controlled. The flaxen skin of Doops, induced by the Atabrine and enhanced by the fever raging within him, matched the oriental hue of the other. They made no motions now. And no sounds. There was a steady calm in each of them and their breathing was stable and even. There was a stillness in the tropics neither of them had known before. Fronds and palmettos held in curbed parenthesis, hushed as stalagmites in a cave. The falling of the rain disturbed nothing. It was as if nothing existed except the two of them facing each other, tuned and blended.

The man motioned to the wine bottle lying beside the pit. It had not been touched since Doops had found it in the ruins of the thatch hut. Doops picked it up without looking at it and without instruction poured all of the wine into the canteen cup. He handed it to the man and stepped back, waiting. Reuben gazed into the cup without expression, then turned and looked into the sun, a sun wrestling with the pluvial haze and casting lustrous corrugated streamers directly at them both. When Doops saw him lift the cup to his lips, the same feeling of floating, sinking, blurred consciousness fusing with adumbration returned. It passed as quickly as it came.

When he finished the wine, he motioned for Doops to take the

130

cup. Doops, seeing that it was empty, placed it beside the decanter on the ground and waited. The man pointed again, almost casually, to the M-1 rifle lying beside the field pack and continued to hold the soft and sober aim until Doops obeyed. Doops walked over and picked the rifle up, hesitated, then stopped completely, waiting for the next bidding before returning to his station and pose. He stood with the weapon at a stilted port-arms position. The man, hovering now like an eagle, and without relaxing his gaze, motioned again to the rifle in Doops's hands. Doops waited. Pointing to a spot just above but directly between his own eyes the man bowed gently from the waist, then slowly stood erect, rigid and sublime. His motions were not rushed, as if without purpose or design.

With both hands he lifted the canvas half-tent to his head, holding it taut so that it formed a tidy mask over his face, outlining his nose, sunken eyes, and cheeks in a strained, Veronica-like distortion.

Doops did not feel the jolting thud against his shoulder. He did not hear the thunderous explosion that reached into and filled every inch of the rain-soaked jungle, the brief sloshing in the sordid hospice, the loving sepulcher. Nor did he hear himself, running wildly through the jungle to the west. Screaming.

10

"What are you doing?" the nurse asked. Doops was sitting on a packing crate between two Quonset huts, those hideous corrugated structures, prefabricated first in Quonset, Rhode Island, and dispersed thereafter to every rear echelon of World War II. Looking like a huge torpedo sliced down the middle, the semicircular roofs provided little shade and the heat from the metal discouraged one from sitting close. The nurse, a short, stocky woman whose gray-streaked hair blended with the stiffly starched cap she wore over an almost invisible hairnet, was older than the other army nurses moving to and fro on the walkway in front of the row of Quonsets. She was the only one who had noticed Doops sitting alone halfway between the front and rear of the buildings. She had dropped by each afternoon since he had started coming there, almost two weeks now. She did not say the same thing each time. At first she just nodded and when Doops did not nod back, she moved on. Then she began offering routine greetings. "Good afternoon." "Hey there." "And how are we to-day?" Things like that, leaving when he did not respond. On the day before this one, she had not slowed down as she approached him, saying as she moved, "One day I'm going to walk by here and you're going to say something and I'm not going to answer." This time she stopped suddenly, asked, "What are you doing?" and moved a step closer to him.

"I'm writing a story," Doops said, not taking his eyes from the red writing tablet with a black silhouette head of an Indian and the word *Chief* printed on the front. It was the kind of tablet he had bought at Miss Flora's store and used in school at Claughton Station. They were the first conscious words he had spoken during the nine weeks he had been there.

"Oh," the nurse said, answering as if she had asked a soldier what he was doing and he had said he was cleaning his rifle or shining his boots. As she said "oh," she turned and walked away in the same direction she had come from.

The soldiers had found him wandering through the jungle but he would not talk to them, would not tell them anything at all. He was fully clothed but had no identification. His wallet and dog tags were gone. He had no pack and no rifle. They tried to find his serial number, the one the GI laundry always stamped on every item of clothing. On each garment the number was either faded beyond recognition or had been torn off. On the inside of his belt they found three digits—301. Army serial numbers had eight digits and they could not tell if the three they found were middle or last numbers, so they were of no use to them at all. The medical records in the 109th Station Hospital had "Private John Doe—301" typed on them. The charts showed that when he was admitted to the 38th Field Hospital on Guadalcanal, he had been diagnosed as having viral pneumonia. Underneath that had been written, "Severe malnutrition and dehydration." A second chart, the one started when he had reached the station hospital on New Caledonia, showed that the admitting officer had diagnosed him "Acute psychosis—suspected of malingering." The chart also showed that since he had been there, he had been treated for dengue fever. The daily records showed the same entry each day: "Acute psychosis—suspected of malingering." Occasionally there was the notation, "Patient refuses to speak."

Each afternoon now he sat in the same spot, always wearing a green army fatigue uniform and a khaki bandana tied around his neck, falling loosely on the back of his shoulders. Sometimes he was barefooted and sometimes he wore wooden clogs held in place with a single strip of rubber cut from an airplane inner tube. He sat each day between the same two Quonset huts, on the same packing crates and with the same writing tablet on his lap. But he had not written anything at all. This day, as soon as the nurse asked him what he was doing, and he had replied that he was writing a story, he began to write, moving the yellow pencil back and forth across the page as a secretary might do taking dictation.

"*Where are the other ones?" Cecelia Geronymus asked.*

"Gillis will not be here," Goris Cooman said. "I saw him yesterday in Hoorn. He said he will never see us again. He sends regrets, says to tell you that he is sorry. His fear of death is too much."

"Will he betray us?" Cecelia asked.

"He says that he will not. Maybe he is leaving because he is not sure. He has signed as a merchant seaman. He says he leaves tomorrow for the East, China he believes. And he says he is sorry."

"We have reason to be more sorry than he," Cecelia said, turning aside. "But so might it be." She stood by the window staring into the darkness of Amsterdam, pretending to smooth the wrinkles from the broadcloth curtain as she spoke. "Gillis baptized more than three thousand of us. I among them. And you and Pieter Boens as well." She sighed deeply and turned back to face Goris. "He has the list. When he gives them the list, they will come for us. We will all die. Until they come for us, there is much to do."

He continued to write until it was almost dark, until a young corporal came and nudged him on the elbow, pointing without speaking in the direction of a row of ward tents on the far side of the hospital.

"**W**hat's the story about?" the nurse asked. Her voice sounded as if no time at all had elapsed since she had asked him what he was doing the day before.

Instead of answering, he turned to a clean sheet in the writing tablet and wrote something down, tore it out, and handed it to her. "Do you know where Kingston and Model T are?"

She read the words and answered. "I don't know *where* they are but I know *who* they are."

"Who told you?" he wrote on the sheet she had handed back to him.

"You did," she replied, responding as if he had asked the question aloud.

134

"Oh," he said, not taking the paper back from her. He said it the same way she had said "oh" the day before, showing no more surprise than she had shown. She moved directly in front of him, placed all her fingertips under his chin, pulling his face upward so that he could not avoid seeing her face. Their eyes touched briefly and as they did she smiled gently and assuringly, then as quickly pushed his face back toward the writing tablet and walked away.

"**P**ieter Boens will be here soon," Goris said. "He is hiding the boat. And canvassing the docks to be sure we were not followed. He escaped two days ago. You know he does not hear well now."
"Yes, I know." Her voice was sad as she moved back to the window.
"It was the molten lead," Goris continued, speaking in nervous gasps. "While he was their prisoner. The margrave did it himself. When the bailiff could not make him talk, the margrave poured the sizzling potion into his ear, then cooled it at once with the water cup, sealing it forever shut."
"Not forever," Cecelia said, putting her hand on his shoulder. "Forever is not a calendar word."
Pieter Boens entered the room as Cecelia spoke, embraced her modestly, and sat down.
Amsterdam was a city of harsh persecution in 1549. The same bitter wind that had swept over most of Europe was now blowing furiously over the Low Countries, leaving countless martyrs in its wake. The Calvanists and Lutherans had become the established church and were no more tolerant of those who disagreed with their doctrines than the Church of Rome had been with the Reformers not many years earlier. Lumping all disidents together and calling them Anabaptists, they exercised barbarities on them that knew few boundaries or limitations.

Doops read over what he had just written, corrected the spelling of *Calvinists* and *dissidents*, added a description of Cecelia's house where his characters were gathered.

The house was a short walk from the Amstel River, and they were in a large upstairs room. When Cecelia was a young girl she had been in a convent in East Friesia. A servant girl in the convent gave her a Latin Testament and from curiosity and boredom with convent life, she read it and was converted to the Anabaptist faith by the young

135

servant. Gillis, an itinerant elder who had recently arrived in Amster-
dam, baptized her and her father when she was on her next holiday.

Doops wrote a paragraph describing the baptism, read it twice, then tore it out, wadded the sheet, and dropped it at his feet. He wrote of a communion service where Cecelia, Goris, and Pieter stood together eating a loaf of plain bread and drinking red wine from pewter cups. There were four cups, one intended for Gillis. When they finished she poured the wine from the fourth cup into a small decanter and hid it in back of other bottles, cups, and earthenware utensils in a large oak cupboard.

"**W**hat's the story about?" She asked him the question on the third day as if she had not asked it before. It was a breezy Monday afternoon and she was taking a break from her rounds. She pulled up a packing crate and sat down beside him, not facing him.

Doops turned to a clean sheet and wrote the answer. "It's about how there aren't any Baptists left in the world." Instead of tearing the sheet out he held the tablet up for her to read.

"That doesn't strike me as being a big seller among the troops of World War II, but . . ." She pushed herself backward, letting the crate fall on its side, turning to face him as the crate turned, and she stood up.

"Look, 301." She pulled his face toward her. "It's time we quit the waltzing and get some things straight. Now, I guess you know that there are some folks in this hospital who think you're crazy. I'm not one of them. There are some others who think you're a fake. I'm not one of those either and I've fought that lieutenant like a tiger. Partly because I just plain don't like the bastard. And partly because I do like you. But all I know about you is what I heard when you were ranting and raving. I'm supposed to be a psychiatric nurse. I'm not that any more than that lieutenant-gynecologist-supposed-to-be-psychiatrist is a real psychiatrist. I'm a country nurse. A country nurse from Monroe County General Hospital. That's in Rhode Island. Twenty years of it. And that's where your real crazies, your full-time crazies are. Not just the full-moon crazies." Though she let go of his face, Doops continued to watch her. She pulled a Philip Morris from her breast pocket, lit it, and inhaled the first long pull, letting the smoke out through her nose and mouth as she continued to talk. Doops rocked back and forth on the crate.

"I've watched you for two months now. I made sure you had something to eat, that you got alcohol rubdowns every day, that you took your medicine when they brought you in with pneumonia. And when you had dengue fever. You were almost dead when they brought you in here. For two days and nights you were delirious. And for two days and nights I didn't take my clothes off. I brought ice from the kitchen and packed you down in it like beer for a picnic, trying to keep the fever from frying your brain. When you were talking out of your head, that damned lieutenant—and I'm a *captain*—that arrogant little bastard, I outrank him. He wanted me to keep notes on everything you were saying. I never wrote a word of what you said. I made stuff up just to keep him off my back. And off yours too. But you did talk, 301. You said a lot of things. Lots of things. None of it made much sense to me, though some of it made me feel strange. I mean real strange inside. But I knew it wasn't the lieutenant's business and he never knew about it. And won't. At least not from me.

"All I'm saying is that I want to help you. Not help you get uncrazy because you're not crazy. Help you get the hell out of here." She had finished her cigarette and was cupping his chin and face in her hands again, following his rocking motions, leaning closer as she talked. "But you've got to help me too, level with me. For instance, I don't even know your name." She dropped her hands to her knees and shrugged. "All I know is three digits of a serial number. You rambled and raved about Model T and Kingston, wherever they are, and a lot about Baptists and drownings and burnings. But you never said what your name is. I'm not playing psychiatrist. I'm playing buddy. For God's sake, tell me your name." She sat waiting for him to answer.

"This story is about some people who lived a long time ago and aren't around anymore," he wrote. "An extinct species, I think." He handed her the tablet. She read it, sighed, and handed it back.

"I just want to write a story about them. And that's all I want." She read the words but did not hand the tablet back to him this time.

"Extinct people," the nurse said, looking confused. "What kind

137

of extinct people?" Doops reached for the tablet, but she held it behind her back. "What kind of extinct people?" she asked again.

"Baptist people," Doops said feebly after a long pause.

"Oh," she whispered, a glimmer of half-understanding showing in her face. "Well, if you want to talk about your story, if it means that much to you, you know my name is Williams and I'm from Rhode Island and one of my three-hundred-years-ago grand-daddies was named Roger, or so they tell me, so . . . well . . . it isn't that I mind talking about your story. But I would like to know your name first."

Doops spat on the ground, raked some sand over it with the toe of the wooden clog, and reached his hand out again for the tablet. At first she hesitated, then handed it to him. He sat holding the tablet on his lap, studying the page. She gestured for him to go on.

"I don't know what my name is," she read from the tablet when he handed it back to her. He seemed embarrassed, hesitant to write again when she gave him the tablet. She looked at him with both pity and acceptance. He stood up and paced nervously around the area between the Quonset huts.

"I just want to write my story," he said aloud.

She beckoned for him to sit on the same crate with her, put her arm around his shoulder. "Okay. I believe you. If you say you don't remember your name, well, you don't remember your name. Aside from being a little inconvenient where the army is concerned, not getting paid and all, I guess it doesn't make any difference. What else did you forget?"

"Nothing," he wrote on the tablet.

"Where you're from? You remember that?"

Again he wrote the answer to her question. "Claughton County, Mississippi."

"Your mamma, your daddy's names? You remember that?"

"Harry Momber. Christine Momber." He continued to write the answers and hold the tablet up like a flash card.

"All right. Good man," she said. "Momber is your behind name. We know that much. That's more than a lot of people know. That's what we'll call you for now. Then we'll put the Red Cross on the case. They'll find out your front name."

"I'd rather find Model T and Kingston than know my name,"

Doops said hurriedly, his voice more confident than when he had spoken the other words.

The afternoon sun had moved around the far edge of the Quonset hut and was striking her hair, which the breeze had scattered over her face and shoulders. Doops noticed that she was not wearing the hairnet she generally wore. The gray streaks in her hair matched the color of the sand. The fading peroxide yellow reminded him somehow of the wind, which was blowing stronger across the ocean from the west. She sat staring at Doops, both hands resting in her spraddled lap, holding her skirt between her legs as the wind sought to lift it above her thighs. Perspiration beaded on her neck and face, catching in the shallow wrinkles as she arched her brow into the sun, the sweat dropping occasionally as it drained down the sloped furrows of her forehead. For a brief moment Doops felt a stirring in his loins that he thought at first was the onset of the symptoms. He realized quickly that it wasn't, that what he was feeling had to do with the woman who turned to face him. He held the stare as long as she did, trying hard not to blink, watching the pupils of her deep-green eyes dilate and rapidly shrink again as the direct sunlight shone full into them.

When she stood up and turned to walk away, saying nothing, Doops called after her, his voice stronger and still more confident. "Do you want to read my story, Miss Williams? I mean, when I get through with it?"

She was grinning broadly as she turned around and walked back. She stood in front of him and he didn't get up. She smoothed and stroked his cowlicked hair, which was no longer crewcut, then began to curl each side of the cowlick around her index finger, pulling each sweaty ringlet slightly and watching them fall on his forehead.

"Tomorrow, when I come back, let's just talk. Okay? I mean, enough of this 'Me write, you read' routine." Doops did not answer, just sat gazing across the beach and into the distance long after she had gone.

When the nurse arrived, Doops handed her several pages he had written. Neither of them spoke. She smiled, shook her head slightly, and began to read. It was in the form of a letter.

Dear Miss Williams:

You see, this story is about three people who didn't believe the way most people did. Actually, I got most of this stuff, at least some of it, out of a book our preacher back home gave me when I was just a yearling boy. The ideas I mean. I must have read it a dozen times. It told all about what happened to the people they called Anabaptists. They didn't call themselves that. It was what other people called them. They wouldn't baptize their babies, claimed that wasn't really baptism. They would baptize one another, most of the time in secret, beside a well using a dipper, sometimes in a river or canal. But that really wasn't why folks hated them so much. It was just that not baptizing their babies was against the law and they could kill them legally for that. They actually hated them more for some other things, but they couldn't kill them for the other things. Not legally anyway. And my story is about three of them who knew they didn't have long to live. They were being hunted because they were Anabaptists and everybody hated them, the Calvinists, the Lutherans, the Catholics, the government, everybody.

They shut themselves up in Cecelia's house. Cecelia was obsessed with the notion that she had to write it all down before the officials came for them. That was all she did, day and night, working on her book about what was happening to them. Goris, he was a big, rough, Spanish-looking fellow, a baker. He would bring other folks who believed like they did to the house for Cecelia to talk to, to interview. Pieter, he had once been a Catholic priest, real smart, knew four different languages. He helped with the writing, translating, and all that. People told them all kinds of stories. One fellow told how he had seen people die. He had seen one of his friends chained to a stake and a fire built close to him but not really on him, so he just parched real slow until the marrow was trickling down from his thighbones. Another was found dead in his dungeon cell from smoldering straw that was too wet to burn. Because the law said a criminal had to be present when the judge sentenced him, they tied him to a chair and took him to the court where his corpse was sentenced to be burned. Another fellow, he was eighty-seven years old, Miss Williams, had his head cut off and put on a pole in a public place and they put his body on a wheel outside for the birds and varmints to eat. Just all sorts of things.

140

When I was a kid, Miss Williams, I used to wonder how those folks felt. Now when I tell you this you're probably going to think I'm crazy too. But I remember one time my daddy was burning brush heaps and I had this colored fellow I played with tie me on a ladder, then pretend he was pushing the ladder over on the fire. My daddy caught us and threatened to whip the tar out of both of us. Another time I had him put me in a gunnysack and throw me in the creek. I told him not to pull me out until he had counted to fifteen. While I was at the bottom of the creek I remembered that the fellow had never been to school and probably couldn't count. But he pulled me out in plenty of time.

Miss Williams, you asked what my story is about. Well, that's what it's about. I'm sorry about writing all this down but I hope you understand.

> Your friend,
> Momber

P.S. Miss Williams, I'm doing the best I can to help you help me.

"Thanks for the letter," she said when she finished reading it. She folded it twice and stuck it in her uniform pocket. "It's been a long time since I got some mail." As she turned to walk away she saw that he had already started to write again. "Remind me not to give that book you read to my kids," she called over her shoulder. "Not that I'll ever have any. This goddamn army!"

"*W*hat is it about us they hate the most? We will not baptize our young because it is nothing more than the State's manner of enrolling us, the king keeping tabs on his vassals. We believe that the State and the fellowship of the faithful should never be one. We will not kill for them, will not fight their wars. We will not swear in their courts. Yet, these things are not the true reasons for their persecution of us. Then what is? What do we do that strikes them as being so heinous a crime?"

Goris and Pieter had returned to the bench before her, sitting like schoolboys. "I believe you have asked us a question you are about to answer," Goris said, poking Pieter with his elbow.

"I can tell you what I believe," she said. "And I will write it down for all eternity to know."

141

Pieter raised his hand to be recognized.

"You need no permission to speak, dear Pieter," Cecelia said.

"I think it is community of goods," he said, his smile widening as Cecelia nodded her head in approval. "They call us communists," he added. "Der Kommunist, Communiste, Communist!" shouting now, repeating the word in German, French, and Dutch.

"But," Goris interrupted, "we have no common treasury. We care for each other. We may be communitarians but we are not der Kommunist."

Doops was not aware that the word he was ascribing to Pieter Boens was not a word at all in the period of which he was writing.

"To them we are what they say we are," Cecelia said. "It is community that they fear will be their undoing."

"But it is their churches that accuse and oppose us most. More than the temporal powers," Goris answered.

"That is because the two of them are one," Pieter said. "That is what our sister is writing. As long as the two of them are one, there can never be community. There will not be Church. There will be State."

"Who is Cecelia?" the nurse asked on the following day, pulling the packing crate a little closer than usual to where Doops was sitting, watching him as he continued to write, his hand and pencil moving across the page like sails driven by the wind.

"Cecelia?" Doops said. "She's my main character. She's the one writing the book." He was reading over the last sentence he had written as she spoke.

"Is Cecelia in love with Pieter?" she asked, pretending not to notice that he was speaking.

"I don't know," Doops said, flipping the pages of the tablet back to something he had written earlier. "At least I don't know *yet*," he added, reaching over and touching her cheek, trying to suppress a laugh as he did.

"I'll let you read something that happened yesterday that made me wonder," he said, still looking for the right page. "It was after you left. Here. Start reading right here. It sort of made me wonder."

"You just tell me about it," the nurse said, touching him as he had touched her. "It isn't time for me to read the story. We'll know when the time comes. Just tell me about it."

"Well, like I said. After you left, Goris brought this woman in who told about her sister and her sister's husband. They were hauled to the scaffold on the back of a two-wheel cart. The husband kicked his slippers off, told the crowd there wasn't any point in burning them, that some poor person could wear them. The executioner sprinkled gunpowder all over his beard and dusted it in his hair. They did that sometimes, saw it as an act of mercy. You know, so they would catch on fire and burn quicker. The man yelled out, 'They have salted me good, my friend.' Sometimes they would strangle them with a rope and twisting stick—more mercy—so they would be unconscious when they lit the fire. Only this time the rope was loose and the executioner raised hell with his assistant, got mad because he had to twist the rope himself. The wife—now she was some tough woman— wouldn't quit preaching at the jail and they had fastened her tongue to the roof of her mouth with a screw to keep her quiet. They did that, you know. Called them tongue screws. Logical enough name for them, I reckon. Anyway, this woman told Cecelia that the couple's two little children dug in the ashes the next day to find the tongue screw as a souvenir of their mamma. Cecelia was shook up by all that and Goris and Pieter knew it. But here, I'll just read you this little bit."

The nurse tried to show no hint of satisfaction in hearing him speak freely. She continued to sit as Doops read.

"*Cecelia placed her pen in the well and asked the woman no more questions. For a long time they talked of pleasant things, ate bread and cheese, took turns singing songs of their native countries and making up limericks.*

"*Margraves and executioners and bailiffs were for the moment beyond their concern.*

" '*Life was so good,' Cecelia said as she bade each guest good-bye.*

" '*Life is so good,' Pieter said when they were all gone, taking Cecelia by the hand and leading her up the stairs into the darkened room.*"

"Just made me wonder," Doops said when he had finished reading. "But like I say. I really don't know."

"I think you really do know," she said, tapping him playfully on the jaw with her fist. "And you know what else?" she said, hitting him again and laughing. "I think you're an ole rascal."

"**D**id Cecelia and Pieter have a good time last night?" Miss Williams asked. She had slipped up behind Doops and put her hands over his eyes.

"Don't make fun of me," he said, handing her a single sheet of paper.

"I'm not making fun of you," she said, stepping in front of him. "And I'm not going to read this either. You tell me what's on it or I won't ever know."

Doops looked pleased, as if he'd been hoping she would say that, expecting it. He took one of her hands, kissed her palm, and began to speak. "Well, Pieter and Goris had this conversation this morning while they were cooking breakfast. Actually it was before I got up. See, they're afraid Cecelia is losing her mind. She is so wrapped up in her story that she's losing weight, turning pale, and they're really worried about her. They went upstairs and tried to get her mind on something else, tried to talk her into going walking with them on the frozen river after dark, when they could trust being outside the house. She didn't even seem to hear them, just said, 'Listen to this,' and started to read what she had written about a baptism.

" '**H**ow did he do it?' Cecelia asked. 'Tell me every word and every motion. Leave nothing out. Exactly what did he do? I have to write it down just as it happened.'

" 'Here is what I remember,' the man said. 'And I think it is all that happened that day at the well. He asked if I was heartily sorry for all my sins and I replied that I was. "Do you desire the baptism?" he asked me. "Yes," I answered. "Who will forbid me, that I should baptize him?" "No one," the four others replied together. "Humble yourself before God and His Church and kneel down," he instructed me.

" 'The man took a metal dipper, not the large one that was at the well but one he had tied upon his saddle. He filled the dipper with water from the well and poured it over my head as I knelt, saying, "I baptize you in the name of God the Father, God the Son, and God the Holy Spirit." And that is all that he said.' "

"Are you Cecelia?" the nurse asked as soon as Doops stopped reading, patting his knee. There was no sound of probing in her voice. She asked the question with the same matter-of-factness one might ask the time of day.

"I thought you said we weren't going to play psychiatrist," Doops said. There was no anger in his voice but a kind of assertiveness, which seemed to please her. He sat rolling the tablet into a cylinder, looking at the ground, slipping his feet into the wooden clogs lying on the sand in front of him. She thought he was going to walk away and wondered if she would try to stop him. Instead, he kicked the clogs away from him, turned casually to a new page and began to write.

"There are things more important than your project," the man seated in front of Cecelia said to her.

"What?" she snapped, impatient and irritated at this delay.

"That of which you write is more important than whether or not you write it down. What was, is, and will be. You seek to conquer with your words. But conquering, winning, is a dangerous thing. For the victors seem always to accept the gods of the vanquished. We can see it in what has happened to us. The Reformers have won over the Papists throughout Europe. Everywhere the people saw and believed and followed because of the oppression and corruption of the Roman Church. But before their castles were even aired out they were inhabited by the Reformers who now use no different methods to oppress and persecute us." He spoke calmly but with a solid sternness.

Doops was writing frantically, flipping each page as he finished it, without looking up. Miss Williams continued to sit quietly beside him.

"Is that what you wished to tell me?" Cecelia asked, not quite so testy now.

"No," he said. "What I want to tell you is that within their understanding of truth they can justify the persecution, even the torturing of us. It is not that they are liars and rogues that they do these things. Your honor, your integrity, your passion for truth are all admirable things. But they may also become idols. It is God who must be honored, not our honor of Him."

Goris had finished his chores and stood attentively before the fire.

Pieter looked at the man with astonishment. "How then are we saved?
Certainly not by worshipping worship as the Papists do." He was trying
to mask the irritability he was feeling.

Doops handed the nurse the last page he had written, nodded for
her to read it, and continued with the same furious pace.

    "It is by faith, as Luther says," Jacob Cool replied, still calm.
"But it is not my faith. It is the faith, the faithfulness of God."
    "By that logic then how do we differ from the Roman Church?" Pieter
asked, standing directly in front of the man, his voice rising. "Why
could we not simply have said, 'We are saved by good works but it is not
my good works but the good works of God which redeem us'? Then we
could all be good Catholics again."
    "Perhaps we could," Jacob sighed. "Yes, perhaps the line is that thin."

"You've led me into some deep water, Momber," the nurse
said, standing to leave. "You sure you learned all that stuff out of
one book? I mean, well, I always went to Sunday school—not always, but until I was old enough that my mamma couldn't make
me go anymore. But I never heard of all that. I just thought religion was about God and love and doing things for folks. Why I
became a nurse. You may be teaching me more than I want to
know."
    She took a stethoscope from her pocket, hung it in her ears, and
pretended to listen to his heart. "Anyway," she said straightening
up, "what's all that got to do with getting you the hell out of
here?"
    "Nothing," Doops said. "It's just a story. It doesn't have any-
thing to do with anything." He put the page she had handed him
back in place and tried to catch her eye, tried to look at her the
way he had on Monday. She gazed down the alley and into the
distance, a hint of a smile locked on the corners of her lips, looking as if she were entranced by something she did not wish to
discuss.

    "I didn't mean to vex you yesterday, Momber," the
nurse said, straddling the packing crate, kicking it sprightly on
the sides with her heels like one might a horse.

146

"Don't let him run away with you," Doops said.

"I mean about your story. I really want to see all of it. When it's time. I even dreamed about Cecelia last night. But there's more we have to do. We'll never get you off this island until we find out your name. Of course, the army will find it out in time. But their missing-persons bureau isn't too swift. There are a couple of things we'll try in the meantime. But not until you're done. Not until you have finished your story."

"I'm done," Doops said, pointing to the stack of writing tablets beside him. "I finished an hour ago. Didn't turn out the way I thought it would, though. Folks have a way of going where they want to go and you can't guide them like you can that horse you're riding." He took the tablets in his hands and spread them like large playing cards. "A hundred and twenty-six pages. Pretty long story, huh?"

"A good week's work I'd say," she said, smiling with approval. "At least we know what you'll be doing when this man's war is over."

"This *man's* war?"

"That's right. Women don't start wars. They stopped one one time but they don't start them. They're just soldier factories."

Doops sat down, took the last tablet and began to read to her.

" '**P**erhaps the smoke from what we do will float over all of Europe,' Cecelia said. 'And also to England. And the New World—what are they starting to call it—America, I believe. Yes, perhaps it will spread there too, new as it is. For no land will long survive without its tyrants.' "

"What are they doing?" the nurse asked, taking a more dignified pose on the crate. "What smoke? Is she talking about the smoke they get burned up in?"

"Partly," Doops said. "That's part of it. But see, after she finished writing her book, after she had chronicled everything she knew about the Anabaptist people, writing down everything the witnesses told her, well, then she decided to burn it all up. See, they got word that the bailiff and his troops were coming for them next morning. They have this all-night ceremony and she burns her book. One page at a time.

" 'A finished story that has no ending,' Cecelia said as they reached the last page, which was the first she had written. 'We have reached the beginning. There is no ending.' Goris continued to sit between them, whimpering softly, making no effort to conceal the sound. 'Jacob Cool was right,' she continued. 'Writing the story is not the story. The story will go on. With or without our help.'

"For an hour they sat staring out the window at the white smoke flying and scattering in the early morning wind, blowing downward into the city streets, upward and away in the direction of the North Sea, skipping and dancing like a kite.

" 'That has been our sin,' she began again. 'At least, my sin. To end the story. The end of a story can only be defended with violence. Nothing else is left.' Pieter sat now with his arms folded across his chest, watching with Goris as the smoke blended with the gathering clouds, the clouds accepting and embracing it now like a vacuum. Cecelia continued to speak, softer now. 'The tattered coat can never be possessed.' The wind had shifted and a slight gust down the chimney livened the coals, blowing a wisp of the white smoke, the very last of it, back into the room. Cecelia leaned into it and inhaled deeply. Goris and Pieter did the same, saying nothing, Goris no longer sobbing. 'Until we came together we knew the words,' Cecelia said. 'Now we know the tune.' "

"That's downright beautiful," the nurse said, not moving from where she sat. "You know what, Momber? I'm damned proud of you."

As she stood up Doops caught the clean, natural smell of her skin. For a moment it was replaced by the wretched scent of Reuben in the pit. And just as briefly he felt the near panic of sinking to the bottom of the ocean. As she nudged him in the direction of the dense thicket behind the hospital, the fresh smell returned, more pleasant than before. Doops moved along beside her with all the tablets under his arm except the one he was reading from. He continued to read as they approached the heavy wooded area.

"Without moving from the bench where they sat they heard the hoofbeats of what sounded to them like a legion of horsemen, approaching slowly and deliberately. They were quiet now, sitting as close to each other as they could get, sitting as one person. They did not move and did not speak again until there was a loud knocking, fol-

lowed by a continuous rattling of the latch chain. Goris started for the stairs.

" 'No,' Cecelia said, catching him by the hand, her voice calm and warm.

" 'We will let them in together.

" 'And together we will go with them.' "

The nurse was holding Doops's free hand as he finished reading, their fingers laced tightly together. She led him through the tight underbrush as one might lead a blind man, paying no attention to branches and brambles that plucked at her clothing. Assorted sounds of war were all they heard. Giant seaplanes dropped into the bay. An artillery battalion slammed practice rounds into the side of Mt. Humboldt in the distance while navy pilots returned to their anchored carriers near the harbor, all the sounds together reminiscent of the bailiff at Cecelia's door.

"I guess we haven't come very far in four hundred years," Doops said as she led him deeper and deeper into the dense thicket.

"Your story is finished. Let it be," she said. "For everything there is a season. That's in the Bible, I believe."

"Yeah. Ecclesiastes."

When darkness came they loved on the cool jungle carpet, an occasion flowing more surely from some mysterious remnant of long-ago time than from the mild and puerile flirtations that preceded it, yet in itself a path of tenderness and emotive madness, a procession of awe and wonderment Doops apprehended, recognized, and appropriated in silence and in crying out. And when it was over they lay for a long time in stillness, the quietude evoking blurred and jumbled thoughts of Amsterdam, Rhode Island, Mississippi, and the two of them together, their thoughts and silence bespeaking the cumulative histories that led to where they lay.

11

"Where the hell you guys been?" Doops said. He was stretched out on a canvas cot, lying on his back, his hands behind his head. The thick stack of Chief writing tablets was on the cot beside him. Two clean sheets and a brown woolen blanket were folded on the locker at the foot of the bunk.

"Where the hell you guys been?" he asked again.

Kingston and Model T were standing on either side of him, just standing there looking down at him. He had been dozing lightly when they came in, and as he looked up at them, his eyes squinting into the morning sun streaming in through the pyramidal tent flap, he did not rise and did not take his hands from behind his head.

"Model T here, he got sort of hurt," Kingston said. "When the lieutenant stepped on that land mine, he got sort of hurt."

"Really?" Doops said. He spoke without expression, as if he had not even noticed the grotesque appearance of the figure looking down at him. Model T's face and head were almost completely covered with Ace bandages, the bandages holding a stack of four-by-four gauze squares over his right eye and another stack over his left ear. His head was shaved clean and he was wearing a pair of white hospital pajamas and a red Medical Department robe. He was shaking his head from side to side.

Miss Williams and another nurse, an orderly, and a doctor stood at the entrance of the tent, out of sight but where they could hear.

"I told you that phony could talk," the doctor said.

"I never said he couldn't talk," Miss Williams said curtly. "I said he *wouldn't* talk. And if you made your rounds more often you would have known that he *is* talking. For over a week." She stood a conscious short step behind the doctor. The other nurse stood beside her, saying nothing. The orderly, a fat, smooth-faced technician fifth-grade, smiled faintly, pretending not to listen as he shuffled the stack of medical records he held.

"Wouldn't talk, couldn't talk. What's the difference?" the doctor said, walking around her, patting her on the rump and laughing.

"A lot of difference," she said, moving away from him. "Unless you don't understand about verbs."

"I didn't go to Monroe County General, nursie. I went to Yale. We didn't study verbs. We invented them."

"We invented some adjectives," the woman mumbled to the other nurse, who was nudging her in the direction of the next tent.

The doctor turned to follow them, still chuckling. "I still say the lad is clever. Just wants to go home. For two months he hasn't spoken a word. Now he's in there chattering like a parakeet. If I were his CO I'd court-martial his butt from here to Alabama. Or wherever rednecks breed. 'Whea thu hail you guys been?' " he drawled, trying to sound the way he thought Doops sounded. "He didn't learn to talk like that in my part of the world. And maybe I'm only a gynecologist—I didn't *ask* to be put in charge of a bunch of male nuts—but I know this much: The guy is a fake."

The nurse whirled around and faced him squarely, making no effort to conceal the anger and contempt in her voice. "I may be nothing to you but a Monroe County nurse, sir, lieutenant, sir! But I know something too. I know that if a man wants to go home badly enough to be quiet for two months he is in need of more than the half-baked psychiatric bullshit of a spreader of old wives' tails!" She handed the stethoscope and blood-pressure cuff she was carrying to the grinning orderly and walked away.

The doctor, feigning loud laughter, called after her, "You're cute when you're mad, nursie."

Doops had gotten up and was sitting on the footlocker at the end of the cot, lacing his boots. The other nurse came back in and

151

sat down beside him. She was a small woman, young, and wore the shiny gold bar of a second lieutenant opposite the brass caduceus pinned to her collar. She put her arm around his shoulder and kissed him on the cheek. "Welcome back, 301. I'm sorry for what you heard from that one. But somebody'll clean his plow before it's over."

"No problem, Miss Rhea," Doops said, pulling the laces tighter. "I may be half a bubble off-plumb but I'm not stupid. I've seen his likes before."

Kingston and Model T continued to stand beside the cot, still looking down at him.

"You're not even off-plumb," she said, smiling as she thought about what he had said. "Miss Williams told me that right off. And she's one smart nurse. She said she could always tell. And she's smart. When the moon is full. She can tell who's crazy when the moon is full. And it's been full twice since you've been here." She started to leave the tent but when she got to the opening she turned back toward him. "By the way, 301. Just what the Sam Hill is your name?"

"Sam Hill," he said, looking up at her. "God, it's been a long time since I heard that. Where're you from? No, let me guess. Sam Hill."

"Kentucky," she said, not waiting for him to guess. "Madison County, Kentucky. Berea College. That's where I went. It's not Yale, but it's not bad."

"Close enough," Doops said. "I'll tell you my name."

He got up and turned to face Kingston, squinching his face into a garbled mask, his eyes studying Kingston's eyes, inquiring, probing for any hint at all Kingston might give him. He turned to Model T with the same begging quest, tapping his forehead with his fingertips, still giving no indication that he had noticed Model T's condition. They looked at him as imploringly, reaching out, but telling him nothing.

"Don't try too hard," Miss Williams said calmly. She had returned to the tent opening and was watching and listening to the other nurse. She moved beside Doops and put her hand on his arm, turning him around to face her. "Don't try too hard," she said again. "We thought it might work. But don't worry about it. We thought seeing them might do it."

152

"My name?" Doops whispered, the lines of his face drawing tighter. "I have to tell this Kentucky lady my name." Miss Williams did not move. "My name is Momber. I'm from Claughton County, Mississippi, and my number is 38483013." He was looking at Miss Rhea as he spoke.

"We already knew that much, hon," Miss Williams said, rubbing and patting his shoulder. "But it's all right. Don't worry about it." She turned and looked at Kingston and Model T. "Tell him his name, boys. In a homecoming everybody has to have a name." She spoke gently, but with a note of disappointment.

"Tell him, T," Kingston said.

"*Sacré misère!*" Model T said. "*Fut putain!* And a big *poo yie!* A friend without a name! *Sacré misère!*"

A sort of befuddled glaze came to Doops's eyes, a faraway look. "*Sacré misère?*" There was a pathetic quality in his voice as he repeated the two words as a question. Model T moved a short step closer to him, still shaking his head from side to side. Doops stood motionless for a moment, the others backing slightly away as if they were expecting the two of them to attack each other. Model T became like a statue, his head still now, staring intently at Doops with his one eye. Suddenly the leaden confusion lifted from Doops's face, and for a moment he stood with no expression at all. Just as quickly, a smile of recollection and pleasure and approbation shone in lustrous boldness on his face, unmistakable to them all. Kingston and the two nurses moved in close as he continued to smile and nod his head up and down, the beaming incandescence seeming to light the darkest corners of the tent.

"You know!" Miss Williams shouted, grabbing him around the neck and jumping straddle of his waist, almost knocking him down. All the others, except Model T, who had not moved and had not changed expression, began mauling, pummeling, hugging, and slapping. "He knows! He knows!"

When the excitement subsided and there was quiet again, Doops moved to where Model T was standing. For the first time he seemed to notice the bizarre wrappings on Model T's face and head. Model T did not move. The two of them stood facing each other, stood close but did not touch. The others moved slightly away again, watching, quiet now.

"Say it," Model T said softly, still not moving.

"You're a great little Cajun, *mon ami*," Doops said, grabbing him, holding him close in a long embrace. Model T hugged him back.

"My name is Doops," he said at last. As he spoke his name a collective sigh went up from the little band gathered around them, followed by prolonged applause as Doops continued to hold Model T.

"At least as far as my daddy knew," he said, letting go of Model T. He sat down on the footlocker again, a trace of the earlier consternation returning to his face.

"What does that mean? 'As far as my daddy knew,' " Miss Rhea asked as she and Miss Williams were walking away.

"I think what it means is that he still doesn't know his name."

"I thought he remembered," the nurse said.

"He did. He remembered as much as his daddy remembered."

The nurse shook her head in confusion. "Well, Doops is good enough for me."

"Yeah. Me too," Miss Williams said. "But it isn't good enough for him."

"What?" Miss Rhea said, slowing the pace.

"Never mind. You're a Methodist. There is no way you could understand."

"**L**et's go to the PX," Doops said. "Let's go get some beer."

"Doops," Kingston said. "Do you know where you are?"

"Yeah. I'm right ahead of you. One step ahead of you."

"I mean, do you know where we all are? Do you know what day this is?"

"We're in the chickenshit army. That's where we are. And today is Monday. And if you were a Pisces it would be your birthday. Like it's mine. So let's go get a beer."

"Doops. You can't get beer on this island. I mean, not unless you're at least a second lieutenant. And I don't think you've been promoted that much in two months' time. Now tell me, just what the hell is going on with you?"

"What's going on is that today is my birthday. And what's going on is that we got scattered like a 'thirty-eight Chevy running through a covey of quail on the public road. And what's

154

going on is that I've been in this hospital for going on two months waiting for you guys. And I've had pneumonia and dehydration and malnutrition and, they think, a case of the crazies."

"And a case of the malingerings," Kingston said. "I heard the lieutenant say it to the nurse."

"That was the only thing he got right. Malingering I have been doing. A sweet case of the malingerings."

They walked past the long row of hospital tents, weaving in and out, behind some and in front of some. When they reached the last one, they walked in the direction of the ocean. The tide was moving out and they edged out with it as they walked back and forth, never moving beyond the marked hospital boundaries.

"Well, I guess we have to regroup," Doops said as they moved back to the dry sand and sat down. "Guess we've got some catching up to do. You go first, Kingston."

"Why do I go first? I think Fordache ought to go first. He got hurt."

"You want to go first, Model T?" Doops said, looking at him but still showing no indication that he even saw the swathing about his head.

"Maybe you're right," Kingston said, not giving Model T time to answer. "The last shall be first. Redbones should go first because they are the last."

"Good Lord," Doops said. "I see you're still on that kick."

"Okay. Okay," Model T said. "I'll go first." He spoke with only the slightest touch of his Cajun accent.

"I got half my head blown off, Doops," Model T began. He spoke as if he had memorized and rehearsed what he was going to say. He tugged at the elastic bandage, pulled it slightly away from his chin, and let it snap against his skin. Doops shifted his position in the sand, reached for a large shell he had picked up when they were following the tide, held it to his ear, and listened to the protracted din and roaring of the ocean sounds. He did not respond to what Model T had just said, and did not look directly at him.

"Model T got half his head blown off," Kingston said, reaching over and tapping Doops on the arm. "Didn't you hear what he said? Can't you even see the shape he's in?"

When Doops didn't answer, Model T continued. "I was in the

foxhole next to the lieutenant. First, I heard him calling the names of the guys on the first watch. You know. Stelling and Wardlow and them. Then I heard him walking back toward where I was in that foxhole. He stopped by where I was hunkering in that hole in the ground, stooped over and touched my helmet and said, 'Good-night Arceneau.' And that's the last thing I remember. Kingston said there was a big explosion. But I didn't hear that. I didn't hear nothing at all. Kingston said the lieutenant cried, 'Mamma!' but I didn't hear that either. The next thing I knew some medics were hovering over me. I had gone over and got in the foxhole with the lieutenant. I don't remember doing it. But that's where they found me. There wasn't much left of the lieutenant but I was in there with whatever was left of him. They said my shirt was wrapped around the piece of his neck where his head used to be—you know, like I was trying to stop the bleeding. But I don't remember doing that either. I just remember them pulling me out and putting me on a stretcher, two of them, and walking off through the jungle. And I remember hearing one of them say, 'The burying detail will get him.' "

As Model T was speaking, Kingston was watching him, grinning with doting pride. "Just listen at those verbs," Kingston said, looking at Doops. When Doops continued to sit in the same aloof, disaffected manner he added, "And listen to my prepositions, huh?"

Doops had broken a smaller shell in half and with the jagged edge was scratching his name on the larger shell. When he finished he wrote the names Fordache Arceneau and Kingston Smylie underneath his own name, the calcium from the white shell crumbling against the rough surface of the large blue one. He drew a small cross above the names, using the last piece of the chalky shell. When he finished he walked slowly down to the water's edge and dropped it in the surf.

As he took his place again on the sand beside the two of them, Model T continued, as if there had been no interruption. "I don't remember much that happened the next few days. They put me on a ship but I don't know how long it took us to get back here. Anyhow, after I got back here, I reckon maybe it was three, four days, this doctor came in the tent where I was and said they had to start operations on me, that my right eye was gone and a big chunk of my cheekbone. And my left ear was gone too."

"And, guess what," Kingston interrupted. "This crazy coonass told them to get lost. Can you believe that, Doops? This idiot won't let them operate on him. Says he's going through the rest of his life with half his head gone. One ear gone and one eye gone and a hole you can stick your fist in where his eye is supposed to be. Talk to him, Doops. They said they can do plastic surgery. You know, graft skin and all that business. Make him an ear and all that. And fix his face up—bone graft too, and all that business— and put a glass eye there. 'Course he couldn't see through it. And he couldn't hear with the homemade ear. But shit. You talk to him, Doops. Tell him he's a dumb coonass. Teach him a lecture, 'fesser. He'll listen to you." Kingston tried to laugh, started to rub Doops's cowlick, pulled his hand back quickly.

Doops still had not said anything.

"Your eye is to see through and your ear is to hear with," Model T said. "If they won't do that it's like a car with no motor. It ain't for shit."

"Why the hell don't you say something, Doops?" Kingston asked. "Don't you understand? Model T's got one eye blown away forever. Look at him! Don't you even care anymore? What happened to the neighborhood? One of us is bad hurt and you sit there like a knot on a log. Damned if I understand what's going on."

"In the country of the blind a one-eyed man is king," Doops said, and began to play tic-tac-toe on the sand, making X's with his right index finger, zeroes with the left, winning each time with horizontal zeroes. "Seems like I heard that somewhere once," he said finally, wiping all the games away with his foot. "Wells? Yeah. H. G. Wells."

"You sure it wasn't Zane Grey?" Kingston said.

Doops did not answer. He stood up and started to walk away, mumbling some words to himself. "There is the land of broken hearts, and the land of broken heads. I think Chesterton said that one first."

"Get your ass back here, Doops," Kingston yelled at him.

Doops came back and sat down. "Okay, Kingston, you're next," he said in the same detached manner. "Catch us up on what you've been doing. War is hell. Seems like I heard that somewhere too. We don't have time to whimper."

"Who's whimpering?" Kingston said, the irritation in his voice growing. "Have you heard anybody whimper? Hey, T. You whimpering? Jesus! I just said he's half deaf and half blind and looks like some goddamn mummy. And he wants to be a war freak in a circus the rest of his life. Wants to go around showing everybody what WW II looks like. That what you want him to do? You want to have a fucking freak for a friend the rest of your born days? A freak! You hear that? A goddamn freak for a friend." His face was red and he was screaming, talking faster and faster with each word. Model T was shaking his head in a near cadence with the words.

"Maybe all *friends* are freaks," Doops said, his voice still calm. "Maybe you have to be a freak to be a friend, Kingston. I really don't know. I just said maybe. Catch us up."

Kingston stood up and walked round and round the two of them, kicking sand ahead of him. "Yeah. I'll catch you up, Doops. But before I do there's one little thing I want to tell you. Me and Model T here, we've been together almost the whole time since they brought him in. Maybe we've changed some. I know we've learned a lot of things. Thought about a lot of things. Talked about a lot of things. Things we used to all talk about, and then some. You know, the neighborhood and all. Maybe it's what they used to mean when they said the army would make a man out of you. I just know we're a lot older. We read books—hell, Model T here, he's read ten books all the way through. Me and him read the fucking Bible all the way through. Every last bit of it down to the last begat. Didn't we, T? Damn right we did. And listen how he talks. We went through these exercises every day. We missed the hell out of you, but Godamighty, we did the best we could. We got by. Anyway, what I want to tell you is that the neighborhood is intact. And you're part of it, like it or not. Just the way you always said. You know, it ain't something you join—or quit."

While Kingston was talking, Doops never took his eyes off Model T. He couldn't understand why Model T was shaking his head from side to side, as if he were disagreeing with everything

Kingston said. Doops was conscious for the first time that he had not actually seen the bandages before, that he was looking so intently at Model T himself that he had looked past the sad and outlandish headdress. He felt a deep something within him, a longing, a nagging, a wanting to move to Model T, hold him close and tell him how sorry he was that this had happened to him, to ask him all about how it hurt, why he wouldn't agree to have the surgery, what he was thinking, to tell him how glad he was to see him. But he just sat staring at him, trying to figure out why Model T kept moving his head from side to side. Suddenly, he understood. Model T could not listen to someone and look at him at the same time. He could hear with his right ear and see with his left eye. But he couldn't do both at once. The thought of Model T going through the rest of his life shaking his head, saying no to everything, gave him a renewed urge to comfort him. Or be comforted by him. But he just sat. Maybe that's his call now, he thought. His vocation. To say no to the world for the rest of his days. Great God Almighty! He was remembering Cecelia and Goris and Pieter.

"Did you read the part about Jonathan and David?" he asked. It was his only response to what Kingston had said to him.

"Yes," Kingston said. "I told you we read it all."

"Catch us up." His voice was hard but there was a slight tremor in it.

"When the lieutenant stepped on the land mine that night, I took off running," Kingston said, matter-of-factly. "Just like we all did. Everybody but Model T, and the lieutenant, I mean. Only I ran right back the way we had come in. I didn't know it but that's what I did. Maybe it was just instinct. My daddy—granddaddy— used to call me a homing pigeon. Used to try to get me lost when I was little. But he never could. Maybe that's the Indian in me. Or the nigger. The Indian, I reckon. Anyway, I got back to the camp at Henderson Field in not more than an hour. I crossed the Lunga River and I could hear airplanes revving up their motors. I got back in less time than it took us to get where we got split up. 'Course, I was hauling ass running. Rifle, pack, and all hanging all over me. Damn near got shot myself by the guard posted out by the runway. He yelled at me, you know, all that crap: 'Halt!

Friend or foe?' " Kingston had backed several yards away from them and was reenacting both parts, changing his voice the way he remembered the guard shouting. "Friend!" he yelled, excited and out of breath. "Advance, friend and be recognized," he said for the guard, facing Model T and Doops when he was playing the guard's part, turning his back when he was himself. "So I started easing up, real slow now." He moved down the beach away from them. "He couldn't see me in the dark and so he asked for the password. Hell, I didn't know any password. The lieutenant didn't give us any password. Least, I don't think he did. Did the lieutenant give us a password? Hell, I don't remember." He was talking fast and moving rapidly from one place onstage to another. Model T was trying to keep up with his seeing eye and hearing ear, still shaking his head. Doops listened from where he sat on the sand, most of the time watching Model T.

"Shit, son. I don't know no password but let me the hell through because I've got something hot to tell the captain." He moved to a spot offstage, a place he had designated for commentary. "Well, that gung-ho sucker, he wouldn't let me through. And when I moved in, that dumbass, he shot right over my head. *Boom!*" Kingston fell flat on his belly, onstage now; then jumped up as quickly and moved to the guard's position.

"The password is *coconuts*, and you'd better say it!"

"Okay. Okay! Coconuts!" He was on his belly again.

Model T had heard the story many times before but was laughing and shaking his head and beating the sand with his fists. "Tell ole Doops what that shithook said next. Tell ole Doops!"

Kingston moved to the offstage position. "Well, he realized he had shit in the nest, but he was flustered, that dumb bastard, he hollered out . . ." He moved back to the guard's position. "No. You're supposed to say, 'Coconuts!' and I'm supposed to say 'Make soap!' and then you're supposed to say . . ." He spoke as commentator again. "By then the sergeant had come running out and grabbed the gun away from that pissant, told me to get the fuck up off the ground and come on up to headquarters with him. Can you believe the shit that goes on in this man's army?"

Doops had stood up and was cracking his knuckles, first on one hand and then the other, staring all the while, gazing out across

160

the ocean. After cracking each knuckle until they stopped popping, he picked up a small feather that was blowing along the beach, split the quill end in half with his thumbnail, and began picking his teeth, still staring at the horizon.

Kingston moved back to Model T. "The others came straggling in all next day. It was almost sundown, though, when they came in with Model T. They had patched him up a little but, Jesus Christ, he was a mess. I never saw such a mess. He was mostly out of his head, talking nothing but that coonass talk of his, and nobody could understand him. I played like I knew what he was saying, just made up bullshit to tell the captain, made up this whole spiel about how many Japs he had seen come by before they picked him up. Just a bunch of shit—you know. Anyway, the captain was real interested in all that, was writing it all down on a scratch pad, me just making it up as I went, jabbering what little Cajun I knew to Model T, saying mostly the same thing over and over. Just as luck would have it, the next morning there was a hospital evacuation ship pulling out to bring casualties from Talagi and Rendova back here, and the medic told the captain he didn't think Model T could make it in the field hospital. The captain said he needed all the details about the Japs, all my bullshit—you know. So he told the medic he was going to send me along to interrogate him on ship and told me to get in touch with the ship's executive officer and they would radio the information back. Did you ever hear of such bullshit? There was so damned much confusion on that hospital boat, guys lying on stretchers on the deck—Jesus God, nobody knew what the hell was going on. Some sergeant running around tagging everybody, asking things like, 'Where's your injury?' if they could talk and just scribbling what they said on a tag. Hell, I scoped that one right off. You'd have been proud of this country Redbone, neighbor. Some poor guy lying next to Model T croaked before the ship pulled anchor and, Godamighty, it was so hot on that fucking deck, he started stinking before he was dead good. Everybody was running around, screaming, giving orders. They stuffed him in a bag and took him back on the Higgins boat that had brought us out there and—shit. I just stretched out on the litter next to Model T after they moved that guy and when the sergeant asked me what was wrong with me I just mumbled, 'Back,' sort of weak like, and for the rest of the day I never got off that stretcher except to go to the head and to help Model T with one thing and another. When they moved us down in the hold they moved me right along with Model T. And when we got here they just brought me right on to the one-o-nine with the rest of them and I've been here ever since. I told a nurse the whole truth when we got here and she laughed her ass off. Asked me if I knew how to take temperatures and blood pressures. When I told her I didn't, she laughed some more and said she'd teach me and meanwhile I could empty bedpans. So, Doops, old neighbor, you're looking at a bedpan commando. The swiftest shit-slinger in the South Pacific."

Model T was laughing again, snapping the elastic bandages against his chin with both hands in two-four time, patting his foot in perfect cadence with the sounds.

Doops shifted the feather toothpick from one side of his mouth to the other, back and forth, his eyes still fixed on some far-distant point. He had not moved.

"Now it's my time," he said, spitting the tiny feather from his mouth, the wind catching it and blowing it back over his head.

Model T stopped his antics and moved a bit closer to Kingston, both of them facing Doops, who stood directly in front of them, his hands behind his back.

"Yeah, it's your time," Kingston said. "Catch us up."

"Well," Doops said, shifting his feet uneasily in the sand. "I killed a man." He said it impassively, almost coldly, not looking directly at them. Model T looked quickly at Kingston again, asking this time with his dexterous blink if what he had heard Doops say was what he had said. That was all Doops said. As soon as he said it he took his place beside them. They sat cross-legged on the sand, a silent and motionless triad.

They sat for a long time with no one speaking a word. The sun had inched its way over the trees and mountains behind them and they were in the sweltering heat of midafternoon. A miscellaneous line of sick and wounded soldiers, returning from assigned therapeutic walks, filed past them, some with plaster of paris casts, some with pigments of their skin thrown into garish disarray by the pranks and mischief of malaria, some barely moving as their crutches struggled with the sand, the weight of their mangled bodies digging in. The motley procession seemed proper and relevant to the silent rite of understanding and acceptance and absolution in which the passing soldiers showed no interest at all.

It was almost sundown when the last group of soldiers passed them, each throwing a long ghostlike shadow away from the shoreline as the sun touched and sank into the ocean in the distance. The last one to pass was wearing a half body-cast, his right elbow straight out from his shoulder, the forearm sticking straight up with just his hand showing above the cast. His fingers trembled and the shadowed motion on the sand looked like a torch.

"Going to Olympia," Doops said as the man disappeared. It was the first word anyone had spoken since Doops's brief report.

"Looks like they're coming after us," Kingston said. Two people were moving swiftly down the beach in their direction, a man and a woman.

"Where the hell have you fellows been?" the doctor asked, looking straight at Doops as they approached.

"We've been right here," Kingston said.

"I'm talking to him, Jack," he said, pointing to Doops.

"He's been right here too," Kingston said.

"Don't get cute with me, Slim," the doctor said. "I'll bust your ass from here to Birmingham."

"I've heard tell that's a mighty fine town," Kingston said.

"Come with me, Doops," the nurse said, extending her hand to him as he continued to sit on the sand. He stood up, brushed the sand from his clothes, took the nurse by the arm, and started to walk away.

"Keep it in the yards, boys," he said, turning quickly to Kingston and Model T. "Gotta go back to the loony hatch."

12

"**A**re you ready, nursie?" the doctor said.

"Ready for what?" the nurse asked.

"Ready for the session to begin. You're supposed to be a psychiatric nurse. Do you know what a psychiatric nurse does? This is a therapy session. Do you know what you're supposed to do?"

"Do you?" the nurse asked, smiling, just smiling, winking at Doops when the doctor glanced away.

The three of them were seated in a pyramidal tent with all the flaps rolled down, four days after the reunion. The tent was bare except for three chairs and a wooden filing cabinet. The only light was a forty-watt bulb attached to a plaited yellow-and-green cord, the cord wound around the center tent pole. The doctor had fastened the entrance flap by making a neat bow with each of the inside ties. Two orderlies stood outside the entrance on either side of the closed flap. The nurse sat slightly behind the doctor, a yellow writing pad on her lap. Doops sat facing them a few feet away.

"Have you ever had mental problems before?" the doctor asked.

"Before what?" Doops said.

"Before now."

Doops did not answer. The nurse had not made any notes, had not even taken the lead pencil from where it was tucked between her cap and ear. The doctor glanced at her impatiently but she showed no concern.

The doctor fidgeted in his seat, searching for the next question. For a few minutes no one spoke. The doctor lit a short, bulldog-style pipe and leaned forward, blowing clouds of rich aromatic smoke directly in Doops's face.

He began speaking slowly, tamping the hot ashes down with his thumb. "On the beach the other day . . . when you said . . . uh . . . what was it he said, Nurse Williams? . . . 'Keep it in the yard' to your friends. What exactly does 'keep it in the yard' mean?"

"I don't know," Doops said. "I never thought about it. I say that a lot. We all do. All three of us, I mean. It just means what it says. It's just a saying. It means . . . keep it in the yard."

"I see," the doctor said, scratching his closely cropped mustache with the end of the pipestem, the corners of his mouth curling slightly.

"Let's look at that 'keep it in the yard' business. I think it means something very deep within you. Something personal, I think. Let's take one word at a time. What is *it?* for example. *It* has to be something. What is *it?*" There was another long silence, the nurse staring at the floor, looking uncomfortable, Doops looking at her, the doctor sitting with his arms stretched over the back of the chair like a fighter in his corner watching a knocked-down opponent.

"And where is the *yard?*" he said, grinning, rushing in now.

"Oh, for Christ's sake!" Doops whispered, standing up and walking about the darkened tent, his vexation mounting.

The doctor seemed pleased with the response, standing up also and following Doops as he moved about the tent. "You see? You really don't want to talk about it. Why do you think you aren't willing to talk about it?" The nurse watched helplessly but with amused satisfaction at the doctor's uncertainty.

"No, you're right," Doops said, turning to look at him for the first time. "I don't want to talk about it because there isn't anything to talk about. And I don't want to talk about why today is Friday either. Or—"

"Ah," the doctor interrupted, pleased and encouraged. "You see? It's significant that you said you don't want to talk about Friday. Friday—ah, how interesting, Nurse Williams—you see, Friday is late in the week. It's an old day. Monday is a young day.

You wouldn't mind talking about a young day. But, you see—how very interesting—you don't want to talk about an old day."

Doops had returned to his chair and the doctor, more sure of himself now, pulled his own chair closer to him, leaning over and patting him on the knee. "Son, you're afraid of old age already, aren't you? And how old are you? Twenty-two, twenty-four? You're afraid of death, aren't you? Yes. You're afraid of death. He's afraid of death, Nurse Williams. We're getting somewhere now, son, but you have to trust me. I want to help you. I want to be your friend. But you have to trust me. Talk to me now. Tell me whatever comes to your mind. That was good. You not wanting to talk about Friday. But there is a lot more we have to discuss if you're going to be well again. You do want to be well again, don't you, son?"

"But, sir. Today isn't Monday. Today is Friday. And what is there to talk about? So it's Friday. So what?"

The doctor kept moving in. "Is there anybody you dislike, Doops? I believe you said his name is Doops, didn't you Nurse Williams? Funny name, but no more than some others, I suppose. I mean *really* dislike." Doops did not change expressions, sighed deeply but did not answer. "You really don't dislike anyone, do you son? And that isn't normal. It isn't healthy. You don't really dislike anybody."

"Wanna bet?" Doops said, smiling at the nurse.

"Good. Good!" the doctor said. "Good now. You're saying me, aren't you? What I hear you saying is 'I actively, honestly, without evasion of mind and without equivocation, dislike Lieutenant Thomas Rollins.' Now that's what you're saying and that's all right. That's good. Go ahead. Say it out loud. Hear yourself say that you really don't like me. Don't think of me as an officer and yourself as a private. Think of me as just another person. Someone you have recently met and suddenly detest. Go ahead. Say it. Let yourself hear it. You can do it. Go ahead now. Say it."

Doops was not even hearing him any longer. He had turned to thinking of Kingston and Model T and wondering how they had found him. Suddenly he realized that they had been in the same hospital for two months and although the psychiatric wards were separated from the rest of the hospital by a small lagoon, he won-

166

dered how they had found him when they did and if they had told Miss Williams his name before he remembered. The doctor fumbled with his pipe again. When it would not light he knocked the ashes out, tapping the pipe against the heel of his shoe, letting them fall on the floor. The silence continued while he filled the pipe, fumbled in his pockets for fresh matches, lit it again.

"I think he has read the book, lieutenant," the nurse said, obvious pleasure in her voice.

"Write it up, nurse," he said angrily, walking to the entrance and untying the flaps to let himself out. "I don't have time to play games. If he doesn't want to be helped, if he refuses to let me help him . . . I still think he's a fake. There are sick people in this hospital who want to get well. I don't have time for this one."

He finished with the last tie and pushed the flap open. Doops and the nurse blinked as the sun struck their faces. The two orderlies outside snapped to attention and saluted. The doctor returned the salute, turned around, and spoke through the opening.

"Read him a bedtime story and tuck him in, nursie. Maybe he'll talk in his sleep."

"Good-day, lieutenant," the nurse said, lifting her collar with the silver captain's bars on them, breathing lightly on them, pretending to shine them with her fingertips.

"I hope he's good at delivering babies," she said when he was gone. "But I don't believe he'll ever be much at delivering minds." Doops smiled but did not reply.

She put the yellow pad on top of the filing cabinet. "Let's get some air in this place," she said, starting to roll up the side flaps of the tent. Doops got up and helped her. When they finished, she went to the entrance and told the orderlies the session was over, that they could go back to the office. After they had gone, she picked up one of the chairs and moved it outside.

"Let's sit here."

Doops followed and sat down on the ground a few feet from her. He watched as she inhaled the first long pull of a cigarette. He had not had a cigarette since he'd been there. She handed him one, leaning over to give him a light from her own. He took a few short puffs, felt dizzy, and snuffed it out in the sand, then field-stripped it the way they had taught them to do in basic training, splitting it down the middle with his thumbnail, letting the tobacco scatter on the ground, then wadding the paper into a tiny, almost invisible ball.

"They say that's the mark of a good soldier," she said. "You a good soldier?"

"No ma'am," Doops said without hesitating. She smiled as he called her ma'am. "I'm not a good soldier. I'm not a soldier at all. And never will be. I tried to tell them that before they drafted me. Tried to tell them that I loved my country and if they loved it too it would be best for the country and everybody else if they didn't draft me. But they did it anyway. No ma'am, I'm not a good soldier."

She reached over and touched his lips. "It seems rather silly for you to call me ma'am now," she said. "I mean . . ."

"Just a habit," Doops said, blushing slightly.

"What are you, Doops?" she asked. "That's not a question that means anything except what it says. To hell with the lieutenant's therapy. He does cerebral Pap smears. Forget it. Me, I just like to know what makes somebody tick. You know that. Or you should. I'm not after a damn thing. I'm not trying to heal you. I'm trying to get you out of here."

"I guess I'm supposed to say something," Doops said. "But I don't know what it is. If what you're trying to do is get me the hell out of here, well, I'm sympathetic to your cause. But I don't know what I'm supposed to say."

He wanted to cooperate for her sake, wanted to tell her something that would please her. But he did not want to betray her by making something up.

"You're not supposed to say something, Doops. Not unless you want to."

He felt drawn to her, close, the way he had felt the first time he really looked at her as they sat between the Quonset huts. He wished that she would take him by the hand and lead him back into the jungle, and wondered if they would ever go there again.

"You know, it's against their rules for officers to fraternize with enlisted men, Doops," she said, eyeing the line of nurses and doctors moving by. Doops wondered if she had read his mind.

168

"So. I guess we'd better act professionally." She held the yellow tablet on her lap and pretended to write, looking at Doops all the while.

"Doops. That's a pretty name. Do you like it?"

"Not especially. But I guess I'll get used to it again. Maybe that's why I forgot it." He stood up nervously and moved about the area. For a moment she thought he was going to cry.

"You'll be okay," she said, touching him on the head.

"How do you know?"

"I don't know how I know. Maybe because I'm from Rhode Island. And my name is Williams. But you'll find out."

Doops looked at her curiously, a mixture of confusion and admiration. "Blood will tell," he said, then wondered why he had said it. And what it meant.

"Let me ask you something," she said, her manner different. "You know, I'm the one who left that stack of writing pads by your bunk. You kept asking for them. When you were so sick and out of your head. And I used to follow you every day after you got better, or better enough to walk around, when you wouldn't talk to anyone. You left every day as soon as we had made rounds and you sat in the jungle for hours, holding that tablet on your lap. Sometimes you wrote things down but you never brought it out with you. But you sat out there day after day. And sometimes I followed you, watched you through the brush, wishing you would talk to me and wondering why the hell I had cut you out of the herd for such special attention. God knows I—"

"Will you read my story to Kingston and Model T?" Doops interrupted, appearing not to be listening to what she was saying.

"I don't know." She answered almost before he had finished. She did not seem surprised that he had asked. "Before I answer your question, let me ask you one. The one I was about to ask. All the time you were out of your head, you kept talking about trying to find somebody to baptize you. Now, I'm not very religious, as you might have gathered, and I'm still not asking clinical questions. But that's when you would get almost raving. In your ranting you would wander all over the globe looking for a Baptist. From Claughton Station to Amsterdam. Maybe it has something to do with my genes—or yours. I mean, I'm just curious."

"Will you read my story to them?" he asked again, asking as if he had heard nothing of what she had said.

"Yes," she said. "I'll read it to us." Their eyes met and each one tried to hold the stare longer than the other, trying not to blink, and when they did she spoke again. "But you said 'to *them*,' didn't you?" Doops did not answer.

She found them sitting in their usual place, facing the ocean, the morning sun to their backs. They were seated in a circle and Doops had clawed a deep hole in the sand in the middle of the circle they formed. He had torn all the pages from the tablets and they were in a neat stack beside him, a green coconut palm weighing them down. When she sat beside them forming an imperfect circle as she took her place slightly outside their own already defined periphery, no one spoke. Kingston changed places with Model T, putting Model T's good ear nearest her. They sat quietly and comfortably with no one moving. She looked steadily at the stack of paper but did not touch it until Doops took the palm branch off and handed the manuscript to her. When he did, she began to read.

" 'Where are the others?' Cecelia Geronymus asked."

She read Cecelia's words in a high soprano voice, dropping to her own normal pitch for the narrative.

" 'Gillis will not be here,' Goris Cooman said."

She had chosen a gruff, raspy voice for Goris. For Pieter's words she used a serious, scholarly tone. She read expressively, often with a manner one would use when reading to small children. There was an obvious pride about her, touching and handling each word like a midwife might do a newborn child, knowing she was not responsible for what she held but feeling a part of it too.

The melancholic procession of disabled soldiers had already begun their morning exercise when she started to read. The man with the arm cast stuck up in the air led the way, just as he had been the last when they had seen them before, returning then to their hospital beds. They were an indifferent party to it all again, a visible background dirge as they labored over the loose sand, unknowing patrons, a silent commentary.

As she neared the end of the first page, she could see from the corner of her eye that Doops was trying to get one of the palm leaves to burn. The flame from a new Zippo lighter flickered in the wind, blowing back against his hand. He turned to shield it with his body but the green palm simply smoked and cracked, would not catch. When she finished the page she passed it casually to him, did not begin a new page but sat watching him. As he started to touch the flame to the corner of the sheet she reached over and popped the lighter shut.

"You're not Cecelia," she said sternly, the snapping of the Zippo lid punctuating her words.

Kingston and Model T watched them with curious interest but did not comment. Doops placed the page beside him, removed one of his shoes and put it on top of the paper which the wind sought to blow away. Then he began pushing the sand into the hole with his bare foot, burying the palm branch as he did.

"Or are you?" she said before she began the next page.

She continued to read in a loud, distinct, and eloquent fashion with frequent overtones of insight and understanding showing in her voice, the pride increasing. Kingston and Model T did not move as they heard the stories told to Cecelia by sixteenth-century cutlers, tanners, chairmakers, ribbon weavers, barbers, and shoemakers, stories of death and persecution of Christian by Christian—Calvinist, Lutheran, and Catholic against Anabaptist— stories Cecelia wrote down and Doops reported in his own telling and now a nurse named Williams read in her turn. They dug fuel from Haarlem peat bogs, smelled Goris's bread rising in big stone ovens, heard the freezing rain of Amsterdam's winter of 1549 rapping on the shutters of Cecelia's house as the three Anabaptists awaited the day of their own execution, writing their story. The three soldiers, sitting on a South Pacific island, knew as they listened, knew in their bones, that they were hearing history that had to do with them all, and knew that Doops's telling of it made it even more their own. A history of a tenacious little band of fanatics who would not go to war, serve on juries, allow their babies to be enrolled by the state in the rite of infant baptism, who believed that true freedom could exist only when the affairs of state had no bearing ever on the affairs of church, and whose issue four hundred years removed no more believed what they believed than the three of them believed, as they listened, that Model T's wounds would stop the reign of the universal soldier. Kingston and Model T intuited but did not fully fathom the gentle warning to Cecelia that what she was doing in her zeal might itself be an act of hubris, replacing the love of God with the love of the love of God, more dangerous to what the Anabaptists were about than all those who hunted them down on horseback to do them harm. Model T and Kingston listened in quiet horror as Doops's words were read—believers sentenced by believers to be led like calves to the place of execution, their tongues cut out and thrown on the fire, their hearts to be cut out, while alive, and thrown into their faces, their bodies quartered and hung on the town gates.

Doops stacked each page as it was read.

During the four hours it took Miss Williams to read all the pages, she stopped but once. That was when Cecelia, Pieter, and Goris were in a lengthy discussion of the true meaning of the passage "Where two or three are gathered . . ." "What about four?" Goris had asked. "What about where four are gathered?" They had agreed that it could not mean one, for one person cannot gather. The Bible said where two or three are gathered. They were having trouble agreeing if it could be more than three. The nurse stopped reading, pulled a mayonnaise jar filled with black coffee from a paper sack, drank from it, and handed it to Model T. He and Kingston joined her in sipping from the jar as they passed it around but Doops politely declined each time.

"Does that mean it cannot be four?" she asked Doops the last time he passed it on, loud enough for all of them to hear. When he did not answer, she started reading again, a bit more hurriedly. As she began, Model T put his hand on her back and nudged her gently toward the inner edge of their circle. Without hesitation she scooted forward. But not enough to be completely in the circle. Her voice was not quite as stable and sure as it had been, but she did not stop again until she reached the end.

" 'No,' Cecelia said, catching him by the hand, her voice calm and warm.

" 'We will let them in together.

" 'And together we will go with them.' "

Her heavy inflection on *together* was more resignation than emphasis. She stood up, brushed the sand from her dress, and watched Doops as he straightened the pages into a manageable stack.

Doops was humming an unfamiliar refrain and when he started to sing she strained to hear the words:

> "God, it's almost Easter Sunday,
>   And I can't even spell salvation right.
> Here it is Good Friday morning,
>   But for fools like me, it's still Thursday night."

A different group of wounded soldiers had passed them while she read. As she turned to walk away, the last of them were moving down the beach. She hurried to fall in behind a soldier who was moving slowly along with the aid of one crutch. She walked as one of them. When she had established herself as part of their procession, she gestured up and down the line of pathetic figures with a sweep of her outstretched arm, pointing then back to herself, and finally to the three of them sitting together on the sand.

"Hey Doops," she called. "Do you think *we* came out of the same quiver?"

"What about the lieutenant?" Doops called back.

"That's the toughie," she said.

There was a long pause as she continued to move down the beach, looking over her shoulder. "At least for you," she yelled, turning her head and continuing with the soldiers.

Doops started to sing again, louder now, facing down the beach so that she could hear him. Kingston and Model T stood behind him, Model T humming in harmony, Kingston listening.

> "God, it's almost Easter Sunday,
>   And I can't even spell salvation right.
> Here it is Good Friday morning,
>   But for fools like me, it's still Thursday night."

13

"**W**ell, Mother, this is our little neighborhood. This is it. This is what you've heard so much about. You must be tired of hearing it by now, but now you see it. Kingston Smylie. Fordache Arceneau. Doops Momber. That's it. Ain't we something? Soldiers home from the war. Three of us."

They were seated around a table laden with food—crisp fried chicken, slices of beefsteak that had been pounded thin with the edge of a plate, fried brown in a heavy batter, and smothered with thick gravy, mashed potatoes, creamed corn, a plate of sliced tomatoes and green onions, corn bread and yeast biscuits, fried okra, three kinds of pie, a chocolate cake, milk, and ice tea. It was being served by a skinny, brown-skinned Negro woman who edged her way from one of them to the other placing big helpings of each dish on their plates without asking and without speaking at all.

The house had been built by Doops's father twenty years earlier. It was not a large house but was neat and well furnished, painted white inside and out, roofed with aged cedar shingles. Heavy crepe myrtle bushes, red blossoms already beginning a late summer shedding, overhung the tall picket fence that enclosed the yard. Dozens of purple martins, those swallowlike creatures said to have a diet of two thousand mosquitoes a day, nested in gourds hanging on crosspieces nailed to a slender pine pole in the backyard. One continuous porch completely encircled the house. Wisteria vines growing on a lattice structure shaded the west porch from the afternoon sun.

"Just three?" his mother said. "Aren't you forgetting someone? Doesn't Mother count just a little bit? Mother wants to be in your little group." She faked a shallow laugh and asked the Negro woman to bring more ice.

"Yes, ma'am," Doops said. "But we aren't exactly a group. We just called ourselves 'the neighborhood' during the war and all. You know what I mean."

"Oh, I was just teasing you, sugar. You know I'm just teasing. Mother knows you wouldn't leave her out. You boys make out your dinner." She put a spoonful of sugar in her tea, stirred it noisily, and dropped some more ice into the glass as the woman stood beside her holding a green mixing bowl.

"I don't guess it will ever seem right with your daddy gone. It was just so sudden. Not even fifty years old and dying on a tractor. His heart just playing out right in the middle of the field. It still doesn't seem right. But I never was one to question the Lord's will. He knows what's best." They continued to eat without answering what she had said. "He was quite a bit older than I am. As you know. Almost raised me, you might say. It always seemed like me and you were about the same age. Almost like you were my little brother, sort of." She spoke as if Kingston and Model T were not even there. "He created this place. Took it from nothing and made it into the best place around. Maybe it was time for him to go. He created all this. Now it's up to us to do what we can with it. It's all up to us. He's gone now, sugar. But listen to me. We've been through this every day since you've been home. Time to stop. You enjoy your company. You boys make out your dinner."

They had been out of the army three weeks. When the war ended they were in Letterman General Hospital in California. Model T had been sent there from New Caledonia for plastic surgery, which he steadfastly refused. They continued to keep him in case he changed his mind. Doops was sent for an undiagnosed nervous disorder, which he told them repeatedly he didn't have. Kingston had been shipped along with them simply because they didn't know what else to do with him. His records had been sent to the 109th Station Hospital when he went with Model T and he was never reassigned. When the war ended, they were sent immediately to Camp Fannin, Texas, to be discharged. The process was outlined when they arrived. If a soldier wanted to keep his GI insurance and if he agreed to remain in a reserve status, he was discharged the day he arrived and was free to go home. If he chose not to remain in the reserves, he was told that it would take two days to get the discharge papers in order. If he chose not to keep the insurance, it would also take two days. If he neither wanted to stay in a reserve unit nor keep the insurance in force, it would take three days. It was an effective gimmick and many soldiers were so anxious to leave they readily agreed. With the three of them, there was no question. Kingston said after all they had been through they could hold a bear in a bathtub for three days in order to get it all behind them. There was no further discussion of it.

The final ceremony was solemn but brief. High-ranking officers, with no further duties to justify their existence, were assigned to the various mustering-out programs around the country. A Protestant chaplain who was a full colonel began with a prayer. The soldiers to be discharged that day sat in a large theater and were told to bow their heads and close their eyes. Doops did neither. As an electric organ droned "America the Beautiful" softly in the background, the chaplain thanked God for America, for brave and gallant soldiers, for victory, then asked God for His continuing blessing upon our land and heritage. Then a one-star general stepped to the lectern and read the same prepared speech he would continue to read every day until the last soldier had passed through. He read with exaggerated sentiment, his voice cracking at previously marked points, stopping occasionally to wipe his eyes as he quoted the Constitution or recited random and unrelated patriotic trivia. "America and defeat cannot be made to rhyme." "Without a sign, his sword the brave man draws,/ And asks no omen but his country's cause." "And for our country 'tis a bliss to die." "One flag, one land, one heart, one hand,/ One nation, evermore!" When he finished, the men came by, each to receive the document he longed for, each to execute a snappy salute one last time. The chaplain returned to the microphone and led them in "The Star-Spangled Banner," the bashful voices of the men heard hardly at all above the electronic reverberations of the giant Baldwin organ and the chaplain's own voice. Then one last formation as they lined up outside while some unseen and faraway bugler played the doleful Taps. No one spoke as the general strode to the front of the ranks.

"Com-pan-ee! A-ten-shun!" Five hundred men, hearing that familiar command for the last time snapped their heels together, chin up, chest out, stomach drawn in, elbows bent slightly at their side, thumbs in a line with the seam of the pants, eyes staring straight ahead at nothing, minds thinking mixed and garbled thoughts of what lay in the future along with a creeping nostalgia for years of wretched soldiering. The depressing silence held for a long sixty seconds, and when the general's voice was heard again—"Com-pan-ee! Dis-missed!"—a concerted sigh was the only response.

They still did not speak and as they milled around in place, each one feeling isolated and alone in a way he had not felt since his number was called to go to war, each one seeking to find a direction, a place to walk where there would be no one else walking, the collective loneliness was overwhelming. As they began to drift away in small groups and pairs, aimless still, someone in the center of the crowd broke the spell. "Ya-hoooo!" Then a spontaneous cheer as they quickened their pace, remembering Trailway bus and eastbound-train schedules, casting about for vacant telephone booths. It was Kingston who summed it up.

"Whoever would have thought that getting out of the army would be like swallowing a goddamn quince." World War II was over.

The next day and the next, five hundred others would hear the same prayer, the same speech, go through the same ritual, until they were all gone. Five hundred men who were children when they left home and country for what would come to be called "the last of the good wars." Returning now to the confusion of national realignments, new definitions of friend and foe, being called on to consider those they had hunted down and killed for five years as new friends and those who had been their allies as the present menace. New slogans and new politics as the eternal struggle between pieces of geography continued. Back to wives and girl friends who had changed as they had changed, each never again to be certain of the fidelity of the other, starting a chain of catching-ups and getting-evens for what the other might have done in the long interim, an unconscious and irreversible sequence of events and crosscurrents that in their generation would be discussed in theological schools and newspapers and journals of social concern as the New Morality, stripping fiber and sinews from the society they had gone away to defend to a point almost beyond recognition. But they were thinking of none of that. They were simply going home. The war was over.

Doops, Model T, and Kingston had agreed to regroup in Claughton Station, then visit the homes of the other two. Doops had not been told his father had died until he got home. He felt some strange obligation to mourn, but grief for someone who had been dead for more than a year seemed inappropriate. His mother had insisted that he visit the cemetery the day after he arrived, but she did not go with him. His father had given him a watch fob, a small gold cross, when he graduated from high school and Doops carried it in his pocket all during the war. He dug a hole at the base of his father's tombstone and dropped the cross in it, carefully replacing the sod.

His mother was a beautiful woman, looking much younger than her years. She had an almost frail appearance about her but a certain radiance. Her cheeks seemed to reflect her red hair, which was cut short. She was known for her good works in the community and taught Sunday school in the Claughton Station Baptist Church.

Now as they sat at her table, she made a pretense of welcome but Kingston and Model T felt they were in a hostile atmosphere. They spoke few words as they hurried to finish the meal. When they excused themselves, saying they were going to the bus station to see if Model T's suitcase had come in, she soon indicated to Doops how she felt about them.

"How long are your little friends going to stay?"

"They aren't my *little friends*, Mother. They are Kingston and

178

Model T. They mean a lot to me. We have been through one hell of a lot together and I had hoped you would be nice to them."

"You don't talk like that in this house, Claudy Momber," she said sternly, twisting a white lace apron in her hands. "What would your father think. Now you watch your tongue." Then her voice took the same cloyingly sweet tone it had before. "Darling heart. Your mother will not be mean to your friends. You know that Mother has always wanted you to be popular, to have lots of friends. I wouldn't mistreat your friends for the world. But you know, we have lots of nice boys and girls right around here. People you have known all your life."

Doops was trying not to feel what he was feeling. He got up and walked out the kitchen door, onto the screened back porch and began commenting on the lush hanging baskets of ferns and blooming geranium.

"Do you think they will still be here for the baptizing?" she said, not responding to what he had said about the plants.

"Who's getting baptized?" he asked, not acknowledging that he knew what she meant. "They're both Catholic. I doubt if they would want to go to a Baptist service."

"Now you know very well who I'm talking about, sweet Doopsie. You know how your father always wanted you to be baptized. And I promised him when he was lying a corpse, I promised him over and over that as soon as you got home from the army I wouldn't rest day or night until you joined the Church and got baptized." She had walked out on the porch and put her arm around his shoulder, kissing him lightly on the cheek.

Doops tried to move away but she pulled him closer. "Now you know how determined this old hardheaded mamma of yours can be. And I've prayed over this thing ever since you were old enough to walk down the aisle. And my prayer will be answered. When I was getting dressed this morning, I felt a burden lift from me like somebody had rolled a bale of cotton off of me. I had just been praying about it and all at once I just felt the weight fall off of me. I knew it was the answer to my prayer. I knew then that you would be the first one to be baptized in the new baptistry. Oh, you haven't even seen it yet. You haven't even been inside the church house since you've been home, have you. When Ed

Hamlett got killed in the war, right over there close to where you were—oh, I'm thankful that you got home safe. Oh, I knew what they said about your . . . you know, your nerves and all, but you're just as sane as you ever were. I mean, just as sane as I am. There isn't a thing wrong with your mind. I'm just so thankful that God watched over you through all you had to go through. Anyway, when he got killed, he was some kind of kin to us, you know. Your father used to tell us that, you know. Well, his mother said she couldn't stand to spend one dime of his government insurance money. And there's people right here in this county riding the roads in brand-new cars from their dead sons' insurance money. But she gave every red cent of his insurance for a new baptistry, and now we can have baptismal services summer or winter and day or night, rain or shine. And it's the prettiest thing, the painted scene, an artist came here from New Orleans and spent over a week working on it. Jesus being baptized in the River Jordan. With a dove right over his head. You know, before, we could only baptize in the summer when the river warmed up. And then half the time the river would freshen and we would have to put it off. The new baptistry is heated, they can put water in there and in half an hour it's just as warm as you would want it. Brother Moss said he had a nice prize for the first one to be baptized in it. He wouldn't tell what it was but his wife told me. It's a brand new Holy Bible. A Scofield Bible, with all the maps and teaching aids and everything. And a Bible dictionary in it, too. I remember how you always loved a Bible more than anybody I ever knew, how you read it over and over, and how you stood up on the back of the church bench when you were four years old one night and said the Twenty-third Psalm by heart. Your Aunt Alice held you up there, you with your little striped coveralls and barefooted as a jaybird. People around here are still talking about that." She kissed him on the cheek again, started to speak but began crying. She turned away as if she was trying to hide her face. When he didn't move to comfort her, she turned to face him again.

"Oh, Doops, honey, wouldn't it be wonderful if your father was here to see you baptized. I'd give anything in this world, I'd give this whole place, if he could be here to see you baptized."

"You reckon Brother Jesus was baptized in one of them electric pools, Miss Mother?" It was a way he teased her when he was a young boy. She moved in again.

"Now, don't you try to make one of your jokes, Claudy Momber. Don't you have the least bit of respect for your dead father? You know how he pleaded with you to be baptized and live like other people." She spoke harshly, making no effort to conceal the anger and impatience.

He tried again to humor, to tease her. "I had a buddy who told me about getting baptized in one of those electrified bathtubs. Up in North Carolina. They had a revival and the preacher was taking the ones who had got saved into the water one at a time. Every time one of them waded down in the pool they commenced to shake and shimmy and carry on and, man, he thought the Spirit was really moving in their midst. They would jerk and cry out till he took them under and got them out of there. Come to find out the damn thing had a short in it. He had on that fancy rubber suit so as not to get his preaching clothes wet so he could climb right back to the pulpit soon as he was done and he couldn't feel it. Naw, Miss Mother, I don't believe I better do that."

She didn't think it was funny. "Is that all the respect you have for your dead father?" She had twisted the lace apron around both her hands and was having trouble getting them untangled, trying to look hurt, trying to appear incredulous. But failing.

Doops raised his voice for the first time. "Mother, I didn't bring this subject up. You did! Now, I don't want to argue with you and I don't want to hurt your feelings. But for Christ's sake, let's stick to the truth. My daddy never said one word to me about getting baptized. Never! Not one time in his lifetime or mine did he ever mention it to me. I have, yes, I have a lot of respect for my father. One hell of a lot of respect for my father. But . . . not but! And And I'm not getting baptized in no damned tub full of water spitting electrons on my ass!"

He expected her to scream, to throw herself across her bed crying and trembling and kicking her feet the way she used to do when Doops's father lost his patience at one of her unyielding whims. Instead she followed him into the yard and opened the gate as he climbed into the pickup truck. As he backed the truck through the gate opening she tapped him gently on the arm.

"You sweet ole thing. Mother will go right on praying for you. And prayer changes things. The prayer of a righteous man availeth . . ."

She was still talking as he drove out of hearing. As he sped away he knew that he would not get very far.

14

Kingston and Model T found him lying by the side of the road, the motor of the truck still running. His lips and fingernails were a cyanotic blue, the skin under his neck shriveled like an old man's. He appeared not to be breathing at all. He was lying on his back, his mouth and eyes open. Without saying a word Kingston grabbed one of his shoulders and flipped him over. His body landed limp and flaccid like Jell-O.

"God save the neighborhood," Kingston said, jerking him up by the midsection into a jackknife position, holding him in that position with his feet and head touching the ground.

"If it ain't something you join, it ain't something you bail out on," Model T said, walking round and round them, moving his head from side to side, gesturing for Kingston to tell him what to do.

"Hit him! Hit him! You remember what the nurse told us to do. God damn it, do what she told us!"

Model T began to pound him on the back with his flattened hand, pressing down hard with each stroke. A constant stream of clear fluid began to drain from Doops's mouth and nostrils. Model T continued to hammer his back, at the same time looking at his face turned sideways on the ground.

"It's stopped! It's stopped! The water's stopped!" he screamed. "Remember what the nurse told us? Remember? Drop him!"

Kingston dropped him, making no effort to be gentle. The deep gurgling sound from Doops's throat and the sloshing from his chest were faint. His body dropped, floppy and loose.

"Remember! Remember!" Model T yelled. "Do it! Do it! You remember!"

Kingston dropped over him, astraddle of him, his buttocks on Doops's buttocks. With his cupped hands he began to press down and forward on the back bottom of the rib cage, pushing down and then releasing suddenly. As he began, Model T turned Doops's head to the side, pulling his jaw forward, fishing with his thumb and forefinger for his tongue.

"Pump! Pump! You remember what she told us. Now pump!"

"Out goes the bad air," Kingston said as he mashed down against Doops's listless body. "In comes the good," he whispered as he pulled his hands away.

"Out goes the bad air. In comes the good.

"Out goes the bad air. In comes the good.

"Out goes the bad air. In comes the good." He said it over and over, pressing down hard, a little harder each time when there was no response, glancing from time to time at Model T, who stood to one side watching Doops's face.

Suddenly they heard a slight gasp, like a hiccup. Then a long, steady moan, growing louder as Kingston pushed down, softer when he let up. Doops's body heaved and he began a spasm of coughing.

"He's breathing! He's breathing!" Model T said. Kingston stopped the pumping and stood up. Doops rolled over, started to sit up, but fell back. They took him under each arm, lifted him to a sitting position and steadied him for a moment and then sat down on each side of him. Doops blinked his eyes as one awakening in the sun from a deep sleep. He looked first at one and then the other, not fully aware of what was going on around him. A confused, bewildered look, but not agitated, like one immured in some strange but not altogether unpleasant dream.

"How did you guys know what to do?" he said at last, rubbing his eyes, still squinting from the sun.

"We just knew," Kingston said. "That's all. We just knew."

"Yeah, we just knew," Model T said, then adding, "the nurse told us. After she read us that story you wrote that time."

"How'd she know what to tell you?" Doops asked.

"Don't know," Kingston said. "After she read it to us she asked us a lot of questions about you. Said this was apt to happen sometimes. Told us what to do in case it did. We told her everything we knew about you—you know, how you act sometimes. We told her everything she asked us. Didn't we, Coonieboy?"

"Yeah. But we didn't mean any harm. I mean, we thought we were supposed to tell her. She said she wouldn't tell anybody. Not that doctor. Not anybody. We thought we were supposed to. You're not mad at us or anything, are you? We did it for you." Model T had inched his way a little closer to Doops and was leaning sideways in front of him, looking him in the face.

"I just feel silly," Doops said. He did not say it but he also felt impaled, imprecated by some far-off and long-ago something he did not understand and did not want to understand. "I just feel silly," he said again. No one answered and they sat in a lonesome quiet.

Across the road was a row of unpainted shotgun houses, the "quarters," residences of Negroes who worked for the Geringer Lumber Company. The houses, made of faded oak-boards, the twelve-inch boards running from the roof almost to the ground, the cracks battened with three-inch strips, all looked exactly the same, distinguishable only by which one had a washing machine on the small front porch, a porcelain nightjar with petunias growing out of it, a tire swing hanging in the yard, or an artificial tree made from blue milk of magnesia bottles. The same six-inch stovepipe stuck through the back roof of each one. The same black smoke rose from each one, pine knots burning in the kitchen stove, a signal that the company whistle would soon blow and the menfolk would leave cant hooks, circle saws, and green chains behind until the whistle blew again at five o'clock the next morning.

A dozen or more Negro children of varying ages had gathered along the barbed-wire fence that separated the houses from the gully-washed dirt road. They had started gathering as soon as the truck stopped and had stood peering at all the proceedings, saying nothing, not even to one another. They all knew Doops but would not speak until he spoke first, even though they had not seen him for two years. "Tommy Lee. Bennie Earl. Jimmy Ray." As he called their names they crawled through the fence or rolled under the bottom strand and came toward him. Doops stood up and as each one arrived they slapped each other on the back, jostled one another around, and Doops gave them birthday spankings, one lick for each year. He knew how old each one of them was. He asked about their brothers and sisters by name, about school, and a lot of little things he remembered about them.

"What ch'all doin'?" one of the older boys asked.

"Nothing," Doops said. "Just messing around."

"What was they doing to you?" another one asked.

"You sick or something?"

"Nope, not sick. We're just messing around."

"You get hurt in the war, Mr. Doops?" the first one asked. "Papa said you got messed up in the war. You get bad hurt?"

Doops began to do a buck-and-wing dance and make funny faces at them. "Naw, man. I ain't bad hurt. I'm just crazy. I always been crazy. Everybody in the quarters knows that. I'm just a nut. A loony." They giggled and teased him back, dancing the same way he did.

"You ain't crazy, Mr. Doops. Don't nobody in the quarters believe you crazy. You the mos' kindest white feller we knows. Everybody in the quarters tell you that."

"Thank you, Bennie Earl. Maybe that's what makes me crazy. Hey. This here is Model T and this here is Kingston," he said to them, tapping each on the shoulder as he introduced them. The children nodded to each of them but didn't say anything, eyeing them timidly and suspiciously.

"*He* get bad hurt in the war?" the youngest one said, pointing to Model T. Then all of them moved closer to him, looking curiously at the concave scar on the side of his head where his ear had been, and at the depression in his face where his eye, upper cheekbone, and brow used to be. They circled him, as if they were seeing some strange animal for the first time. Kingston stood glowering at Doops, wanting him to make them go away. But Model T turned to face them, bending over closer to them, close enough for them to see the network of minute blood vessels that crisscrossed the thin, transparent layer of deep-pink skin covering

186

the bone. It irritated him when people, even his own kin, refused to acknowledge what they saw, would dismiss it with one swift, all-encompassing glance, would look past him when they talked to him as if he were a shadow. There was something refreshing to him about the children's inquisitive concern.

"Yeah. I got bad hurt in the war," he said, patting the one who had asked the question on the head. "But I'm okay now. I'm alive. That's more than a lot of people can say."

"Did you bleed bad?" another of the children asked. Model T answered each question as it was asked.

"You sweat there?" one of them asked, touching the red scar tissue with one finger, quickly jerking it back.

"Nope. Don't sweat there. No sweat glands."

"Bullet git them too?" one of them asked.

"Look like it's made out of crepe paper," another one said.

"My daddy bled bad," the same little boy said.

"Was he in the war?" Model T asked him.

"No, sir. He wasn't in no war. He fainted on the carriage at the sawmill and it pulled him across the headsaw. Cut his head clean off. Mamma saw it. Mr. Doops here saw it too. She had just took him his dinner and was standing there and she saw his head roll off down the sawdust pile. Eyes still open too, she said. Like he was lying there looking at her. Mamma said he had the high blood and didn't have no business working that close to the saw. But he did, though. I wudden even born then, though. Was I, Mr. Doops? Mr. Doops went for the doctor the night I was born but he wouldn't come. He had to go get Aunt Ella Mae to come stork me."

The children began to drift back across the fence as their curiosity about Model T was satisfied. And after Doops had verified the story of Bennie Earl's father.

"Those kids are almost pretty enough to be free," Doops said when the last one was gone.

"What?" Kingston asked.

"Never mind," Doops said.

"Don't you think we ought to take you to the doctor?" Kingston asked "You could have died right here, you know."

"No. No, I don't think you ought to take me to the doctor.

Forget it. I'm not sick. And if he wasn't good enough to come deliver that little black baby, him coming two months early because his mamma had seen his daddy's head roll down a goddamn sawdust pile and stop at her feet . . . well, if he couldn't deliver him he sure as hell can't deliver me."

"What's with you and all them folks in the quarters?" Kingston asked. "You going to get yourself in trouble."

"Really?" Doops said, shrugging his shoulders, the corners of his mouth turning down. "We got to go to the sewage plant and get a load of sludge. They give it away this time of year. We always get it for the tomato field."

"You don't even want to talk about it? Man, you had the symptoms bad. Worse than we ever saw. Don't you know you could be fucking dead right now? What the hell happened to you anyhow?"

"Same thing, I reckon. I don't know what happened. Me and Mamma. She wants me to get baptized in their electric River Jordan. That's always trouble. I don't know what happened." He started to hum, then began to sing. "I get that ooold feeling." He laughed and shrugged again.

"What's wrong with getting baptized?" Kingston said. "Hell, me and Model T, we been baptized since we were born. It don't hurt . . . doesn't hurt much. Does it, T?" Model T didn't answer. "Does it, T?" he asked again. He still did not answer.

"Nothing wrong with it," Doops said. "Nothing *wrong* with it. But who would do it?"

"Who would do it? What the hell kind of a question is that? You a Baptist ain't you? Aren't you? Well, some Baptist would do it. Just like some Catholic did it to me and Model T. Jesus! What's the big deal?"

"And where would you find him?" Doops said.

"Find who?" Kingston asked, more confused than vexed.

"A Baptist. Where would you find one?"

Kingston had picked up a handful of gravel and was throwing the rocks against one of the truck tires, seeing if he could catch them as they bounced back toward him. "Jesus!" he whispered. "I thought this was Mississippi. Find one? The woods is full of them. Go out on the street and trip a hundred people and ninety-nine of them are Baptists."

"Really?" Doops said sarcastically. "Let's go get the sludge."

188

"Look," Kingston said. "Why don't you just let the bastard baptize you? What difference does it make? My mamma said the priest who did it to me was a first-class shithook. What difference does it make?"

"None to you," Doops said, starting to throw rocks at the tires the way Kingston was doing. "But I ain't you."

"But we're us," Kingston said.

"Yeah, we're us. But even identical twins are born one at a time. I ain't you."

They were scooping the sludge out of long shallow pits with flat shovels. All the sewage from Claughton Station was pumped into large tanks where it was churned and chopped with huge steel rotary blades. From there it was channeled into settling vats where it went through a heat process. Then various chemicals were added and it was emptied into the narrow pits to dry and further decay. It was used by the farmers as a high-nitrogen fertilizer.

The September sun was bearing down on them and they had stripped to the waist. Only material that would rot was supposed to be in the sewage but a few items had successfully avoided the settling process. Occasionally they would uncover a clump of human hair, and cigarette filters would not decompose. They laughed and teased one another about what Kingston called "sapphire rings," small rubber bands used in the manufacture of cheap condoms.

"You know what you're standing in?" Kingston asked Model T as he heaved with a bigger shovelful than he could handle. "You're standing in a big pile of shit." He laughed and pretended to empty his shovel over Model T's head.

"You ought to be right at home, then," Model T said. " 'Cause you're full of it."

"It sure will make tomatoes grow," Doops said, not laughing with them.

"What you and your mamma fight about religion for?" Kingston said, leaning on his shovel handle.

"That's what religion is," Doops replied. "Somebody told me a man's religion is what he'll get mad enough to fight about."

"I thought religion was about God," Kingston said.

"God is about God," Doops said. "Religion is about us." All of them had stopped working and were sitting on the tailgate of the pickup.

"Thick cream, Model T. Did you hear what ole Doops said? He said, 'God is about God.' Wonder what that's supposed to mean." When no one answered he said, "The nun told us God is love. But I reckon I never understood that either."

Model T had stood up and was facing them, the sun striking the two indentations in his head, outlining the tiny veins like a county road-map held against a lantern. "I t'ink God is sludge, me," he said, saying it in his old Cajun manner, something he did only when he intended to be utterly frivolous or wholly serious.

"Now hold it, coonass boy," Kingston said. "Not even I can be that irreverent. That sounds like something I might say. But I didn't. You're saying God is shit. Jesus Lord, Doops. Make him take it back. He's going to get hit by a bolt of lightning. God ain't going to put up with being called a pile of shit."

"God is sludge," Model T said it again, as if he wanted to hear the sound of it, as if he hadn't been listening to himself when he said it the first time. And as if he was prepared to defend it now that he had listened to the way it came out.

Kingston stood up and started to say something but Doops jerked him back down. "It's his sermon. Let him preach it. Come on, Amos. Prophesy."

Model T was embarrassed. He ducked his head and shifted uneasily from one foot to the other, turning half to the side. "Aw, I was just messing around."

"No, you weren't," Doops snapped. "Come on, champ. Tell us a sermon. You've jumped a rabbit. Now let's see you run him in a log."

"Well, I was just thinking," he began.

"Thinking what?" Doops prompted. "You said God is sludge. Tell us what that means."

"Well, I just got to thinking about what this stuff does—you know. I mean you said it makes things grow like nothing else in the world. But the truth is it's really what nobody else wants. I mean it's what everybody throws away, wants to get rid of, think they don't need—you know. And . . . aw, this sounds silly." He became awkward again, pushing the ground about with the toe of his shoe.

"No it isn't. Now go on," Doops said.

"Well, I was just thinking about when the baby Jesus was born in Bethlehem. You know, they wouldn't have him. Wouldn't even let him be born except in a barn. And then when they killed him—you know—how they buried him under these big ole rocks. Just threw him away, you might say." Kingston sat in rapt attention now, approving with his eyes what he was hearing. "But there was some kind of power there. Something just made him grow up out of there. And then that gives us . . . what do you call it? . . . salvation? And—you know—makes us grow and even when we're dead we grow again. I was just thinking about all that . . . and that's why I just said what I said, that God is sludge. You know, makes life and all."

Doops and Kingston sat on the tailgate looking at him when he finished. Neither of them said a word. Model T, like a little boy who had just done his assigned recitation in school, came back and sat down too.

"I ought to cut you with my knife," Kingston said finally.

Doops got up and started shoveling the sludge with renewed energy, not saying anything at all. Kingston and Model T stood and watched him, knowing that they weren't supposed to help him now.

"Where'd you get all that stuff the nurse read out loud to us at the hospital?" Kingston asked as they drove back to the farm.

"God is sludge," Doops said, continuing to drive. Kingston didn't reply.

They began to talk about what they were going to do. "You know, we can't just go around being war veterans wearing these damned little ruptured ducks the rest of our lives," Doops said, referring to the little gold-colored eagles the army gave them to wear in their lapels. They discussed some of the options. There was a form of veterans' unemployment compensation. They called it the 52/20 Club. Anyone who had been in the service could draw twenty dollars a week for one year. If the Employment

Security Office found you a job you had to take it, but you were allowed to list the jobs for which you were qualified. Model T said that would be easy for him. He could say that all he knew how to do was trap nutria and pick moss. "Bet they don't get many calls for moss pickers," he laughed. But in the end they agreed that none of them wanted to be a member of the 52/20 Club.

They talked about college. The GI Bill of Rights would pay all tuition and fees plus a living allowance. Kingston and Doops wanted to go back to college but both said they would not accept government money for it. "If they won't ever bother me again, I won't ever bother them again," one of them said. They all agreed.

Doops's quandary was that his mother expected him to live at home and run the farm. "I guess I'll have to do it," he said. "At least for now. We don't have any money, she says. Daddy left this place but nothing else. But I'm going to school somehow. It's less than forty miles to Baton Rouge. I can drive back and forth in the winter and still do what I have to here. I don't care that much about going to school just to tell you the truth, but they don't hire many people to write fresh in off the street."

"What you going to do about the baptizing?" Kingston asked, reaching across Model T, who sat in the middle, to brush Doops's cowlick.

"God is sludge," Doops said.

They were passing the Geringer Lumber Company again, the only industry in Claughton Station. Beyond the quarters, separated from the houses by a little distance, a woven wire fence, and a tall stand of privet hedge, was a medium-sized mobile home. The yard was well kept and young slash pines lined the winding driveway. All of it looked new. The Negroes who lived in the quarters called it "Mr. Geringer's other office." All of them knew, but did not discuss, why it was there. As they drove by, Doops thought he saw his mother's car, a black 1940 Ford sedan, parked behind the butane tank that was on a scaffold. He was not sure that it was hers. There were many 1940 black Fords. He said nothing about it.

That night when she came home to serve them supper, she had a new permanent wave. As they sat around the table, eating for

192

supper what was left from the bountiful dinner, she told Doops that she was taking two courses at Fort Warner College in nearby Sterlington and that maybe he would like to go to school there too. When he told her he thought he was going to LSU, she said maybe that would be better.

"You studying typing, bookkeeping, and all that?" Doops asked her.

"Oh no. I don't want to learn all that stuff. I'm taking one course in philosophy and one in sociology. I just want to broaden myself. And it'll help me in my Sunday school work too. You know, I always was sorry I didn't get to finish my education. I was barely through high school when your father and I got married. And I've just been a little country girl ever since. Papa wanted me to go to college, had money all saved up. Wanted me to go to Blue Mountain. You're going to be proud of this ole mamma of yours."

"I think we're going down to Mermentau tomorrow," Doops said. "Model T's going to show us how to catch nutria."

"I wish you'd call him something besides Model T," she said.

15

"**W**here the hell we going?" Kingston said.

Model T was moving frantically about in the dim light of a coal-oil lantern. They were on the bottom deck of a two-story houseboat. The house was secured to two large cypress trees with one-inch steel cables, the cables looped so they could slide up and down the tree trunks as the water of the Mermentau River rose and subsided, something it did often without warning.

"We're going where nobody has ever been but me," Model T said, rushing about in the shadows, throwing things into a small, flat-bottomed boat tied onto the deck railing.

"Nobody?" Kingston said. "How do you know?"

"I just know. You'll see. I'll show you."

Doops had stretched out on the deck and had gone back to sleep. Kingston kicked him hard on the bottom of his feet. "Hey Doops! You going with us where nobody else ever been?"

"Knock it off!" Doops grumbled. "Wake me up when we get there."

Model T's mother yelled something in French from the top deck, leaning over the rail.

"What'd she say?" Kingston asked.

"She asked if we wanted some coffee. Or some red soda pop. *Ya oui*," he yelled back. "*Café*. And she called me *cayenne*," he giggled.

She disappeared for a minute and came back with two quart jars full of jet-black coffee. She placed it in a bucket with a small rope tied to it and lowered it to him. "That's good stuff," Model T said. "Community Brand. That's what it says on the label. Community Brand Coffee and Chicory. It's done in Baton Rouge. Get it?" he giggled, obviously pleased with himself.

"Get what?" Kingston said.

"Community Brand. Baton Rouge. Don't you get it?"

Kingston started to say he got it and it was corny, but instead said, "Oh yeah. Yeah, that's pretty good, T." He had never seen Model T so excited. "Get your ass up, Doops. We're going where nobody has ever been but T," he said, kicking Doops on the feet again. "You better slow down, coonie pal," he said to Model T. "You're going to blow a gasket."

"Damn, hell, no, *mon ami*. We got to get there before the sun goes down. Nobody ever been there but me." He picked up a paper sack containing a thick piece of unsliced bologna and some biscuits and jumped into the flat-bottomed boat. Above their heads, roosting on a limb, an assortment of bantam chickens stirred and complained at the noise, already awakened by the first light of day.

"I didn't know chickens would roost above water," Kingston said.

"Them will," Model T said. "That way they feed the catfish too. There goes one now!" he screamed, pointing to a big channel cat scudding lazily through the murky water, his long whiskers moving with the grappling of his broad jaws for the chicken droppings.

"Throw me them quilts," he said, moving to the back of the boat. "And that lantern. We might need it if we stay in the marsh tonight." He pushed the globe of the lantern to one side and blew it out. "Don't guess Doops is going," he said, reaching for the starter cord of the Johnson outboard motor. The engine fired after a few pulls and churned steadily, the chickens scattering to the bank from their perch above them. Kingston jumped into the boat and sat down. Doops leaped to his feet and got in beside Kingston. Model T revved the motor to top speed, spun the boat around, and headed to the middle of the river, moving south.

"How far is it to DeRidder?" Kingston yelled above the noise of the engine. "We going to see some Japs?"

"Long way," Model T yelled back. "Wrong way too." He was

moving the boat as fast as it would go, controlling its every motion, the early morning mist stinging his face. For the first time he noted that the scar tissue on his face had no feeling. But it didn't bother him. This was his place. He was at home, at one with everything about him, taking his friends to a spot where no other human being had ever been in all of eternity. He tried to estimate how many muskrats he might have brought home in this same boat. And nutria. Even alligators. From the time he was ten years old he had gone to school in it. To mass in Abbeville on Easter Sunday when he was fourteen. To Gueydan, Erath, Delcambre, Jefferson Island, and New Iberia, spending as long as two weeks at a time with his daddy trapping and fishing. He had been the length of every bayou around Lascassine, Queue de Tortue, des Cannes, Plaquemine. And once they had gone almost to Alexandria on the Calcasieu River. His daddy had been drunk and had told Fordache, his youngest son, that they weren't going home until the four bottles of whiskey in the boat were gone. He had been thirteen and had consumed almost as much of the whiskey as his father, not because he wanted it but to keep his father from having more. When it was gone, they took turns at the motor day and night until they got home.

On his sixteenth birthday his father told him they were going to Grand Chenier to spend the night. His mother had followed the boat down the river as far as she could, crying and screaming at his father not to take the boy with him. It took them most of the morning to get there, down the river to Lake Arthur, across the widest part of Grand Lake, across Upper Mud Lake, and on down the Mermentau to Grand Chenier. His father tied the boat to a wharf leading to a long, barnlike building with a boxcar-lettered sign on the side of it facing the river. MERRY WIDOW LOUNGE. His father gave him twenty silver dollars, told him to have a good time and that he would see him at the boat at noon the next day. But he had not had a good time. When he realized what the place was, saw the women wearing long stockings that looked to him like crawfish nets, low-cut blouses, and skimpy tight pants, bustling about from table to table, giggling and pairing off to side rooms with various men and not coming back, he slipped out a side door, got back in the boat, and didn't stop until he reached the very end of Hog Bayou, halfway to Pecan Island.

196

He intended to sleep there in the boat but decided to wander around in the marsh looking for mayhaws, tart little berries his mother used to make jelly and on which he had survived many a day in the swamps. Less than twenty feet from where Hog Bayou ended abruptly without coming to a point was the beginning of a narrow slough, going back in the direction of Lower Mud Lake. He had an overwhelming urge to pull the boat across the strip of marshland and see where the slough led. He loosened the brackets that held the motor in place and heaved it onto the bank. The pirogue was still too heavy for him to carry but by pulling and rolling it over and over sideways he managed to complete the portage. With a paddle he began to move the boat along. The beginning of the slough was exactly the width of the ending of the bayou, like some giant alluvial hand had broken it in two and turned the end piece around. Instead of growing wider as he moved along, it continued to narrow to a point, so that finally the boat would not move, lodged against each bank. Determined now to find the end of it, he left the boat and started walking, jumping from one bank to the other, back and forth.

What he had found was what he was taking them to see.

The boat lunged and churned, sometimes jumping completely out of the water as larger craft they met sent big waves in all directions. Occasionally, Model T would point out familiar landmarks, places where they had caught an unusually big fish, where their trotlines had been, muskrat burrows, or where they had stalked and shot an alligator. He screamed the words above the roaring of the motor and they seldom tried to answer. He stopped to let them see spoonbills feed in the shallow waters, swinging their big beaks back and forth like prospectors sifting for gold, the slim and graceful blue herons patiently searching for frogs or small fish the spoonbills had stirred up but missed. And to watch the ridiculous brown pelicans plunging headlong into the water, almost always coming up with a fish. Commenting on it all, whether in flight or perched on buoys or utility poles, "Kak-kak-kak. Kee-ow, kee-ow," the populous herring gulls.

"That's the pogy plant," Model T yelled as three tall chimneys billowing white smoke came into view through the breaking fog.

"The what?" Kingston called back. Model T cut the engine and pushed the stick down, lifting the motor out of the water, letting

197

the boat coast to a spinning stop. "The pogy plant. They go out with great big nets and catch millions of pogies. They make fertilizer out of them."

"Smylie doesn't know what a pogy is," Doops said. "And just to tell you the truth, I don't either."

"Pogy? That's a little fish. Looks something like a sardine, only you can't eat them. Other fish do, though. Menhaden—that's the real name. Some places they call them mossbunkers. But around here they're just plain pogies." They could tell by his expression that he didn't like the idea. "Papa worked there for a while. Not long, though. Couple of weeks. Said he couldn't work by no whistle. Said they're going to starve all the big fish in the gulf, too, taking all their food out. So he quit."

"God ain't pogy, I reckon you'd say," Doops said, remembering their conversation at the sludge pits.

"God for damn sure ain't pogy," Model T said, laughing and pulling the cord to start the motor again.

They stopped twice at shore-side restaurants for sandwiches. Each time, Model T insisted that he pay. "This is my trip. Going to take you where nobody ever been but me."

The sun was going down when they reached the end of Hog Bayou. Model T left the engine running full-throttle until they were almost to the end, then cut it and let the force push the boat almost out of the water.

"Is this it?" Doops asked. "This where nobody else ever been? God, I can believe it." The last hour had been through heavy swamp. It reminded him a little of the jungles of Guadalcanal but felt even more faraway and isolated. They had not seen a house or another boat in more than two hours. Model T had told them that where they were going would be close to the gulf and they listened for sounds of ships or any sound at all, but heard nothing.

"No, this ain't it. Not yet."

"This *isn't* it," Kingston corrected. He had started them on a campaign of improving their grammar. "We have to get back to decent society," he had said.

"Then where in hell is it?" Doops asked, ignoring Kingston.

Model T explained that they had to carry the boat over to a

small slough. And then ride some more. He lifted the motor and told them to bring the boat. They stumbled and complained as they followed him. When they reached the slough and were settled back in the boat, Model T reached for the starter cord but then stopped short. Somehow it didn't seem appropriate. He pulled the motor out of the water and began to paddle. No one spoke as he eased down the slough, stopping the paddling when the current began to thrust them forward, gaining momentum until the banks closed in on each side, the sudden stop throwing them forward.

"Is this it?" Doops asked again.

"No. Not yet. This ain't . . . this isn't it. Come on." Model T jumped out of the boat, took the sack with the coffee, bologna, and biscuit, and told them to get the quilts. They walked single file down the edge of what had become a tiny, but swiftly flowing stream. They began to hear a muffled roaring ahead of them, and Model T quickened his pace. "Just about there now," he said, almost running. The sound grew louder and they recognized it as water falling. Model T told them to close their eyes and walk close behind him and not to look up until he told them.

"Now!" he yelled over the noise of the water, stopping suddenly, the two of them bumping into him. "There it is! *Sacré misère!* Nobody ever been here but me. Kingston went to New Orleans when he was sixteen. I came here. By myself. There it is."

They saw it then. A perfect circle, about fifty feet in diameter, sloping affably into the earth, forming a pool. The water level was forty feet or so below the surface of the ground where they stood. The slough flowed to the edge of the circle and fell free. As the falling water hit the pool surface, it did not disturb it, did not splash, just seemed to fuse into and join it, becoming one with it. Floating gently around, slowly turning this way and that, were hundreds of water lilies. They were not the blue hyacinths generally found in swamp ponds and lakes. They were lilies. The colors varied—goldmist, celeste blue, mikado red. The gemlike green leaves formed a cozy nest for each blossom. Huge cypress trees stood at regular intervals around the circumference of the pool, their branches reaching and touching as a peak in the center, looking like an enormous summer parasol, boldly proclaiming mercy and defense. In the sharpest contrast, delicate ferns lined the sloping inside banks from the water's edge to the top, the fronds waving unassertively in the downward draft. Directly across from where the water fell into the pool, presiding over it all, stood a human-sized cypress knee. Except for the oxblood bark, it looked like a carved wooden statue. There was no mistaking what it was. Standing straight and majestic. Sure and utter and complete. Untouched. A perfect Madonna.

Kingston fell instinctively to his knees the moment his eyes touched it, his hand moving by some ingrained, if not congenital, force to his forehead and breast, and then to cross each side of his heart. Model T was beside him. Doops took his cap from his head and stood behind them, his head bowed.

"Hail Mary, full of grace, the Lord is with you," Kingston began.

"Salut Marie, pleine de grâce . . ."

Doops started to say the words along with them, moved his lips, then stopped, feeling that it would be somehow inappropriate.

Model T and Kingston stood up laughing, slapping each other on the back and dancing about the area as if in celebration.

"How do you know nobody has ever been here before?" Doops asked, trying to act as excited as they were.

"You never been a Catholic. That's for sure," Kingston said. "Huh, Model T?"

"I'll show you," Model T said, motioning for Doops to follow him around the pool to where the Madonna stood. As they walked around the edge of the pool, the centuries of humus soft under their feet, he explained. "We're in the middle of coonass Catholic country. I mean, it's a big thing with us, religion. There are businesses in every little town that do nothing but make statues out of cement. People put them in their yards, alongside the roads, in churches, schools, even offices have them. Now I want you to take a good look." They were standing beside it. It stood taller than Model T, its perfection and beauty defying complete comprehension. "Just look at it," he kept saying, pointing to various features—hands, feet, eyes, flowing hair, the slightly tilted head. "Now, if somebody else had been here, anybody, one of two things would have happened. Either they would have cut it down with a crosscut saw and hauled it out of this swamp by sundown, or else they would have slapped down a concrete road where that bayou is and they'd be charging folks a dollar a head just to come in here and see it. Man, believe me, this place would be a shrine by now, and folks would be pouring in here from everywhere. I mean, just look at it!" He pointed all around him, to the trees, the lilies, the waterfall.

"Yeah, and more than that," Kingston said. "The first time some coonass got cured of a hangnail they'd be hauling folks in here in wheelchairs and stretchers from here to Boston. *The Lourdes of Louisiana!*"

"I guess so," Doops said. "But what if one of *my* people had found it? We don't pray to statues."

"They would have grabbed my dollar," Model T said. The first time he had been there he had taken one of the silver dollars his father had given him, drilled a hole in it with the leather punch in his knife, and hung it around the Madonna's neck with a piece of fishing line. He reached up and lifted the necklace over her head, cut the string off, and threw the dollar into the middle of the pool. "At the least they would have grabbed my dollar."

They stood watching the water, curious that the dollar had not made a sound when it hit, and that the ring of tiny ripples which would ordinarily move out from the spot did not appear.

"How deep you reckon that thing is?" Kingston asked.

"More than a hundred feet. I know that much," Model T said. "Because one time when I was in here I tied a rock on a line and let it down. The line was a hundred feet long and the rock was still sinking. It's more than a hundred feet deep. I know that."

"How many times you been down here?" Doops asked.

"Lots of times."

"What for?" Kingston said. "I mean, it's beautiful, but man, it's a long way in here."

"Lot of things I guess," Model T said. "When things got tough. Papa would get drunk. Or him and Mamma would have a fight. The day before I went to the army. When my dog got run over. Lots of things, I guess."

"You said if anybody else had been here they would have cut it down," Doops said. "You didn't cut it down. You said they would have laid a claim and made a tourist trap out of it. You didn't."

Model T dropped his head and started walking back to the

other side. They followed along behind him, stepping only where he stepped. When they got back to where the water fell into the pool, Model T turned and surveyed it all again. It was almost dark now and they still heard no sound at all except the falling water. No human sounds and no swamp sounds, a settling balm.

Model T began to spread the quilts out on the ground near the edge of the pool. He took the bologna and began to cut heavy chunks off it, putting it between the biscuits.

"It's Community Brand," he said, holding a jar of the coffee in his hand. "But it's got chicory in it."

"Chicory?" Doops said.

"Yeah," Model T said. "That's a chicory question you asked, *mon ami.*" He took a long pull from the jar, then handed it to Doops, who tasted it and frowned.

"Bitter, huh?" Model T said. He threw his hands above his head and waved them impatiently. "I brought you guys!"

"Okay, *mon ami,*" Doops said. "I get it. You brought us. I got you. You brought us."

Kingston had lighted the lantern and hung it on a limb above their heads. As they ate the bologna and sipped the coffee from the jar, Model T told them about the way he had found the place, about his sixteenth birthday and the Merry Widow Lounge. Trying to tease him. Kingston asked why he had not stayed at the lounge. "Don't you get horny like the rest of us mortals?" he asked.

"Yeah, I get horny," he answered. "But I get scared too. And chicken, I reckon you might say. Maybe I was scared I'd pick the same woman my daddy had already picked." He took a big bite from one of the biscuits, chewed it for a long time before washing it down with the coffee, then continued. "Or maybe I already knew you can't pay somebody to love you."

"You ever going to get married?" Kingston said, wanting to change the subject. As soon as he asked the question he was sorry, knew he shouldn't have asked it. Model T dropped his head and smiled wryly. With both his hands he touched the deep scars where his eye and ear had been, indicating with his forefingers the depth they sunk into his head, tracing the outline of them and scratching the flesh stretched across them, noticing again that they were devoid of any feeling.

"Look at me," he said, smiling again.

"Hey Doops, you ever going to get married?" Kingston asked, turning from Model T. Doops was lying on his back with his eyes closed, munching one of the biscuits.

"Married? Hell, I can't even get baptized."

"Sure you can," he said, relieved that they were talking about something else. "Nothing to it. You know, maybe we're lucky, me and Model T. Catholics, I mean. That's one thing no Catholic has ever had a fight with his mamma about."

"Guess not," Doops said. "You know, I was just thinking how it would be to get baptized in that pool down there. Wouldn't that be pretty?"

"I didn't know it was supposed to be pretty," Kingston said. "But the way y'all do it, it would take one hell of a tall preacher."

"Yeah," Model T laughed, pleased that Kingston was comfortable again. "He'd have to be over a hundred feet tall."

"You ever think about being a preacher?" Kingston asked. "You talk about religion a lot. 'Course, you talk about everything a lot."

"I *am* a preacher," Doops said. "Everybody is a preacher."

"I mean a real preacher. You know. A Baptist preacher."

"You mean like Cecelia? That what you talking about?" He sat up as he spoke, his voice agitated.

"Who the hell is. . . ? Oh yeah. I didn't know she was a preacher, though. I'm talking about—you know—Baptists like we have in these days."

"Guess I don't know any Baptists," he said quickly. When neither of them answered he added. "Less it's Fordache there."

"I ought to cut you with my knife," Kingston laughed. "Model T ain't no . . . isn't a Baptist. He's a coonass Catholic. And I'm a Redbone Catholic. And you're some kind of a halfass deepwater Baptist—"

"Baptists don't kill," he interrupted under his breath, though both of them heard what he said.

He stood up and began to stroll around in the shadows of the coal-oil lantern. He had never told them the story of Reuben. That day on the beach, after they found him in the hospital, he had said that he killed a man. That was all he said. They had asked no questions about it and he had not told them more. Now he told it all.

"His name was Reuben," he began. "That may seem like a funny name for a Japanese, but his name was Reuben. I found him sitting in a pit, in a pool of . . ." He had spoken easily at first, but now his voice cracked and he turned away for a moment. When he turned back, his voice still breaking, he said, "But . . . it . . . wasn't like this pool." He came over and sat down again on the quilt, pulled his knees up under his chin and laced his hands over them, facing closest to Model T's good ear.

He talked for an hour without stopping, describing each day in the jungle in meticulous detail. He described Reuben as he had found him, how he looked, smelled, every symptom of his illness. He talked of how mad he got at him when he wouldn't eat or drink or talk to him, and the melodrama he had performed with the GI condom. He told them of the pitched battle in the middle of the night, how they were caught in the cross fire and how he had crawled into the pit with him. He described the bamboo shelter he had made to protect the man from the sun and rain, and the way Reuben had told Doops things about himself, that he was a priest, that he was not a soldier, and all the other things. He talked of how they had shared the tea and food, of the Christmas service, and of how he had imagined he heard the voices of Model T and Kingston coming out of the jungle. Finally, he told them of his own sickness, and how Reuben had hypnotized him and got complete control over his will, down to the final recollection of the man directing him to get the M-1 rifle, and the forming of the Veronica mask over Reuben's face with the canvas. He did not report the firing of the shot, for he had not heard it, did not remember it at all. When he finished, he repeated what he had said when he began. "His name was Reuben. And he was sitting in a pool. Reuben," he said again, softer. "Genesis 37:22. Great God!"

Neither Kingston nor Model T had moved during the time he talked. And when he stopped, they continued to sit as still as the cypress Madonna across the way. The pouring of the water over the ledge was the only sound. But they did not even hear that, absorbed in a collective meditation. The kerosene lantern had burned itself out, and the light of a descending moon in its third quarter cast distinctive beams through the marsh.

After about five minutes Doops spoke again. "Do you forgive me?"

"Forgive you for what?" Kingston said raucously, trying to sound nonchalant and unrestrained, not impressed by what he had heard, his voice piercing through the hushed swamp.

"Do you forgive me?" Doops said again, the same as before, not fooled by Kingston's bluff.

"Who you think we are? God?" he answered impatiently. "First place, you haven't done anything wrong. War is war. Next place, now I'm not making light of what you told us, you understand. I know it kind of got to you. Would have me too, I reckon. But the Man upstairs forgives. That's not in my M.O. That's His department."

"But we have to start with each other first," Doops said, a sound of entreaty, a sound of testimony.

Doops continued to sit with his hands holding his knees, his chin resting on them, his eyes averted. A warm, ghostly breeze was moving in from the coast, ruffling the cypress branches lightly. A random cloud, retiring inland, moved beneath the moon, dimming the light in the marsh like a rheostat.

Model T spoke softly but commandingly out of the darkness. "We forgive you."

16

On the third Friday of each month they got together. For seven years they did not miss one of their meetings. At first they met at Baton Rouge, where Doops was attending LSU, at one or the other's home, or at Mississippi State, where Kingston was enrolled. Later they gathered wherever the host said.

Their favorite place was with Model T in Mermentau.

"The home team makes the rules," Kingston said. That meant the one they were visiting planned the entertainment. Model T took them fishing, to run the traps along the rivers and bayous, to French honky-tonks with names like The Step-Inn Club, Kinder Garden, or Big Mamou Fe Do-Do Hall. They drank beer and listened to Cajun bands, the accordions, fiddles, and guitars played by local folk with names like Cleveland Crochet, LeRoy Broussard, Iry LeJune, J. D. Fusilier, and Linus Touchet. Doops was fascinated by the way the singers could go back and forth from French to English in the same song, even in the titles. "La Valse de Poor Boy." "Le Petit Two-Step de Chagrin." "La Valse de Love Lane." He wrote an article about them for the campus literary magazine, which he edited. He titled it "Smile When You Call Them Coonasses." "Only they can take two languages, mix them up, and come out with a better one," he wrote.

Model T especially liked a snappy tune called "Sha Ba Ba." He knew all the words and would sing along with the band, keeping perfect time as he beat on the table with two spoons, striking beer bottles, cups, and plates for a snare-drum effect. Sometimes he arranged dates for all of them, sometimes they would dance with girls they met at the beer joints, and sometimes his sisters and cousins would go along. He also had an uncanny instinct for knowing when a fight was about to start. When he sensed one on the way, he would calmly say, "Let's go to Gueydan. That's where the action is tonight." Kingston always objected, saying he wanted to see what a good Cajun brawl was like. Model T already knew and moved them on. Sometimes they stayed until daylight. Other times they would get beer to go and camp in the woods, sleep on the houseboat deck, or near where they were going to fish the next day.

If they were at Kingston's he took them to local parties—peanut boilings, watermelon cuttings in the summertime, roller-skating in the winter. Once he surprised them with a trip to Nashville to see the Grand Ole Opry, driving all Friday night to get there. He knew some of the girls at Mississippi State College for Women in nearby Columbus. For a while he occasionally took them there for movie dates or some program on the campus. Model T took a special liking to a girl Kingston had known in Cummings. Angie Simpson. She was a quiet, shy, wholesome girl who came from a poor family and was going to school on an academic scholarship from the local Lions Club. They stopped their visits there when the dean of women at MSCW called the dean of men at Mississippi State and told him that the girls were afraid of Mr. Smylie's little friend from Louisiana. "You know. The deformed one," she said. Model T had sensed it already and told Kingston that he didn't like those classy ladies over there and didn't want to go back. But he continued to see Angie when they were in Cummings and seemed to enjoy it when they teased him about her. "Yeah, she's my sweetie," he would say.

They were never as relaxed at Doops's house. It was something Kingston and Model T could not understand and never talked about. His mother was generally busy with her own activities and they seldom saw her. Only Doops, and perhaps the Negroes in the quarters, knew of her frequent visits to Mr. Geringer's other office. At first Doops could not handle it, thought of moving away and never coming back. It was not so much the carnality of it. He could accept that she was a young and beautiful woman. But the fact that she spent all the money on herself—from a permanent wave to a college education to a remodeled house. Forever building bigger and better barns, Doops thought. But they were her barns. He knew a woman in Baton Rouge who was an avowed and notorious streetwalker. She said she did it to support her three children. He had once interviewed her for a free-lance article, trying to draw a parallel between what she was doing and what a large, downtown church located in a slum area was doing in its massive building campaign. But he gave it up, deciding that there was no analogy to be made. "A Christian is someone who loves the Lord so much that he is willing to risk going to hell for the sake of the brethren," he began the piece. He ended by saying the greatest evil was not the harlotry of the Church but what it did with the revenue from the harlotry. Spending it on itself. But when he finished the piece he threw it away, never submitting it.

To the others around Claughton Station, his mother was seen as a good and respectable woman. And she was. There had been some rumblings when she went to the courthouse soon after her husband's death and had her name changed legally from Mrs. Harry S. Momber to Miss Christine Fenner. But her life in the months and years that followed dispelled any scandalous notions this might have precipitated. She was seen as one who had moved from being a faithful and dutiful wife, denying her personal ambitions and aptitude for the sake of her husband and son, to become a sophisticated woman who overcame her grief by finding fulfillment in academic, religious, and civic activities. In addition to her work at the college, she organized a book circle, helped start a center for the elderly, and served as a volunteer teacher of English and Bible studies for Negro ministers in the area.

The fact that her son persisted in his refusal to be baptized and enter into the social and religious life of the community was not held against her, was seen as her burden, which she did not deserve but carried bravely. She was a good woman.

Doops harbored no particular ill will toward Mr. Geringer. He was the sole owner of the only industry in town and half the people who lived there worked for him. He did not flaunt his power, treated his workers well, and had the reputation of being fair and honest in his business dealings. Before the war, there had been an effort to organize the workers by the CIO. Mr. Geringer quietly and politely opposed it and the organizers soon left town, unable to convince a single worker. He had been the biggest contributor to the library where Doops had spent most of his time as a child and young man. He had been a deacon in the Baptist church for many years, but would never agree to be chairman. He served on the school and hospital boards and refused to let the new hospital carry his name. At Thanksgiving and Christmas, he gave fifty turkeys and food baskets anonymously to a local charity. Everyone knew that Luther Geringer was a good man. But Kingston and Model T were never quite comfortable in Claughton Station.

They had various names for their monthly meetings, depending on what they did. And who the host was. With Doops, it was generally a conference, seminar, colloquium, or church meeting. With Kingston, they were shindigs or shebangs. With Model T it was always a *fe do-do*.

Once, Model T had an invitation engraved in script. It was a combination of Emily Post and Cajun.

> *MONSIEUR ET MADAME COONASS ARCENEAU*
> *request the pleasure of your company*
> *to be held at La Maison bateau*
> *on the evening of Friday, the seventeenth of November*
> *at half past six*
> *honoring*
> *their son*
> *SCARFACE*
> *ADMISSION: du JAX froid, et du pop rouge*

"I hope you know when you've had something rammed up your ass," Kingston said as he and Doops left the campus of LSU and started for Mermentau. Doops had just asked him what he thought of Model T's invitation.

"I don't get it," Doops said. "Why me?"

"Why you? Because you're starting to take all this education shit too seriously. Getting too couth. Go to school? Yeah. If they can teach you something, fine. But there are a lot of places to learn. My granddaddy taught me how to run a chain saw. But he never neglected to tell me that the damn thing could get away from me and cut my head off. That's the difference between his teaching and theirs."

They were starting across the Huey P. Long Bridge, moving west. "I think you're trying to tell me something but I'm not sure what it is," Doops said, driving behind a slow-moving line of afternoon traffic.

"I'm not trying to tell you something. The little coonass genius we're going to see is trying to tell you something. Maybe me, too. Only I'm listening."

Doops drove along in silence for several minutes. Kingston opened a beer and passed it to him. "I just thought it was funny," Doops said, taking a sip of the beer.

"Hard sayings usually are," Kingston said.

"I'm damned if I know what you're pissed at me about," Doops said. "I haven't done anything to you."

"I'm not pissed. I'm just telling you Model T is judging us, telling us something. I think he's learning things we aren't learn-ing. And I don't want us to miss it. Look. I stopped at your mamma's house on the way over. She's proud of you. And that's okay. My old mamma is proud of me too. I'm doing my thing at Mississippi State. But she went and got your grades. Showed me the letter from the dean. Showed me the article in the Baton Rouge paper about the stuff you're writing. Hell, I'm proud of you too. I know you're gonna make it. But there are different kinds of smarts." They finished the beer, and Kingston opened another one. "Gotta get right for the *fe do-do*," he said. "Yeah. Guess so," Doops said.

"You know what I do?" Kingston went on. "I don't mean to dwell on it. Hell, we're going down here to have a good time. This isn't one of your seminars. No offense, ole buddy." He reached over and started to brush Doops's cowlick, noticed that Doops was letting his hair grow longer, and pulled his hand back. "What I do is, every other quarter . . . you know, I'm making pretty good grades too. But I'll make these As and Bs, and then about every other quarter I'll just up and flunk something flat. I mean, a great big goose egg. And I always try to make it something easy. Something any idiot could pass."

"Afraid I'm not following you, neighbor," Doops said. "I don't get it. Why do you have to fail something?"

"Pride," he said. "Just plain pride. I'm not going to let that little Cajun get too far ahead of me. I'm going to follow him where I can. I'm going to hang in there with him. He knows something I don't know. He knows what's important, what counts. I guess he was born with it. And maybe it can't be learned in school. But I'm going to give him a chance to teach it to me. And I'm going to give myself a chance to learn it. And the only way I know how to do it is not to take the schoolhouse too seriously."

It was the first time Doops had felt threatened by one of them. He felt suddenly alone. Kingston knew it and turned to talking about other things. Football, what they might do next summer, Hank Williams drunk in Shreveport. Doops answered his questions, but that was all.

"**T**he big dance is in Abbeville tonight," Model T yelled at them as they turned down the driveway that led to the river. He was waiting for them at the main road. He was wearing new clothes—a white shirt with the cuffs turned up two rolls, maroon rayon pants, a white, John Dillinger–looking straw hat, and wing-tipped brown-and-white shoes. They could tell he was excited.

"Man, if you ain't a sharp dude," Kingston said, jumping out of the car and walking down the oystershell driveway with him while Doops parked the car on the edge of the riverbank. "You must have thought Angie Simpson was coming."

"Wish she had," Model T giggled. "Instead of you turds. Shore wish she had."

"She sent you a letter anyhow," Kingston said. "It's in the car. Don't let me forget it."

"Hoboy. I won't do that. A letter from my sweetie? I won't do that, me."

"Ole Doops there, he's not feeling so hot," Kingston said as they walked along. "We have to cheer him up."

"Going to done it," Model T laughed, slapping Kingston on the back. "Going to have us a blast. That Abbeville, that's one hot town, yah. I'm gon' tole you, me."

"How now brown cow," Kingston said, in a way that suggested to Model T that he approved of his Cajun accent.

"And how now Monsieur Jax, mah fran," he said, drinking the beer Kingston had handed him without stopping for breath. He crushed the can with his thumbs and tossed it to Kingston, who batted it back with his open hand like a tennis ball. "Don't worry none 'bout ole Doops. We'll patch him up. He be good as new."

Doops met up with them, shaking Model T's hand but omitting the usual banter. "How've you been?" he said.

"Better'n you I t'ink, me," Model T said, shaking his hand again.

"Watch your verbs," Kingston whispered.

"Hey man, we going to have us a time in Abbeville. Gumbo and *etouffee. Boudin* too. And scatman Jax til daylight. Alka-Seltzer for breakfast. God bless, yah!"

"Sounds all right," Doops said, not smiling. Model T glanced at Kingston and shrugged his shoulders.

"First we'll check in at the old Abbeville Hotel. Never stayed there. Big place. I got the money. Me and pa-pa. Man, we made some kind of money last week. God bless!"

They sat on the lower deck of the houseboat, Kingston and Model T doing most of the talking. Occasionally, Model T's mother yelled something in French from the upper deck. Model T would laugh and say something back. "She wants me to take my new britches off," he said. He talked to both of them the same way he always had, did not acknowledge that Doops was not doing the same.

"Hey man. You know something," Model T said excitedly. "I know a better idea. Let's don't go to Abbeville. Let's go to Church Point. In the pirogue. What you say? We can get there before dark. What you say? We'll mess around up there. Go to the Dentelé Fin Club. Hear some music." He was throwing things over the rail into the boat as he talked. His mother called over the rail again. "Got to take off my new britches," he laughed, disappearing inside.

"You want to go?" Kingston asked Doops.

"Suits me," he said. Kingston went to the car and got Angie's letter and some more beer and the red pop the invitation had called for—Nehi cherry. He put the pop in the bait box, which still had ice left from the day's fishing.

When Model T had the boat headed upstream, he told Kingston to steer while he read his letter. "Got to read my sugar report," he said. They watched him as he read the one page over and over, sometimes smiling, blushing, sometimes laughing out loud. When he finished, he tore it into tiny pieces and threw it over his head, the wind catching it and spreading it along in the churning waters behind them. "Going to be some sweet fishes in this river now," he yelled at them above the roar of the engine.

"Looks like this one is going to be a church meeting, T." Kingston said as Model T was tying the boat to a pier on the edge of Church Point.

Dozens of fishing and pleasure boats were streaming in from down the Plaquemine Bayou, outrunning the darkness, tying up all around them. They paid them no mind.

"Good place for it," Model T said, sitting down again in the boat. "Church Point. Mass or confession?"

"Confession," Kingston said. "Who's the priest?"

"Everybody," Model T said.

"Okay," Kingston began. "I confess. It's my fault. Me and Doops got into a little bit of a fracas coming along. I told him you are smarter than both of us put together and I guess it sort of hurt his little feelings. I didn't mean it to come out the way it did. But anyway . . . I'm sorry, neighbor." He extended his hand to Doops and Doops shook it firmly. Then he extended it to Model T.

"No, wait a minute," Model T said without taking his hand. "First there's got to be a penance. What kind of a Catholic are you anyhow? You don't get absolution yet. Not from this priest anyway." Model T had cut a slit in a wide piece of cardboard he found on the bottom of the boat and was holding it up between them, pretending it was a confessional stall. They were feeling the effect of the beer. "You have sinned, my child. Now here is the penance. You give le frère Doops your next two beers. Now what that means is while he is drinking two beers you don't drink any.

213

You just sit there and watch him. Or us. I can have mine too."

As Kingston nodded in agreement and reached into the bait box for one of the beer cans Doops was interrupting. "No, Father. That's not it. That's not what's eating at—"

Model T didn't let him finish. "Look, son," he said to Doops. "Penance ain't got nothing to do with the one who got sinned against. But then you ain't no Catholic. It's just got to do with the one who sinned. *Sacré misère!*"

"It *doesn't* have *anything* . . ." Kingston stopped when he saw Model T hold his hand up, motioning him to be quiet.

"Now you drink the beer. and *le frère* Smylie is going to watch."

Doops drank the beer as fast as he could, in long, steady swallows. As soon as he finished the first one, Kingston handed him the other. He drank it the same way, only a bit slower.

"Now," Model T said when he had finished. "Your sins are forgiven. My son, your sins are forgiven." He dropped the piece of cardboard and moved to the end of the boat with the bait box. "Now we got to catch up," he said, opening the box. Doops, standing to let him pass, almost fell out of the boat. "Bes' you have de pop rouge," Model T said.

Model T found a can of sardines and some crackers in a sack beside the bait box. "We got supper right here," he said, looking for the key to open the sardine box.

"If this ain't a bitch," Kingston said. "Sitting here in the seafood capital of the South, eating possum sardines from Maine. I ought to cut you guys with my knife."

They ate in silence for a few minutes, then Doops began telling them about a book idea he had, how he was going to use that story he wrote on New Caledonia.

"It's all about how there aren't any Baptists left in the world."

"That sounds familiar," Kingston laughed. "Hey T, Doops is going to write his life story at twenty-eight."

"When you going to write yours?" Model T said. "When you're eighty-two. Now back off."

"Of course, that was a pretty good story you wrote on New Caledonia, the part I understood," Kingston said, his voice more friendly. "I never did know where you got all that stuff. Were you just crazy and dreamed all that stuff? Where'd you get it?"

"I told you where I got it. Made it up. Most of it anyway. Got the rest of it out of a book. Anyway, guess most folks around Claughton Station do think I'm crazy."

"Wonder why?" Kingston said. "Jesus! It's a miracle they didn't haul your ass clean to Whitfield, Parchman one, that kooky thing you pulled last Easter."

Model T hadn't heard the story and Doops was denying it ever happened. It was dark now and the last of the boats had come in and they were talking louder than before.

"Hell yes, it damn sure did happen. Your mamma talked to me about it the next time we were there. Said she worried about you and maybe we could do something with you. You didn't know about this, T? This crazy bastard went to church Easter Sunday, one of his rare visits, drunk as shit. Stood right up in the middle of the sermon and yelled, 'He is not here! He is risen!' and stumbled out. But that wasn't enough. Then he goes from one church house to another—Methodist, Presbyterian, Holiness, didn't go to one of ours because there wasn't one there—goes from one to another, screaming through the door, 'He ain't here. He done got up and run off.' Or some crazy shit like that. Don't you sit here in this pirogue and tell me it didn't happen because it did. Tell Model T what you told the deputy when he ran your ass in. Tell him!"

"I don't know. I didn't tell him anything. I don't remember any of that stuff. I just remember waking up in that jail with one hell of a hangover."

"The deputy said, 'What you think you're doing, boy?' when he pushed him in the police car. Now tell him what you told him."

"They said I told him I was just looking for some Baptists. I guess that's what I said but I was drunk at the time. You're right about that much."

"Yeah, and then the idiot deputy said, 'In a *Methodist* church? Boy, you been drinking.' And crazy Doops said, 'Is that why I can't find no Baptists?' "

Model T did not seem amused any longer. He tried to laugh with Kingston but the seriousness showed through. "That's our Doops all right. Looking for some Baptists." He appeared confused and awkward as he moved about the boat. "Looking for some Baptists."

"Yeah. I think they call that an obsession," Kingston said, noticing Model T's change of mood.

"Well, come on, you turds," Model T said, trying to act casual. "It's nine o'fucking clock. I'm not missing the *fe do-do* for this kind of crap."

"Yeah, let's go," Kingston said, running down the wharf and into the darkness ahead of them.

"He's a big ole God," Doops said to Model T, touching him on the shoulder as they followed Kingston. "I thank you for that, Father."

"*Sacré misère*," Model T said, not as an exclamation the way he generally said it, serious again. "Your father is dead. Let's go to the *fe do-do*."

"That Redbone was right," Doops said. "That damned Redbone was right."

"Right about what?" Model T asked.

"Never mind," Doops said. "The Redbone was right. Now let's go to the *fe do-do* and dance till daylight. Bet they got pretty women in Church Point."

17

"**A**fraid we got troubles, Doops," Kingston said. Doops had answered the phone in the kitchen where he and his mother had been having breakfast. Kingston was agitated and Doops had trouble understanding him. "Can you get over here in a hurry?"

Doops did not ask what the trouble was, just said that he would be there in about two hours.

"They picked Model T up about half an hour ago," Kingston said, his voice trembling.

"Picked him up? Who picked him up? What the hell you talking about? Settle down. You're about to blow a Redbone gasket."

"The sheriff! And another man," he said. "They came knocking on the door before we even got up. My mamma let them in and they came straight past her to where he was asleep. You know, in that back room where he sleeps when he's here. Shook him and yelled at him and hauled him out of here. They didn't even let him put his shoes on. We got troubles, neighbor. You better get on over here."

"God damn it, Smylie. You're not making any sense. Or else I'm not hearing too well. What the hell would the sheriff want with Model T? Now tell me what the shit is going on."

He had stretched the telephone cord down the hallway and his mother, listening from the kitchen table, came and closed the door. "You should watch your language, Doops Momber."

"Great Jesus," Doops mumbled.

"Murder! That's what they said. And rape! And they threw him in the back of that sheriff's car like a sack of potatoes. Slammed the door and took off with the sirens blaring all the way to Cummings. He needs us, Doops. Get on over here." Doops had left them about ten o'clock the night before, deciding to drive home and go to work early on a story he was trying to finish.

"Kingston. Hey, Kingston. Will you slow down? Look. Take a deep breath, hold it in until you count to ten, and let it all the way out. Jesus! Are you drunk? Did you guys go out again after I left from over there? Are you standing there telling me that somebody is damn fool enough to suspect Fordache Arceneau of molesting some woman, of hurting a single soul in this whole fucked-up world? Is that what you're telling me? Christ Almighty!"

"What I'm telling you is that Model T is locked up. What I'm telling you is that Angie Simpson got killed last night down at the marina and they're saying Fordache Arceneau did it. That's what I'm telling you. Now are you coming over here or not?"

When Doops arrived at the Smylie place he found Kingston sitting on a hammock under a cottonwood tree in the front yard. Kingston came to the car and got in beside Doops.

"We got troubles, Doops," he said. Doops had never seen him look like this. "It looks bad for us. We were the last ones seen with her. Must have been fifty people saw us at the drive-in restaurant with her. And that many more at the movie. It looks bad for us."

Doops sat for a minute without answering. "It can't be all that bad," he said. "Model T went to her house and got her at three o'clock in the afternoon. Her mamma and daddy and sister were in the house. We went swimming at the marina, rode around in your boat for an hour, went to the movie, ate hamburgers at the drive-in, and took her home. We were with him the whole time. This idiot sheriff just got a little overzealous. When we tell him we were with him all the time, that he never left our side for one second until we got here . . . well, he'll turn him loose. Now let's get with it. Let's go."

"Afraid it won't be that simple, neighbor," Kingston said. "Angie was pretty badly mutilated. Her right eye was gouged out and her left ear was cut off. And they found her with no clothes on. This whole town has gone crazy. My mamma is scared to death and my daddy is sitting inside with a shotgun in his lap. We've been getting threatening phone calls ever since the word got out. People call, scream something, and hang up. Mamma wants us to leave. Of course, that old man. They would have to shoot him first. He's not going anywhere. I'm telling you, it's going to get nasty. Awful damn nasty."

Doops sighed deeply and stared out the window. Cars and trucks were passing the house in rapid succession, all of them driving fast, the dust floating up the lane in continuous clouds. "They go up to New Mars Road and turn around. It's the same ones. Going and coming," Kingston said. "Been at it for an hour now."

That was the way it began. Now it was October and the fall term of criminal court had just impaneled the jury. Model T had been in jail for five months. Bail had been set at fifty thousand dollars, and Doops and Kingston had tried to raise it. Kingston's grandfather offered his farm, but for property to be accepted by the court, it had to be free and unencumbered. There was a long-term Federal Home Administration loan against his property. Doops tried to persuade his mother to sign the bond and she agreed to if Doops would become a Christian and be baptized. That way she'd know the Lord's hand was in it all. In desperation he relented, decided to make the swap. But the night he was going to do it, going to walk down the aisle and join the Baptist Church, he had the symptoms and Kingston had to revive him the way he had done in front of the quarters right after they were discharged from the army. His mother went on to church and told the preacher that her son had always been sickly, that he wasn't feeling well, but that she was sure he would join the following Sunday. When they told Model T of the plan, he was unbending in his refusal to accept it. "This is not a trading item," he said. "Don't worry so. It ain't the end of the world." From the beginning he had said he did not want them to hire a lawyer for him, that they would plead their own case before the judge and jury.

He talked as if all of them had been indicted. When they told him that if he did not have an attorney the court would appoint one to represent him, he found that even more offensive. "I said I never would ask them for anything and I won't." They talked to a man named Walter Corbitt, a young attorney in an adjoining county who had just graduated from Harvard Law School. He agreed to take the case for whatever they could pay him. He had recently been admitted to the Mississippi bar and had never defended a murder charge except in moot court at school. They liked him and insisted that he set a fee and they would pay it. Kingston had long since finished college and was helping his grandfather run the farm. Doops was working for a new magazine called *The Southern Supposer*, a journal in New Orleans, which combined satire on Southern customs and serious social criticism. It paid him little, but he lived in his mother's house and had few expenses. They pooled everything they made, both of them finding it hard to believe that they were working to defend so gentle a man of so horrendous a crime. Model T encouraged them on each visit, kept them going with his unwavering confidence that he would be turned loose as soon as they had a chance to tell the truth.

The lawyer was less assuring. The State, he said, had everything going for it. Model T had little. He was an outsider. He had a funny-sounding name, at least to the provincial folk of Cummings, Mississippi. He looked strange and suspicious. He was a Catholic in a region that was overwhelmingly Baptist. Feelings still ran high about the murder and he feared it would be impossible to pick an impartial jury. The prosecutor would certainly parade the still-grieving parents and sister through the court and all the sentiment would be with them. But he would do the best he could.

The lawyer painstakingly covered every possible courtroom development with them. There was one brief period of time for which they could not account. After they had taken Angie home the night of the murder, Kingston's mother had said she was out of cigarettes and asked the three boys to go to the store for her. Doops was in a hurry to leave and Kingston was supposed to get up at four o'clock to go to Jackson for a load of feed. Model T said that he would go. Kingston said that he would testify that he had gone with Model T to the store and sat in the car. Neither Model T nor the lawyer would agree to that. "There may be perjury committed in that courtroom, but it won't be by us," the lawyer said. Model T said simply that he wanted everyone to tell the truth. "Anyway," he kept repeating, "the storekeeper and his wife both saw me there. Do you think they're going to forget this face?"

"People forget all sorts of things when they're supposed to," Kingston said.

But Model T would not relent. He had read the entire Bible three times since he had been in jail and had committed long passages of it to memory.

"Ye shall know the truth and the truth shall make you free." He repeated it over and over.

"There's a difference between truth and fact," Kingston said each time.

The prosecutor, Attorney General Theodore Sikes, was a well-dressed, handsome man in his middle forties. He was a large man but not fat, muscular and athletic-looking. He wore heavy tortoiseshell glasses, which he apparently did not need. They were in his coat pocket as much as they were on his face and he took them on and off as he spoke. He introduced himself to the twelve white men seated in the jury box and explained in meticulous detail what it was the State would prove to them. He moved about the courtroom with ease and confidence, speaking with a mellow baritone, his manner fitting the seriousness of the occasion.

When he called the first witness, a frail, ashen-faced woman of about fifty entered the courtroom. She was wearing a medium-length, dotted Swiss dress with a sailor collar and a stiff-brimmed straw hat with a band made of the same material as the dress. She had on new patent-leather shoes, white with a black bow. As she walked across the room, her gait showed she was not used to wearing high heels. She appeared frightened as she glanced quickly at the defense table where Model T and the lawyer were seated.

"I wouldn't hurt little Angie, Mrs. Simpson," Model T called in a normal tone, waving at her, his smile tightening the celluloid-looking scar tissue on his face.

She did not respond and the judge mildly rebuked him, telling the lawyer to instruct his client to remain silent. Mr. Corbitt reached over and patted his shoulder.

After the woman had taken the oath and the prosecutor had asked her to state her name for the court, he spoke to her in a patronizing, saccharine manner.

"Mrs. Simpson, I know this is not easy for you. I will not keep you long and if you do not feel like continuing at any point, I will ask His Honor for a recess. All of us in this court know how you have suffered."

He paused, holding the heavy glasses in his hand. "Will you tell the jury how you were related to the victim?"

"You mean to Angie?" she said nervously. "What kin I was to Angie?"

"Yes," he said. "What kin were you to Angie?"

"I was her mother," she whispered, about to cry.

The prosecutor led her through the events of the evening of the murder, when Model T came for her, where they said they were going, when they would return, how Angie was dressed. When he asked, "And that's the last time you saw her alive?" the woman broke into a hysterical fit of crying. He handed her his handkerchief and waited, watching the jury from the corner of his eye. A few of the men were wiping their own eyes and several women in the audience were sobbing along with her. The prosecutor did not ask for a recess, just stood waiting. When she stopped crying and he knew that she would be able to speak again, he began to question her about a scene she and her daughter had witnessed a month before the murder. She spoke freely now, her composure regained.

"Well, me and Carol, that's her sister, we was in the front room listening to some records and they was on the porch. We heard them drive up but we wasn't paying no attention to them. All of a sudden we heard this racket, it sounded like Angie was hurt or something. We both just went over to the window and looked out."

222

"And when you looked through the window, exactly what did you see?"

"Well, this fellow . . ."

"When you say, 'this fellow,' to whom are you referring?" the prosecutor said. "Is the man to whom you are referring in this courtroom?"

"Yes, sir," she said. "He's a-sittin' right there." She pointed directly at Model T.

"All right. You are referring to Fordache—or however he says his name—Arceneau. Go on, please. Just tell the court in your own words what you saw."

"Well, like I say, he was hugging her and trying to kiss her in the mouth, and she was turning her head like she was trying to get away."

"In other words, she was rejecting his advances toward her?"

"Yes, sir. I reckon that's what you'd call it. She wasn't letting him kiss her anyhow. She was trying to get away. Reckon that's what you'd call it. Rejecting him, you might say."

"And when did she get away? How long were they on the porch before she came inside?"

"I'd say, maybe five or ten minutes."

"And when she came in, was she crying?"

"Yes, sir. She was crying."

"Thank you, Mrs. Simpson. You are a brave woman. That's all."

Mr. Corbitt stood in front of the table and spoke to her as gently as the prosecutor had. "Mrs. Simpson, how long had your daughter been going out with Mr. Arceneau?"

"You mean when that happened?" she asked.

"Yes, ma'am. How long had they been going together?"

"About three years, I reckon."

"And when she came in crying that night, did she say Mr. Arceneau had abused her, had hurt her?"

"No, sir. But we knew it, though. We knew he had hurt her, for she was crying."

"Did you or Carol ask her what was the matter?"

"Yes, sir. We both asked her what was the matter."

"And will you tell us what she said?"

The woman looked at the prosecutor and he nodded for her to

answer. "Well, she said Fordie, she always called him Fordie, she said Fordie had tried to kiss her."

"And is that all she said, about why she was crying, I mean?"

"Yes, sir. That's all she said about it." She looked at the prosecutor again but he did not let their eyes meet.

"Mrs. Simpson, I will ask you if she didn't say that she was crying because she wished she had let him kiss her. Didn't your daughter say that?"

The woman dropped her head and fidgeted in the seat, twisting the prosecutor's handkerchief in her hand. "I don't remember. I mean, I remember her saying something but I don't remember what it was she said." She tried again to catch the prosecutor's eyes.

"Mrs. Simpson, didn't your daughter tell you that she thought she was in love with Fordie, but she wasn't going to let him kiss her until she was sure that she didn't just feel sorry for him?"

"Objection," the prosecutor called, not rising. "Counsel is leading the witness."

"Sustained," the judge said, routinely.

"Mrs. Simpson, you have testified that your daughter said that Mr. Arceneau tried to kiss her. You remember her saying that. Then you testified that she said something else but you don't remember what it was. Will you try to remember just what it was she said after she had said that Fordie had tried to kiss her. Take your time. Just try to remember."

The woman looked at her husband, who was seated in the front of the courtroom. He was trying to get the prosecutor's attention but the prosecutor was studying the faces of the jurors.

Finally she said, "Well, she might have said something like that, something like what you said she said, but I don't remember the exact words. And that's the God's truth."

"Thank you, Mrs. Simpson. I have no further questions."

When the woman moved from the witness stand there was a general restlessness in the courtroom. They did not like the way the testimony had gone, but a voice from the rear seemed to restore their confidence.

"Just wait," the voice said.

The judge stared at the back of the room but did not comment.

224

The second witness was Angie's sister. When she walked into the courtroom and the bailiff instructed her to take the oath, Model T waved and spoke to her the same way he had her mother. She smiled faintly and turned to face the court, took the oath calmly, and sat down. She was dressed exactly as her mother was.

The prosecutor asked her the same questions he had asked her mother, emphasizing that Angie came into the room crying, making the same point about Angie rejecting his advances.

"Miss Simpson," Mr. Corbitt began, moving around the table, his voice a bit more assertive. "When your sister came into the room and said that Mr. Arceneau had tried to kiss her, who was in the room at the time? Were you alone with her?"

"No, sir. My mamma was there too."

"Your mamma was there too? And she heard every word that was spoken? Is that correct?"

"Yes, sir. I mean, I reckon she did. She was there."

"Miss Simpson, you were not in the courtroom but I am sure you are aware that your mother's testimony as to what was said that night has already been heard in this court. Am I correct?"

The prosecutor objected sternly, seeing the lawyer's strategy. The judge sustained the objection but let the lawyer rephrase what he had said. The girl answered that she knew her mother had already been a witness. Mr. Corbitt moved closer to where she was seated, looking her directly in the face.

"Miss Simpson, why did your sister say she was crying?"

"She said something like, 'Fordie tried to kiss me.' Something like that."

The lawyer moved as close to her as he could get as he asked the next question.

"Didn't she say she wished she had let him kiss her?"

"She didn't say that, no, sir."

"And didn't she say she thought she was in love with him but she wouldn't let him kiss her until she was sure she didn't just feel sorry for him?"

"She . . . I didn't hear her say that. No, sir."

The lawyer's questions were coming in rapid succession, the girl trying to keep up with her answers. "And didn't—" The prosecutor was on his feet, waving his hands in the air, almost running into the bench, screaming, "Objection!" The lawyer didn't stop his questions, didn't slow down, his voice rising higher with each word, waving with one hand for the prosecutor to sit down. "And didn't you say to your sister, 'You better not ever kiss that circus freak'? And didn't your dead sister slap you in the face and start crying again? And didn't she say, 'You'd better not ever call him that again! He's not a circus freak. He's a dear, sweet man, and I think I'm in love with him'? And didn't she run to her room and lock the door for the rest of the night? Now isn't that the way it happened, Miss Simpson?"

His booming, still-resonant voice echoed through the hallways as he turned and sat down.

The spectators were making no effort to keep their voices to a whisper as they talked excitedly in small clusters. The judge was pounding hard and rapidly on his desk, telling the bailiff to prepare to clear the courtroom. The girl sat frightened, her look at the prosecutor a plea for help. The mother was clutching her husband's shoulder, screaming above the other noises.

When order was restored, the judge spoke first to the spectators, telling them that if the slightest hint of such a scene happened again he would clear the courtroom for the remainder of the trial. When he finished with the audience, he motioned both attorneys to the bench and addressed them in a dour but fatherly fashion.

"Now boys, this court is not going to put up with this. Both of you should know better. We have an added burden in this trial. Feelings in the community are still fierce. Both of you know that. You have a duty to your task but you also have an obligation to this community. Mr. Corbitt, I admonish you heartily to contain your passions. I know you are new to the scene of criminal court. I appreciate your zeal for your client. I have personally welcomed you to this bar and when you walk away from this case I do not believe you will say you have been treated unfairly. But if there is a repeat of this outburst, I will hold you in contempt. In my court, that's pretty serious. Now the objection is unwaveringly sustained. If you wish to continue your questioning, Mr. Corbitt, you may do so."

226

Mr. Corbitt nodded and walked slowly back to where the girl was seated. "Miss Simpson, I have one further question." He spoke softly now, and the girl appeared calm, no longer afraid of what he might ask her, no longer looking at the prosecutor or her mother. "The question has to do with a precious and sacred moment in your life. I do not wish to destroy or tamper in any way with that moment. Will you tell this court the last thing your sister said to you when Mr. Arceneau came to get her, as she was going out the door?"

The girl did not hesitate, did not seem at all nervous. "Yes sir. She leaned over and whispered, 'Sis, I'm in love!' "

"Thank you very much, Miss Simpson. You may step down now, at least as far as the defense is concerned.

"I wish you hadn't done that," Model T said to the lawyer during the noon recess.

"But that's the way it happened, isn't it?" the lawyer replied.

"That's exactly the way it happened. She told me all of that. But I didn't tell you."

"I know you didn't," he said. "But you told your friends. And they want to help you. And so do I. We're talking about your life now, son. I know you still love the girl. And I know you won't do anything to mess up your memories. But you'll have to let me try the case. That's my line of work."

After lunch, the prosecution called the county sheriff. He was a popular man in the county. He had run for office on the same platform that Mississippi sheriffs had run on for fifty years, a promise to put the bootleggers out of business. Unlike many who were elected on that promise he had kept his word. He was tall and thin, wavy-haired, attractive. Dressed in a neat business suit, he had ceremoniously removed his gun and holster and handed them to one of his deputies as he approached the witness stand. The little shield pinned on his lapel was the only indication that he was the sheriff. As he sat down, a ripple of applause began in the courtroom, then quickly subsided as they remembered the judge's warning. He testified that he and a deputy had found the girl's body. He told of the physical surroundings, answered affirmatively to a question as to whether the fact that the mutilation of the girl's face, corresponding to that of the defendant's face,

had been a factor in the reasonable-cause warrant he got before
making the arrest. The prosecutor asked if he had found any
other evidence near the body. He said that he had found a silver-
plated Zippo lighter. The prosecutor handed him a lighter and
asked him to identify it. He said that was the one he had found.
The prosecutor asked him to read the initials etched on the side
of the lighter. "F.A.," the sheriff said, a professional air about him,
no editorial inflection in his voice. He testified that the lighter
was not found among the young woman's personal effects but was
discovered in a trampled area where a scuffle had apparently
taken place, fifty yards from where the body was found.

"That's my lighter," Model T whispered to the lawyer. "I gave
it to her while we were watching the movie, when she whispered
in my ear that she loved me." The lawyer placed his hand on
Model T's knee.

"Do you think I'll get it back when this is over?" Model T
asked. "I gave it to her."

"We'll see," the lawyer whispered, patting him lightly.

"Will you tell the court if the lighter was later identified by
anything other than the initials?" the prosecutor asked him.

"Yes, sir. It was sent to the state crime lab and later to the FBI
lab in Washington."

"And what identification was made there?"

"A fingerprint identification."

"And will you tell the court what that showed?"

"Yes, sir. The prints matched the army fingerprints of Private
Fordache Arceneau."

The prosecutor asked him if there were any other prints on the
lighter and he said that none had been found.

"Was Angie wearing gloves when you handed her the lighter?"
the lawyer whispered to Model T.

Model T said he didn't remember, that she always wore thin
white gloves when she dressed up but he didn't think she had
them on when he slipped her the lighter that night at the drive-
in movie.

The prosecutor asked the sheriff if any kind of weapon had
been found and he answered that one of the deputies had found a
pelting knife, explaining that a pelting knife was a type of hunt-

ing knife, generally used by trappers for removing the hides from small animals. The knife had been found about a hundred yards from where the body was found.

In the cross-examination, Mr. Corbitt asked two questions.

"Sheriff, do you remember what the personal effects of the victim to which you referred contained?" He answered that there had been the usual odds and ends found in a woman's purse—hairpins, lipstick, nail clippers, chewing gum, things like that. Mr. Corbitt did not rush him, gave him time to continue. "And a pair of gloves, I believe." He said it as a sort of afterthought. He added without being asked that the purse had been returned to the family.

"Were any fingerprints found on the pelting knife, sheriff?" The sheriff answered that the knife appeared to have been wiped clean.

The rest of the afternoon was spent with the testimony of the storekeeper and his wife. Both swore that they did not remember seeing Model T in the store the night of the murder. They were also witnesses for the defense and Mr. Corbitt had been counting heavily on their testimony. The man had told him earlier that maybe he remembered seeing Model T but that he couldn't be sure, that he would have to see him face-to-face before he could be sure. The lawyer knew that if he could place Model T in the store between 10:15 and 10:45, and assuming that the jury would believe Kingston's mother, who would testify that he was not gone from the house for more than half an hour, he would have a good case. Without that they were in trouble. Throughout two hours of the most intensive questioning, spaced by numerous objections, exceptions, and rulings, and several heated exchanges between the two attorneys, the storekeepers did not waver in their claim that they had never seen Model T before.

"Mr. Stelling, I don't want to offend this defendant's sensitivities," the lawyer said with exasperation at the end of the questions. "I hesitate to allude to his physical appearance. But, do you mean to tell me that it is your testimony before this court that someone who looks like he does could walk into your store, pay for a pack of cigarettes, and get change from a twenty-dollar bill and that you would say, as Mr. Arceneau will swear you did say, 'You're the one who's sweet on the Simpson gal, ain't you?' and that five months later you would not remember it? Is that what I am to understand?''

The prosecutor objected and was sustained.

The following morning, Mr. Corbitt began presenting the defense case. He knew that most of his arguments were gone already. What the State had offered was circumstantial. Yet it had made a deep impact on the jury. The prosecutor had introduced witnesses with whom they were already friendly and sympathetic. He would have the obstacle of suspicion and hostility to overcome. He had decided to start with Model T. He knew there were hazards in it, but thought that a direct exposure to the jury might be helpful.

"The defense calls to the stand Mr. Fordache Arceneau," he announced, trying to sound confident. The courtroom was more crowded than it had been the day before. All of the downstairs benches were jammed and the balcony was almost full. No one made a sound as Model T walked around the table and sat down in the witness chair, not stopping beside the bailiff, who stood holding the Bible in his hand.

"The defendant will please rise to be sworn," the judge said, fumbling with some papers a secretary had brought him to sign.

"I don't swear, Mr. Judge," Model T said, showing no sign of being nervous. The judge stopped writing in the middle of his signature and looked down at the lawyer, who had already taken his stand in front of the witness chair to begin the questioning.

"Mr. Corbitt, I don't mean to sound harsh, but it is customary to inform the court if a witness will refuse the oath."

The lawyer, surprised himself, hurried to the bench and asked for a brief recess to confer with his client. The prosecutor objected to the recess on the grounds that Mr. Arceneau was not a client when he took the witness stand. He then became a witness. The judge granted the recess and asked the jury to leave the room.

It was the first time the lawyer had become impatient or abrasive with Model T. He was embarrassed and knew the prosecutor was laughing at him. "Look son, what the hell is that all about? Now, damn it, I'm trying to save your life. Can't you understand that? Why in hell didn't you tell me you wouldn't take the oath?''

"You didn't ask me," Model T said, not discourteously. "The Bible says, 'Let your communication be, yea, yea; nay, nay: for whatsoever is more than these cometh of evil.' That's what it says in the book of Matthew."

"Okay. Okay. That's what it says in the book of Matthew. But what it says in the book of this courtroom is that if we don't win this trial you're liable to go to the electric chair. Now how about it? Just put your hand on the Bible and say that you solemnly *affirm* that the testimony you are about to give will be the truth, the whole truth, and nothing but the truth so help you God. Will you do that?" He was trying to keep his voice low so the prosecutor could not hear him.

"That's the same thing. I'll just tell the judge that I will tell the truth. I won't swear and I won't affirm. That's the same thing. Jesus said not to swear at all, not by anything."

The judge, hearing the conversation, called the lawyer over and told him that the witness did not have to swear, did not have to take an oath against his religious convictions, and said he would explain to the jury that the law did not require a witness to take the oath.

For more than an hour, the lawyer questioned Model T about every aspect of his life, trying to convey to the jury his germinal innocence. At times Model T was of little help, adding things about himself the question had not called for, leaving the lawyer staring blankly.

At the end, the lawyer said, "Mr. Arceneau, did you kill Angie Simpson?"

"I love Angie Simpson," he replied.

"Mr. Arceneau, I know you loved Angie Simpson. But for the benefit of this jury, and for the benefit of the State, which has charged you with a terrible crime, will you just answer the question? Did you kill Angie Simpson?" he was trying hard not to let his uneasiness show through.

"Mr. Corbitt, you can't kill someone you love. I love Angie Simpson." The lawyer was afraid to risk asking the question again and accepted that as his answer. He knew what the prosecutor would do with it. "Thank you, Mr. Arceneau. I know you can't kill someone you love," he said. "I have no more questions."

The prosecutor poured a glass of water from the silver pitcher and stood drinking it slowly. He moved the seersucker coat he was wearing and hung it neatly on the back of the chair, thumping some specks of dust off the shoulders. Everyone waited for him to speak.

"He's your witness, general," the judge said curtly as the spectators grew restless.

"Sorry, Your Honor. I was just wondering. Just wondering how a man could carve up so lovely a creature as Angie Simpson with a pelting knife, could violate her body like a butcher would a hanging carcass, could cut off her ear and gouge out her eye like one might do skinning a wild animal, and then refuse to take a legal oath in his own . . ."

The defense lawyer was on his feet, momentarily unable to make a sound. Even before he could voice his motion the judge was instructing the jury that they should disregard what the prosecutor had said. He reprimanded the prosecutor and told him he would declare a mistrial if it happened again in his court.

"I'm sorry, Your Honor. It is not easy for me to hide my deepest feelings."

"But that is what the people of this county pay you to do," the judge said brusquely.

"Mr. Arceneau, I believe you're a Catholic," the prosecutor said, after another long pause.

"Objection. Immaterial," the lawyer said.

"Sustained," the judge said, a note of disgust in his voice.

The prosecutor was visibly annoyed at the way Model T shook his head from side to side all the time. He turned to the jury and made the same motions with his own head, frowning as he did. One of the jurors, an older man, was doing the same thing.

"Mr. Arceneau, will you state your religion to this court?" the prosecutor said, still shaking his head.

"I'm a Catholic," he said.

The judge denied Mr. Corbitt's objection.

"Mr. Arceneau, have you been visited by a priest since you have been in this trouble?"

"No, sir."

"Have you been visited by any minister of the Gospel of any faith?"

232

"I have been visited by Doops and Kingston. Every week, sometimes twice."

"I believe, however, those gentlemen are hardly considered ministers of the Gospel." Model T curled his lips down but did not answer.

"By the way," the prosecutor said hurriedly, as if something had occurred to him for the first time. "I believe you do not have a Social Security card. Is that correct?"

"Yes sir," Model T answered.

"And would you please explain to us why you refused to get a Social Security number?"

"Well, I'll tell you, general," Model T said. "When I got out of the army I said I wouldn't ever be a number again."

"I see," the prosecutor said, picking a thick file from the table and opening it. "But you're a number now," he said, pulling a sheet from the file and holding it up. "You're number 15062. That's your number. Did you know that?"

"No, sir," Model T said. "That's not my number. That's your number for me. But it's not my number."

The judge rapped for order as the spectators stirred at what they saw as Model T's impudence.

"I see," the prosecutor said again, glancing at the crowd.

"When you were growing up, Mr. Arceneau, did you go to catechism classes?"

"Yes, sir."

"And did the nuns ever tell you that if you told a lie the booger man would get you?"

Mr. Corbitt stood, started to object, but then sat down.

"Mr. Arceneau, is the reason you refused to take the oath because you were afraid you would swear something was true when it was a lie and the devil would get you?" Model T's expression was blank, as if the prosecutor had not said anything at all. When he continued to sit, holding his ear as he was straining to hear the next question, the prosecutor turned to the court reporter and said, "Let the record show that the witness refused to answer the question." He moved back to the table and sat down, looked across the room at Mr. Corbitt, and said, "He doesn't seem to hear what I say, counsel. Sorry."

Kingston's mother took the stand next, telling about Model T going for the cigarettes and insisting that he was gone no longer than half an hour. She agreed that he could not have gone to the store and the marina and got back in the length of time he was gone from her home. The prosecutor did not question her, leaving the impression that he already established that Model T did not go to the store at all, that he had gone directly to the marina where he secretly met Angie Simpson. The defense then called several people who testified that they had seen the four of them together at the movie and the drive-in restaurant and that Model T and Angie seemed happy. Mr. Corbitt called the sheriff to the stand again and questioned him about the lighter and the gloves. The prosecutor did not cross-examine any of the witnesses.

The room was hushed as Doops walked in and stopped at the witness stand, not sitting down. No one believed that he would put his hand on the Bible and take the oath, based on a story about Doops that had appeared in the morning paper. Their speculation had been that it was he who had influenced Model T about true believers not swearing. As the bailiff approached him the crowd leaned forward, straining to hear and see. Doops looked at Model T and smiled as he stood waiting. The bailiff held the Bible by his side, not presenting it to him, expecting him to refuse. They stood looking at each other, neither of them moving for several awkward seconds. The judge swung his chair around and watched as intently as the others. When the bailiff did not move, did not speak, the judge cleared his throat and addressed him. "The court instructs the bailiff to present the book." When he held the Bible out, Doops glanced quickly at the jury, trying in that evanescent moment to read them, to know what they were thinking, what possible influence he might have on them if he refused as the lawyer had told him Model T had, or if he swore the oath. The ceiling fan droned steadily above the judge's head. Angie's sister, sitting in the second row with her parents, popped her bubble gum loudly and a few people giggled nervously.

"Do you solemnly swear that the testimony you are about to give will be the truth, the whole truth, and nothing but the truth so help you God?"

"I do," Doops replied distinctly, keeping his right hand up and the other firmly on the Bible until the sheriff pulled it away. A general sigh, followed by scattered murmuring and whispering, arose from the crowd. The judge rapped once with his gavel and cautioned them again about any display of feeling, not saying anything about clearing the courtroom this time.

When Doops had taken his seat, Mr. Corbitt stood in place, not moving around the table. "Mr. Momber, how well do you know the man seated beside me? The man at this table?"

"I know him as well as I know anyone in this world." His voice was clear and calm and easily understood throughout the courtroom.

"Would you say that you know him better than anyone else knows him?"

"Unless it is Mr. Smylie," he said, an air of formality about him. "Yes, sir. I would say I know him better than anyone else unless it is Mr. Smylie."

The lawyer backed slowly away from the table and stood directly behind Model T, placing both his hands on his client's shoulders. "Mr. Momber, do you believe this man killed Angie Simpson?"

"I do not believe it now and I will never believe it," he said, louder than before.

"Thank you, Mr. Momber. No further questions."

The prosecutor took a stand in front of the jury, facing them, his back to the witness. "Mr. Momber, do you believe Mr. Arceneau killed Angie Simpson?" he asked, trying to ask the question in exactly the same tone of voice Mr. Corbitt had asked it.

"No, sir," Doops said, leaning forward, trying to see his face.

"Mr. Momber, before me are seated twelve of the finest men in this county. Two of them teach Sunday school. Three of them are deacons in their Baptist churches. The youngest among them is a student at the New Orleans Baptist Theological Seminary, studying for the ministry. Another is a scoutmaster. Another works for the United States government. Mr. Momber, let's suppose that these twelve men, after hearing and viewing all the evidence this state has to offer, some of which you have not heard and seen, after all this what if they told you that he did kill Angie Simpson? Would you believe it then?"

"Objection," Mr. Corbitt said, pushing himself halfway to a standing position. "That is hypothetical. Immaterial."

"Your honor, this court has heard the witness testify that he would *never* believe something. Never is a long time. Never is all-inclusive. It is not immaterial to establish if this witness is in contempt of this honorable court. This jury has a right to know what estimate the witness has of them. May it please the court, the State insists that the witness be instructed to answer the question."

"General, the court will decide on any incident of contempt," the judge said, rapping with his gavel to quiet the scattered whispering in the courtroom. "But I am overruling your objection, Mr. Corbitt, since you brought up the matter of the witness's opinion first. The witness will answer the question."

Doops had used the time to prepare his answer. "I would believe that they believe it," he said.

"That is not my question, Mr. Momber. I will state the question again. It requires one of two words as an answer. You may say yes, or you may say no. Now. Would you believe it if these twelve men told you that he did it? That he did kill Angie Simpson?"

"I would believe that they believe it," Doops said again, turning to the judge. "That is my answer, Your Honor."

The prosecutor moved slowly toward him, hunching over when he stopped so that he was at face level with him. He turned slightly sideward and made sweeping eye contact with each of the jurors, a kind of sneer on his face, which he held until he turned back to face Doops. Doops was leaning forward in the chair, his legs crossed, his right hand resting on his knee, his left hand almost touching, but not touching, the arm of the chair. The prosecutor moved closer, his face not more than two feet from Doops's face. Suddenly he straightened up and whirled around, speaking as he turned.

"So he took the oath!" he said, looking again at the jury.

"Objection," Mr. Corbitt said. "The prosecutor is addressing the jury."

"Sustained." The judge motioned for him to continue.

"Why did you take the oath?" he said, turning back to face Doops.

"Objection," the lawyer said, his voice rising as he stood. "Taking the oath is standard courtroom procedure."

"Too bad you couldn't convince your client of that," the pros-

236

ecutor said as the judge was sustaining the objection.

"Your Honor, may it please the court, my line of questioning is not designed to discredit the witness. It is designed to enlighten the jury. If the witness is discredited it will be by his answers and counsel's obtruding interruptions, not by my questions."

"The witness need not answer the question," the judge said.

The prosecutor turned again to the jury as he asked Doops the next question. "Why are you holding your left hand off the arm of the chair? Are you afraid the chair is dirty?" His voice was loud, bellicose. "Or do you feel your left hand has been somehow defiled by coming into contact with the greatest book ever written, the Holy Bible?" He had turned as he spoke to survey the spectators, his manner one of outrage, the same smirk as when he had faced the jury. Again he did not wait for an answer, spinning around to face Doops.

"Mr. Momber." He held the word *Mister*, drew it out with exaggerated emphasis, leaning toward him again. "Mr. Momber," he repeated, easier now. "How does it happen that you Communists are able to—"

Mr. Corbitt was on his feet, pushing his hair back with both hands, his face flushed with anger. "Your Honor! I take the most extreme umbrage at what is . . . Your Honor! Please! This witness is not on trial in this court. This outrageous line of questioning, this affront to this honorable court, surely sir, surely Your Honor will not allow it to continue."

The prosecutor edged calmly toward the bench, then turned so that the jury could hear what he was saying. "Your Honor, may it please the court, if counsel does not wish all the facts known in this case, if it is his intention to stifle this court by such childish outbursts . . . I heard no objection stated. If there is objection or exception he has only to state it. I heard an oration, a presumptuous challenge to this court. May I remind counsel that this is a witness for the defense. If he chooses to withdraw him as a witness, the State will obligingly ask him to step down. The State hasn't brought him here. Meanwhile I would mightily appreciate his indulgence as I proceed."

"Mr. Corbitt, if you have an objection to enter, you will please state it to the court," the judge said.

"I object, Your Honor, on the ground that the politics of this witness is not germane to this trial, and that the line of questioning is designed to create a negative response from the jury. That it is prejudicial and is a desperation move to bolster the collapsing case of the prosecution."

"The objection is sustained, Mr. Corbitt," the judge said. "But I remind counsel that procedural objections, not speeches, are in order. General Sikes, the court reminds you that you are to confine yourself to direct questions of the witness."

"Mr. Momber, I will ask you if you work for a magazine called *The Southern Supposer?*"

"That is correct."

"Mr. Momber, I have in my hand a deposition—do you know what a deposition is?"

"I do."

"I have in my hand a sworn deposition from one Gerald Sleath. Does that name mean anything to you?"

"No, sir."

"Very well, I'll enlighten you."

Mr. Corbitt stepped to the table and asked to see the paper the prosecutor held. Without looking up he handed it to him and continued. "Mr. Gerald Sleath is a staff attorney for the United States Department of Justice. He has testified that a magazine called *The Southern Supposer,* published in New Orleans with an address on Poydras Street, is on the attorney general's list of subversive organizations. Are you aware of that testimony?"

Mr. Corbitt interrupted before Doops could answer.

"Objection! Objection! This witness is not on trial. And there is no way he could have known of this deposition."

"The objection is sustained," the judge said.

"Mr. Momber, I will ask you if you knew, prior to coming into this courtroom, that the magazine for which you work is considered subversive by the attorney general of the United States?"

"Objection," Mr. Corbitt said, not rising.

"Sustained."

"I will ask you if you know a master sergeant named Cleanth Gaines?"

"I once met someone by that name. I did not know him."

"I will ask you if counsel has informed you that Sergeant

Gaines in sworn deposition testified that you once declined an offer to serve your country by reporting on subversive activities while you were a member of the armed services of this country."

"Objection," Mr. Corbitt called calmly. "The witness has no counsel. The witness is not on trial."

The prosecutor argued that he had a right to examine the witness as to his credibility and the objection was denied.

"I recall a conversation with Sergeant Gaines. But at the time it was my impression that we were at war with Germany and Italy and Japan. I declined an offer to spy on Jews. That was the impression I got from Sergeant Gaines. I would do the same again."

"I will ask the court to instruct the witness to answer the question. The question is, did you refuse to honor the request of Sergeant Gaines? Yes or no?"

Mr. Corbitt's objection was overruled and the judge nodded to Doops that he should answer the question.

Doops replied that he had declined the offer, but that he had not disobeyed a direct order of a superior.

"And you would do the same thing again? Is that your testimony?" Doops said that he would do the same thing again.

"Now, I ask you if you recognize these words?" He handed him a single sheet of paper. Doops sat staring at the words on the page, excerpts from the story he had written about Cecelia and Goris and Pieter, phrases and sentences that in context would have been harmless, but in this succession gave a different meaning to what he had written. He glanced at Mr. Corbitt for assistance. When the lawyer asked permission to see the paper, to read what the witness was holding, the prosecutor grabbed the paper from Doops's hand.

"The witness has no counsel. I believe those are your words, Mr. Corbitt. I intend to enter this as an exhibit of the State. You are entitled to see the document at that time. May I continue with this witness, Your Honor?" he said, turning to the judge. The judge appeared baffled by what was happening, but nodded for him to go on.

"Now, I ask you, Mr. Momber, are the words on this sheet of paper your own words? Yes? Or no?"

Doops looked again at Mr. Corbitt, who was trying to phrase an objection but was confused as to what it should be. "They're my words but they're out of order. They're bits and pieces from a longer manuscript I wrote years ago."

"Yes or no, Mr. Momber."

Doops sat in cautious silence looking at Model T, who was whispering something to the lawyer. The court reporter sat with her pad in her lap, glad of a chance to rest her fingers. There was a general murmuring in the courtroom, and the judge tapped lightly with his gavel until it stopped. The lawyer continued to whisper with Model T, still searching for some ground for objection, trying to determine what was on the paper.

"Yes," Doops said finally. "But let me—"

"That's fine," the prosecutor said. "Thank you. Now I will read to you, and to the jury, the words you have acknowledged are your own."

"Objection," Mr. Corbitt said, but tentatively.

"To what?" the prosecutor said, as if he had been expecting it, wanting it.

"Your Honor, I object to something written on a piece of paper being admitted into the record. What possible bearing could it have on this trial?"

"Denied," the judge said. "Counsel may state his objection when he hears what the words are."

"Mr. Momber, gentlemen of the jury, I will read you these words." He raised his voice as he started to read. "The words come from a manuscript written by this witness, an exhibit duly subpoenaed, supplied by the witness's own mother.

" 'We will not kill for them.' " He removed his glasses and faced the jury squarely. "That means they will not serve their country in time of war," he said, holding his glasses to his eyes but not putting them on. " 'We will not baptize . . . '; that is, they will defy the Church as well as the State," he said making a sweeping motion with his glasses. " 'We will not serve on their juries. . . . But it is not for those things that they hate us.' " He moved in close to the jury and waved the paper in the air. "Now listen closely," he said in half a whisper. "These words belong to the witness." He turned the page toward the jury as if to let them read the most unbelievable words for themselves, then pointed his forefinger at them as he read again, pausing after each word. " 'They hate us because of community of goods. We are . . . *der Kommunist! Communiste!* Communist!' " He had moved to the railing of the jury box, his voice booming through the courtroom. "Ladies and gentlemen, those are the acknowledged words of this witness!"

Mr. Corbitt was standing, facing the judge, outraged by what he had just heard but trying not to show it. "May it . . . Your Honor . . . never in . . . " The prosecutor crossed in front of him and was presenting the sheet of paper to the bailiff to be labeled.

"Your Honor!" the lawyer screamed, still not composed. "I move for a mistrial on the grounds that the State has led and badgered this witness, has entered irrelevant, immaterial, and prejudicial evidence and has so poisoned the minds of this jury that they could not possibly accept his testimony as to the character and reputation of the defendant. Your Honor, may it please this honorable court, my motion is for a mistrial." He returned to the defense table and sat down, his hands trembling, his face wet with sweat.

Before the judge could address the jury, the prosecutor was in front of them, laughing loudly as he spoke. "You have just been told that you are stupid. Learned counsel has been to Harvard, so please consider yourselves stupid. Consider yourselves incapable of hearing evidence and weighing it on its merit. Had I known of your backwardness . . . well, I would have moved for a change of venue so that a more sound panel might have been selected." He was slapping his hands on his thighs and the jurors were trying to stifle their laughter as the judge pounded his desk for order.

The judge sent the jury from the room, explaining that there was a point of law that must be discussed.

The two attorneys approached the bench. "Your Honor," the prosecutor began. "Counsel did in fact ask a question and the witness answered. He admitted that he wrote the words on the paper. That is what I wished to establish. The jury could not know what the witness acknowledged unless I read the words to them." Mr. Corbitt tried to interrupt but the judge motioned him to silence and the prosecutor continued. "Surely the defense counsel will agree that it is judiciously proper to establish the credibility of a witness. And certainly I concede that he may establish whatever he wishes in his redirect."

The judge nodded for Mr. Corbitt to speak. "Your Honor, my motion is based on the introduction of immaterial and prejudicial evidence that is so dissembling that this jury, in this day, will be incapable of rendering a fair decision."

"This jury? This day?" the prosecutor interrupted. "What day? How is this day any different from any other?"

"I'll tell you how it's different. It's different because we are in the midst of mass political hysteria. Every man on this jury has heard the live radio and television accounts of Senator McCarthy's witch-hunt."

"Witch-hunt?" the prosecutor countered. "I was under the impression that Senator McCarthy is presiding over a duly constituted committee of the nation's Senate, seeking to protect us from alien ideologies in the Department of State. If counsel's witness shares those ideologies, then it becomes my duty to expose it here in this court. Witch-hunt? Really, counsel!"

"Yes, witch-hunt!" Mr. Corbitt repeated. "And you, sir, are supplying the tinder."

"Gentlemen. Gentlemen," the judge cautioned. "Now here's something for both of you. Mr. Corbitt, I will deny your motion for a mistrial."

"But judge. My client's very life—"

"Hold on. Settle down," the judge admonished him. "I will deny the motion and then you may move to strike. I will sustain such a motion and instruct the jury to disregard the words the witness admitted having written. That seems fair enough to me. Now, what do you say?"

The prosecutor protested mildly, knowing that it really did not matter, that he had made his point with the jury.

"No, sir. Your Honor," Mr. Corbitt said, glancing at Doops, who was straining to hear what they were saying. "It is your decision to make. The defense will not seek remedies in special deals. No disrespect, Your Honor, but we are not here shopping for bargains. We are here in the name of justice, and pray that the integrity of this court might be preserved in the process."

"Attaboy, son," the prosecutor said, slapping Mr. Corbitt on the back. "You'll get over Harvard yet. You're gonna be all right. We'll wait around for you."

"You do that," the lawyer snapped, moving back to the table beside Model T.

When the jury returned to the room, the judge announced that he was denying the motion for a mistrial and that the court was ready to continue.

"Does the defense wish to state an objection, make any other motion at this time?"

"No, sir, Your Honor."

The prosecutor took his place in front of the witness stand. Doops did not move, just sat staring at him the way one might look at the most ordinary object.

"Mr. Momber," he began, glancing over his shoulder to be certain the jurors were all listening. "Those words you wrote, and which I read, they must be very important to you. You wrote them in three languages. And . . . a funny thing. You wrote them as if they were actually spoken in 1549, as if you were simply reporting something that actually happened."

"State your question, general," the judge said as Mr. Corbitt started to stand.

"Mr. Momber," he said sternly, turning to face the jury as he spoke to Doops. "Are you aware that the first written record of the word *communist* being used was in 1785, used then by a French revolutionary and filth writer named Restif de la Bretonne? Were you aware of that? You used it as if it had been a household word two hundred years before it was a word at all. Before it was in anybody's dictionary. And you wrote it in three languages. Yes, it must be a pretty important word in your vocabulary."

Without waiting for Doops to answer, he acknowledged the instruction of the judge not to make a speech, turned back to face Doops, and moved closer to him.

"Mr. Momber, what is your religion?"

"Baptist," Doops replied.

"And will you tell us where and when and by whom you were baptized?" He was smiling as he spoke. "You see, I'm a Baptist too. So is His Honor. Most of the jurors too. We're glad you're

243

one of us. As a matter of fact," he said, interrupting himself, "so is the president of the United States. Does that bother you Mr. Momber?"

"Yes, sir," Doops said emphatically, not hesitating.

"I thought it might," the prosecutor said caustically. "But I daresay the rest of us are quite proud that Mr. Truman is one of us too. But never mind all that. Would you just tell this jury where and when you were baptized?"

"I have never been baptized," Doops said.

"No further questions," the prosecutor said quickly, turning back to his table, shrugging, winking at the jury as he sat down.

Mr. Corbitt moved slowly around the table, stopping directly in front of the prosecutor, facing Doops.

"Well, Mr. Momber," he began. "They have no case against the defendant so they have decided to try the witnesses. I am very saddened by such abuse of this honorable court and I apologize to you."

"Objection," the prosecutor said, getting up.

"Sustained," the judge said. "Mr. Corbitt, please confine yourself to questioning the witness."

"Mr. Momber, will you state the occasion of your writing the words that were read in this court and which have now been labeled and entered as what the State is calling evidence in this murder trial?"

"They were taken from a story."

"And did you write the story?"

"Yes, sir."

"The characters in the story—you were not referring to yourself in the story, were you?"

"Objection. Counsel is leading the witness."

"Sustained."

"Mr. Momber, were you referring to yourself or to any other person in the courtroom?"

"No, sir."

"To whom were you referring?"

"The story is about three people who lived in Holland in the sixteenth century. They were Baptists. They were called Anabaptists at the time."

"Anabaptists. And what happened to them in the story?"

"They were all executed. One by drowning and two were burned alive at the stake."

"By whom?"

"By the government."

"And would you outline to this court what the charges were?"

"Sedition. That was the official charge."

"And what exactly did that mean? What had they done wrong?"

"Objection, Your Honor." The prosecutor stood up and moved to the bench. "Your Honor, we all admire learned counsel's expertise in the field of sacred history. But would the court remind him that this is a court of law. What a bunch of people believed four hundred years ago may be of interest to Harvard scholars but it can have no possible bearing on the heinous crimes of the man at counsel's table. And I doubt if this jury cares to be further enlightened on that subject."

"Your Honor, I believe I sought earlier to make that point, that the words on the paper were not relevant, without success. If the state moves to strike and withdraw the exhibit I will desist in my questioning."

"Overruled," the judge said to the prosecutor. "Counsel will continue."

"What did the people you wrote about believe?" he said again. "What made them different?"

"They did not believe in baptizing infants. And because they did not believe in taking human life, would not go to war. They did not believe in the death penalty, so they were not allowed to serve on juries. They believed that the Church and the State should be completely separate. They would not swear, because they understood the scripture to forbid it. They led simple lives, did not engage in politics. And some of them, a few of them, practiced community of goods."

"And what exactly was that? 'Community of goods'?"

"They had a common treasury. Property and possessions were owned by the community, not by individuals. It was the only way they could survive in times of persecution."

"And that is what you were writing about, is that correct?"

"Yes, sir."

"When you were writing about them, did you believe they were Communists?"

"I believed they were Christians."

"Mr. Momber, the material contained in the story those words came from—was the material a figment of your own imagination? Did you make it up, or did you draw on actual historical data available to you?"

"Some of both," Doops replied. "I always read a lot when I was a boy. Our preacher once gave me a book about how the early Baptists, the Anabaptists, were persecuted. The story drew heavily on that book. But the characters were from my own imagination."

"And do you recall the name of the book?"

"Yes, sir. *Martyrs Mirror.* That was the name of it. I still have the book."

"And will you tell the court how long ago the book was written?"

"Yes, sir. Sixteen sixty. That was when it was written. In Holland. It was written in Dutch. Of course, the one I read was translated. But when it was first written, it was in Dutch." The lawyer stood looking at him, wondering if what Doops had just said would have any meaning at all to the jury, wondering if it would occur to them that 1660 was more than a hundred and fifty years before Karl Marx was born and two hundred and fifty years before Senator McCarthy's time.

"*Martyrs Mirror.* Without an apostrophe," Doops said, looking at the court reporter. "That was the name of it."

"Mr. Momber, you admired the people you wrote about, didn't you?"

"Yes, sir. I still do."

"Do you know anybody like that today? Like they were?"

"No, sir. Not so far."

"And if you found someone like they were, would you ask them to baptize you?"

"Yes, sir."

"Thank you, Mr. Momber."

It was after five o'clock and the judge recessed until the next morning. As the people filed out of the building, going in pairs

246

and small groups to their cars, or walking around the square toward the residential area, most of them were talking about Doops's testimony.

"Where did he come from?" one woman asked another.

"Claughton County," she said. "He is a friend of the Smylie boy. They were all three in the army together, or so they tell me."

"Well, he's plenty smart."

"Smart. Yeah, and crazy," the woman said. "I been a Baptist all my life and never heard anything about the folks he was talking about."

"Me neither. You coming back tomorrow?"

"You bet. This is better than the picture show. I think they might wind it up tomorrow. They're going to put that Smylie boy on tomorrow. That's what I heard."

When Kingston entered the courtroom the next morning, he walked over to the defense table and started to shake hands with Model T, whom he had not seen since the beginning of the trial.

"How's it going, T?" he called.

The deputy grabbed him and spun him around, leading him to the witness chair.

"You're not supposed to talk to anybody until after you testify, boy. Sit down," he said to him.

"I'm fine," Model T called after him.

Mr. Corbitt questioned Kingston briefly about his relationship with the defendant, about Model T's general character, what kind of a person he believed him to be, and something of their war experience. He asked specifically about the time he and Doops had found Model T praying beside the disabled tank before they were going into battle and how he had said he would never kill anybody. He covered everything they had done the night of the murder, when they had picked the girl up, who was there, what was said, where they went, when they took her home. He dealt in detail about exactly how long Mr. Arceneau had been gone, when he went to the store to get the cigarettes for Kingston's mother, the precise distance and how long it would take to drive there and back.

"Mr. Smylie," he asked finally, "do you believe this defendant murdered Angie Simpson?"

"No, sir. I know he didn't."

"Object," the prosecutor said. "That is opinion. Not admissible. Move to strike."

"Motion denied," the judge said. "The jury knows it is opinion."

Before the prosecutor began his cross-examination, he reached into his briefcase and unfolded a letter-size sheet of paper.

"Here we go again," the lawyer whispered to Model T. "Wonder what we got this time."

"Before I begin my questioning, may it please the court, I have here a sworn statement from Dr. Irvin Morton, professor of sociology and anthropology at Pennsylvania State College. I would like to read this document, and then offer it as an exhibit for the State." He paused, glanced at the defense table and then at the judge, waiting for an objection and ruling. Mr. Corbitt did not move, did not speak.

"Let me preface the reading of this document by stating that there is a statute in the state of Mississippi—now I know, counsel for the defense, they don't have this in Massachusetts, at Harvard—but in the sovereign state of Mississippi, it is against the law for white people and colored people to live under the same roof together. The law defines 'colored' as any person having one sixty-fourth of African or Negroid blood. The notarized statement from Dr. Morton of Penn State—Dr. Morton wrote a book on ethnic minorities in America called *Ethnic Minorities in America*. On page 231 he discusses a small group in Frilot Cove, Louisiana, called Redbones. In it he says that it has been established by the finest minds in the field of anthropology that said Redbones are a mixture of Spanish, Indian, and . . . *Negroid*." He stopped completely, looking hard at the jury.

"That's right," a voice in the back of the room said, loud enough for everyone to hear. "Huh," said another one nearer the middle of the audience. A few giggles of agreement and approval came from various areas about the courtroom. The prosecutor raised his hand slightly and the noise stopped. There had been gossip and rumors about the Smylie family during all the years they had lived there, things about Kingston and his mother look-

248

ing like colored people, but no one in the room had ever heard the term *Redbone* before. The expression on most faces was that of someone suddenly having a mystery cleared up, an unexpected enlightenment, a sort of bonus.

Model T was whispering to the lawyer, telling him what Kingston had told him and Doops about his mother and father. When he understood enough of what Model T was saying, he quietly stood up and went to the bench. The prosecutor was proceeding to read the statement as the lawyer approached the judge. The lawyer leaned over and asked the judge for a short recess, told him he had become suddenly sick and needed a recess. The prosecutor was continuing to read from the document he held, reading about the incidence of sickle-cell anemia in Frilot Cove, explaining that it was a disease only colored people had. The judge called him to stop and asked the jury to leave the courtroom. When they were gone, Mr. Corbitt stepped to the far left side of the bench, where he could see the judge, the prosecutor, and the spectators and began to speak.

"Your Honor, ladies and gentlemen." Everyone was leaning forward, straining to hear what he was going to say. Except for the ceiling fan humming over the judge's head and the ticking of the clock mounted at the back of the room, there was no sound. Mr. Corbitt moved in a few feet, took a stand right beside the state flag, which was posted beside the American flag. He began talking slowly, his voice low, saying each word distinctly and deliberately.

"Your Honor, I approached the bench and said that I was sick. May it please the court, I wish to explain the ailment which suddenly afflicts me." He reached down and picked up the bottom end of the Mississippi flag and stretched it to its full length and held it there as he continued. "Your Honor, I love this flag. My family has lived in this state for going on two centuries. They came to these hills from Georgia and South Carolina, came in search of freedom and security. They were here when this state was still a territory. They had been indentured servants from Scotland and Ireland, had worked for seven years in exchange for being a part of this country. My great-grandfather homesteaded a section of land in the Homochitto swamps, cleared it with a broadax and, with his brother, built two houses. The brother fell outside of New Orleans, fighting the British. My grandfather was wounded and almost died at Gettysburg. My father fought as a Marine at Belleau Wood and I at Salerno twenty-five years later. Yes, Your Honor, and General Sikes, I studied law at Harvard. With the money from the GI Bill of Rights I earned fighting for my country, and the sale of a hundred acres of this geography. It was more than half of what my daddy owned. Today my widowed mother makes a living teaching the young of Pitkin County. Let no one say I am not a native son. I know and love it all. From Natchez to Pascagoula. From Moss Point to Corinth, through the red clay hills of Tupelo to the flatlands of Coahoma County and down the river to Vicksburg. I know and love it all. But, old flag . . ." He bowed low, fondling and addressing the flag itself. "In the words of a great Englishman, 'I could not love thee, dear, so much, loved I not honor more.' " He dropped the end of the flag, watching it settle in place, and stood erect, talking directly to the people. The prosecutor sat glowering from his table, the judge making no effort to stop him.

"Yes, my friends," he said, his voice rising. "I am sick. Sick at heart and mind and stomach. And for the first time in my life, embarrassed and ashamed of my own people." He took one step and held up the American flag in the same manner he had held the other one. "I was taught at home and school that one cannot love one of these flags without equal affection for the other. One nation! With liberty and *justice* for all! What happened to that notion? What became of the idea that *all* men are created equal? Where hides the lady who beckoned, 'Give me your tired, your poor,/ Your huddled masses yearning to breathe free,/ The wretched refuse . . .'? Has the torch flickered its last and died forever? I say you nay. The dream lives on. The great American experiment continues. And there is yet honor left in the land. In the midst of bigotry and little minds, it will prevail. Ladies and gentlemen, we have here on trial a poor and powerless little man. A Cajun. That's what we call him. One whose ancestors fled from the kind of tyranny that is this day rearing its ugly head in this courtroom. One whose body bears the horrid scars of war. Mr. Smylie is of complexion dark. So are some of us. His hair is black

250

and wavy. So is mine. Out of his genetic past you are about to see the unruly horse of intolerance parade by you. Watch it well. For one good day you will see that steed no longer. Precisely what some primeval combination of genes might have to do with the matter before us eludes me. But let it be."

The lawyer turned and faced the judge. "Yes, Your Honor, I am sick. But I ask for no notation of exception. I offer no objection. Let the jury return. We will act out the drama."

No one stirred while the lawyer spoke and when he had finished, they continued to sit like wax figures. The prosecutor walked over to where Mr. Corbitt was seated beside Model T. "That was a pretty good speech, son. But you should have saved it for the jury. Those folks out there don't have a vote."

"But you do, general," the lawyer said. "And you have cast it well. Congratulations." The prosecutor chuckled nervously and walked away.

"Does counsel wish to offer any objections? Any exceptions to be noted?" the judge said, as the last of the jurymen took their seats. When Mr. Corbitt did not respond he waited a full minute before indicating that the questioning could continue.

"Kingston," the prosecutor began, his tone somehow different.

"Notice he ain't calling him Mister now," one of the women in the back of the courtroom said, not to anyone in particular.

"That other little lawyer better not neither," a woman beside her whispered.

"How long have you known the defendant?"

"Ten years," Kingston said.

"And how long have you known Mr. Momber?"

"The same time. Ten years. We met in the army."

"And during that time have you been close? Have you continued to visit and keep in touch with each other?"

"Yes, sir."

"You were sort of a clique, sort of a separate little group in the army, is that correct?"

"You might say that. We were special friends."

"All right. And was there any particular designation, any certain name you called yourselves?"

"Well, we sometimes referred to ourselves as 'the neighborhood.' Sometimes we called ourselves 'the community.' Things like that. But it didn't mean anything."

"It didn't mean anything. But you did have a name for yourselves?"

"Yes, sir. Sort of."

"And it was . . . the *community?*" In this *community,* as you called yourselves, did you ever dance together?" Kingston did not answer and the lawyer did not move.

"Great God!" Doops said from the front row.

"Humph!" grunted a man seated right behind Doops.

The judge rapped one time for order, more for his own sake now than for the decorum of the court. The prosecutor moved quickly to his next question.

"And in the community did you kind of look out for each other?"

"Well, like all friends do, I suppose."

"All right. Now I will ask you if you ever pooled your money, so that one of you didn't have more than the other."

Kingston started to tell him about the time at Camp Polk when they were not getting paid and did odd jobs and extra-duty things for the other soldiers, but he was interrupted. "Just answer the question, Kingston. Was there *ever* a time, you don't have to say when, that you pooled your money?"

"Yes, sir."

"And did you refer to it as 'community of goods'? "

"No, sir. Not that I remember. It was just something we did."

"Just something we did," he said aloud, smiling. "Kingston, do you believe in the free-enterprise system?"

The judge eyed the defense table, but Mr. Corbitt did not move. He sat with his hands on the table, his head down. When he did not object the judge turned to the prosecutor. "General Sikes, let's don't get into that again," then swinging around told the jury not to consider that question in arriving at a verdict.

"Thank you, Your Honor," the prosecutor said.

"Kingston, I want you to remember that you are under oath. You doubtless know the penalty for perjury. I want you to answer truthfully. I have but one further question to ask." He walked over and leaned against the railing where the jury was seated, folding his arms across his chest. "Did your father ever tell you that you have colored blood in you?"

The judge began to pound the bench before any noise from the crowd could begin. But except for a few low, almost inaudible sighs, there was no noise. They continued to sit in place, no one moving, waiting for Kingston to reply. Kingston, the judge, and even the prosecutor looked expectantly at Mr. Corbitt. But he did not move, did not object.

"I have never seen my father," Kingston began. And then he told the story precisely the way he had told it to Doops when Doops had found him crying in the forest at Camp Polk. He left none of it out and the audience sat quietly, absorbed in what he was saying. He was not awkward, not excited as he talked. The judge seemed as engrossed in the tale as the others and did not interrupt. Kingston looked at the jurors as he spoke, looking each one in the eye, not embarrassed by what he was saying.

He told them of the trip to New Orleans when he was sixteen, when his granddaddy had told him he was not his father, and about how he had made him drive the new pickup truck onto the ferry and through the New Orleans traffic. He talked about his granddaddy adopting his mother and moving from Frilot Cove to Mississippi when he found out that she was pregnant by his son, and how the girl's father had made his granddaddy stop beating the boy for what he had done. He told them all his grandfather had told him about the Redbone people. Doops sat in the front row of the courtroom, watching him, proud of what he was hearing, yet knowing that the testimony of neither of them had done anything to help Model T. When Kingston finished, he turned to the prosecutor, who had taken his seat at the table. His voice was still calm as he turned away from the jury. He moved to a standing position as he continued. "So no, general. My *daddy* never told me that I had colored blood. My daddy never told me anything. My daddy is one of you."

The people continued to sit solemnly, some of the women fanning with the cardboard fans put there by the Cummings Funeral Home. The prosecutor was watching the faces of the jurors, trying to decide if he should question him further or leave the story alone. The judge had pushed his robe slightly down his back, almost off his shoulders. He was looking at Mr. Corbitt, who had held the same pose throughout Kingston's story. "Are there any motions to come before the court?" he asked, almost pleading.

The lawyer slowly shook his head from side to side, then glancing at the court reporter said, "No motions, Your Honor."

The judge made a note on his pad, a reminder to explain to the jury when he was instructing them that the racial background of a witness need not be considered a factor.

"I have no further questions, Your Honor," the prosecutor said.

Mr. Corbitt continued to sit beside the defendant, still staring at his hands.

"Does Counsel wish to redirect?" the judge said.

"No, Your Honor. The defense rests."

"**W**ell, there you have it boys," Mr. Corbitt said to Doops and Kingston as he drove them home two hours later. "How did you like the witch-hunt?" He had made an impassioned plea to the jury, trying hard to dispel the notions the prosecutor had left in their minds. The prosecutor did not mention Kingston and Doops's testimony at all. He talked only of what the girl's parents had said about her rebuffs of Model T's advances, of his lighter, which was found near the body, of the storekeeper's testimony that they did not see him the night of the murder, of the twenty minutes unaccounted for, and the mother and sister's insistence that Angie never came home that night. He reminded them that she had been disfigured exactly as Model T was disfigured and said that the State had proved beyond a reasonable doubt that the crime committed was a deliberate act of revenge on her and on society in general. He asked them to show no mercy as none had been shown to Angie, and told them repeatedly that the State was seeking the death penalty.

"Will they find him guilty?" Doops asked as they approached Kingston's house.

"Yes," the lawyer said, his voice tired and weak. "They really didn't try Model T. They tried all three of you. And it was an effective device. Perhaps I would have done the same. In law, the name of the game is winning. I was thinking of running against Sikes for district attorney next year. And I could have whipped him. But that's over now. He can have it. I wanted to be governor of this state someday. And I still do. But I won't be. Your friend got to me. God, he got to me. I'll fight them until the day I die. And if they think I learned it at Harvard, fuck 'em. I learned it in these hills. Sikes knew that boy didn't kill anybody as well as you know it. But he'll celebrate the victory. He'll feel fresh and clean inside like a Black Draught commercial, and he'll thank God at his family altar tonight that he was used by Him as an instrument of justice. We lost, boys. Lost. And we'll go on losing for a long time. How one demented senator could come from the same state that produced Bob La Follette and do that to this country is more than I am able to understand. But he has put a Commie under every bed and all the king's horses can't pull them out because as fast as one clears himself, he'll put a dozen more in their place. Mississippi didn't beat us. Wisconsin beat us. Sure, the race thing was part of it. And how long do we have to go on paying? A case in Cummings, Mississippi, is lost because some rich Yankees sold human beings three hundred years ago to some rich Southerners, and because one sonofabitch from Wisconsin says Washington is being run from Moscow. Jesus God! Boys, we're in a heap of trouble."

When he drove up to Kingston's house, he turned the motor off and continued to talk. "Yeah, they'll find him guilty. They've already found him guilty. Oh, we won't give up. We'll go on trying. But whoever said the devil is stupid was bad wrong. We'll appeal. But the judge was pretty clever, too. I really don't believe he made any procedural errors.

"We won't get a reversal on that. I know you thought I just gave up there toward the end, just quit. Well, I did. There were half a dozen valid objections and exceptions I could have made. But I figured the only possible hope for a new trial or a reversal would be on the basis of inadequate counsel. And we'll thank God for *Powell* versus *Alabama*. Shades of Scottsboro. Now ain't that a bitch! When a man's only hope is for his lawyer to do the worst job in the courtroom he can. Jesus God! But that isn't much to go on. No, boys, it's over. Your friend, and now mine, is going to die. All we can do is put it off a while. Fordache Arceneau is going to die."

He draped his arms over the steering wheel and hid his face in them. They thought he was going to cry, but he didn't.

"God damned death," Kingston muttered.

"Yes. He did," Doops said. "And Model T knew it all along." He reached over and squeezed Kingston's shoulder, both of them trying hard not to believe what the lawyer had told them.

18

"**D**r. Jamison is coming up from the seminary to preach on Sunday," Doops's mother said. "Are you going to be back?" Doops was packing to go to east Tennessee to begin a story for *The Southern Supposer.* Kingston was going along for the ride. Since the trial, Doops had tried to write at least one story a week and had made a sharecropping arrangement with his mother so that he would get a larger percentage of the crops. Kingston had moved to Baton Rouge to work for the Ethyl Corporation. He and Doops were saving their money to take the verdict through all possible appeals even though Mr. Corbitt had told them not to worry about the money, that he was going to do everything that could be done whether they paid him or not.

It had been six months since the trial. They had a schedule: Doops visited Model T on Tuesday, Kingston drove from Baton Rouge to Cummings on Thursday evening, and on Sunday afternoon they both went to see him.

"You going to be back?" his mother asked again when he didn't answer.

"I doubt it, Mamma. This story is going to take me through the weekend. There will be services Friday night and Saturday night. They never meet in the daytime. Kingston and I have arranged to see Model T on Monday instead of Sunday. No. I'm sure I won't be back."

"Services? What kind of services? You writing a story about

something civil for a change? Is it a church service?" She asked all the questions all at once, not waiting for him to answer.

"It's a story about a church service," he said. "But it won't be civil. It's a different kind of church. It won't be civil."

"What kind of church? Is it a Baptist church?"

"Naw, that would be civil, I'm afraid," Doops said. "It's called the Church of the Almighty in Jesus Name Amen." As she started to leave the room, he called after her. "They're a cult. They lift up serpents."

His mother did not turn around, walked on down the hall to the kitchen. In less than a minute she was back. The same brown-skinned woman who had worked for them for years was with her. "I just want Ina to hear this. I just want her to hear what you said, where you said you were going." When he continued to throw things in the Gladstone bag he was packing, she moved to the opposite side of the bed, the woman right beside her.

"Ina, do ya'll pick up snakes in your church?" she said in a tone of ridicule.

The woman giggled nervously, pushed her hands out, and moved backward. "No ma'am," the woman said. "I done a lot of things the preacher told me to do. But he better not ax me to pick up no snake. Mr. Doops, you gon' git yoreself killed." The woman was still snickering as she hurried back toward the kitchen.

"You see," his mother said, standing with her hands on her hips. "Not even the most ignorant darkies do that sort of crazy thing. And I've seen them do some crazy things, too, in their church, moaning and screaming and all that business."

Doops did not answer her.

She had not mentioned getting baptized to him since she had made the offer about signing the bond for Model T if he would agree to join the church. Doops knew that she was about to do it now. She moved to the dresser and began helping him with his toilet articles.

"Do you have your toothbrush?" she asked, no longer defiant.

Doops pointed to it in the corner of the bag, wrapped in a washcloth.

"Honey," she said, pleading, placing her hand on his shoulder. "I know you still have it in your craw that I wouldn't put the place up to get your little friend out of jail. But, honey, this place is all we have. Your daddy worked himself to death to make it the good farm it is, to leave it for us. And, well, I just think it was too much to ask to risk it for somebody like that. I mean, you don't ever know what someone like that will do."

"I do," Doops said, moving out of her reach. "I know. But it's all right. I guess I really didn't expect you to know."

"Honey, I didn't come in here to argue with you. I know you think a lot of the boy, know you were in that terrible war together and all that. But have you ever really looked at him? Honey, he looks like something in a carnival. What would somebody like that have to lose? Looking like that and staring the electric chair in the face. I mean, don't you know that he would have just disappeared if we had got him out of jail? And there we'd be, left in the road. I just think you're being unreasonable. And what do you think the people around here would have thought of me, what kind of a woman do you think they would have thought I was, putting my husband's place up for somebody who had done what he did?"

"He didn't *do* anything," Doops sighed, snapping the bag shut and starting to leave the room, his mother following as he headed for the kitchen.

"How can you say he didn't *do* anything, honey?" she said, trying to hide her annoyance. "Twelve of the finest men in that county. They said he did it. They had his fingerprints, honey. And even you said that you couldn't account for the half hour, when he was supposed to have been going to the store. How can you say he didn't do it?" She was talking louder and faster, her face red.

Doops sat at the table and Ina brought him coffee. "You want some more coffee, Miss Christine?" she asked.

"No, Ina. I don't," she said, sitting down across the table from Doops. "But I tell you what I do want."

"What's that, Miss Christine?" She said it as if they had rehearsed the lines before.

"I want this old precious boy of ours here to experience Christ in baptism."

"Yes, ma'am. I reckon you told me that a million times. But I reckon we all gonna do what we gonna do."

Doops's mother looked at her as if she had missed her cue.

"No, Ina. We can do the right thing. We can be baptized and live a Christian life the way you and I do. I've done a lot of things these past few years that I feel good about. I went back to school and finished my education when I was too old to be going to school. And I'm proud of that, proud of the fact that I wasn't satisfied to sit around and be a simple country woman. But the thing that makes me the happiest is to know I'm a Christian. You know Christian people, black or white, are the happiest people in the world. Don't you agree?"

The woman seemed uncomfortable, scampering about the kitchen with busywork, as if she knew what was coming next and dreaded it. Doops sat sipping his coffee, looking through the *Jackson Clarion-Ledger*.

"Now, come over here and sit down at the table with us," his mother said to the woman. "In the eyes of the Lord, you're just as good as we are. I really do believe that. I know you're a Christian because you've been too good to me when I needed you to be anything else but a Christian. I want you to join us in prayer that Doops will accept Christ as his personal Savior and follow Him in baptism. Come on." She motioned to the chair she wanted her to sit in. "Sit down right here with us. Put your paper down, honey." The woman untied her apron, hung it on a nail by the door, and sat down. His mother began to pray the bedtime prayer she had used every night when he was little.

"Now I lay me down to sleep. I pray Thee, Lord, my soul to keep. If I should die before I wake, I pray Thee, Lord, my soul to take."

Doops and the woman said amen but his mother continued to pray. "And our dear heavenly Father, thou knowest all the burdens of our hearts. Thou knowest our deepest secrets."

Without meaning, without thinking, Doops murmured, "Yesss, Lord."

His mother seemed baffled but went on. "Thou knowest the love we have for those Thou hast given us. And, our dear heavenly Father, we are weak, but Thou art strong. Thou canst do all things and without Thee we can do nothing. We pray that Thou wilt touch the heart of the unsaved, and dear heavenly Father, we just pray that they will know no peace until they give their heart to Thee."

260

Doops sat casually but respectfully. Occasionally he opened his eyes enough to see if Ina had her eyes closed. She seemed to be sitting more through duty than participation. His mother prayed by name for several people with minor problems or illnesses. She talked about how we never know the day nor the hour when the Lord would come back to earth, and of the awful day of judgment. "And dear heavenly Father, we never know when we lay our weary bodies in the bed at night if we will wake in the morning. And the traveler knows not what peril lies in store." Once he thought she was going to mention Model T when she began praying for those in bonds, but she was talking about the bondage of sin.

"That shore was a mighty pretty prayer, Miss Christine," the woman said when the prayer was over.

"Thank you, Ina. You know, God does answer prayer. I know that for a fact."

"Yes, ma'am. That's the truth. 'Course, sometimes he answers in funny ways. My old man say he prayed for the Lord to teach him patience and the Lord give him me to put up with." She laughed and slapped her hands as she reached for her apron. She turned back as she tied the strings in place, glancing quickly at Doops as she did. Doops winked lightly, grinning behind his coffee cup.

They were going through Cummings to see Model T before they headed north to the mountains. Kingston picked him up on time and they got to the jail in Cummings a little after ten o'clock. The deputy told them Model T was in the exercise yard and they would have to wait. Only one of the sheriff's deputies bothered to search them anymore when they came, and Kingston said he thought that was more because he liked to touch men's bodies then because he was expecting to find contraband. The deputy on duty let them wait in Model T's cell. Prisoners awaiting execution were kept in a special cell adjoining the office. The cell opened onto a hallway that went the length of the jail. There were no windows and little ventilation, but Model T could see through the front door of the jail when it was open. It was a small room, six feet wide and ten feet long. There was no movable furniture in it. A heavy metal bunk, made of one solid piece, was welded to the steel wall. There was a small washbasin with one faucet and a lidless toilet. When Model T was first placed in the cell, the toilet ran over whenever it was flushed. The only way Kingston could get it fixed was to bring his grandfather's tractor with a front-end loader and dig up the septic tank and feeder lines. He simply showed up one day and did it. When the sheriff drove up just as he was finishing and told him he couldn't do work on county property without authorization, Kingston asked him if he wanted him to unfix it.

The bunk in the cell had a thin cotton pad on it and at first there was no pillow. The sheriff said they could not bring him sheets because prisoners sometimes hanged themselves with sheets. He did agree for them to bring him a pillow.

Model T was cheerful when the deputy locked the door and walked away. He slapped them both on the back, rubbed his hand across Doops's cowlick, which he had cut short again, and teased Kingston. "Which fountain you drinking out of these days?" he asked him. "Whichever is closest," Kingston said.

"Did they give you your cap yet?" Doops asked.

"Not yet," Model T said. "I don't think they're going to give it to me. I asked the sheriff about it again last week. He just laughed. Said, 'You'll get your cap all right.' "

"That lousy sonofabitch," Kingston said. *"Sacré misère!"*

"I guess he's just doing his job," Model T said.

"Yeah, I guess so," Kingston said. "So was Hitler."

"And so was Judas," Doops added.

The cap was the only thing Model T had asked for after they brought him to death row. His sister, Cécile, had sent it to him before they left New Caledonia to go to Guadalcanal. She'd seen an advertisement in a *Grit* newspaper saying that, for selling twenty-four boxes of White Cloverine Salve from Tyrone, Pennsylvania, you could get your choice of prizes. She chose the Chesapeake captain's cap. It was quite ordinary looking, made of white twill with a black bill and band around it. She bought three of the boxes of salve herself with money she had made helping their daddy pick moss and gave them to school friends for Christmas presents. A Syrian merchant in Mermentau bought the other twenty-one boxes when she went to his dry-goods store and told him that she wanted to send a cap to her brother who was overseas. Model T treasured it and kept it with him wherever they went.

The day they brought the cap to the jail the sheriff said he would have to look at it, that men on death row were required to wear clothing issued by the jail. He said he was not sure that he wanted to set a precedent by letting him have the cap. When Doops questioned him on just what sort of a precedent he would be setting by letting Model T wear a ship captain's cap, the sheriff said he had to take unusual precaution with men sentenced to die because there was always the possibility that they would try to kill themselves.

"Just leave it here with me. I'll look at it. I have to make sure there isn't a poison needle in it, dope, nothing like that. Just leave it here." But he never gave it to him.

"Don't worry about the cap," Model T told them. So they talked about trivial things and then about Mr. Corbitt's motion for a new trial. Model T said that if the storekeeper and his wife would come to the jail to see him, he was sure they would change their testimony. Kingston asked if he would take the oath if he did get a new trial. He and Doops had agreed that his refusal to swear on the Bible had hurt him with the jury.

"Oh, no," Model T said. "Couldn't do that. I'd have to do it the same way again. I told them everything I knew. If they didn't believe me then, they won't believe me next time."

"And why the hell not? You crazy coonass," Kingston said. "Why can't you *swear* you're going to tell the truth? You know you are."

"I told you already," Model T said. "I read the Bible. And it said not to swear. Remember that book?" He grinned at Doops and did his awkward wink. "That's one of the ones we read in the hospital when we were waiting for Doops. Remember? It said not to swear."

"Look," Kingston said, his voice a mixture of concern and pride. "The Bible says a lot of things. It says let your conversation be yea, yea and nay, nay. Now, when we're talking you don't just sit around babbling, 'Yea, yea. Nay, nay. Yea, yea. Nay, nay.' Jesus! They'd haul you out of here and take you over to Whitfield in a straitjacket. Talk to him, Doops. This crazy coonass wants to help them bastards kill him." Doops did not answer.

Model T moved to the cell door and faced the hallway, holding on to the bars with both hands. "Maybe he shouldn't have given me the book," he said, shaking the bars slightly as he spoke. "The other book, I mean."

"Book? Which book? I've brought you a hundred books. What book?"

"You guys ever do this kind of exercises?" Model T asked, pressing his hands toward each other. "One of the deputies took a Charles Atlas class. He told me how to do them. I do a lot of them these days. Clears the head."

Doops sat on the far end of the bunk, his head down, still saying nothing.

Kingston moved beside Model T and leaned backward against the bars, trying to see his face. "What book?" he asked again. "What the hell you talking about? What's come over you, T? Where's the coonass boy from Mermentau I used to run with? What book you talking about?"

"Doops's book," Model T said, almost matter-of-factly. "You know . . . Cecelia. The book he wrote. I guess I've read it fifteen times since the prosecutor gave it to me. I asked him for it one day when he was here to see the sheriff and he sent it to me. Said he was supposed to give it back to Doops's mamma."

He turned around and looked down at Doops, who continued to sit with his head bowed. "They were up to something, Doops," he said, sitting down beside him. "Those folks. They were up to something. I guess it never hit me before. I mean, when the nurse read it to us that time on the beach, I just thought it was pretty words. I liked it but I thought it was because you had written it. I would have liked anything I was so glad we were back together." He reached under the bunk and picked up the crinkled and faded manuscript and held it on his lap, snapping the wide rubber band that held it together. "They knew something, Doops," he said. "Those folks knew something. And you know it too, don't you."

"One of us does," Doops said, his voice sounding faraway. "But I'm not sure I'm the one."

"It's a good book, *mon ami*," Model T said, placing the manuscript in Doops's hands. "I'm glad the nurse didn't let you burn it. I've read a lot of things now. Since you birds came along and told me there were things in the world besides muskrats and Jax beer." He stood up and began to pace the length of the cell. "You've been good teachers, neighbors," he said as he walked back and forth. "Real good teachers. And I appreciate it. I just wanted to tell you."

The deputy came to the cell door and told them it was time for them to leave. "Two minutes," he said, tapping his billy club on the bars as if playing a xylophone.

"We'll see you on Monday," Kingston said. "When we get back from Doops's holy-roller meeting. That's if we don't get snake-bit." He spoke as if he had not heard what Model T had said to them.

Model T sat down and motioned for them to sit down beside him. The deputy was waiting to unlock the door for them to leave. "You want to hear something funny?" Model T said.

Neither of them answered.

"They're talking about killing me for rape." He whispered so the deputy could not hear him, leaning over to Kingston and then to Doops. "And I'm still a virgin."

When he saw that they were not going to answer, he began to laugh, nodding for the deputy to unlock the cell.

"Now all I have to figure out is whether I'm a wise virgin or a foolish virgin."

"I think you trimmed your lamp," Doops managed to say, still not laughing.

"I guess we're going to have to talk about it," Kingston said as they walked toward the car from the jail. They had never discussed the possibility of it actually happening.

The closest they had come to talking about it was the day the judge pronounced the sentence. After the sheriff had led him back to his cell and Doops had come in to see him, Model T stood up and faced him squarely as he entered.

"Will you go with me?" he asked, a seeming acceptance in his voice.

"Yes," Doops replied.

They had embraced and turned to talking of other things.

"This thing is starting to hit me," Kingston said to Doops as they were driving out of town, heading for Tennessee. "Looks like time is running out on us. I mean, good God! We can't let it happen to him."

"We'll keep doing everything we can. That's all he expects from us," Doops said.

"The thing that tears my guts is that he doesn't even expect *that* from us," Kingston said, looking back until the jail faded from sight.

"Get the map," Doops said. "You'll have to navigate. I've never been farther in this direction than Corinth."

It was late afternoon when they left the U.S. highway in Sanborn, Tennessee, and asked directions to the village of Zion Mountain. Doops's editor had told him that the preacher's name was Edward Vinsang and that he worked at a cannery in Zion Mountain. He was friendly and would let them go to the service. The editor wanted a story on primitivity in America.

Primitivity? Doops thought. "Primitivity in America," he mumbled, thinking of Model T.

They found the preacher operating a forklift at a little cannery built beside a mountain stream. He remembered the exchange of letters with Doops's editor but said a lot of things had happened since then and he was not sure what the service would be like that night. He was cordial enough, but a bit suspicious too.

"You boys ain't from the government, are you?"

Doops showed him his press card, explained to him that they had their own problems with the government. He told him about Model T and when he finished, the man got off the forklift, closed the doors of the big tractor truck he was loading with cartons of canned string beans, and motioned them to a darkened area in the corner of the big warehouse. He sat down on a stack of wooden pallets and began telling them of his own troubles, appearing to trust them fully.

"Three weeks ago tonight. That's when they come in and arrested me and Brother Busby. He's from North Carolina and was in here preaching a revival for me. They busted right in on us while we was worshiping and praising God, handcuffed the two of us together and hauled us off to jail. Wouldn't even let us finish the service or tell our women folks good-bye. 'Course, we was just in jail overnight, but if a body can't pray to his God in a free country . . ." His voice trailed off and he gazed into the last of the mountain sun.

Doops, making rapid notes on a small pad, asked him why they arrested them.

"Well, we believe in the Bible. We read it and whatever it says we believe." He pulled a small New Testament from his shirt pocket and began to read.

> And these signs shall follow them that believe; In my name shall they cast out devils; they shall speak with new tongues; They shall take up serpents; and if they drink any deadly thing, it shall not hurt them; they shall lay hands on the sick, and they shall recover.

He closed the little book gently and put it back in his pocket, stood up, and began prancing around where Doops and Kingston were standing. "Now we believe that. And we practice it. But they got a law in this state that says you can't pick up snakes, which we don't do in the first place for the Bible don't say nothing about snakes. It don't even mention snakes. It says 'take up serpents.' Anyway, this law says you can't do that and you can't tempt or harass anybody else into doing that. Of course, we don't do that neither. I never preached a sermon in my life when I didn't warn the people, when I didn't exhort them in just the direct opposite direction. I tell them not to touch them deadly devils until they are anointed by the Spirit to lift them up 'cause they will flat kill you. But that's what they arrested us for. In court I told the judge that. He told us he would just let us go with a fine if we would promise not to handle any more snakes. I told him we didn't handle snakes, that we took up serpents. Like the Bible says. The Bible don't mention snakes. It says serpents. And I told him we don't do that unless we are anointed by the Spirit. He sent this feller, the bailiff I think you call him, out to get a dictionary. Said, 'Now boys, let's us see what Mr. Webster says *anoint* means.' Then he read out of the dictionary and then said, 'Now boys, that's what Mr. Webster says *anoint* means. Is that what happens to you before you do whatever it is you do with the snakes . . . the serpents?' I said, 'But judge, we don't live by Mr. Webster. We live by the Bible. And we already know what anoint means.' Well, he got powerful mad then and that's when he sentenced me to thirty days in jail and Brother Busby to twenty days. I don't mind telling you I can't afford to spend no month in jail. I got a family to feed and if I don't work they don't eat."

"Don't you get a salary from the church?" Doops asked, continuing to write on the note pad.

"Oh, nosirree. We don't hold with that. That was when the trouble started with most churches. When they started paying one another to preach and pray. When they started talking about 'full-time Christian service.' Can you tell me how in the world somebody can be in part-time Christian service? Either you're saved by the blood of the lamb or you ain't. And if you are, well, then you're saved full-time. You can't be a Christian part of the time and a heathen part of the time. That's like saying I'm Edward Vinsang part of the time and somebody else the rest of the time. I got to be Edward Vinsang all the time, for that's who I am."

Doops had stopped writing and was following him around the area as he talked, listening, studying his person. "But Paul and Silas went to jail for preaching the Gospel," he went on. "And I don't reckon we're any better than they were."

"Why did you say you don't know what kind of service you will have tonight?" Doops asked him.

"Well, I said it because a lot of people around here are scared. I mean folks don't know what to make of it when the law comes in their church houses and drags their preachers off to jail. But we'll be there. Brother Busby will be back and I'll be there and my family will be there. I can't predict how many people will come but the faithful ones will be there all right. So y'all come if you want to."

Kingston had moved to the pallets. "Will you be picking up any . . . lifting up serpents?" he asked.

The preacher came over and sat down beside him. "When somebody tells us they're telling the truth, I believe them," he said. "You say you're not from the government and I believe you're not from the government. But that's the same question a deputy came out here and asked me yesterday. He brought some papers, said it was an injunction. Said the judge sent them. He read it out loud to me. Like I can't read. My mamma said I was a-readin' before I went to school. Anyway, what they said was that if we lift up serpents while the case is going through the appeals, we'll be in contempt of court. I'm going to answer you the way I answered him. We're going to do what the Spirit leads us to do. And that's all I can tell you."

"Look, Brother Vinsang," Doops said. "I don't want to do anything to disturb your service. I respect you. I respect your beliefs. And your rights. If our coming to the service will be in any way unsettling to any of your congregation, will be disruptive in any way . . . well, we just won't go. I don't have to write this article. We can get back in the car, go over the mountain, and forget it."

The preacher walked over and put his hand on Doops's shoulder and looked him directly in the eye. "You saluted me as 'brother.' When a man does that I know that he is after the truth. And that's all we want. There has been a lot of lies told about us in the newspapers. And on the radio. In Third John we read, 'For I rejoiced greatly, when the brethren came and testified of the truth that is in thee, even as though walkest in the truth.' That's all I ask. That you walk in the truth, that you write the truth you find in our midst. No sir. You won't interfere. Some folks say because our little church is way down at the very end of a mountain trail we hide out to worship. Well, we built it there because one of our members gave us some land and that's where the land was. Some folks have to walk across the mountain to get there or drive thirty miles around on the road to get to a place that ain't no more than a mile from where they live. The county won't build a road so we can get in and out and then they say we hide out. You see what kind of lies I'm talking about."

The man told them how to get to the church and said he would be on down as soon as he went home and cleaned up. Doops drove past the First Baptist Church of Zion Mountain and turned at the second road to the right, the way the preacher had told him. Just before that road came to a dead end at a row of tobacco barns, there was a descending wagonway veering to the left. They followed it across a shallow ford and Kingston opened a barbed-wire gap stretched across the trail. Doops told him the man had said to leave it open.

The church was a small, one-room structure with buckeye siding of random widths and lengths. There was one door at the front and the wooden shutters were propped open. There were no glass windows. There was a graveled parking area but theirs was the only car there. Doops turned around and parked the car so that it was heading back in the direction they had come from.

"Think you might want to be the first to leave?" Kingston said.

"Never can tell," Doops said.

Above the door was a neatly painted sign: THE CHURCH OF THE ALMIGHTY IN JESUS NAME AMEN. The pulpit was a slanted stand made of the same wood as the siding on the building. It was on a slightly elevated stage. On one side of it was a quart bottle half filled with a clear fluid.

"That'll be strychnine," Doops said.

"How you know?" Kingston asked him.

"And that one will be arsenic," Doops said, pointing to a glass jar on the other side of the pulpit.

"How the hell . . . uh . . ." He glanced quickly about the room. "How you know that?"

"I've read about them," Doops said. "And didn't you hear the preacher read to us? 'If they drink any deadly thing, it shall not hurt them.'"

"You're shitin' . . . whoops . . . you're kidding me!" Kingston said. "You telling me they actually drink that stuff?"

"So they tell me," Doops said. "My first trip, too."

"And my last," Kingston said. "What the hell . . . God damn it . . . I keep forgetting we're in a church house. Let's get out of here."

"I've got to get a story. Got to write about primitivity in America. Well, here it is. I can't leave until it happens."

"I don't mean for always. I just mean let's get out of here for right now. So I can talk right. I keep forgetting where we are, that we're in a church house."

"That's because you're a bigot," Doops said. "Bet you wouldn't forget if you smelled incense."

They walked back outside and stood beside the car.

"Looks like it's going to be a slim congregation," Kingston said.

"Can't tell yet," Doops said. "The preacher said they didn't start at any certain time."

They heard talking from the direction of the main road and several people moved into view. When they saw the car and Doops and Kingston standing beside it, they stopped walking and stood silent, watching. Then a car pulled alongside the little group and the driver said something, and they began to move on in the direction of the building.

"That must be the preacher," Doops said. The car drove to the door and parked. Preacher Vinsang walked toward them carrying two small boxes crudely constructed of pine lumber and glass. "Don't be nervous," he said, smiling at them. "They can't get out. These in this box never had a handle on them."

They could tell the boxes were heavy and he dropped them clumsily on the ground. Both of them looked at the box closest to them. Through the glass they could see a coiled and tangled mass of slithering, glistening, tremoring diamondback rattlesnakes.

"Those folks left their cars somewhere else," he said, ignoring the continuous buzzing of the rattlers inside the cage, motioning to the group continuing to move toward them. "Don't want the law to be gettin' their tag numbers. I told them who you were. Be more coming along soon and we'll get started."

He picked up the two cages and moved through the door.

"What the . . . what does that mean? Never had a handle on them?" Kingston asked when he had disappeared.

"Means no one has ever handled them before," Doops said. "I suppose that's what it means. I told you it's my first trip too. I guess it means they have never been lifted up."

They watched as several other small groups drifted down the hill. A few cars, moving almost as cautiously as the pedestrians, pulled onto various spots about the parking area. A panelbody truck with *Cherokee Plumbing* lettered on the side drove off again after three men got out, two carrying guitars and one a double bass fiddle. Doops and Kingston continued to mull around in the shadows of the trees, listening to the men tuning the instruments inside. When they heard them singing, they moved

271

inside and sat on one of the benches about halfway down the single aisle.

> "Canaan land is far away
>   Will I see you there?
> There will be so many joys
>   You and I will share."

"I could improve on those lyrics," Doops whispered to Kingston, who looked confused. They played in peppy ragtime, their voices sometimes a whole beat behind the music. Doops wondered if Kingston had ever attended any kind of religious service other than Catholic and what he was thinking. The preachers sat in the front row with the congregation. There were several ladder-back chairs on the platform but no one sat on them. There seemed to be no particular order to the service. Sometimes the people sang along with the band and sometimes they sat and listened. A few clapped their hands with the rhythm of the music but most of them seemed subdued. For nearly an hour, the singing continued, the enthusiasm mounting gradually as they went along. Occasionally one of the preachers would jump to the pulpit and say a few words, speaking of the lack of unity in the church. And of coldness. Once they stood up together and talked to each other, meaning for the people to hear what they were saying.

"You know, a fellow, I believe he was a Methodist, asked me the other day if we lifted up serpents before the sermon or afterwards," one of them said, laughing loudly.

"And I wonder if you told him what I would have told him," the other one said.

"Yeah, I bet I did. I told him we don't have a printed bulletin that's sent to the printer on Tuesday for next Sunday's service. You know what I'm a-talking about!" he screamed to the applauding congregation. "They'll have all this fancy stuff. Processional. Call to Worship. Invocation. Or whatever they call it when the preacher gets up and reads something out of a book. Congregational Hymn. Offertory. First Lesson. Second Lesson. Responsive Reading. And all that. Sermon. Recessional. Prayers of Intercession. All that. I just told him, 'Now brother, we don't write it down in advance because we don't know what the Spirit has in mind for us to do until He leads us to do it. We don't have printed on a piece of paper Processional, Call to Worship, Hymn, Sermon, Lift up Serpents! We lift up serpents when the Spirit of the living God tells us to lift up serpents! Not when some elder or bishop or pope tells us to. You know what I'm a-talking about out there!" Most of the people were on their feet, laughing, clapping their hands, and some dancing in the aisle.

"Don't you think we ought to clear out of here?" Kingston said.

"Not yet," Doops whispered.

Doops wondered how he would respond if they really did start handling the snakes and passing them around the room, for snakes had been one of his worst fears as a child. He had expected the service to be pitched at a much more frenzied level and wondered if they were subdued because of his and Kingston's presence. Or perhaps because they feared the officers would come back.

One of the preachers invited the worshipers to come forth and give their testimony. Some of them told of being delivered from drunkenness, from various illnesses and vices. One woman said the Lord had rescued her from certain divorce and restored her husband's love. Her husband, a very bald and very fat man with no bottom teeth, stood beside her, holding her hand. There was more handclapping, cheers, and cries of "Amen!" "Praise God!" and "Hallelujah!" but still not the frenetic outpouring that Doops had anticipated. The other preacher asked if there were any sick in their midst who desired to be healed. A few came forward with an assortment of minor complaints. The preachers placed hands on their heads, exhorting them to total and unconditional belief, chiding the demons that possessed them to depart, and then declaring them whole. But this too seemed stilted and routine, if not downright contrived.

But then it happened. A slender woman of about forty had moved out of the congregation and seated herself at an old upright piano with yellowing keys and no front panel. The band moved in around her. She was wearing a full-length velveteen dress, solid white with half-sleeves and a close-fitting collar that covered her neck completely. Her hair was a moderate brown, gathered in two half-buns over each shoulder. She paused for a moment as she sat down, opening and closing her hands, stretching her fingers. As she began to play, the movement of her fingers, hands, and arms gave a stroboscopic effect, moving from one end of the keyboard to the other in rapid succession. She followed her hands with the upper part of her body, leaning to the left as her fingers moved, her torso stretching as far as her arms did. Then swaying back to the right as her hands moved to the opposite end of the keyboard. Doops did not recognize what she was playing and the people did not sing. Only Doops and Kingston remained seated. The others were shouting, sighing, dancing in place, their bodies divested of all control, their cares released.

As soon as she started to play, a young man who looked no more than twenty ran to the raised platform and flipped open the two cages, threw his head straight back so that he could not even see inside, reached his hands into each of the boxes, and when he stood up he was holding three of the snakes in one hand and two in the other. The three in his right hand were cottonmouth moccasins. The other two were rattlers. There was a sort of faraway, glazed look in his eyes. It was not fear. Nor was Doops afraid as the man strolled up and down the aisle, passing a few feet from where he and Kingston remained seated, flinging the serpents over his head and waving them round and round, occasionally clutching them to his chest, sometimes looking at one or another as he exposed his neck and head to their fangs. The sounds coming from the congregation now were indescribable, aspects of rushing water, the whimper of a newborn baby, the fury of a tornado, the fragility of a lullaby, the frenzy of a giant airplane about to leave the ground.

"But judge, we don't live by Mr. Webster. We live by the Bible." The words kept running through Doops's mind.

"Great God!"

The young man with the snakes was the center. Sometimes some of them formed a circle about him as he moved. The woman at the piano continued with the same tune as when she began. Suddenly the music stopped as if by some prearranged signal. When it did the young man let one of the moccasins slither from his hand onto the floor, and one of the rattlers onto the huge Bible resting on the pulpit, then dropped the others in the box. He kicked his unlaced shoes off and stood victoriously, massaging the lengthy spine of the cottonmouth with his toes. The big rattler lay on the open Bible, moving only its tongue, a rhythmic in-and-out oscillation possible only among the cursed ophidians. There was no more music, no shouts, dancing, or handclapping in the aisle. Only the silence. The man began to speak.

"They say it takes music for us to do this—what I been a-doing." Apparently he was not unmindful of the skeptics who tried to explain their behavior. "Well there ain't no music now. And look at them!" He spoke slowly and softly. "Only God can do that. I can't do it. You can't do it. *Them things'll kill ya!*" he screamed. "Only God can do that. I can't. You can't. That's the devil lying there. Oh, he won in the Garden of Eden. But just like God said, 'Upon thy belly shalt thou go, and dust shalt thou eat all the days of thy life.' Look at the devil eat the dust and go on his belly. Oh, he's powerful all right. He's strong. And he's dangerous!" He reached down and picked up the moccasin again, leaving the rattler wriggling in place. "But he's second best. But *look out!*" He jumped straight at the congregation, all seated now, exhausted. "Look out," he said again, whispering. " 'Cause he *is* second best. He's the next most powerful thing to God. But just look at him now. He's helpless. He didn't bite me and if he had of, it wouldn't of hurt me. He's conquered. The devil is conquered. *Hallelujah! Hallelujah! Hallelujah!* " The people were on their feet again, shouting with him.

He flung both snakes in the box, secured the latch, and sat down. As soon as he did the woman at the piano stood up, moved forward, and began to speak. She wandered in and out among the congregation, not looking at the people, up and down the aisle, giving the impression that she did not care if they saw her, heard her or not.

> "Ah 'ach ma hah moora, ay *doopsgesinde*
> andorra ay ach-ah ha moora
> Ammtee muhr ah had melah, ay *doopsgesinde*
> ah nahah mahah murch *doopsgesinde* mahlan."

At first Doops tried to write down the ciphers. But as the tongues continued his pen dropped from his hand to the floor. Kingston picked it up and tried to hand it back to him but he did not move to take it.

"You getting the symptoms?" Kingston asked him.

"Afraid so," he muttered panting heavily.

"Let's go," Kingston said, taking him by the arm and standing up.

As they moved toward the door, Doops stumbling along behind, some of the people smiled and waved cordially. The same young man was speaking again as they left the building.

"If they take me to jail tonight, for being here tonight, for doing what I'm a-doing tonight, they can keep me there forever and I won't pay no fine. I ain't got no fine money for Caesar. I give my money to the Lord. If they come and put a padlock on the church door tonight while I'm a-sleeping, I'll come saw it off in the morning and go on confirming the mighty acts of God like the Bible tells me."

Kingston pushed Doops into the car and got in on the driver's side.

"You feeling better?" he asked, driving away. "You look like a ghost."

"Maybe I am," Doops said.

"No, you're not. Now tell me how you feel."

"I feel like I just learned something I never knew before."

"Like what?" Kingston snapped. "Hell, I was scared of those vipers. What the devil did you learn in there?"

"My name," Doops said. "But never mind. Drive this thing. We have to get back."

"You mean tonight? What's the hurry?"

"I've got to get Model T to baptize me. It's time for me to get baptized."

Kingston answered him but not right away.

19

"**I**s this everybody now?" the sheriff asked Doops as the prosecutor and the judge edged their way into Model T's tiny cell. "I still think this is damned irregular. You want me to lock the cell, general? Or leave it open?"

"It's your jail, sheriff," the district attorney said.

"But he's your prisoner," the sheriff said, trying to be casual.

"Not anymore," the prosecutor answered. "I finished my job with him. So has the judge. You're the only one not done."

"I know," the sheriff said, hurrying down the hallway, leaving the cell door open.

"I still wish you would stay," Doops called after him.

"No thank you, Mr. Momber. I appreciate it, but I think I better not stay."

"You sure you don't want to do it in the courtroom?" the judge asked when the sheriff had disappeared. "There's a lot more room there. And the sheriff said he would send a couple of his deputies with us. Seems to me it would be a lot more dignified."

"That's still up to Model T," Doops said. "He's in charge."

"What about it?" the judge said, looking at Model T.

"No, sir. Holy things ought to be done at home. This has been my home for a long time now. And I guess it is going to be for a while longer. Holy things ought to be done at home."

The judge and the prosecutor were trying to move about the cell but there was room to do little more than shift from one foot to another. Doops had asked them to be present and they had agreed.

"Where are you from?" the prosecutor said restively to the woman standing beside him in a stiffly starched nurse's uniform.

"Rhode Island," she said, moving slightly away from him.

"Rhode Island?" he said. "You came all the way from Rhode Island for this?"

"Yes," she said, somewhat shortly.

"What for? I mean . . . you know these boys?"

When she did not answer, Doops said, "She was my nurse in the war. Her name is Williams. She knows us well."

The prosecutor turned to the judge, shrugged, and said nothing more.

Kingston and Mr. Corbitt stood at the foot of the bunk, saying nothing. Three prisoners sat on the edge of the bunk, all of them handcuffed together. There had been four but one had been released that morning. The prisoners knew no more what to make of what was taking place than the judge and the prosecutor.

"Wonder why his mamma didn't come," one of them whispered.

"I don't know," the one in the middle answered.

"I heard she wanted it done in church," the third one said.

"I heard she don't think it's a baptizing," the first prisoner said.

Doops and Model T moved to face each other squarely. The others moved closer together, leaving them as much room as they could.

"You have shown me the truth, my friend," Doops began. "Now I am asking you for the sign." He spoke in a clear, eloquent, and oratorical fashion.

"Are you asking to be baptized?" Model T said with equal fluency.

"Yes," Doops replied. "I am asking for the sign."

"Are you heartily sorry for all your sins?"

"Yes."

"Do you desire the baptism?"

"Yes."

"Who will forbid me, that I should baptize him?" Model T said, looking around the room at the group.

"No one," Kingston, Mr. Corbitt, and the nurse said in unison.

"No one," the three prisoners mumbled in hushed tones after them.

"Humble yourself before God and His Church and kneel down," Model T said. Doops, wearing seersucker trousers and a new white shirt with the collar unbuttoned and the cuffs turned up, knelt as close to the small washbasin, already filled with water when they came in, as he could get. Model T cupped both of his hands together and dipped into the water.

"I baptize you in the name of God the Father," he said, letting the water trickle over the tips of his fingers and onto Doops's bowed head. "God the Son," pouring another handful of water. "And God the Holy Spirit," the water running off Doops's cow-licked head, down his back, and onto his shirtfront.

Doops stood up, making no effort to dry the water from his face and clothing. The judge and prosecutor edged their way toward the open cell door. All the others formed a circle around Doops, embracing him, the prisoners joining in the embrace as best they could with their hands cuffed. The judge and district attorney moved back in and shook Doops's hand.

"Did I read your story to *them?*" Miss Williams whispered when she was the only one still embracing him. "Or to *us?*"

"It was always *us*," Doops replied, not surprised by her question.

"Then it can be more than two or three?"

"It can be everybody in the whole wide world," Doops said, holding her tighter.

"Why didn't you tell me that then? And that night on the jungle floor?" she asked, returning the tight embrace.

"Maybe I didn't know it then," Doops said.

"It's a long way from Bethlehem, isn't it?" Kingston said as they drove away from the jail.

"No," Doops said. "Not really. That's as close as we'll ever come."

The baptism was over.

20

"You know where we have to take him, don't you?" Doops said.

"Yes, I know. We'd better get started."

Kingston had waited in the whittling room of the new courthouse. He had told Doops that he would wait there because the room was never used. In the old county courthouse, the older men used to sit on the benches in the hallways, and on the steps when the weather was fit, and whittle cedar sticks all day. They called it "going to the office." They would be waiting when the building was opened in the morning and did not leave until it was closed. Each one would leave behind a bushel of the finely curled cedar shavings. Some of them called the little curled shavings "angel pubics." The courthouse officials complaind about the litter and some of the merchants on the square accused the old men of looking up the women's dresses as they got out of their cars. When the new courthouse was built, a boxlike room with no windows and one door was put in the very middle of the building. A solid concrete bench lined the four walls. The day it was dedicated a special part of the ceremony was reserved for the whittling room. The old men went to the door and watched the proceedings, listened to the preacher pray for them, but did not go inside and never went back, sitting after that on the curbs around the building, whittling as they had before.

Once Doops, Kingston, and Model T had been in a state-line tavern near Pearl River and Kingston told the story to a down-and-out guitar picker who sat at the bar playing songs he had written. He sang for drinks and whatever anyone left on the bar beside him. He said that for a dollar he would write a song on any subject. "You ought to write a song about that," Kingston said after he had told him about the whittling room. "We'll give you three dollars. Won't we, T?" Model T said they would. The man said he would write it for nothing. On the door of the tavern a sign written on a piece of butcher paper read SID PLAYS TONIGHT. They had seen him there several times before. There was always the same quiet, dark-haired young woman with him. Occasionally when he finished a song, he would pause, look at her, and say, "Huh Debbie?" She sat alone in a corner, watching him sing, and no one ever bothered her. They said someone bothered her once, that Sid had taken time out from his picking to explain to the molester that he had made a mistake. They said that no one ever bothered her again. The bartender said she was his sister. When someone came in and said, "Sid who?" she would reply under her breath, "You'll know soon enough." The man took a dingy and ruffled notebook from his guitar case and sat down beside the woman. She looked over his shoulder as he wrote. In a few minutes he came back to the bar and started to sing, looking directly at the three of them.

> "Kingston still walks by the courthouse
>   When he's out taking his stroll.
> But the one he is seein' ain't what he remembers.
>   There's concrete where grass used to grow.
>
> "There ain't no more trees and benches out back
>   Where the horses used to be tied,
> Fannin' the flies, in the cool of the evenin'
>   While the old men whittled and lied."

When he reached the chorus he dropped to a lower key and his voice, which had been singing with a timbrel quality, boomed with a steady baritone. No one moved as he sang.

281

"Well, the young men plan for things better
Like the old men had in their day;
But sometimes the plan for the progress of man
Just don't seem to work out that way."

He moved back to his high tenor as he went into the next verse, still picking the deep blues.

"The young planners planned in seclusion;
    The old men hoped it was fair.
The young men wanted a whittlin' room!
    For the old men who wanted the square—

"Now the young men live in their future.
The old men live in their past;
But some men who plan for the progress of man,
    Live with their heads up their ass."

The tavern was filled with cheers and applause at the last line, then quieted again when they realized he had not finished. The woman sat quietly through it all, not moving, her face showing no feeling at all.

"So there in that new courthouse lobby,
    The whittlin' room was unveiled,
For men like ole Doops and Kingston and T
    Who'd just as soon whittle in hell."

The man moved from the barstool and dropped the guitar to his side and held it in a precise parade-rest position as a soldier would a rifle. He recited the final dolorous words in a whisper, looking at the people. They strained to hear him, the woman watching from the table, the guitar quiet.

"So it's a big empty room, full of brand-new spittoons,
And benches the old men ignore.
A tourist attraction of concrete and steel,
And the old men don't whittle no more."

282

No one applauded as the man handed the crinkled sheet of paper to Kingston, placed his guitar in the case, and walked into the night, the woman close behind him.

It was the first time Doops ever felt old. Now, as he walked into the whittling room the stranger named Sid had written about, he felt a lot older than he had then. Kingston did not move when Doops entered the room, just continued to sit on the long concrete bench, his hands folded in his lap, legs stretched to their full length, his chin resting on his chest, eyes closed. Doops came over and sat beside him but did not speak.

After a few minutes they stood up as if on a given signal. That was when Doops said, "You know where we have to take him, don't you?" And Kingston had replied, "Yes, I know. We'd better get started."

They left the building in silence, walked out the back door to where the station wagon was parked, and Doops eased it around the corner without turning the headlights on. He backed up to a cement ramp that led to the side door of the jail.

They walked down a wide hallway between a long row of cells. The hallway was a flurry of reporters and photographers. Flash-bulbs blinded them as they walked toward the end of the hall where the sheriff was talking to the newsmen. The reporters fired questions at them as they walked. "How do you feel Kingston, Mr. Momber?" "Will you ever say if you have been a Communist, Mr. Momber?" "Do you still believe that he was innocent?" "Do you wish you had gone to a colored college, Kingston?" "Is it true that you lost your job with the magazine?" "Have you talked to the girl's father? Don't you have sympathy for them?" "Were any of Arceneau's people here tonight?" Neither of them responded to the questions.

The sheriff stepped out of the circle as they approached, the reporters close behind him. "What can I do for you boys?" he said.

"We have come for the body," Doops said.

"The body belongs to the family," the sheriff said, reaching in his back pocket. He took a sheet of paper out of a folded envelope and began to read. It was typed on the official stationery of the sheriff's office.

TO THE STATE OF MISSISSIPPI, COUNTY OF THURSTON, OFFICE OF
THE SHERIFF:

This gives you the authority to bury the remains of our son,
Fordache Arceneau, following his death, at a time and place of
your own choosing, the expense of such interment to be borne
by said state or county, or both.

He read the message hurriedly but making sure all the reporters
could hear him. His voice was quivering, the paper trembling in
his hands. When he finished, he held it to one side so that Doops
and the newsmen could see it.

"Now, you'll notice that this is a legal and official document,"
he said, his voice calmer now. He pointed to the letterhead and
the date on the notary-public seal.

Doops reached inside his coat pocket and handed the sheriff a
short white envelope. The sheriff opened it and read the words,
but not aloud.

TO WHOM IT MAY CONCERN:

This gives permission to Claudy "Doops" Momber and/or
Kingston Smylie to claim the remains of our son, Fordache
Arceneau, and to conduct a memorial service at a time and
place they may select and to bury the deceased wherever they
may so choose.

"Who wrote this?" the sheriff asked, handing it to a deputy
who stood beside him.

"I did," Doops said.

"Oh, that's right, you're a writer. I'm sorry. I forgot," he said,
winking at one of the older reporters.

"Who wrote yours?" Doops asked.

"The district attorney did, that's who," he snapped, winking at
the reporter again.

"It doesn't matter who wrote them," Doops said. "What mat-
ters is who signed them."

"Well, it looks like you got a document, and it looks like I got a
document. But, I'm the sheriff of this county."

"Yes, sir. You're the sheriff of this county. And you have a document and we have a document. But there's just one difference. Our document was signed two days ago. And yours was signed two months ago. No disrespect, Sheriff Higgins, but we've come for the body of Mr. Fordache Arceneau."

The reporters were listening carefully to every word, flashbulbs going off from every direction.

"What's in the other letter?" several of the reporters asked at once.

"I'll have to show it to the DA," the sheriff said. "I can't show it to you now."

Doops took several typed, but unsigned, copies of the letter from another pocket and began passing them around. The district attorney had come in and was standing directly behind the sheriff but had not heard the exchange.

"There's the DA," Doops said to the sheriff. "We've come for the body," he said to the prosecutor.

"What's the trouble, sheriff?" the DA said, moving in closer.

"No trouble, general," he said. "These boys here just still want to stir up some trouble in my county." He handed him the letter Doops had brought, then stood mumbling in his ear as he read it. When the DA finished reading and studying it, he put it in his pocket and motioned for Kingston and Doops to follow him to his office.

"If I ever catch them boys in my county again without important business, I'll move them sombitches from here to Jericho," the sheriff said to the newsmen as the three of them walked out of the jail and started for the courthouse.

The district attorney sank down behind his desk into an overstuffed swivel chair. He opened the envelope and read the document again, holding the notary seal up to the light and rubbing across it with his fingers.

"Why do you boys want to do this?" he asked, rocking back and forth in the chair. "I mean, what's your angle now? What are you trying to prove? Why can't you just leave well enough alone?"

"Well enough?" Kingston said.

"It's just something we have to do," Doops said. "We don't have an angle. We're not trying to prove anything. We just want to have a service for our friend."

"I can understand why you don't like me. I guess I was pretty rough on you fellows. And you heard me say a lot of harsh things about your friend. But that's what the good people of this state pay me to do, to prosecute criminals. I do my job the best I can. I know I make some people mad. But you shouldn't take it out on the good people of this county. They've been through a lot in this case. She was a good girl. From a fine family. Don't you think we ought to . . . well, just let things settle down a bit? I mean, there'll be a nice, dignified service for Mr. Arceneau. The chaplain from Parchman has already made arrangements. And if you boys want to attend, want to bring some flowers, I'm sure that it will be more than all right with the chaplain. Might even let you say a prayer. Whoever you pray to."

Doops and Kingston sat looking at him, not answering.

"By the way," he said. "You say you've come for the body. What do you plan to do with it? We have a hearse waiting. We've bought a casket. You know there are some pretty rigid statutes in this state about decency, propriety, and doing certain things, like burying the dead, with some dignity. You planning to take the body in that station wagon I saw by the jail? Well, you can't do that."

Neither of them answered.

"And the state has to do an autopsy. The body has to be embalmed. It's a state law. Any person who expires in a state-operated institution, no matter what the circumstances, well . . . the law was originally written, intended for mental patients, indigents, charity cases, things like that. But there are no exceptions made in the statute. So there has to be an autopsy on everybody. And it's part of our contract with the undertaker." He shifted uneasily in his chair, pouring water from a tall silver thermos.

Doops eyed the engraving on it as he poured: *Blue Room, Roosevelt Hotel, New Orleans.* "Of course, the coroner does the actual autopsy," he said, sipping the water.

Kingston looked at Doops, his expression a mixture of incredulity, revulsion, and amusement. "Autopsy, Doops. Autopsy. Understand?" He spoke with dubiosity and offense. "That's to determine cause of death."

When Kingston spoke, the DA's face flushed red with rage.

"Look, boy . . . uh, son. Now, don't you get cute with me. Now, you're not the most popular commodity in this county right now and I guess we both know why. Now, that doesn't mean a thing to me. I mean, I deal with what's the law. I don't make it. I enforce it. Far as I'm concerned, all the rumors about whether you're a . . . about, uh, what you might be . . . this or that . . . that doesn't concern me one way or the other. And I'd defend your rights just the same . . . just as quickly as I would the whitest . . . same as I would anybody else. But don't go getting cute with me or I'll haul your tail into court and cite you for contempt."

Kingston leaned forward as if he was going to answer, but Doops motioned with his hand for him to keep quiet.

"And another thing. You fellows claimed to be such great friends of that . . . of . . . of the deceased. And you claimed to be such believers, though I never could quite pin you down on just what it is you believe. . . . Now I never said in court, and I'm not saying out of court, that you're Communists. And, God knows, I don't have anything against Catholics, but in my Baptist church, and I know that's not the only church, we're taught to have respect for the dead. And hauling somebody's remains around in a frazzling pickup . . . station wagon, well, that isn't showing much respect for the dead."

"Yes, sir," Doops said. "And no disrespect to you, general, but maybe we have more respect for the dead than some people have for the living. We just want to do what we have to do. And we'd rather do it with your cooperation. We've come to claim the body of Fordache Arceneau."

They stood up to leave and the DA followed them to the door. "Thank you for your time, general," Doops said.

"Yes, sir," Kingston added. "Thank you very much for your time."

"By the way, general," Doops said. "Not trying to hoe your furrow or anything, but I've searched the statute, too. It doesn't say there has to be an autopsy. It says there has to be an inquest."

The prosecutor blocked the door with his arm and stood facing them.

"Look, fellows." He turned and walked toward his desk but before he got to it, he came back and put his hand on the doorknob, pulling it completely shut. There was a long pause as the prosecutor stood there with his hand holding the door shut. Then he put his arm around Doops's shoulder and pulled him toward him. "May I ask you a question? If you object, I'll play judge and sustain you. I just been wondering about something." He held Doops tightly in the half embrace. Doops wished he would not touch him. "Why did you invite me to your service? I mean . . . why? I haven't been able to bring it into focus. I mean . . . hell, I'm the bad guy in this. Church is for good folks. Why did you want me there?"

Doops answered without hesitating. "The wind bloweth where it listeth."

"I think that means church is for folks, period," Kingston said as the prosecutor dropped his arm from Doops's shoulder, shaking his head.

"You guys ever hear of plea-bargaining?" the prosecutor said. Both of them nodded that they had. "Well, it's the criminals who're supposed to do that. So that's not what I'm doing but . . ." He walked over to the window and looked out, his gaze sweeping in all directions, came back and opened the door slightly, looking up and down the hallway.

"Look. I'm in the middle of this term of court. Arceneau is not the only murderer I have to convict. I won that case and I won it good and I won it fair. I have no regrets. Now, there's a statute in this state against body snatchers." He went to the window and peered out again. "I'm damned sick of this thing. Now, I'm not saying you won't get caught. All I'm saying is that I'm the one who has to take a case before the grand jury. And that's all I'm saying."

Neither of them answered. Kingston pretended not to be listening and Doops stood facing the DA squarely, studying his countenance.

"This might surprise you, Mr. Momber. But in three years at Ole Miss Law School, I was the only man there who belonged to the American Civil Liberties Union." He lowered his voice and glanced quickly over his shoulder as he spoke. "Times might change a man, but a man can't change the times. But I try. And I'm going to be gov— going to be a leader in this state in some most difficult times ahead."

288

He stepped to the side of his desk, picked up his briefcase, and followed them into the hall. He stopped at a new shiny water cooler and pushed the pedal down with his foot, letting the stream of water flow over his brow and eyes.

"Like I say," he said, drying his face with his handkerchief. "I'm the one who takes a case to the grand jury."

They were moving away from him toward the exit. They heard him whistle to them and turned around.

"Or I'm the one who doesn't take a case to the grand jury."

As soon as they were outside, they saw a hearse moving slowly away from the jail. "That's not from Cummings," Kingston said. "They're taking him to Jasper. That's from Jasper. I know that guy. Go get the wagon. We can beat him there." He stepped back into the shadows while Doops hurried around the building to get the station wagon.

The sheriff was leaving the building with two state troopers when Doops walked up the ramp.

"Okay, son. The show's over. The press is all gone and they've taken him to the funeral home. You can go home now."

Doops slid behind the wheel without answering.

"You drive," Doops said as Kingston stepped out of the darkness. "You know where we're going."

"No big hurry," Kingston said. "He'll take the highway. They don't like to get mud on the carriage. I'll go through Otis Springs. We'll beat them there by ten minutes."

"Did he suffer much?" Kingston asked after they had driven out of the lighted streets and picked up the rutted gravel road moving south. Doops started to answer but couldn't. He was trying hard to blot it all out, to deny that he had actually seen what he had seen, to so concentrate and commit himself to the mission they were about that he could ignore the vision fashioned and fastened in his head. All the things that Model T's one eye told him in that final minute, those sixty ticks of the official timepiece, filled with all satanic residuum. An interminable forever when the world stopped utterly and death stepped aside until one execrable click on a dial decreed that yesterday is today and time can resume with the pilfering of Genesis by the downward stroke of a human hand.

The final minute of waiting had been worse than watching the dying itself. Because the death warrant said that he would be executed on May 18, it could not be done until it was at least one minute past midnight. The final preparations had gone faster than they had rehearsed them. The two deputies had strapped his arms and legs to the big chair made of four-by-four timbers. Then they had buckled the electrodes to his calves, placed the cap soaked in wet acid on his head, and secured it with a strap under his chin.

It was the cap with the wet acid dripping out of it and the electrodes hanging from all sides that bothered Doops most of all. The sheriff had been so inflexible in his refusal to let Model T have the little sailor cap his sister had sold White Cloverine Salve to send him. That's what the sheriff was talking about, he thought, when he told him, "You'll get your cap all right." That's his cap. *Sacré misère.* Doops tried consciously to faint, to pass out. Then he tried to induce the symptoms. He could do neither. I'm not sure I want to be this strong, he thought.

"*Sacré misère. Sacré misère.*" He whispered it over and over as the deputies tightened the strap under Model T's chin. Vinegar and gall. It was the first time he really knew what it meant. *Sacré misère.* Creation in retrograde. *How are the mighty fallen in the midst of the battle! O Jonathan, thou wast slain in thine high places. I am distressed for thee, my brother Jonathan: very pleasant hast thou been unto me: thy love to me was wonderful, passing the love of women. How are the mighty fallen, and the weapons of war perished! O brother of Cecelia, brother of the world, fly away. Come quickly, my sister. Claim your own joint heir. Even so, come, quickly.*

When the deputies stepped back and looked at the sheriff, who was sitting beside the executioner, the official clock showed exactly twelve o'clock. The sheriff began to count each second aloud, holding his right hand above his head until he reached sixty. It was during that minute, from the time all was in readiness until the sheriff dropped his hand, that Doops could see the words from Model T's eye, an eye fixed indelibly and resolutely and finally on Doops. He noted in that moment that Model T was not shaking his head from side to side. Either he sees it all now, or he hears it all now, Doops remembered thinking. Doops had never experienced visible sounds before. What he could hear was like words from a record in a doll's belly. What he could see was not the words themselves but depictions of what they said. I am helpless and you are helpless. I love you and you love me. I love life and I am about to die. You can do nothing, and I can do nothing. My life is ending. There is a pool. There is a river, the streams whereof shall make glad the city of God, the holy place of the tabernacles of the most High. The heathen raged, the kingdoms were moved; he uttered his voice, the earth melted. The Lord of hosts is with us; the God of Jacob is our refuge. There is a river. There is a pool. Selah.

"It was quick," he said finally.

Neither of them spoke again as Kingston drove the twelve miles to Jasper over the rough and muddy back road. It was starting to drizzle when he pulled out of the light shining from the loading dock at the back of the funeral home and parked under the branches of a large sweet-gum tree. They had been there less than a minute when the hearse made the turn around the building and backed to the door. As the driver opened the rear door of the hearse and started to pull the slender cart with the corpse on it, the small wheels making a scraping sound, they walked toward him.

"We have come to claim the body of Fordache Arceneau," Doops said, stopping on the side of him where the most light shined.

The startled driver stepped back, pushing the corpse back into the hearse as he did. "I don't want any trouble," he stammered, quickly closing the door and securing the latch.

"There is no trouble," Doops said calmly and reassuringly. "We have a legal document. We are friends of the deceased, his family. His mother and father are not here. We are here in their place. I am sorry if we frightened you. If you would help us load the corpse we would be much obliged."

"But I . . . I . . . I'm just doing my job. I work for Mr. Delaughter. I . . . I . . . I . . . you better call him."

"If you wish," Doops said. "But it is quite late. We don't want to get you in any kind of trouble with him, calling him this late and all. We have a document here. And we have just come from Cummings. We talked to the sheriff and the district attorney. You had gone already when we got back to the jail for the body." He spoke as one with authority, one with uncontested jurisdiction.

Doops unfolded the letter and handed it to him. "I . . . I'm by myself here. I'm just supposed to put him in the cooler till morning. And I don't have my glasses. My reading glasses. I don't need them to drive. I'm just the driver. I don't have nothing to do with anything official."

"It's all right," Kingston said, patting him on the shoulder. "Mr. Momber will read it to you if you want him to. We talked to the district attorney. If it's the money you're worried about, tell Mr. Delaughter to just send the bill to me. He knows my daddy. I'm Kingston Smylie."

Kingston began opening the door of the hearse and as he did Doops read the letter in the same composed, calm manner in which he had spoken.

"Here, you'd better keep this copy," he said. "Just give it to Mr. Delaughter in the morning. Of course, if you want to call him now, we'll be glad to wait."

The confused and frightened driver took the letter and put it in his back pocket.

"You're very kind to help us," Kingston said, continuing to pull the cart out, motioning for Doops to open the back window of the station wagon and let the tailgate down.

"One dying and a burying," Kingston said casually, motioning with his head for the man to lift the other side of the cart. They placed the cart on the ground behind the station wagon. Kingston leaned over, picked the limp body up, lifting it under the knees and arms, and pushed it through the opening, sliding it forward on the metal bottom, which was the back of the folded-down rear seat.

"Thank you very much," Kingston said, closing the tailgate and starting to roll the window up. "Guess I better give you this," he said tugging at the blanket which was over the corpse.

"No, no!" The man said, grabbing Kingston's hand and pulling it back through the window. "You can have it! I mean, it goes with the body! Uh . . . O shit, mister. It belongs to you. Don't take it off! It goes with the body!"

"Don't forget to give the letter to Mr. Delaughter," Kingston said warmly, shaking hands with the bewildered driver. "And tell him to forward any expense he might have had to me."

292

They both got in, and Kingston pulled slowly out of the driveway, leaving the man alone beside the hearse.

"Why we going this way?" Doops asked as Kingston headed toward Cummings.

"Because they won't be looking for us in this direction. If they're going to chase us, they'll cover every road except this one. They don't think we're stupid enough to go this way. And they for sure won't look for us in my granddaddy's shop."

"We're going to your house?" Doops asked.

"Yeah. To get the box. I made a box for him. And to lay him out. I have his clothes there."

The clock on the dashboard showed two-thirty.

"Turn the radio on," Kingston said, gaining speed as they drove out of town and hit the same gravel road they had come in on. "Get the Jackson station. It's the last number to the right."

Doops turned the volume just loud enough for them to hear, at the same time moving the needle as fast as he could with his right hand.

"That's it," Kingston said as the static stopped and the clear channel sounds of WJBX became louder.

"That clock must be fast," he said.

Ernest Tubb was singing "Walking the Floor over You." The announcer faded it out before the record finished, gave the call letters and the time, and read a Jitney Jungle grocery commercial as the clacking and stuttering of a simulated teletype machine sounded in the background.

"Almost two years ago, Angie Simpson, a twenty-year-old white woman was brutally raped and murdered in rural Thurston County. Her body, nude and mutilated, was found beside what local residents described as a popular lover's lane. Fordache Arceneau, a thirty-year-old white male from Mermentau, Louisiana, was tried and convicted of the crime. At exactly one minute past midnight this morning, he paid for that crime by dying in the state-owned electric chair in the sleepy little town of Cummings. A spokesman for the sheriff's office said there were no incidents and that everything had returned to normal in Thurston County.

"Meanwhile, Senator James Eastland, commenting on yesterday's Supreme Court ruling—" Doops switched off the radio.

"Well, at least we didn't make the news," he said. "At least not yet."

"That means they won't be looking for us," Kingston said.

"Or else it's a trick," Doops said. "Let's don't bet on it. But I guess it depends on whether or not the general can handle the sheriff."

"Yeah, the high sheriff is going to be plenty mad. But he won't know it until morning, and by then we'll be clean gone."

"Let's don't bet on it. Drive this thing."

Kingston shut the lights off as he turned onto a narrow dirt lane leading to a structure made of corrugated roofing, with no windows. A wide double door was open and he pulled the station wagon inside. When he had closed it, latching it from the inside with a piece of galvanized pipe that slipped into a larger piece, he stumbled around in the darkness until he found a switch on the opposite side of the door. The building was bigger on the inside than Doops had remembered. Various pieces of farm equipment, two tractors, a combine, a flat-bed two-ton truck, heavy disk harrows, and planters were lined neatly in the center. Light equipment and tools of all kinds appeared to have their own individual places. Underneath the pickup reel of the combine was the box. It was made of old barn lumber, heavy oak boards twelve inches wide. The coarse grains were a dull gray, rotting in places, fatigued by wear and time and weather. The boards ran up and down, not lengthwise, nailed to an inner structure made of new pine two-by-fours. A lid running half the length of the box and hinged with thick pieces of harness leather was swung open. A small pillow with *Panama City, Florida*, and a picture of a tarpon printed on it was tacked on the bottom of the box at the very head. Kingston had brought it to Model T after he had taken his mother to Florida soon after they came home from the war. They used to tease him about it because he took it with him from place to place. It had been at Kingston's house since the night he was arrested.

The box did not look like a casket on the outside, more like a bin for storing grain.

"Why don't you wait outside?" Kingston said. "I can do this part. You did the other."

"I'll help you," Doops said. "None of it is very pretty. But nobody is running for champion. I'll help you."

A few feet from the box was a green oilcloth which had once been a table covering. Beside it was a five-gallon bucket filled with water and a small basin. To one side were towels and washcloths, and a new bar of Lifebuoy soap.

Kingston opened the back of the station wagon and pulled Model T's body toward him, then lifted it in the same manner he had from off the cart at the funeral home and placed it on the tablecloth. Model T was not limp, as he was before, but his arms and legs still dangled and his head fell back when Kingston picked him up, the thorax making a deep bubbling sound.

"Why don't you wait outside?" Kingston said again, not taking the blanket from the body. "You watched him die. I can lay him out."

"We will do it together," Doops said. "It wasn't your fault they wouldn't let you go inside."

"You're not going to have one of your symptoms, are you?" Kingston asked, trying to manage a smile.

"I don't do that anymore. You know that."

"You mean . . . since . . . after . . . he . . . uh . . . after . . ."

"Yes. After the baptizing. I don't have the symptoms anymore."

A fawn-colored milk cow in a nearby lot had stood calm as a statue, silently chewing her cud when they drove in. Now she was bellowing and snorting, pawing the ground and trying to jump through the fence. "She's smelling death," Kingston said, matter-of-factly.

Kingston took his knife and began slitting the trousers from Model T's body, starting with the inseams, which were torn already to allow the deputies to fasten the electrode straps. As he did, Doops unbuttoned the prison shirt. They had heard the revolting stories of involuntary bowel and kidney actions and had prepared themselves for what they might find when they removed his underwear. But his body was clean. Except for the slight swelling on his arms and legs where the straps had been tightened, and a blackened, almost charred, area on his shaved head and around his face, there were no marks on his body.

Kingston lathered Model T's entire body, trying to scrub the seared coloring from his head but failing. The water beaded on the scar tissue as it would on cellophane and neither of them made any effort to wipe it off. Doops moved behind him with another cloth, rinsing the suds with clean water from the bucket. When they finished, they each took towels and dried every part of his body, sponging the excess water from the oilcloth as each towel became wet.

Kingston went to the cab of the truck and came back with a pair of pajamas. At first Doops was shaken at the sight of them. The colors and printed patterns looked like a Polynesian sarong, a caricature of the most absurd, a funereal outrage bordering on sacrilege, even to Kingston himself. Yellow, orange, pink, white, and royal blue. Starfishes, tiger heads, and buttercups.

"Think these'll do?" Kingston said.

"Yeah. They'll do just fine. But where in this world did you find them?"

When they had him dressed and lying in the box, his hands down by his thighs, they stood at one side of the box together looking down at him. They had made no effort to close his eye and mouth. The big scars which had continued to contract and dry and tighten over the years, looking now like old parchment, would not conduct the electricity and glistened pink in the light, outlined by the darkened skin and tissue surrounding the sunken areas, skin and tissue killed by the heavy charge of power as quickly as his eye and ear had been killed by the charge of the land mine. They knew that it was time now to cry, but they didn't.

"Shall we try to close his eye?" Kingston said.

"Can we remove the scars?" Doops replied.

"No," Kingston said. "But that's what he saw with."

Doops did not answer. He wanted to say, "He wasn't shaking his head at the end," but he couldn't.

"Something just doesn't seem right about him," Kingston said. "There is something else, one more thing that we're supposed to do."

They stood for several minutes saying nothing, not taking their eyes off his face.

"I know what it is," Kingston said finally. "Remember how he would never go anywhere at all with his shirttail out? No matter where. Even if he was wearing a sport shirt, T-shirt, or whatever. Playing ball, working outside, anything. He always had to have that shirttail tucked in." Doops crossed to the other side of the box and together they stuffed the buttoned pajama jacket inside the pants. Kingston tied the drawstring into a neat bow.

"Okay, T," Kingston said. "Now it's time to go." He closed the lid and fastened it with a piece of baling twine he had attached to the top, wrapping the twine round and round a short nail he had driven in the side. Both of them stepped back.

Then there was one minute of ineffable pain, which they shared.

21

"**I** think we ought to cross the river at Saint Francisville, on the ferry," Doops said.

"Why's that?" Kingston asked.

"Well, if we cross at Baton Rouge, on the bridge, they have that Department of Agriculture booth there—you know, asking if you have any live plants. Or animals. Sometimes they search the car. Maybe we ought to cross on the ferry."

It was four o'clock and Doops turned the radio on again. Except for the time, it was the same broadcast they had heard before. Doops turned it off when the announcer began to talk about Senator Eastland's response to the Supreme Court's decision.

"Reckon we'll ever find out how the senator is going to save the South?" Kingston asked.

"I doubt if we ever will," Doops said. "What time you think we'll get there?"

"The way I figure it, about three this afternoon. We'll be driving slow, of course."

"That's a good hour," Doops said. "Where we going to get a boat?"

"Already got one," Kingston said. "In Grand Chenier. That'll save us some time too. We won't go through Mermentau."

"You think you can find the place?"

"Know I can. Went there two days ago. When I drove down to rent the boat. After I got the letter signed and all."

"Is everything still there?"

"Everything. It's exactly the same. Exactly."

They reached the Saint Francisville ferry a few minutes before five. It was a clear morning and they could see the ferry pulling away from the opposite side of the river. Though there was no fog and no traffic on the river, they could hear the long plaintive bass horn as the boat moved along, and when it drew closer, the bells.

"Anybody on it?" Doops asked.

"Looks like two cars and a pickup on this side. Maybe more on the other side. Can't tell yet. No one on there going to be looking for us, though."

"How you know?"

"They'd wait on the other side. They won't be looking for us. Couldn't arrest us on the high seas anyway."

Kingston had thrown the spare tire, sundry tools, and some burlap sacks on top of the box, giving the inside of the station wagon an extemporaneous appearance. When the ferry docked and the last of the vehicles, seven in all, drove up the one-lane ramp, the attendant motioned for them to move forward.

"Looks like we're going to have it all to ourselves," Kingston said, looking behind him through the side mirror. He maneuvered the station wagon onto the deck, and the attendant pointed him to a position in the middle. The captain reversed the engines almost immediately and started to back away as soon as the man had pulled the last of the big manila hemp ropes off the pilings that jutted up from each end of the dock.

Both of them got out, stretched, and walked casually to the stern, watching the big paddlewheel churning the water. They noticed the man glancing occasionally into the back of the wagon as he went about his duties. He worked his way in their direction and asked them if they had a match.

"Got a lighter in the car," Kingston said, walking over and pushing the dashboard lighter into the socket, reaching through the window. When it popped out he handed it to the man, who stood looking hard at the box. He lit his cigarette and reached through the window, putting the lighter in place himself.

"Going fishing?" he asked.

"No. Not right now. Going to Cajun country. Maybe later. Just messing around."

"What you got in the bin?" he asked, moving back to the window.

"Seed," Kingston said quickly, glancing at Doops.

Doops flinched, then smiled as he thought about Kingston's answer. The man walked away and began to get ready for another docking.

"You think he had heard something?" Doops asked after they found the highway to New Roads.

"Naw. Just being friendly. And curious. Not everybody who pulls on that ferry has a big oak bin with them."

"Well, anyway," Doops said. "You told him the truth."

Kingston did not answer, just continued to drive, watching the speedometer and looking behind him often through the rear mirror.

"Seed," Doops said reflectively. He spoke with approbation and pride and satisfaction. "Yeah, seed," he said again, wiping his eyes. "And God is sludge. Lordy mercy." He sighed deeply and leaned his head out the window, the bugs stinging and sticking to his cheeks.

From New Roads they drove along the west bank of the river for several miles, sometimes atop the levee, where they could see the tugs pushing the long barges loaded with oil and rice and cotton bales, and big seagoing vessels moving north and south. When they turned back west on a narrow macadam road that led to Livonia, Doops asked about Model T's family.

"Do they still think he did it?"

"I'm not sure they ever thought he did it. They were just poor, confused, ignorant moss pickers. I don't think it was because they didn't want to help him. They just didn't know how to go about it. They've never been out of those swamps. I don't think the mamma has ever been further from home than Mermentau. And daddy no further than Lafayette, drunk to get nerve enough to go that far. Can't half speak English. Living in a houseboat on a few dollars a week. Pitiful. I don't think they thought he did it. They wouldn't ask that question any more than we would. They just didn't know how to go about doing anything."

"Did you ask them if they wanted to bury him?" Doops asked.

"When the constable brought them the paper giving the sheriff authority to bury him they thought they had to sign it. Thought they had to sign it because the priest had told them the Church couldn't bury him. They were helpless. They don't understand any of it. Pitiful. That's all. Just pitiful."

"Where in hell all these people coming from?" Kingston said. They were meeting a solid line of traffic—cars, some old, some new, pickup trucks with homemade campers on the back, old school buses with the yellow partially painted over to indicate that you didn't have to slow down for them anymore.

"Going to Baton Rouge," Doops said. "Leaving the pirogues and trotlines and muskrat hides, the little piece of ground their papa left them where they used to raise enough sugarcane and sweet potatoes to get by. Going to work for Mr. Standard Oil of New Jersey, Mr. Kaiser of California and his aluminum plant. Baton Rouge has a television station now. They'll have to have a TV set or their kids will get behind in school. Be culturally deprived. Have to have one of the big high aerials to draw in New Orleans too. Electricity to run them. Cars to go buy what they tell you to buy and money enough to do it with." He rolled the window down and stuck his open hand out the window, letting the wind bump it against the side of the car. "No more Cajuns," he said. "It won't be a world for Model T."

"How long you reckon he would have made it without a Social Security card?" Kingston asked.

"Oh, he would have made it. They never would have got him. But they don't make them like that anymore. He's the last of the Model Ts. V-eights from now on. V-eights."

In order to resurface and widen the U.S. highway, sacked by the dealings and commerce of war and the Louisiana maneuvers of World War II, the giant live-oaks, with Spanish moss hanging low enough from their boughs to touch the travelers passing underneath, had been cut down. Already they were being replaced by fast-growing, but short-lived, mimosa and willows.

"Nobody expects anything to be around for very long anymore," Doops said, commenting on the mimosa sprigs and the way he remembered the old live-oaks.

"Why don't you stop and let me drive awhile?" Doops said. "You've driven the whole time."

"You got the roughest duty," Kingston said. "Take a nap. We'll stop in Grand Coteau, if you're awake. Get us a dope. Some gas too."

Cankton, Ossun, Sunset, Duson, Rayne. Villages and small towns, some without a traffic light, places along the ride. As Doops dozed and nodded, Kingston drove in silence, thinking his own thoughts, thoughts he generally did not speak, leaving words to Doops and others, content to know what he knew.

"Thirty more miles and it'll all be over. . . . No more Model T, Doops, and a half-ass Redbone. . . . No more neighborhood. . . . Just passed Pecan Island. Thirty miles from Pecan Island to Grand Chenier. Thirty miles of desolation. Brand new road . . . big LeTourneau earth movers on tank tracks still here. . . . Man said some of the women threw their aprons at them when they passed . . . didn't want the road. . . . No more mail boat . . . mail boat brought them thread and things from the store . . . post office department mail rider can't do that. Mail boat came twice a week—Big Al Fontenot had it. Folks on the bayou paid him . . . little extra sometimes when he had to walk to the drugstore to get their medicine. . . . Earth movers tore up the bayou . . . messed up the fishing . . . pushed down big trees. . . . Looks like Guadalcanal the day we got there. Crying my ass off in the middle of the woods . . . ole Doops Momber . . . gave me his handkerchief . . . I know the feeling, neighbor. Fordache Arceneau . . . standing by the bulletin board . . . *Ton parle!* I don' understan' dat, me . . . *Poo yie!* Ah got tuh say you somet'ing, me . . . Ah pick de moss, trap de nutria, t'ings like dat. . . . Mop the floor, coonass boy. . . . Two dogs caught in a muskrat trap . . . saddest thing I ever saw . . . five pennies and two dimes in a roadhouse urinal. . . . *Sacré misère* . . . Returnable souls . . . no throwaways . . . two cents apiece . . . Model T . . . I wouldn't hurt little Angie . . . I love Angie Simpson . . . *Salut Marie, pleine de grâce.* . . . Sherman tank for an altar. Shithook lieutenant. . . . Going to DeRidder to find some Japs . . . we never knew the porter's name . . . kept T's money. Mine, too . . . wouldn't bet with the others . . . guess he knew it all. Wonder where my daddy is right this minute . . . Wonder if he thinks about how he never saw me? Community of goods. Don't even know what it means. Love thy neighbor. Miss Christine . . . Get baptized . . . who'd do it . . . *Doopsgesinde*. Know my name and got to get baptized . . . Father, Son, and Holy Ghost. Virgin with his lamp trimmed. Ah t'ink it's time to open de club, me. . . . God is sludge . . . sweet loving brothers . . . *Sacré misère*. Twenty-five more miles."

"They tell me Mr. LeTourneau gives ninety percent of everything he makes off those things to the Lord," Doops said, rubbing his eyes and pointing toward one of the dirt movers beside the road.

"Good for him," Kingston said. "Wonder what the Lord does with it? Dirt movers for Christ. *Poo yie!*"

Doops stuck his head out of the window for a moment and let the wind blow against his face. "How much farther?" he asked, rubbing his eyes.

"Not far," Kingston said. "Maybe ten miles. Not sure. Why?"

"It's starting to hit me," he said. "I guess last night the overload switch took over. When it was all happening so fast. There's only so much you can carry. Like packing feathers on a mule cart. It comes on gradually and it looks like he will go on pulling forever, no matter how many you pile on. But then you throw a goose on the wagon and he stops. He doesn't pull anymore. You take the goose off and he still doesn't pull. I guess we've known for two years that it was coming to this. That one day we would be driving down this road. Going where we're going." He leaned his head back against the seat and closed his eyes again. "I'm just not sure I can make it."

"You remember the first words you ever said to me?" Kingston said. "Must not be over forty miles from here, way the gull flies. You remember? Well, that's all I have to say to you now. 'I know the feeling, neighbor.' "

There was more silence and Kingston was not driving as fast as he had been. Doops did not try to answer, did not lift his head or open his eyes. He wished that he could cry, call out, make any sound at all. He studied the dark marshes on each side of the road. Since their first visit he had thought of them as being unspoiled, full of life, one noble and authentic bit of geography left in America, a refuge for so much of creation. The big lamprey eels and carp moving optimistically through the arcane marshes, the low-flying gulls and heron just above the mucky waters, the lines of turtles sleeping confidently in the sun on rotting logs, the venerable cypress trees not only surviving but thriving where logic would say they would drown in infancy, warm rivers that had once run to the sea as ice water from melting glaciers—the silent swamp, outranked at last by the noise of due process, yet willing still to accept and welcome one of its own.

"You'll make it," Kingston said. "The overload will kick off again. God Almighty, I know it isn't easy. Like you say, nobody is running for champion. You'll make it."

He rounded a sharp bend in the road and began to count piers jutting into the lake. "Now tell me I'll make it too," he said, stopping at the seventh pier from the Skelly gas station.

"There's the boat," he said. "The man said it would be at the seventh pier."

"What'd you tell him we wanted with it? I mean, why did he think we didn't just come to his place and get it like other people do?"

"He didn't ask," Kingston said. "I just told him we didn't want anybody around when we got the boat. Maybe he thinks we're a couple of bootleggers." He started to chuckle as he began untying the plow lines holding the box in place.

"And I guess we are," Doops said, opening the door and walking to the back of the station wagon.

"We'll need some skids," Kingston said. He took a hammer from the station wagon and walked toward the opposite end of the pier, found two suitable boards, and pulled them loose. "I'll put them back in a minute," he said. He nailed one end of each plank to the pier, letting the other end rest just inside the front of the boat. "It's four o'clock," he said. "Want to get the news again?"

"No," Doops said. "It doesn't matter now. We made it."

They inched the box back until they could lift it from the bottom, then placed it on the two boards. Kingston jumped to the inside of the boat and they gradually pulled and pushed it to the middle of the flat-bottomed trawler.

"You all right?" Kingston said, about to pull the starter cord. Doops was at the front, sitting hunched down on a small tackle box.

"Yeah. Okay. How about you?"

"Let's go then," Kingston said. He turned the boat around and headed south, following the channel but staying as close to the bank as possible so that he would not miss the spot where the Lower Mud Lake defected and became Hog Bayou.

They did not attempt to talk above the roar of the engine and the chopping of the propeller in the water. There was no cause for words now. Each knew the thoughts of the other. Occasionally their eyes met, saying things they both understood. There was plenty of daylight remaining and Kingston moved the boat along slowly, a cortege of reverence and dignity, an affair as incomprehensible to all except the two of them as the thalassic crypt to which they were going would be.

When they had turned the bend that was the beginning of the bayou and were out of sight of the main body and there was no more traffic coming and going, Kingston held his fingers up in a V sign. Doops nodded, smiled, and waved back at him. They knew that what was left was the grievous privilege and duty of ritual, Promethean and enervating, a devastating, devouring, and exhausting presumption. Abba, Father. Baby talk to God.

When Kingston eased the boat to the end of the bayou an hour later, cut the motor, and got out, Doops did not move. He did not seem to be aware that they had stopped. Kingston moved around the boat without speaking. He pulled a folded air mattress from beside the box and began to walk in the direction of the slough, not asking Doops to go with him, the vigil continuing. When he got to where the slough began, he inflated the mattress with a bicycle pump he had brought with him, watching the wrinkles smooth out as the rubber stretched and took shape. Then he placed the mattress in the water and tied it to some swamp grass with ropes that were fastened to the front of the raft.

Doops was standing up, his hands resting on the foot of the box, when Kingston returned to the boat. He was thinking of that first funeral he had attended as a child and the words the widow had said when they told her it was time to return to the carriage.

"I promised to go with him as far as I could go and I won't leave until the last shovel of dirt is throwed." They were just words to him then. He thought of a story a woman he once met on a train told him about the time her three-year-old daughter got a new dog.

"Mommy, I bet God doesn't know we have a new dog," the little girl said.

"Well, you can tell Him," the mother said to her.

"I will when we go to church."

The mother explained that she didn't have to wait until she went to church, that God was in her heart and she could talk to Him anytime.

Little Amy pulled the top of her blouse out and whispered into her tiny bosom. "God, we got a new dog."

He wondered if he had told the story to Model T, sorry if he hadn't.

"Everything is ready," Kingston said.

From inside the boat, they lifted the box to the bank. "I'll go in front," Kingston said. "We'll take twelve steps, put it down and rest."

When they had the casket securely centered on the raft, Doops stood with one of the ropes in his hand, Kingston on the opposite bank with the other one. "Let's go," Kingston said. And the silent procession began.

At first they had to pull gently to float the bier along. Then, as the gradual current began, it drifted on its own. As the water began to move more swiftly, they had to hold back on the ropes to keep the raft from moving so fast they would not be able to stop it. Each of them was thinking the same thing but neither spoke.

When they reached the edge of the pool, they wrapped the ropes quickly around two cypress trees to hold the raft and box in place, the clamorous waters insistent, pushing and slapping, urging the body onward.

Doops stepped to the side Kingston was on. He began a slow and exacting canvass of the entire area, Kingston following. He started with the lilies, seeming to count them, moving to the ferns on the inside bank, on to the cypress trees, his gaze moving from the ground to the top of each one, coming to rest finally on the Madonna. As he held the stare, Kingston began to sing, humming first to get a comfortable pitch. Doops had never heard him sing before. His voice was deep and rich. He started softly.

"I looked over Jordan and uh . . . what did I see?
Coming fo' to carry me home.
A band of angels, uh comin' after me
Comin' fo' to carry me home.

"Swing low, sweet chariot . . .
Coming fo' to carry me home.
Swing low, sweet chariot,
Coming fo' to carry me home."

His body swung to and fro as he sang. His voice was louder with each word and even more resonant, the sounds booming and echoing. Doops had turned from the Madonna, his eyes set, looking at nothing. Kingston continued to sing stanza after stanza, some of them familiar, some he seemed to make up as he went along. He rhymed them if he could, not bothering when he couldn't. "If you get there before I do./ Coming fo' to carry me home." "O God, you've hid yourself so long./ Coming fo' to carry me home." "Sweet Jesus, tell me which way to go./ Coming fo' to carry me home."

Doops stood at the head of the casket, raptured by Kingston's singing. When the singing stopped, he was neither surprised nor daunted by what followed. Kingston fell to his knees, not facing the Madonna, as he had not faced it while he sang. He faced the most dense part of the swamp, his entire body quivering and shaking like one struck with a sudden convulsion. A mergence of grunts, moans, and sighs came from his tremulous voice in rapid bursts. His face was full-blooded and he was breathing in quick jerks, his hands quivering above his head, his skin and clothing wet with sweat.

The trembling oblation continued, Doops remaining fixed, his gaze not changing. When Kingston did stop, it was as quickly as he had begun. He got up and faced the Madonna, genuflected quickly, and began a formal recitation. *"Per dominum nostrum Jesum Christum filium tuum qui tecum. . . ."* He turned and faced Doops, quiet and steady, his sacrifice over, an obsequy as hybrid as Kingston himself.

As Kingston turned, Doops began the eulogy. " 'Before we came together we knew the words,' " he began, recalling some words from his story of Cecelia Geronymus. " 'Now we know the tune.' He refused a number and died a man." His delivery was almost defiant. "We have brought the house he lived in home." His voice was dropping now. "His days of saying no are over.

"We cannot say that he belonged to us. Nothing that has life belongs to another." His tone and manner had become priestly, completely different from the way he began. "It comes as a gift, and when it is gone, we cannot preserve it. We cannot say he belonged to us. But he is of us. And we of him. It is not something we join, get voted into, or killed out of. The neighborhood is intact. And will prevail."

The volume and intensity of his voice rose again, the inflections and gestures those of one speaking to a thousand people. He began to reminisce about their first meeting, recounted incidents and anecdotes, spoke of Model T's resolution in the face of death. He called his name often as he told of his vow in the jungle to die in battle before he would kill another, of how he would not swear an oath even in his own defense, and of how the three of them had pooled their resources when all of them were poor. He talked of the blemishes the war had left upon his face, and of how he had refused to disguise them before the world, and recalled Model T's ecstasy the day he first brought them to where they were standing.

Kingston stood as still while Doops spoke as Doops had stood while he sang, entranced by what he was hearing, absorbed in the purple requiem.

"What the Giver gave so freely, we now return. Without apology for the grudge. We will long harbor and nourish the grudge. Not against the Giver. But against this day and its foolishness.

"He did not make the threescore years and ten, but the visit is not measured in terms of its longevity.

"We had good times together. And bad. We laughed together and we cried together. We opened the club and got drunk when the season beckoned it. We sat on hot ship-decks and talked of God and quivers, and ate ripe olives at suppertime. We confessed our cares in unlikely places. We worked and piddled, sat on rushing riverbanks in the hills, and whiled away many a summer afternoon on sleeping bayous. We read books and learned to talk like each other, argued about trivial things and took hard counsel together about the things that mattered."

His voice faltered and Kingston shook his head up and down, urging him on. Doops cleared his throat, coughed lightly, and concluded.

"But mostly . . . we just loved one another."

Even before he stopped speaking, as he was gaining his composure and Kingston was encouraging him along, Kingston had leaned over and opened the valve in the air mattress. They had not discussed the ceremony, had not even talked before he died about bringing him to the marsh. Now the rite was proceeding as if carefully planned and rehearsed. The air from the valve was soft at first, like the first pianissimo bars of an old hymn, then spurted and bubbled, as the weight of the box pressed it underneath the impetuous waters. For a few seconds the coffin floated free of the raft, not moving. Then it began to inch forward, like a train moved by a seasoned engineer. For one moment it seemed to hesitate again, balanced on the edge of the precipice. Then it tipped forward and cascaded down the rapids. Gone. The sound of it was so mingled with the falling water, so blended with the forever sound they had heard the day they first came, that they hardly heard it at all.

Then there was a perspicuous, tenuring sound, a soft sound, followed by an encapsulating gulp, a sort of echo.

"Model T the Baptist!" Doops screamed, facing the farthest part of the swamp as Kingston had, his declaration reverberating through the evening balm.

They moved aimlessly around the bank for several minutes, no longer possessed, no purpose left for staying. Finally Kingston began untying the ropes from the trees and pulled the deflated raft from the edge of the waterfall, squeezed all the air from it, and folded it into a square.

They looked about to be certain they were leaving nothing behind except what they had brought to leave.

"He was a great little Cajun," Kingston said, walking up the slough in front of Doops.

"Watch your verbs," Doops said.